FOREIGN AFFAIRS

Irresistible Italians...

Gorgeous Greeks...

The world's most eligible men!

Dreaming of a foreign affair? Then, look no further!
We've brought together the best and sexiest men the
world has to offer, the most exciting, exotic locations
and the most powerful, passionate stories.

This month, in *Mediterranean Moments*, we bring
back two compelling novels – by favourite Mills &
Boon® authors Sandra Marton and Meredith Webber.
In warm Mediterranean climes, you'll meet a
gorgeous Greek and a handsome Italian – and both
want to take a wife!   Every month in **Foreign
Affairs** you can be swept away to a new location –
and indulge in a little passion in the sun!

*Don't miss the last book in Foreign Affairs—about
Sydney's most eligible playboys!*
AUSTRALIAN ATTRACTION
by Miranda Lee & Helen Bianchin
Out next month!

SANDRA MARTON

Award-winning author **Sandra Marton** wrote her first novel while still in school. Her doting parents told her she'd be a writer someday and Sandra believed them. In high school and college, she wrote dark poetry nobody but her boyfriend understood. As a wife and mother, she devoted the little free time she had to writing murky short stories. Not even her boyfriend-turned-husband understood those. At last, Sandra decided she wanted to write about real people. That didn't actually happen because the heroes she created—and still creates—are larger than life but both she and her readers around the world love them exactly that way. When she isn't at her computer, Sandra loves to bird watch, walk in the woods and the desert, and travel. She can be as happy people-watching from a pavement café in Paris as she can be animal-watching in the forest behind her home in northeastern Connecticut, USA. Her love for both worlds, the urban and the natural, is often reflected in her books. You can write to Sandra Marton at PO Box 295, Storrs, Connecticut, USA (please enclose a self-addressed envelope and postage for a reply) or visit her website at www.sandramarton.com

Look out for new books by Sandra in Modern Romance™!

MEREDITH WEBBER

Previously a teacher, shop-keeper, travel agent, pig farmer, builder and worker in the disability field (among other things) the 'writing bug' struck unexpectedly. She entered a competition run by a women's magazine, shared the third prize with two hundred and fifty other would-be writers, and found herself infected. Thirty-something books later, she's still suffering. She says, 'Medical romances appeal to me because they offer the opportunity to include a wider cast of characters, and the challenge of interweaving a love story into the drama of medical or paramedical practice.'

Meredith has a heart-warming new novel, *Christmas Knight*, out in Medical Romance™ this November!

mediterranean moments

SANDRA MARTON & MEREDITH WEBBER

**MEDITERRANEAN MILLIONAIRES WITH
SCORCHING SEX APPEAL!**

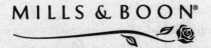

MILLS & BOON®

All the characters in this book have no existence outside the imagination of the author, and have no relation whatsoever to anyone bearing the same name or names. They are not even distantly inspired by any individual known or unknown to the author, and all the incidents are pure invention.

MILLS & BOON and MILLS & BOON with the Rose Device are registered trademarks of the publisher.
Harlequin Mills & Boon Limited,
Eton House, 18-24 Paradise Road, Richmond, Surrey, TW9 1SR

Mediterranean Moments © Harlequin Enterprises II B.V., 2002

The Bride Said Never! and *An Enticing Proposal*
were first published in Great Britain by
Harlequin Mills & Boon Limited in separate, single volumes.

The Bride Said Never! © Sandra Myles 1997
An Enticing Proposal © Meredith Webber 2000

ISBN 0 263 83190 6

126-0802

*Printed and bound in Spain
by Litografia Rosés S.A., Barcelona*

mediterranean moments

THE BRIDE SAID NEVER!

AN ENTICING PROPOSAL

THE BRIDE SAID NEVER!

SANDRA MARTON

CHAPTER ONE

DAMIAN SKOURAS did not like weddings.

A man and a woman, standing before clergy, friends and family while they pledged vows of love and fidelity no human being could possibly keep, was the impossible stuff of weepy women's novels and fairy tales.

It was surely not reality.

And yet, here he was, standing in front of a flower-bedecked altar while the church organ shook the rafters with Mendelssohn's triumphal march and a hundred people oohed and ahhed as a blushing bride made her way up the aisle toward him.

She was, he had to admit, quite beautiful, but he knew the old saying. All brides were beautiful. Still, this one, regal in an old-fashioned gown of white satin and lace and clutching a bouquet of tiny purple and white orchids in her trembling hands, had an aura about her that made her more than beautiful. Her smile, just visible through her sheer, fingertip-length veil, was radiant as she reached the altar.

Her father kissed her. She smiled, let go of his arm, then looked lovingly into the eyes of her waiting groom, and Damian sent up a silent prayer of thanks to the gods of his ancestors that it was not he.

It was just too damned bad that it was Nicholas, instead.

Beside him, Nicholas gave a sudden, unsteady lurch. Damian looked at the young man who'd been his ward until three years ago. Nick's handsome face was pale.

Damian frowned. "Are you all right?" he murmured.

Nick's adam's apple bobbed up and down as he swallowed. "Sure."

It's not too late, boy, Damian wanted to say, but he knew

better. Nick was twenty-one; he wasn't a boy any longer. And it *was* too late, because he fancied himself in love.

That was what he'd said the night he'd come to Damian's apartment to tell him that he and the girl he'd met not two months before were getting married.

Damian had been patient. He'd chosen his words carefully. He'd enumerated a dozen reasons why marrying so quickly and so young were mistakes. But Nick had a ready answer for every argument, and finally Damian had lost his temper.

"You damned young fool," he'd growled, "what happened? Did you knock her up?"

Nick had slugged him. Damian almost smiled at the memory. It was more accurate to say that Nick had tried to slug him but at six foot two, Damian was taller than the boy, and faster on his feet, even if Nicholas was seventeen years younger. The hard lessons he'd learned on the streets of Athens in his boyhood had never quite deserted him.

"She's not pregnant," Nick had said furiously, as Damian held him at arm's length. "I keep telling you, we're in love."

"Love," Damian had said with disdain, and the boy's eyes had darkened with anger.

"That's right. Love. Dammit, Damian, can't you understand that?"

He'd understood, all right. Nick was in lust, not love; he'd almost told him so but by then he'd calmed down enough to realize that saying it would only result in another scuffle. Besides, he wasn't a complete fool. All this arguing was only making the boy more and more determined to have things his own way.

So he'd spoken calmly, the way he assumed his sister and her husband would have done if they'd lived. He talked about Responsibility and Maturity and the value in Waiting a Few Years, and when he'd finished, Nick had grinned and said yeah, he'd heard that stuff already, from both of Dawn's parents, and while that might be good advice for some, it had nothing to do with him or Dawn or what they felt for each other.

Damian, who had made his fortune by knowing not just when to be aggressive but when to yield, had gritted his teeth, accepted the inevitable and said in that case, he wished Nick well.

Still, he'd kept hoping that either Dawn or Nick would come to their senses. But they hadn't, and now here they all were, listening to a soft-voiced clergyman drone on and on about life and love while a bunch of silly women, the bride's mother included, wept quietly into their hankies. And for what reason? She had been divorced. Hell, *he* had been divorced, and if you wanted to go back a generation and be foolish enough to consider his parents' marriage as anything but a farce, they were part of the dismal breakup statistics, too. Half the people here probably had severed marriages behind them including, for all he knew, the mealymouthed clergyman conducting this pallid, non-Greek ceremony.

All this pomp and circumstance, and for what? It was nonsense.

At least his own memorable and mercifully brief foray into the matrimonial wars a dozen years ago had never felt like a real marriage. There'd been no hushed assembly of guests, no organ music or baskets overflowing with flowers. There'd been no words chanted in Greek nor even the vapid sighing of a minister like this one.

His wedding had been what the tabloids called a quickie, an impulsive flight to Vegas after a weekend spent celebrating his first big corporate takeover with too much sex and champagne and not enough common sense. Unfortunately he'd made that assessment twenty-four hours too late. The quickie marriage had led to a not-so-quickie divorce, once his avaricious bride and a retinue of overpriced attorneys had gotten involved.

So much for the lust Nick couldn't imagine might masquerade as love.

A frown appeared between Damian's ice-blue eyes. This was hardly the time to think about such things. Perhaps a miracle would occur and it would all work out. Perhaps, years from now, he'd look back and admit he'd been wrong.

Lord, he hoped so.

He loved Nick as if he were his own flesh and blood. The boy was the son he'd never had and probably never would have, given the realities of marriage. That was why he'd agreed to stand here and pretend to be interested in the mumbo jumbo of the ceremony, to smile at Nick and even to dance with the plump child who was one of the bridesmaids and treat her with all the kindness he could manage because, Nick had said, she was Dawn's best friend and not just overweight but shy, too, and desperately afraid of being a wallflower at the reception afterward.

Oh, yes, he would do all the things a surrogate father was supposed to do. And when the day ended, he'd drive to the inn on the lake where he and Gabriella had stayed the night before and take her to bed.

It would be the best possible way to get over his disappointment at not having taught Nick well enough to protect him from the pain that surely lay ahead, and it would purge his mind of all this useless, sentimental claptrap.

Damian looked at his current mistress, seated in a pew in the third row. Gabriella wasn't taken in by any of it. Like him, she had tried marriage and found it not to her liking. Marriage was just another word for slavery, she'd said, early in their relationship…though lately, he'd sensed a change. She'd become less loving, more proprietorial. "Where have you been, Damian?" she'd say, when a day passed without a phone call. She'd taken his move to a new apartment personally, too; he'd only just in time stopped her from ordering furniture for him as a "surprise."

She hadn't liked that. Her reaction had been sharp and angry; there'd been a brittleness to her he'd never seen before—though today, she was all sweetness and light.

Even last night, during the rehearsal, there'd been a suspicious glint in her dark brown eyes. She'd looked up and smiled at him. It had been a tremulous smile. And, as he'd watched, she'd touched a lace handkerchief to her eyes.

Damian felt a twinge of regret. Perhaps it was time to move on. They'd had, what, almost six months together but when a woman got that look about her...

"Damian?"

Damian blinked. Nicholas was hissing at him out of the side of his mouth. Had the boy come to his senses and changed his mind?

"The ring, Damian!"

The ring. Of course. The best man was searching his pockets frantically, but he wouldn't find it. Nick had asked Damian to have it engraved and he had, but he'd forgotten to hand it over.

He dug in his pocket, pulled out the simple gold band and dropped it into Nick's outstretched hand. Across the narrow aisle, the maid of honor choked back a sob; the bride's mother, tears spilling down her cheeks, reached for her ex-husband's hand, clutched it tightly, then dropped it like a hot potato.

Ah, the joys of matrimony.

Damian forced himself to concentrate on the minister's words.

"And now," he said, in an appropriately solemn voice, "If there is anyone among us who can offer a reason why Nicolas Skouras Babbitt and Dawn Elizabeth Cooper should not be wed, let that person speak or forever—"

Bang!

The double doors at the rear of the church flew open and slammed against the whitewashed walls. There was a rustle of cloth as the guests shifted in the pews and turned to see what was happening. Even the bride and groom swung around in surprise.

A woman stood in the open doorway, silhouetted against the sunlight of the spring afternoon. The wind, which had torn the doors from her hands, ruffled her hair wildly around her head and sent her skirt swirling around her thighs.

A murmur of shocked delight spread through the church. The minister cleared his throat.

The woman stepped forward, out of the brilliance of the light and into the shadowed interior. The excited murmur of voices, which had begun to die away, rose again.

And no wonder, Damian thought. The latecomer was incredibly beautiful.

She looked familiar, but surely if he'd met her before, he'd know her name. A man didn't forget a woman who looked like this.

Her hair was the color of autumn, a deep auburn shot with gold, and curled around her oval, high-cheekboned face. Her eyes were widely spaced and enormous. They were…what? Gray, or perhaps blue. He couldn't tell at this distance. She wore no jewelry but then, jewelry would only have distracted from her beauty. Even her dress, the color of the sky just before a storm, was simple. It was a shade he'd always thought of as violet but the fashion police surely had a better name for it. The cut was simple, too: a rounded neckline, long, full sleeves and a short, full skirt, but there was nothing simple about the body beneath the dress.

His gaze slid over the woman, taking in the high, rounded breasts, the slim waist, the gentle curve of her hips. She was a strange combination of sexuality and innocence, though the innocence was certainly manufactured. It had to be. She was not a child. And she was too stunning, too aware of herself, for it not to be.

Another gust of wind swept in through the open doors. She clutched at her skirt but not before he had a look at legs as long and shapely as any man's dream, topped by a flash of something black and lacy.

The crowd's whispers grew louder. Someone gave a silvery laugh. The woman heard it, he was certain, but instead of showing embarrassment at the attention she was getting, she straightened her shoulders and her lovely face assumed a look of disdain.

I could wipe that look from your face, Damian thought suddenly, and desire, as hot and swift as molten lava, flooded his veins.

Oh, yes, he could. He had only to stride down the aisle, lift her into his arms and carry her out into the meadow that unrolled like a bright green carpet into the low hills behind the church. He'd climb to the top of those hills, lay her down in the soft grass, drink the sweetness of her mouth while he undid the zipper on that pale violet dress and then taste every inch of her as he kissed his way down her body. He imagined burying himself between her thighs and entering her, moving within her heat until she cried out in passion.

Damian's mouth went dry. What was the matter with him? He was not a randy teenager. He wasn't given to fantasizing about women he didn't know, not since he'd been, what, fifteen, sixteen years old, tucked away in his bed at night, breathing heavily over a copy of a men's magazine.

This was nonsense, he thought brusquely, and just then, the woman's head lifted. She looked directly up the aisle, her gaze unwavering as it sought his. She stared at him while his heartbeat raced, and then she smiled again.

I know what you're thinking, her smile said, and I find it terribly amusing.

Damian heard a roaring in his ears. His hands knotted at his sides; he took a step forward.

"Damian?" Nick whispered, and just at that minute, the wind caught the doors again and slammed them against the whitewashed walls of the old church.

The sound seemed to break the spell that had held the congregants captive. Someone cleared a throat, someone else coughed, and finally a man in the last pew rose from his seat, made his way to the doors and drew them shut.

He smiled pleasantly at the woman, as if to say there, that's taken care of, but she ignored both the man and the smile as she looked around for the nearest vacant seat. Slipping into it, she crossed those long legs, folded her hands in her lap and assumed an expression of polite boredom.

What, she seemed to ask, was the delay?

The minister cleared his throat. Slowly, almost reluctantly, the congregants turned and faced the altar.

"If there is no one present who can offer a reason why Nicolas and Dawn should not be wed," he said briskly, as if fearing another interruption, "then, in accordance with the laws of God and the State of Connecticut, I pronounce them husband and wife."

Nick turned to his bride, took her in his arms and kissed her. The organist struck a triumphant chord, the guests rose to their feet and Damian lost sight of the woman in a blur of faces and bodies.

Saved by the bell, Laurel thought, though it was more accurate to say she'd been saved by a C major chord played on an organ.

What an awful entrance to have made! It was bad enough she'd arrived late for Dawn's wedding, but to have interrupted it, to have drawn every eye to her...

Laurel swallowed a groan.

Just last week, during lunch, Dawn had predicted that was exactly what would happen.

Annie had brought her daughter to New York for the final fitting on her gown, and they'd all met for lunch at Tavern on the Green. Dawn, with all the drama in her eighteen-year-old heart, had looked at Laurel and sighed over her Pasta Primavera.

"Oh, Aunt Laurel," she'd said, "you are so beautiful! I wish I looked like you."

Laurel had looked across the table at the girl's lovely face, innocent of makeup and of the rough road that was life, and she'd smiled.

"If *I* looked like *you*," she'd said gently, "I'd still be on the cover of *Vogue*."

That had turned the conversation elsewhere, to Laurel's declining career, which Annie and Dawn stoutly insisted wasn't declining at all, and then to Laurel's plans for the future, which she'd managed to make sound far more exciting than they so far were.

And, inevitably, they'd talked about Dawn's forthcoming wedding.

"You are going to be the most beautiful bride in the world," Laurel had said, and Dawn had blushed, smiled and said well, she certainly hoped Nick would agree, but that the most beautiful woman at the wedding would undoubtedly be her aunt Laurel.

Laurel had determined in that moment that she would not, even inadvertently, steal the spotlight. When you had a famous face—well, a once-famous face, anyway—you could do that just by entering a room, and that was the last thing she wanted to do to the people she loved.

So this morning, she'd dressed with that in mind. Instead of the pale pink Chanel suit she'd bought for the occasion, she'd put on a periwinkle blue silk dress that was a couple of years old. Instead of doing her hair in the style that she'd made famous—whisked back and knotted loosely on the crown, with sexy little curls tumbling down her neck—she'd simply run a brush through it and let it fall naturally around her shoulders. She hadn't put on any jewelry and she'd even omitted the touch of lip gloss and mascara that was the only makeup she wore except when she was on a runway or in front of a camera.

She'd even left early, catching a train at Penn Station that was supposed to have gotten her into Stratham a good hour before the ceremony was scheduled to begin. But the train had broken down in New Haven and Laurel had started to look for a taxi when the station public address system announced that there'd be a new train coming along to pick up the stranded passengers in just a few minutes.

The clerk at the ticket counter confirmed it, and said the train would be lots faster than a taxi.

And so she'd waited, for almost half an hour, only to find that it wasn't a train that had been sent to pick up the passengers at all. It was a bus and, of course, it had taken longer than the train ever would have, longer than a taxi would have, too, had she taken one when the train had first ground to a halt. The icing on the cake had come when they'd finally reached Stratham and for endless minutes, there hadn't been a cab in sight.

"Aunt Laurel?"

Laurel looked up. Dawn and her handsome young groom had reached her row of pews.

"Baby," she said, fixing a bright smile to her face as she reached out and gave the girl a quick hug.

"That was some entrance," Dawn said, laughing.

"Oh, Dawn, I'm so sorry about—"

Too late. The bridal couple was already moving past her, toward the now-open doors and the steps that led down from the church.

Laurel winced. Dawn had been teasing, she knew, but Lord, if she could only go back and redo that awful entrance.

As it was, she'd stood outside the little church after the cab had dropped her off, trying to decide which was preferable, coming in late or missing the ceremony, until she'd decided that missing the ceremony was far worse. So she'd carefully cracked the doors open, only to have the wind pull them from her hands, and the next thing she'd known she'd been standing stage-center, with every eye in the place on her.

Including his. That man. That awful, smug-faced, egotistical man.

Was he Nicholas's guardian? Well, former guardian. Damian Skouras, wasn't that the name? That had to be him, considering where he'd been standing.

One look, and she'd known everything she needed to

know about Damian Skouras. Unfortunately she knew the type well. He had the kind of looks women went crazy for: wide shoulders, narrow waist, a hard body and a handsome face with eyes that seemed to blaze like blue flame against his olive skin. His hair swept back from his face like the waves on a midnight sea, and a tiny gold stud glittered in one ear.

Looks and money, both, Laurel thought bitterly. It wasn't just the Armani dinner jacket and black trousers draped down those long, muscled legs that had told her so, it was the way he held himself, with careless, masculine arrogance. It was also the way he'd looked at her, as if she were a new toy, all gift-wrapped and served up for his pleasure. His smile had been polite but his eyes had said it all.

"Baby," those eyes said, "I'd like to peel off that dress and see what's underneath."

Not in *this* lifetime, Laurel thought coldly.

She was tired of it, sick of it, if the truth were told. The world was filled with too many insolent men who'd let money and power go to their heads.

Hadn't she spent almost a year playing the fool for one of them?

The rest of the wedding party was passing by now, bridesmaids giggling among themselves in a pastel flurry of blues and pinks, the groomsmen grinning foolishly, impossibly young and good-looking in their formal wear. Annie went by with her ex and paused only long enough for a quick hug after which Laurel fell back into the crowd, letting it surge past her because she knew *he'd* be coming along next, the jerk who'd stared at her and stripped her naked with his eyes…and yes, there he was, bringing up the rear of the little procession with one of the bridesmaids, a child no more than half his age, clinging to his arm like a limpet.

The girl was staring up at him with eyes like saucers while he treated her to a full measure of his charm, smiling at her with his too-white teeth glinting against his too-tanned skin. Laurel frowned. The child was positively transfixed by the body-by-health club, tan-by-sunlamp and attitude-by-bank-balance. And Mr. Macho was eating up the adulation.

Bastard, Laurel thought coldly, eyeing him through the crowd, and before she had time to think about it, she stepped out in the aisle in front of him.

The bridesmaid was so busy making goo-goo eyes at her dazzling escort that she had to skid to a stop when he halted.

"What's the matter?" the girl asked.

"Nothing," he answered, his eyes never leaving Laurel's.

The girl looked at Laurel. Young as she was, awareness glinted in her eyes.

"Come on, Damian. We have to catch up to the others."

He nodded. "You go on, Elaine. "I'll be right along."

"It's Aileen."

"Aileen," he said, his eyes still on Laurel. "Go ahead. I'll be just behind you."

The girl shot Laurel a sullen glare. "Sure." Then she picked up her skirts and hurried along after the others.

Close up, Laurel could see that the man's eyes were a shade of blue she'd never seen before, cool and pale, the irises as black-ringed as if they'd been circled with kohl. Ice, she thought, chips of polar sea ice.

A pulse began to pound in her throat. I should have stayed where I was, she thought suddenly, instead of stepping out to confront him...

"Yes?" he said.

His voice, low and touched with a slight accent, was a perfect match for the chilly removal of his gaze.

The church was empty now. A few feet away, just beyond the doors, Laurel could hear the sounds of laughter but here, in the silence and the lengthening shadows of late afternoon, she could hear only the *thump-thump* of her heart.

"Was there something you wished to say to me?"

His words were polite but the coldness in them made Laurel's breath catch. For a second, she thought of turning and running but she'd never run from anything in her life. Besides, why should she let this stranger get the best of her?

There was nothing to be afraid of, nothing at all.

So she drew herself up to her full five foot ten, tossed her hair back from her face and fixed him with a look of cool *hauteur*, the same one she wore like a mask when she was on public display, and that had helped make her a star on runways from here to Milan.

"Only that you look pathetic," she said regally, "toying with that little girl."

"Toying with…?"

"Really," she said, permitting her voice to take on a purr of amusement, "don't you think you ought to play games with someone who's old enough to recognize you for what you are?"

The man looked at her for a long moment, so long that she foolishly began to think she'd scored a couple of points. Then he smiled in a way that sent her heart skidding up into her throat and he stepped forward, until he was only a hand's span away.

"What is your name?"

"Laurel," she said, "Laurel Bennett, but I don't see—"

"I agree completely, Miss Bennett. The game is far more enjoyable when it is played by equals."

She saw what was coming next in his eyes, but it was too late. Before Laurel could move or even draw back, he reached out, took her in his arms and kissed her.

CHAPTER TWO

LAUREL SHOT a surreptitious glance at her watch.

Another hour, and she could leave without attracting attention. Only another hour—assuming she could last that long.

The man beside her at the pink-and-white swathed table for six, Evan Something-or-Other, was telling a joke. Dr. Evan Something-or-Other, as Annie, ever the matchmaker, had pointedly said, when she'd come around earlier to greet her guests.

He was a nice enough man, even if his pink-tipped nose and slight overbite did remind Laurel of a rabbit. It was just that this was the doctor's joke number nine or maybe nine thousand for the evening. She'd lost count somewhere between the shrimp cocktail and the *Beouf aux Chanterelles*.

Not that it mattered. Laurel would have had trouble keeping her mind on anything this evening. Her thoughts kept traveling in only one direction, straight towards Damian Skouras, who was sitting at the table on the dais with an expensively dressed blond windup doll by his side—not that the presence of the woman was keeping him from watching Laurel.

She knew he was, even though she hadn't turned to confirm it. There was no need. She could feel the force of his eyes on her shoulder blades. If she looked at him, she half expected to see a pair of blue laser beams blazing from that proud, arrogant face.

The one thing she *had* confirmed was that he was definitely Damian Skouras, and he was Nicholas's guardian. Former guardian, anyway; Nick was twenty-one, three years past needing to ask anyone's permission to marry. Laurel knew that her sister hadn't wanted the wedding to take place. Dawn and Nick were too young, she'd said. Laurel had kept her own counsel but now that she'd met the man who'd raised Nick, she was amazed her sister hadn't raised yet a second objection.

Who would want a son-in-law with an egotistical SOB like Damian Skouras for a role model?

That was how she thought of him, as an Egotistical SOB, and in capital letters. She'd told him so the next time she'd seen him, after that kiss, when they'd come face-to-face on the receiving line. She'd tried breezing past him as if he didn't exist, but he'd made that impossible, capturing her hand in his, introducing himself as politely as if they'd never set eyes on each other until that second.

Flushed with indignation, Laurel had tried to twist her hand free. That had made him laugh.

"Relax, Miss Bennett," he'd said in a low, mocking tone. "You don't want to make another scene, do you? Surely one such performance a day is enough, even for you."

"I'm not the one who made a scene, you—you—"

"My name is Damian Skouras."

He was laughing at her, damn him, and enjoying every second of her embarrassment.

"Perhaps you enjoy attracting attention," he'd said. "If so, by all means, go on as you are. But if you believe, as I do, that today belongs to Nicholas and his bride, then be a good girl, smile prettily and pretend you're having a good time, hmm?"

He was right, and she knew it. The line had bogged down behind her and people were beginning to crane their necks with interest, trying to see who and what was holding things up. So she'd smiled, not just prettily but brilliantly, as if she were on a set instead of at a wedding, and said, in a voice meant to be heard by no one but him, that she was hardly surprised he still thought it appropriate to address a woman as a girl and that she'd have an even better time if she pretended he'd vanished from the face of the earth.

His hand had tightened on hers and his eyes had glinted with a sudden darkness that almost made her wish she'd kept her mouth shut.

"You'll never be able to pretend anything when it comes to me," he'd said softly, "or have you forgotten what happened when I kissed you?"

Color had shot into her face. He'd smiled, let her snatch her hand from his, and she'd swept past him.

No, she hadn't forgotten. How could she? There'd been that first instant of shocked rage and then, following hard on its heels, the dizzying realization that she was suddenly clinging to his broad shoulders, that her mouth was softening and parting under his, that she was making a little sound in the back of her throat and moving against him...

"...well," Evan Something-or-Other droned, "if that's the case, said the chicken, I guess there's not much point crossing to the other side!"

Everybody at the table laughed. Laurel laughed, too, if a beat too late.

"Great story," someone chuckled.

Evan smiled, lifted his glass of wine, and turned to Laurel.

"I guess you heard that one before," he said apologetically.

"No," she said quickly, "no, I haven't. I'm just—I think it must be jet lag. I was in Paris just yesterday and I don't think my head's caught up to the clock." She smiled. "Or vice versa."

"Paris, huh? Wonderful city. I was there last year. A business conference."

"Ah."

"Were you there on business? Or was it a vacation?"

"Oh, it was business."

"I guess you're there a lot."

"Well..."

"For showings. That's what they call them, right?"

"Well, yes, but how did you—"

"I recognized you." Evan grinned. "Besides, Annie told me. I'm her dentist, hers and Dawn's, and the last time she came by for a checkup she said, 'Wait until you meet my baby sister at the wedding. She's the most gorgeous model in the world.'" His grin tilted. "But she was wrong."

"Was she?" Laurel asked, trying to sound interested. She knew what came next. If the doctor thought this was a new approach, he was sadly mistaken.

"Absolutely. You're not the most gorgeous model in the world, you're the most gorgeous woman, hands down."

Drum roll, lights up, Laurel thought, and laughed politely. "You'll have to forgive Annie. She's an inveterate matchmaker."

"At least she didn't exaggerate." He chuckled and leaned closer. "You should see some of the so-called 'dream dates' I've been conned into."

"This isn't a date, Doctor."

His face crumpled just a little and Laurel winced. There was no reason to let her bad mood out on him.

"I meant," she said with an apologetic smile, "I know what you're saying. I've been a victim of some pretty sneaky setups, myself."

"Matchmakers." Evan shook his head. "They never let up, do they? And I wish you'd call me 'Evan.'"

"Evan," Laurel said. "And you're right, they never do."

"Annie wasn't wrong, though, was she?" Evan cleared his throat. "I mean, you are, ah, uninvolved and unattached?"

Annie, Laurel thought wearily, what am I going to do with you? Her sister had been trying to marry her off for years. She'd really gone into overdrive after Laurel had finally walked out on Kirk.

"Okay," Annie had said, "so at first, you didn't want to settle down because you had to build your career. Then you convinced yourself that jerk would pop the question, but, big surprise, he didn't.''

"I don't want to talk about it," Laurel had replied, but Annie had plowed on, laying out the joys of matrimony as if she hadn't untied her own marriage vows years before, and eventually Laurel had silenced her by lying through her teeth and saying that if the right man ever came along, she supposed she'd agree to tie the knot....

But not in this lifetime. Laurel's mouth firmed. So far as she could see, the only things a woman needed a man for was to muscle open a jar and provide sex. Well, there were gizmos on the market that dealt with tight jar lids. As for sex...it was overrated. That was something else she'd learned during her time with Kirk. Maybe it meant more to women who didn't have careers. Maybe there was a woman somewhere who heard music and saw fireworks when she was in bed with a man but if you had a life, sex was really nothing more than a biological urge, like eating or drinking, and certainly not anywhere near as important.

"Sorry," Evan said, "I guess I shouldn't have asked."

Laurel blinked. "Shouldn't have...?

"If you were, you know, involved."

"Oh." She cleared her throat. "Oh, no, don't apologize. I'm, ah, I'm flattered you'd ask. It's just that, well, what with all the traveling I do—"

"Miss Bennett?"

Laurel stiffened. She didn't have to turn around to know who'd come up behind her. Nobody could have put such a world of meaning into the simple use of her name—nobody but Damian Skouras.

She looked up. He was standing beside her chair, smiling pleasantly.

"Yes?" she said coldly.

"I thought you might like to dance."

"You thought wrong."

"Ah, but they're playing our song."

Laurel stared at him. For the most part, she'd been ignoring the band. Now, she realized that a medley of sixties hits had given way to a waltz.

"Our sort of song, at any rate," Damian said. "An old-fashioned waltz, for an old-fashioned girl." His smile tilted. "Sorry. I suppose I should say 'woman.'"

"You suppose correctly, Mr. Skouras. Not that it matters. Girl or woman, I'm not interested."

"In waltzing?"

"Waltzing is fine." Laurel's smile was the polite equal of his. "It's you I'm not interested in, on the dance floor or off it."

Across the table, there was a delighted intake of breath. Every eye had to be on her now and she knew it, but she didn't care. Not anymore. Damian Skouras had taken this as far as she was going to allow.

"You must move in very strange circles, Miss Bennett. In my world, a dance is hardly a request for an assignation."

Damn the man! He wasn't put off by what she'd said, or even embarrassed. He was amused by it, smiling first at her and then at the woman who'd gasped, and somehow managing to turn things around so that it was Laurel who looked foolish.

It wasn't easy, but she managed to dredge up a smile.

"And in mine," she said sweetly, "a man who brings his girlfriend to a party and then spends his time hitting on another woman is called a—"

"Hey," a cheerful voice said, "how's it going here? Everybody having a good time?"

Laurel looked over her shoulder. The bride and groom had come up on her other side and were beaming at the tableful of guests.

"Yes," someone finally said, after some throat-clearing, "we're having a splendid time, Nicholas."

"Great. Glad to hear it." Nick grinned. "One thing I learned, watching the ladies set up the seating chart, is that you never know how these table arrangements are going to work out.'' He looked at Laurel, then at Damian, and his grin broadened. ''Terrific! I see that you guys managed to meet on your own.''

The woman opposite Laurel made a choked sound and lifted her napkin to her lips.

Damian nodded. ''We did, indeed,'' he said smoothly.

Dawn leaned her head against her groom's shoulder. ''We just knew you two would have a lot to talk about.''

I don't believe this, Laurel thought. *I'm trapped in a room filled with matchmakers.*

''Really,'' she said politely.

''Uh-huh.''

''Name one thing.''

Dawn's brows lifted. ''Sorry?''

''Name one thing we'd have to talk about,'' Laurel said pleasantly, even while a little voice inside her warned her it was time to shut up.

The woman across the table made another choking sound. Dawn shot Nick a puzzled glance. Gallantly he picked up the slack.

''Well,'' he said, ''the both of you do a lot of traveling.''

''Indeed?''

''Take France, for instance.''

''France?''

''Yeah. Damian just bought an apartment in Paris. We figured you could clue him in on the best places to buy stuff. You know, furniture, whatever, considering that you spend so much time there.''

''I don't,'' Laurel said quickly. She looked at Evan, sitting beside her, and she cleared her throat. ''I mean, I don't spend half as much time in Paris as I used to.''

''Where do you spend your time, then?'' Damian asked politely.

Where didn't he spend his? Laurel made a quick mental inventory of all the European cities a man like this would probably frequent.

"New York," she said, and knew instantly it had been the wrong choice.

"What a coincidence," Damian said with a little smile. "I've just bought a condominium in Manhattan."

"You said it was Paris."

"Paris, Manhattan…" His shoulders lifted, then fell, in an elegant shrug. "My business interests take me to many places, Miss Bennett, and I much prefer coming home to my own things at night."

"Like the blonde who came with you today?" Laurel said sweetly.

"Aunt Laurrr-el!" Dawn said, with a breathless laugh.

"It's quite all right, Dawn," Damian said softly, his eyes on Laurel's. "Your aunt and I understand each other—don't we, Miss Bennett?"

"Absolutely, Mr. Skouras." Laurel turned to the dentist, who was sitting openmouthed, a copy of virtually everyone else at the table. "Would you like to dance, Evan?"

A flush rose on his face. He looked up at Damian.

"But—I mean, I thought…"

"You thought wrong, sir." Damian's tone was polite but Laurel wasn't fooled. Anger glinted in his eyes. "While we've all been listening to Miss Bennett's interesting views, I've had the chance to reconsider." He turned to Dawn and smiled pleasantly. "My dear, I would be honored if you would desert Nicholas long enough to grant me the honor of this dance."

Dawn smiled with relief. "I'd be thrilled."

She went into his arms at the same time Laurel went into Evan's. Nick pulled out Evan's chair, spun it around and sat down. He draped his arms over the back and made some light remark about families and family members that diverted the attention of the others and set them laughing.

So much for Damian Skouras, Laurel thought with satisfaction as she looked over Evan's shoulder. Perhaps next time, he'd think twice before trying to play what were certainly his usual games with a woman.

* * *

Gabriella Boldini crossed and recrossed her long legs under the dashboard of Damian's rented Saab.

"Honestly, Damian," she said crossly, "I don't know why you didn't arrange for a limousine."

Damian sighed, kept his attention focused on the winding mountain road and decided there was no point in responding to the remark she'd already made half a dozen times since they'd left Stratham.

"We'll be at the inn soon," he said. "Why don't you put your head back and try and get some sleep?"

"I am not tired, Damian, I'm simply saying—"

"I know what you're saying. You'd have preferred a different car."

Gabriella folded her arms. "That's right."

"A Cadillac, or a Lincoln, with a chauffeur."

"Yes. Or you could have had Stevens drive us up here. There's no reason we couldn't have been comfortable, even though we're trapped all the way out in the sticks."

Damian laughed. "We're hardly in the 'sticks', Gaby. The inn's just forty miles from Boston."

"For goodness' sakes, must you take me so literally? I know where it is. We spent last night there, didn't we?" Gabriella crossed her legs again. If the skirt of her black silk dress rode any higher on her thighs, Damian thought idly, it would disappear. "Which reminds me. Since that place doesn't have room service—"

"It has room service."

"There you go again, taking me literally. It doesn't have room service, not after ten o'clock at night. Don't you remember what happened when I tried to order a pot of tea last night?"

Damian's hands flexed on the steering wheel. "I remember, Gaby. The manager offered to brew you some tea and bring it up to our suite himself."

"Nonsense. I wanted herbal tea, not that stuff in a bag. And I've told you over and over, I don't like it when you call me Gaby."

What the hell is this? Damian thought wearily. He was not married to this woman but anyone listening to them now would think they'd been at each other's throats for at least a decade of blissful wedlock.

Not that a little sharp-tongued give-and-take wasn't sometimes amusing. The woman at Nicholas's wedding, for instance. Laurel Bennett had infuriated him, at the end, doing her damnedest to make him look foolish in front of Nicholas and all the others, but he had to admit, she was clever and quick.

"'Gaby' always makes me think of some stupid character in a bad Western."

She was stunning, too. The more he'd seen of her, the more he'd become convinced he'd never seen a more exquisite face. She was a model, Dawn had told him, and he'd always thought models were androgynous things, all bones and no flesh, but Laurel Bennett had been rounded and very definitely feminine. Had that been the real reason he'd asked her to dance, so he could hold that sweetly curved body in his arms and see for himself if she felt as soft as she looked?

"Must you drive so fast? I can barely see where we're going, it's so miserably dark outside."

Damian's jaw tightened. He pressed down just a little harder on the gas.

"I like to drive fast," he said. "And since I'm the one at the wheel, you don't have to see outside, now do you?"

He waited for her to respond, but not even Gabriella was that foolish. She sat back instead, arms still folded under her breasts, her head lifted in a way he'd come to know meant she was angry.

The car filled with silence. Damian was just beginning to relax and enjoy it when she spoke again.

"Honestly," she said, "you'd think people would use some common sense."

Damian shot her a quick look. "Yes," he said, grimly, "you would."

"Imagine the nerve of that woman."

"What woman?"

"The one who made that grand entrance. You know, the woman with that mass of dyed red hair."

Damian almost laughed. Now, at least, he knew what this was all about.

"Was it dyed?" he asked casually. "I didn't think so."

"You wouldn't," Gabriella snapped. "Men never do. You're all so easily taken in."

We are, indeed, he thought. What had happened to Gabriella's sweet nature and charming Italian accent? The first had begun disappearing over the past few weeks; the second had slipped away gradually during the past hour.

"And that dress. Honestly, if that skirt had been any shorter…"

Damian glanced at Gabriella's legs. Her own skirt, which had never done more than flirt with the tops of her thighs, had vanished along with what was left of her pleasant disposition and sexy accent.

"She's Dawn's aunt, I understand."

"Who?" Damian said pleasantly.

"Don't be dense." Gabriella took a deep breath. "That woman," she said, more calmly, "the one with the cheap-looking outfit and the peroxide hair."

"Ah," he said. The turnoff for the inn was just ahead. He slowed the car, signaled and started up the long gravel driveway. "The model."

"Model, indeed. Everyone knows what those women are like. That one, especially." Gabriella was stiff with indignation. "They say she's had dozens of lovers."

The car hit a rut in the road. Damian, eyes narrowed, gave the wheel a vicious twist.

"Really," he said calmly.

"Honestly, Damian, I wish you'd slow—"

"What else do they say about her?"

"About…?" Gabriella shot him a quick glance. Then she reached forward, yanked down the sun visor and peered into the mirror on its reverse side. "I don't pay attention to gossip," she said coolly, as she fluffed her fingers through her artfully arranged hair. "But what *is* there to say about someone who poses nude?"

A flash fire image of Laurel Bennett, naked and flushed in his bed, seared the mental canvas of Damian's mind. He forced himself to concentrate on the final few yards of the curving road.

"Nude?" he said calmly.

"To all intents and purposes. She did an ad for Calvin Klein—it's in this month's *Chic* or maybe *Femme*, I'm not sure which." Gabriella snapped the visor back into place. "Oh, it was all very elegant and posh, you know, one of those la-di-da arty shots taken through whatever it is they use, gauze, I suppose." Her voice fairly purred with satisfaction. "She'd need it, wouldn't she, seeing that she's a bit long in the tooth? Still, gauze or no gauze, when you came right down to it, there she was, stark naked."

The picture of Laurel burned in his brain again. Damian cleared his throat. "Interesting."

"Cheap is a better word. Totally cheap…which is why I just don't understand what made you bother with her."

"You're talking nonsense, Gabriella."

"I saw the way you looked at her and let me tell you, I didn't much like it. You have an obligation to me."

Damian pulled up at the entrance to the inn, shut off the engine and turned toward her.

"Obligation?" he said carefully.

"That's right. We've been together for a long time now. Doesn't that mean anything to you?"

"I have not been unfaithful to you."

"That's not what I'm talking about and you know it." She took a deep breath. "Can you really tell me you sat through that entire wedding without feeling a thing?"

"I felt what I always feel at weddings," he said quietly. "Disbelief that two people should willingly subject themselves to such nonsense along with the hope, however use-

less, that they make a success of what is basically an un-
natural arrangement.''

Gabriella's mouth thinned. ''How can you say such a
thing?''

''I say it because it's true. You knew that was how I felt,
from the start. You said your attitude mirrored mine.''

''Never mind what I said,'' Gabriella said sharply. ''And
you haven't answered my question. Why did you keep
looking at that woman?''

*Because I chose to. Because you don't own me. Because
Laurel Bennett intrigues me as you never did, not even
when our affair first began.*

Damian blew out his breath. It was late, they were both
tired and this wasn't the time to talk or make decisions. He
ran his knuckles lightly over Gabriella's cheek, then
reached across her lap and opened her door.

''Go on,'' he said gently. ''Wait in the lobby while I
park the car.''

''You see what I mean? If we'd come by limousine, you
wouldn't have to drop me off here, in the middle of nowhere. But no, you had to do things your way, with no
regard for me or my feelings.''

Damian glanced past Gabriella, to the brightly lit entrance to the inn. Then he looked at his mistress's face,
illuminated by the cruel fluorescent light that washed into
the car, and saw that it wasn't as lovely as he'd once
thought, especially not with petulance and undisguised jealousy etched into every feature.

''Gaby,'' he said quietly, ''it's late. Let's not argue about
this now.''

''Don't think you can shut me up by sounding sincere,
Damian. And I keep telling you, my name's not Gaby!''

A muscle knotted in his jaw. He reached past her again,
grasped the handle, slammed the door closed and put the
Saab in gear.

''Wait just a minute! I'm not going with you while you
park the car. If you think I have any intention of walking

through that gravel in these shoes…'' Gabriella frowned as Damian pulled through the circular driveway and headed downhill. ''Damian? What are you doing?''

''What does it look like I'm doing?'' He kept his eyes straight ahead, on the road. ''I'm driving to New York.''

''Tonight? But it's late. And what about my things? My clothes and my makeup? Damian, this is ridiculous!''

''I'll phone the inn and tell them to pack everything and forward it, as soon as I've dropped you off.''

''Dropped me off?'' Gabriella twisted toward him. ''What do you mean? I never go back to my own apartment on weekends, you know that.''

''What you said was true, a few minutes ago,'' he said, almost gently, ''I do have an obligation to you.'' He looked across the console at her, then back at the road. ''An obligation to tell you the truth, which is that I've enjoyed our time together, but—''

''But what? What is this, huh? The big brush-off?''

''Gabriella, calm down.''

''Don't you tell me to calm down,'' she said shrilly. ''Listen here, Mr. Skouras, maybe you can play high-and-mighty with the people who work for you but you can't pull that act with me!''

''I'd like us to end this like civilized adults. We both knew our relationship wouldn't last forever.''

''Well, I changed my mind! How dare you toss me aside, just because you found yourself some two-bit—''

''I've found myself nothing.'' His voice cut across hers, harsh and cold. ''I'm simply telling you that our relationship has run its course.''

''That's what *you* think! What *I* think is that you led me to have certain expectations. My lawyer says…''

Gabriella stopped in midsentence, her mouth opening and closing as if she were a fish, but it was too late. Damian had already pulled onto the shoulder of the road. He swung toward her, and she shrank back in her seat at the expression on his face.

"Your lawyer says?" His voice was low, his tone dangerous. "You mean, you've already discussed our relationship with an attorney?"

"No. Well, I mean, I had a little chat with—look, Damian, I was just trying to protect myself." In the passing headlights of an oncoming automobile, he could see her face harden. "And it looks as if I had every reason to! Here you are, trying to dump me without so much as a by-your-leave—"

Damian reached out and turned on the radio. He punched buttons until he found a station playing something loud enough to drown out Gabriella's voice. Then he swung back onto the road and stepped down, hard, on the gas.

Less than three hours later, they were in Manhattan. Sunday night traffic was sparse, and it took only minutes for him to reach Gabriella's apartment building on Park Avenue.

The doorman hurried up. Gabriella snarled at him to leave her alone as she stepped from the car.

"Bastard," she hissed, as Damian gunned the engine.

For all he knew, she was still staring after him and spewing venom as he drove off. Not that it mattered. She was already part of the past.

CHAPTER THREE

JEAN KAPLAN had been Damian Skouras's personal assistant for a long time.

She was middle-aged, happily married and dedicated to her job. She was also unflappable. Nothing fazed her.

Still, she couldn't quite mask her surprise when her boss strode into the office Monday morning, said a brisk, "Hello," and then instructed her to personally go down to the newsstand on the corner and purchase copies of every fashion magazine on display.

"Fashion magazines, Mr. Skouras?"

"Fashion magazines, Ms. Kaplan." Damian's expression was completely noncommittal. "I'm sure you know the sort of thing I mean. *Femme*, *Chic*...all of them."

Jean nodded. "Certainly, sir."

Well, she thought as she hurried to the elevator, her boss had never been anyone's idea of a conventional executive. She permitted herself a faint smile as the doors whisked open at the lobby level. When you headed up what the press loved to refer to as the Skouras Empire, you didn't have to worry about that kind of thing.

Maybe he was thinking of buying a magazine. Or two, or three, she thought as she swept up an armload of glossy publications, made her way back to her employer's thirtieth floor office and neatly deposited them on his pale oak desk.

"Here you are, Mr. Skouras. I hope the assortment is what you wanted."

Damian nodded. "I'm sure it is."

"And shall I send the usual roses to Miss Boldini?"

He looked up and she saw in his eyes a flash of the Arctic

33

coldness that was faced by those who were foolish enough to oppose him in business.

"That won't be necessary."

"Oh. I'm sorry, sir. I just thought…"

"In fact, if Miss Boldini calls, tell her I'm not in."

"Yes, sir. Will that be all?"

Damian's dark head was already bent over the stack of magazines.

"That's all. Hold my calls until I ring you, please."

Jean nodded and shut the door behind her.

So, she thought with some satisfaction, Gabriella Boldini, she of the catlike smile and claws to match, had reached the end of her stay. Not a minute too soon, as far as she was concerned. Jean had seen a lot of women flounce through her employer's life, all of them beautiful and most of them charming or at least clever enough to show a pleasant face to her. But Gabriella Boldini had set her teeth on edge from day one.

Jean settled herself at her desk and turned on her computer. Perhaps that was why Mr. Skouras had wanted all those magazines. He'd be living like a monk for the next couple of months; he always did, after an affair ended. What better time to research a new business venture? Soon enough, though, another stunning female would step into his life, knowing she was just a temporary diversion but still hoping to snare a prize catch like him.

They always hoped, even though he never seemed to know it.

Jean gave a motherly sigh. As for herself, she'd given up hoping. There'd been a time she'd clung to the belief that her boss would find himself a good woman to love. Not anymore. He'd had one disastrous marriage that he never talked about and it had left him a confirmed loner.

Amazing, how a man so willing to risk everything making millions could refuse to take any risks at all, in matters of the heart.

*   *   *

Damian frowned as he looked over the magazines spilling across his desk.

Headlines screamed at him.

Are You Sexy Enough to Keep Your Man Interested?
Ten Ways to Turn Him On
Sexy Styles for Summer
The Perfect Tan Starts Now

Was there really a market for such drivel? He'd seen Gabriella curled up in a chair, leafing through magazines like these, but he'd never paid any attention to the print on the covers.

Or to the models, he thought, his frown deepening as he leafed through the glossy pages. Why did so many of them look as if they hadn't eaten in weeks? Surely, no real man could find women like these attractive, with their bones almost protruding through their skin.

And those pouting faces. He paused, staring at an emaciated-looking waif with a heavily made-up face who looked up from the page with an expression that made her appear to have sucked on one lemon too many.

Who would find such a face attractive?

After a moment, he sighed, closed the magazine and reached for another. Laurel's photograph wasn't where Gabriella had said it would be. Not that it mattered. There'd been no good reason to want to see the picture; he'd directed his secretary to buy these silly things on a whim.

Come on, man, who are you kidding?

It hadn't been a whim at all. The truth was that he'd slept poorly, awakening just after dawn from a fragmented dream filled with the kinds of images he hadn't had in years, his loins heavy and aching with need...

And there it was. The photograph of Laurel Bennett.

Gabriella had been wrong. Laurel wasn't nude, and he

tried to ignore the sense of relief that welled so fiercely inside him at the realization.

She'd been posed with her back to the camera, her head turned, angled so that she was looking over her shoulder at the viewer. Her back and shoulders were bare; a long length of ivory silk was draped from her hips, dipping low enough to expose the delicate tracery of her spine almost to its base. Her hair, that incredible mane of sun-streaked mahogany, tumbled over her creamy skin like tongues of dark flame.

Damian stared at the picture. All right, he told himself coldly, there she is. A woman, nothing more and nothing less. Beautiful, yes, and very desirable, but hardly worth the heated dreams that had disturbed his night.

He closed the magazine, tossed it on top of the others and carried the entire stack to a low table that was part of a conversational grouping at the other end of his office. Jean could dispose of them later, either toss them out or give them to one of the clerks. He certainly had no need for them, nor had he any further interest in Laurel Bennett.

That was settled, then. Damian relaxed, basking in the satisfaction that came of closure.

His morning was filled with opportunities for that same feeling, but it never came again.

There was a problem with a small investment firm Skouras International had recently acquired. Damian's CPAs had defined it but they hadn't been able to solve it. He did, during a two-hour brainstorming session. A short while later, he held a teleconference with his bankers in Paris and Hamburg, and firmed up a multimillion dollar deal that had been languishing for months.

At twenty of twelve, he began going through the notes Jean had placed on a corner of his desk in preparation for his one o'clock business luncheon, but he couldn't concentrate. Words kept repeating themselves, and entire sentences.

He gave up, pushed back his chair and frowned.

Suddenly he felt restless.

He rose and paced across the spacious room. There was always a carafe of freshly brewed coffee waiting for him on a corner shelf near the sofas that flanked the low table where he'd dumped the magazines.

He paused, frowning as he looked down at the stack. The magazine containing Laurel's photo was on top and he picked it up, opened it to that page and stared at the picture. Her hair looked like silk. Would it feel that way, or would it be stiff with hair spray when he touched it, the way Gabriella's had always been? How would her skin smell, when he put his face to that graceful curve where her shoulder and her neck joined? How would it taste?

Hell, what was the matter with him? He wasn't going to smell this woman, or taste her, or touch her.

His eyes fastened on her face. There was a hands-off coolness in her eyes that seemed at odds with her mouth, which looked soft, sexy, and heart-stoppingly vulnerable. It had felt that way, too, beneath his own, after she'd stopped fighting the passion that suddenly had gripped them both and given herself up to him, and to the kiss.

His belly knotted as he remembered the heat and hardness that had curled through his body. He couldn't remember ever feeling so caught up in a kiss or in the memory of what had been, after all, a simple encounter.

So caught up, and out of control.

Damian's jaw knotted. This was ridiculous. He was never out of control.

What he had, he thought coldly, was an itch, and it needed scratching.

One night, and that would be the end of it.

He could call Laurel, ask her to have drinks or dinner. It wouldn't be hard; he had learned early on that information was easy to come by, if you knew how to go about getting it.

She was stubborn, though. Her response to him had been fiery and he knew she wanted him as badly as he wanted her, but she'd deny it. He looked down at the ad again. She'd probably hang up the phone before he had the chance to—

A smile tilted at the corner of his mouth. Until this minute, he hadn't paid any attention to the advertisement itself. If pressed, he'd have said it was for perfume, or cosmetics. Perhaps furs.

Now he saw just how wrong he'd have been. Laurel was offering the siren song to customers in the market for laptop computers. And the company was one that Skouras International had bought only a couple of months ago.

Damian reached for the phone.

Luck was with him. Ten minutes later, he was in his car, his luncheon appointment canceled, forging through midday traffic on his way to a studio in Soho, where the next in the series of ads was being shot.

"Darling Laurel," Haskell said, "that's not a good angle. Turn your head to the right, please."

Laurel did.

"Now tilt toward me. Good."

What was good about it? she wondered. Not the day, surely. Not what she was doing. Why did everything, from toothpaste to tugboats, have to be advertised with sex?

"A little more. Yes, like that. Could you make it a bigger smile, please?"

She couldn't. Smiling didn't suit her mood.

"Laurel, baby, you've got to get into the swing of things. You look utterly, totally bored."

She *was* bored. But that was better than being angry. Don't think about it anymore, she told herself, just don't think about it.

Or him.

"Ah, Laurel, you're starting to scowl. Bad for the face, darling. Relax. Think about the scene. You're on the deck of a private yacht in, I don't know, the Aegean."

"The Caribbean," she snapped.

"What's the matter, you got something against the Greeks? Sure. The Caribbean. Whatever does it for you. Just get into it, darling. There you are, on a ship off the coast of Madagascar."

"Madagascar's in Africa."

"Jeez, give me a break, will you? Forget geography, okay? You're on a ship wherever you want, you're stretched out in the hot sun, using your Redwood laptop to write postcards to all your pals back home."

"That's ridiculous, Haskell. You don't write postcards on a computer."

Haskell glared at her. "Frankly, Laurel, I don't give a flying fig what you're using that thing for. Maybe you're writing your memoirs. Or tallying up the millions in your Swiss bank account. Whatever. Just get that imagination working and give us a smile."

Laurel sighed. He was right. She was a pro, this was her job, and that was all there was to it. Unfortunately she'd slept badly and awakened in a foul mood. It didn't help that she felt like a ninny, posing in a bikini in front of a silly backdrop that simulated sea and sky. What did bikinis, sea and sky have to do with selling computers?

"Laurel, for heaven's sake, I'm losing you again. Concentrate, darling. Think of something pleasant and hang on to it. Where you're going to have supper tonight, for instance. How you spent your weekend. I know it's Monday, but there's got to be something you can imagine that's a turn-on."

Where she was having supper tonight? Laurel almost laughed. At the kitchen counter, that was where, and on the menu was cottage cheese, a green salad and, as a special treat, a new mystery novel with her coffee.

As for how she'd spent the weekend—if Haskell only knew. That was the last thing he'd want her to think about.

To think she'd let Damian Skouras humiliate her like that!

"Hey, what's happening? Laurel, babe, you've gone

from glum to grim in the blink of an eye. Come on, girl. Grab a happy thought and hang on.''

A happy thought? A right cross, straight to Damian Skouras's jaw.

"Good!"

A knee, right where it would do the most good.

"Great!" Haskell began moving around her, his camera at his eye. "Hold that image, whatever it is, because it's working.''

A nice, stiff-armed jab into his solar plexus.

"Wonderful stuff, Laurel. That's my girl!''

Why hadn't she done it? Because there'd already been too many eyes on them, that was why. Because if she'd done what she'd wanted to do, she'd have drawn the attention of everyone in the room, to say nothing of ruining Dawn's day.

"Look up, darling. That's it. Tilt your head. Good. This time, I want something that smolders. A smile that says your wonderful computer's what's made it possible for you to be out here instead of in your office, that in a couple of minutes you'll leave behind this glorious sun and sea, traipse down to the cabin and tumble into the arms of a gorgeous man.'' Haskell leaned toward her, camera whirring. "You do know a gorgeous man, don't you?''

Damian Skouras.

Laurel stiffened. Had she said the words aloud? No, thank goodness. Haskell was still dancing around her, his eye glued to his camera.

Damian Skouras, gorgeous? Don't be silly. Men weren't "gorgeous.''

But he was. That masculine body. That incredible face, with the features seemingly hewn out of granite. The eyes that were a blue she'd never seen before. And that mouth, looking as if it had been chiseled from a cold slab of marble but instead feeling warm and soft and exciting as it took hers.

"Now you've got it!" Haskell's camera whirred and

clicked until the roll of film was done. Then he dumped the camera on his worktable and held out his hand. "Baby, that was great. The look on your face..." He sighed dramatically. "All I can say is, wow!"

Laurel put the computer on the floor, took Haskell's hand, rose to her feet and reached for the terry-cloth robe she'd left over the back of a chair.

"Are we finished?"

"We are, thanks to whatever flashed through your head just now." Haskell chuckled. "I don't suppose you'd like to tell me who he was?"

"It wasn't a 'he' at all," Laurel said, forcing a smile to her lips. "It was just what you suggested. I thought about what I was having for dinner tonight."

"No steak ever made a woman look like that," Haskell said with a lecherous grin. "Who's the lucky man, and why isn't it me?"

"Perhaps Miss Bennett's telling you the truth."

Laurel spun around. The slightly amused male voice had come from a corner of the cavernous loft, but where? The brightly lit set only deepened the darkness that lurked in the corners.

"After all, it's well past lunchtime."

Laurel's heart skipped a beat. No. No, it couldn't be...

Damian Skouras emerged from the shadows like a man stepping out of the mist.

"Hello, Miss Bennett."

For a minute, she could only gape at this man she'd hoped never to see again. Then she straightened, drew the robe more closely around her and narrowed her eyes.

"This isn't funny, Mr. Skouras."

"I'm glad to hear it, Miss Bennett, since comedy's not my forte."

"Laurel?" Haskell turned toward her. "You know this guy? I mean, you asked him to meet you here?"

"I do not know him," Laurel said coldly.

Damian smiled. "Of course she knows me. You heard her greet me by name just now, didn't you?"

"I don't know him, and I certainly didn't ask him to meet me here."

Haskell moved forward. "Okay, pal, you heard the lady. This isn't a public gallery. You want to do business with me, give my agent a call."

"My business is with Miss Bennett."

"Hey, what is it with you, buddy? You deaf? I just told you—"

"And I just told you," Damian said softly. He looked at the photographer. "This has nothing to do with you. I suggest you stay out of it."

Haskell's face turned red and he stepped forward. "Who's gonna make me?"

"No," Laurel said quickly, "Haskell, don't."

She knew Haskell was said to have a short fuse and a propensity for barroom brawls. She'd never seen him in action but she'd seen the results, cuts and bruises and once a black eye. Not that Damian Skouras didn't deserve everything Haskell could dish out, but she didn't want him beaten up, not on her account.

She needn't have worried. Even as she watched, the photographer looked into Damian's face, saw something that made him blanch and step back.

"I don't want any trouble in my studio," he muttered.

"There won't be any." Damian smiled tightly. "If it makes you feel better, I have every right to be here. Put in a call to the ad agency, tell them my name and they'll confirm it."

Laurel laughed. "You're unbelievable, do you know that?" She jabbed her hands on her hips and stepped around Haskell. "What will they confirm? That you're God?"

Damian looked at her. "That I own Redwood Computers."

"You're *that* Skouras?" Haskell said.

"I am."

"Don't be a fool, Haskell," Laurel snapped, her eyes locked on Damian's face. "Just because he claims he owns the computer company doesn't mean he does."

"Trust me," Haskell muttered, "I read about it in the paper. He bought the company."

Laurel's chin rose. "How nice for you, Mr. Skouras. That still doesn't give you the right to come bursting in here as if you owned this place, too."

Damian smiled. "That's true."

"It doesn't give you the right to badger me, either."

"I'm not badgering you, Miss Bennett. I heard there was a shoot here today, I was curious, and so I decided to come by."

Laurel's eyes narrowed. "It had nothing to do with me?"

"No," Damian said, lying through his teeth.

"In that case," she said, "you won't mind if I..."

He caught her arm as she started past him. "Have lunch with me."

"No."

"*The Four Seasons*? Or *The Water's Edge*? It's a beautiful day out, Miss Bennett."

"It was," she said pointedly, "until you showed up."

Haskell cleared his throat. "Well, listen," he said, as he backed away, "long as you two don't need me here..."

"Wait," Laurel said, "Haskell, you don't have to..."

But he was already gone. The sound of his footsteps echoed across the wooden floor. A door slammed, and then there was silence.

"Why must you make this so difficult?" Damian said softly.

"I'm not the one making this difficult," Laurel said coldly. She looked down at her wrist, still encircled by his hand, and then at him. "Let go of me, please."

Damian's gaze followed hers. Hell, he thought, what was he doing? This wasn't his style at all. When you came down to it, nothing he'd done since he'd laid eyes on this woman was in character. The way he'd gone after her yesterday, like a bull in rut. And what he'd done moments ago, challenging that photographer like a street corner punk when the man had only been coming to Laurel's rescue. All he'd been able to think, watching the man's face, was, Go on, take your best shot at me, so I can beat you to a pulp.

And that was crazy. He wasn't a man who settled things with his fists. Not anymore; not in the years since he'd worked his way up from summer jobs on the Brooklyn docks to a Park Avenue penthouse.

He wasn't a man who went after a woman with such single-minded determination, either. Why would he, when there were always more women than he could possibly want, ready and waiting to be singled out for his attention?

That was it. That was what was keeping his interest in the Bennett woman. She was uninterested, or playing at being uninterested, though he didn't believe it, not after the way she'd kissed him yesterday. Either way, the cure was the same. Bed her, then forget her. Satisfy this most primitive of urges and she'd be out of his system, once and for all.

But dammit, man, be civilized about it.

Damian let go of her wrist, took a breath and began again.

"Miss Bennett. Laurel. I know we got off to a poor start—"

"You're wrong. We didn't get off to any start. You're playing cat-and-mouse games but as far as I'm concerned, we never even met."

"Well, we can remedy that. Have dinner with me this evening."

"I'm busy."

"Tomorrow night, then."

"Still busy. And, before you ask, I'm busy for the foreseeable future."

He laughed, and her eyes flashed with indignation.

"Did I say something funny, Mr. Skouras?"

"It's Damian. And I was only wondering which of us is pretending what?"

"Which of us..." Color flew into her face. "My God, what an insufferable ego you must have! Do you think this is a game? That I'm playing hard to get?"

He leaned back against the edge of the photographer's worktable, his jacket open and his hands tucked into the pockets of his trousers.

"The thought crossed my mind, yes."

"Listen here, Mr. Skouras..."

"Damian."

"*Mr.* Skouras." Laurel's eyes narrowed. "Let me put this in words so simple even you'll understand. One, I do not like you. Two, I do not like you. And three, I am not interested in lunch. Or dinner. Or anything else."

"Too many men already on the string?"

God, she itched to slap that smug little smile from his face!

"Yes," she said, "exactly. I've got them lined up for mornings, afternoons and evenings, and there're even a couple of special ones I manage to tuck in at teatime. So as you can see, I've no time at all for you in my schedule."

He was laughing openly now, amusement glinting in his eyes, and it was driving her over the edge. She *would* slug him, any second, or punch him in the very center of that oh-so-masculine chest...

Or throw her arms around his neck, drag his head down to hers and kiss him until he swung her into his arms and carried her off into the shadows that rimmed the lighted set...

"Laurel?" Damian said, and their eyes met.

He knew. She could see it in the way he was looking at her. He'd stopped laughing and he knew what she'd thought, what she'd almost done.

"No," she said, and she swung away blindly. She heard him call her name but she didn't turn back, didn't pause.

Moving by instinct, impelled by fear not of Damian but of herself, she ran to the dressing room, flung open the door and then slammed it behind her. She fell back against it and stood trembling, with her heart thudding in her chest.

Outside, in the studio, Damian stood staring at the closed door. His entire body was tense; he could feel the blood pounding through his veins.

She'd been so angry at him. Furious, even more so because he'd been teasing her and she'd known it. And then, all at once, everything had changed. He'd seen the shock of sudden awareness etch into her lovely face and he'd understood it, felt it burn like flame straight into the marrow of his bones.

She'd run not from him but from herself. All he had to do was walk the few feet to the door that sheltered her, open it and take her in his arms. One touch, and she would shatter.

He would have her, and this insanity would be over.

Or would it?

He took a long, ragged breath. She was interesting, this Laurel Bennett, and not only because of the fire that raged under that cool exterior. Other things about her were almost as intriguing. Her ability to play her part in what was quickly becoming a complex game fascinated him, as did her determination to deny what was so obviously happening between them. She was an enigma. A challenge.

Damian smiled tightly. He had not confronted either in a very long time. It was part of the price he'd paid for success.

Perhaps he'd been wrong in thinking that he could get her out of his system by taking her to bed for a long night of passion. Laurel Bennett might prove a diversion that could please him for some time. And he sensed instinctively that, unlike Gabriella, she would not want nor ask for more.

The thought brought another smile to his lips. The women's libbers would hang him from his toes, maybe

from a more sensitive part of his anatomy, and burn him
in effigy if they ever heard him make such a cool appraisal
of a woman, but they'd have been wrong.

He was no chauvinist, he was merely a man accustomed
to making intelligent assessments. Laurel was a sophisticated woman who'd had many lovers. Even if Gabriella
hadn't told him so, one look at her would have confirmed
it. A brief, intense affair would give pleasure to them both.

He would go about this differently, then. He would have
her, but not just once and not in a grimy loft. Damian ran
his hands through his hair, straightened his tie and then
made his way briskly out to the street.

CHAPTER FOUR

LAUREL'S APARTMENT took up the second floor of a converted town house on the upper east side of Manhattan. The rooms were sun-filled and pleasant, and the building itself was handsome and well located.

But it was an old building, and sometimes the plumbing was a problem. The landlord kept promising repairs but the handful of tenants figured he was almost as ancient as the plumbing. None of them had the heart to keep after him, especially when it turned out that Grey Morgan, the hunky soap star in apartment 3G, had been a plumber's apprentice back in the days when he'd still been known as George Mogenovitch of Brooklyn.

His pretty dancer wife, Susie, had turned into a close friend, but she was another in what Laurel thought of as a legion of inveterate matchmakers. At least she had learned to read the signs. When Susie made spaghetti and invited her to supper, she accepted happily. When the invitation was for Beef Stroganoff and a good bottle of wine, it was wise to plead an excuse.

Laurel smiled to herself. Susie and George were the most warmhearted people imaginable, which explained why she was sitting on the closed lid of the toilet in her bathroom with a bunch of tools in her lap while George stood in her bathtub and tried to figure out why no water at all was coming out of the shower.

"Sorry it's taking me so long," he said, grunting as he worked a wrench around a fitting. "But I think I've almost got it."

"Hey," Laurel said, "don't apologize. I'm just grateful you're willing to bother."

George flicked back his blond mane and shot her a grin.
"Susie wouldn't have it any other way," he said. "She
figures it keeps me humble."

Laurel smiled. "Clever Susie."

Not that George needed to be kept humble. He was a
nice guy. Success hadn't gone to his head the way it did
with some men. Hand them some good looks, some money,
fame and fortune, and what did you get?

A man like Damian Skouras, that's what. Laurel's mouth
thinned. Or like Kirk Soames. What was it about her that
attracted such superficial, self-centered bastards?

Of course, she hadn't seen it that way, not at first. She
was a woman accustomed to making her own way in the
world; she'd learned early on that many men were threatened by her fame, her independence, even her beauty. So
when Kirk—powerful, rich and handsome—came on to her
with wry certainty and assurance, she'd found it intriguing.
By the time he'd asked her to move in with him, she'd
been head over heels in love.

Annie had told her, straight out, that she was making a
mistake.

"Move in with him?" she'd said. "What ever happened
to, 'Marry me?'"

"He's cautious," Laurel had replied, in her lover's de-
fense, "and why wouldn't he be? Marriage is a tough deal
for a man like that."

"It's a tough deal for anybody," Annie had said wryly.
"Still, if he loves you and you love him…"

"Annie, I'm thirty-two. I'm old enough to live with a
man without the world coming to an end. Besides, I don't
want to rush into anything, any more than Kirk does."

"Uh-huh," Annie had said, in a way that made it clear
she knew Laurel was lying. And she was. She'd have married Kirk in a second, if he'd asked. And he *would* ask,
given time. She'd been certain of that.

"Laurel?"

Laurel blinked, George was looking at her, his brows

raised. "Hand me that other wrench, will you? The one with the black handle."

So she had moved in with Kirk, more or less, though she'd held on to her apartment. It had been his suggestion. He'd even offered to pay her rent, though she had refused. If she kept her apartment, he'd said, she'd have a place to stay when she had shoots or showings in the city because he lived thirty miles out, in a sprawling mansion on Long Island's North Shore.

"Bull," Annie had snorted. "The guy's a zillionaire. How come he doesn't have an apartment in the city?"

"Annie," Laurel had said patiently, "you don't understand. He needs the peace and quiet of the Long Island house."

In the end, it had turned out that he did have a Manhattan apartment. Laurel closed her eyes against the rush of painful memories. She'd learned about it by accident, fielding a phone call from a foolishly indiscreet building manager who'd wanted to check with Mr. Soames about a convenient time for some sort of repair to the terrace.

Puzzled, telling herself it was some sort of mistake or perhaps a surprise for her, Laurel had gone to the East side address and managed to slip inside when the doorman wasn't looking. She'd ridden the elevator to the twentieth floor, taken a deep breath and rung the bell of Apartment 2004.

Kirk had opened the door, dressed in a white terry-cloth robe. His face paled when he saw her but she had to give him credit; he recovered quickly.

"What are you doing here, Laurel?"

Before she could reply, a sultry voice called, "Kirk? Where are you, lover?" and a porcelain-skinned blonde wearing a matching robe and the flushed look that came of a long afternoon in bed, appeared behind him.

Laurel hadn't said a word. She hadn't even returned to the Long Island house for her things. And when the story got out, as it was bound to do, the people who knew her sighed and said well, it was sad but they'd have sworn Kirk had changed, that once he'd asked her to move into that big house on the water they'd all figured it meant he'd finally decided to settle down…

"You got a bad diverter valve," George muttered, "but I've almost got it under control. Takes time, that's all."

Laurel gave him an absent smile. Everything took time. It had taken her months to get over the pain of Kirk's betrayal but once she had, she'd begun thinking about their affair with the cold, clear logic of hindsight and she'd found herself wondering what she'd ever found attractive about a man like that to begin with.

She'd mistaken his arrogance for self-assurance, his egotism for determination. She, who'd always prided herself on her control, had been stupidly taken in by sexual chemistry, and the truth was that not even that had really lived up to its promise. She'd never felt swept away by passion in Kirk's arms.

But Damian's kiss had done that. It had filled her with fire, and with a longing so hot and sweet it had threatened to destroy her.

The tools Laurel was holding fell from her suddenly nerveless fingers and clattered on the tile floor.

"You okay?" George said, glancing over at her.

"Sure," she said quickly, and she bent down and scooped up the tools.

Damian Skouras was not for her. He was nothing but an updated copy of Kirk, right down to the sexy blonde pouting in the background at the wedding.

"Gimme the screwdriver, Laurel," George said. "No, not the Phillips head. The other one."

Had the man really thought she wouldn't notice the blonde? Or didn't he think it mattered?

"Egotistical bastard," she muttered, slapping the screwdriver into George's outstretched hand.

"Hey, what'd I do?"

Laurel blinked. George was looking at her as if she'd lost her mind.

"Oh," she said, and flushed bright pink. "George, I'm sorry. I didn't mean you."

He gave her the boyish grin that kept American women glued to their TV sets from two to three every weekday afternoon.

"Glad to hear it. From the look on your face, I'd hate to be whoever it is you're thinking about."

She'd never been able to bring herself to tell Annie the truth of her breakup with Kirk, not because Annie might have said, "I told you so," but because the pain had been too sharp.

"You were right" was all she'd told her sister, "Kirk wasn't for me."

Maybe I should have told her, Laurel thought grimly. Maybe, if I had, Annie and Dawn and everybody else at that wedding would have known Damian Skouras for the belly-to-the-ground snake he was.

"Got it," George said in triumph. He handed her the screwdriver and flipped the selector lever up and down. "Just you watch. Soon as I get out of the tub and turn this baby on—"

"Just be careful," Laurel said. "Watch out for that puddle of water in the…"

Too late. George yelped, lost his footing and made a grab for the first thing that was handy. It was the on-off knob. Water came pouring out of the shower head.

"Damn," he shouted, and leaped back, but it was too late. He was soaked, and so was Laurel. Half the icy spray had shot in her direction. Sputtering, George pushed the knob back in, shut off the water and flung his dripping hair back from his eyes. He looked down at himself, then eyed Laurel. "Well," he said wryly, "at least we know it works."

Laurel burst out laughing.

"Susie's going to think I tried to drown you," she said, tossing him a towel and dabbing at herself with another.

George yanked his soaked sweatshirt over his head and stepped out of the tub. His sneakers squished as he walked across the tile floor of the old-fashioned bathroom.

"I guess you'll have to phone old man Grissom," he said with a sheepish smile. "Tell him that valve's just about shot and he'd better send a plumber around to take a look."

"First thing in the morning," Laurel said, nodding. She mopped her face and hair, then hung the towel over the rack. "I'm just sorry you got drenched."

"No problem. Glad to help out." George draped his arm loosely around Laurel's shoulders. Together, they sauntered down the hall toward the front door. "As for the soaking— I was planning on entering a wet jeans contest anyway."

Laurel grinned, leaned back against the wall and crossed her arms.

"Uh-huh."

"Hey, they have wet T-shirt contests for women, right?" he said impishly as he reached for the doorknob. "Well, why not wet jeans contests for guys?" Grinning, he opened the door. "Anyhow, you know what they used to say. Save water, shower with a friend."

"Indeed," a voice said coldly.

Damian Skouras was standing in the doorway. He was dressed in a dark suit and a white shirt; his tie was a deep scarlet silk, and his face was twisted in a scowl.

Laurel's throat constricted. She'd been kidding herself. The man wasn't a copy of anybody, not when it came to looks. Kirk had been handsome but the only word that described Damian was the one she'd come up with this morning.

He was gorgeous.

He was also uninvited. And unwelcome. Definitely unwelcome, she reminded herself, and she stepped away from the wall, drew herself up to her full height and matched his scowl with one of her own.

"What," she asked coldly, "are you doing here?"

Damian ignored the question. He was too busy trying to figure out what in hell was going on.

What do you think is going on you idiot? he asked himself, and his frown deepened.

Laurel was wearing a soaked T-shirt that clung to her like a second skin. Beneath it, her rounded breasts and nipples stood out in exciting relief. She had on a pair of faded denim shorts, her feet were bare, her hair was wet and her face was shiny and free of makeup.

She was more beautiful than ever.

"Laurel? You know this guy?"

Damian turned his head and looked at the man standing beside her. Actually he wasn't standing beside her anymore. He'd moved slightly in front of her, in a defensive posture that made it clear he was ready to protect Laurel at all costs. Damian's lip curled. What would a woman see in a man like this? He was good-looking; women would think so, anyway, though he had too pretty a face for all the muscles that rippled in his bare chest and shoulders. Damian's gaze swept down the man's body. His jeans were tight and wet, and cupped him with revealing intimacy.

What the hell had been going on here? Laurel and the Bozo looked as if they'd just come in out of the rain.

Unfortunately, it hadn't rained in days.

He thought of what the guy had said about showering with a friend. It was, he knew, a joke. Besides, people didn't shower with their clothing on. Logic told him that, the same as it told him that they didn't climb out of bed wet from head to toe, but what the hell did logic have to do with anything?

Coming here, unannounced, had seemed such a clever idea. Catch her by surprise, have the limousine waiting downstairs with a chilled bottle of champagne in the built-in bar, long-stemmed roses in a crystal vase and reservations at that restaurant that had just opened with the incredible view of the city.

It hadn't occurred to him that just because the telephone directory listed an L. Bennett at this address was no guarantee that she lived alone.

"Laurel?"

The Bozo was talking to Laurel again but he hadn't taken his eyes off him.

"What's the deal? Do you know this guy?"

"Of course she knows me," Damian snapped.

"Is that right, Laurel?"

She nodded with obvious reluctance. "I know him. But I didn't invite him here."

The Bozo folded his arms over his chest. "She knows you," he said to Damian, "but she didn't invite you here."

"I don't know how to break this to you, mister…?"

"Morgan," George said. "Grey Morgan."

Damian smiled pleasantly. "I don't know how to break this to you, Mr. Morgan, but I understood every word she said."

"Then you'll be sure to understand this, too," Laurel said. "Go away."

"Go away," the Bozo repeated, and unfolded his arms.

His height, and all those rippling muscles, were impressive. Good, Damian thought. He could feel the same sense of anticipation spreading through his body again, the one he'd had this afternoon when he'd wanted nothing so much as to take that photographer apart.

Maybe he'd been sitting in too many boardrooms lately, exercising his mind instead of his muscles.

Laurel was thinking almost the same thing, though not in such flattering terms. What was with this man? She could almost smell the testosterone in the air. Damian's jaw was set, his eyes glittered.

George, his buffed torso and his tight jeans, was oozing muscle; Damian was the epitome of urbanity in his expensive dark suit…but she didn't for a second doubt which of them would win if it came down to basics.

Arrogant, self-centered, accustomed to having the world

dance to his tune, and now it looked as if he had all the primitive instincts of a cobra, she thought grimly. How in hell was she going to get rid of him?

"Laurel doesn't want you here, mister."

"What are you?" Damian said softly. "Her translator?"

"Listen here, pal, Laurel and I are—"

"We're very close," Laurel said. She moved forward, slipped her arm through the Bozo's, looked up and gave him a smile that sent Damian's self-control slipping another notch. "Aren't we, George—I mean, Grey?"

"Yeah," the Bozo said, after half a beat, "we are. Very, very close."

Damian's brows lifted. Maybe George or Grey or whoever he was, was right. Maybe he did need a translator. Something was going on here but he couldn't get a handle on it. He felt the way he sometimes did when he was doing business in Tokyo. Everyone spoke some English, Damian could manage some Japanese, but once in a while, a word or a phrase seemed to fall through the cracks.

"So if you don't mind, Mr. Skouras," Laurel said, putting heavy emphasis on the *mister*, "we'd appreciate it if you would—"

"George? Honey, are you done up there?"

They all looked down the hall. A pretty brunette stood at the bottom of the steps, smiling up at them.

"Hi, Laurel. Are you done borrowing my husband?"

Damian's brows arced again. He looked at Laurel, who flushed and dropped the Bozo's arm.

"Hi, Suze. Yeah, just about."

"Great." The brunette came trotting up the stairs. "Did he do a good job?"

Laurel's color deepened. "Fine," she said quickly.

"You see, George?" The brunette dimpled. "If the ratings ever go into the toilet, you can always go back to fixing them."

Laurel swallowed hard. Damian could see the movement of the muscles in her throat.

"He fixed my shower," she said, with dignity.

Damian nodded. "I see."

"Suze," George said, clearing his throat, "Laurel's got a bit of a problem here…"

"No," Laurel said quickly, "no, I don't."

"But you said…?"

"It's not a problem at all." She looked at Damian. "Mr. Skouras was just leaving. Weren't you, Mr. Skouras?"

"Yes, I was."

"You see? So there's no need to—"

"Just as soon as you change your clothing," he said. He leaned back against the door jamb, arms folded, and gave her a long, assessing look. "On the other hand, what you're wearing is…rather interesting. You might want to put on a pair of shoes, though. You never know what you're liable to step in, on a New York street."

He had to bite his lip to keep from laughing at the expression that swept over Laurel's face.

"I know what *you've* stepped in," she said, her chin lifting and her eyes blazing into his, "but I promise you, I've no intention of going anywhere with you."

"But our reservation is for eight," he said blandly.

A little furrow appeared between Laurel's eyebrows. "What reservation?"

"For dinner."

The furrow deepened. "Dinner?"

Damian looked at Susie. They shared a conspiratorial smile. "I'd be insulted that she forgot our appointment, but I know what a long day she put in doing that Redwood Computer layout."

"Redwood?" Susie said.

"Redwood?" George said, with interest, "the outfit that makes those hot portables?"

Damian shrugged modestly. "Well, that's what Wall Street says. I'm just pleased Laurel's doing the ads for the company." He smiled. "Almost as pleased as I am to have had the good fortune to have purchased Redwood."

"Redwood Comp...?" Susie's eyes widened. "Of course. Skouras. *Damian* Skouras. I should have recognized you. I was just reading *Manhattan Magazine*. Your picture's in it." A smile lit her pretty face. "George?" she said, elbowing her husband in the ribs, "this is..."

"Damian Skouras." George stuck out his hand, drew it back and wiped it on his damp jeans, then stuck it out again. "A pleasure, Mr. Skouras."

"Please, call me Damian," Damian said modestly.

George grinned as the men shook hands. "My wife and I just bought a hundred shares of your stock."

Damian smiled. "I'm delighted to hear it."

I don't believe this, Laurel thought incredulously. Was it a conspiracy? First Annie and Dawn, her very own flesh and blood; now Susie and George...

"Laurel," Susie said, "you never said a word!"

"About what?"

"About...about this," Susie said, with a little laugh.

"Suze, you've got this all wrong."

"You're not posing for those ads?"

"Yes. Yes, I am, but—but this man—"

"Damian," Damian said with a smile.

"This man," Laurel countered, "has nothing to do with—"

"My advertising people selected Laurel. With my approval, naturally."

"Naturally," Susie echoed.

"Imagine my surprise when we bumped into each other at my ward's wedding yesterday." His smile glittered. "In the flesh, as it were. We had a delightful few hours. Didn't we, Laurel? And we agreed to have dinner together tonight. To discuss business, of course."

Susie's eyes widened. She looked at Laurel, who was watching Damian as if she wished a hole in the ground would open under his feet.

"Of course," Susie said, chuckling.

"At *The Gotham Penthouse*."

"*The Gotham Penthouse*! I just read a review of it in—"

"*Manhattan Magazine*?" Laurel said, through her teeth.

Susie nodded. "Uh-huh. It's supposed to be scrumptious!"

Damian smiled. "So I hear. Perhaps you and—is it George?"

"Yeah," George said. God, Laurel thought with disgust, it was a good thing there was no dirt on the floor or he'd have been scuffing his toes in it. "It is. Grey's my stage name. My agent figured it sounded better."

"Sexier," Susie said, and smiled up at her husband.

"Well, perhaps you and your wife would like to join us?"

"No," Laurel said sharply. Everyone looked at her. "I mean—I mean, of course, that would be lovely, but it isn't as if—"

"You don't have to explain." Susie looped her arm through her husband's. "It's a very romantic place, *The Penthouse*. Well, that's what the reviewer said, anyway."

Her smile was warm. It encompassed both Damian and Laurel as if they were a package deal. Laurel wanted to grab Susie and shake her until her teeth rattled. Or slug Damian Skouras in the jaw. Or maybe do both.

"You guys don't need an old married couple like us around."

"Susie," Laurel said grimly, "you really do not understand."

"Oh, I do." Susie grinned. "It's business. Right, Damian?"

Could a snake really smile? This one could.

"Precisely right," Damian said.

"It would be lovely to get together for dinner some other time, though. At our place, maybe. I do a mean Beef Stroganoff—which reminds me, George, if we don't get moving, everything will be burned to a crisp."

George's face suddenly took on a look of uncertainty. "Laurel? You're okay with this?"

A muscle worked in Laurel's jaw. At least somebody was still capable of thinking straight, but why drag innocent bystanders into the line of fire? This was a private war, between her and Damian.

"It's fine," she said. "And thanks for fixing the shower."

"Hey, anytime." George held out his hand, and Damian took it. "Nice to have met you."

"The same here," Damian said politely.

Susie leaned toward Laurel behind her husband's broad back.

"You never said a word," she announced in a stage whisper that could have been heard two floors below. "Laurel, honey, this guy is *gorgeous*!"

This guy's a rat, Laurel thought, but she bit her tongue and said nothing.

Susie had been right. The restaurant was a winner.

It had low lighting, carefully spaced tables and a magnificent view. The service was wonderful, the wine list impressive and the food looked delicious.

Laurel had yet to take a bite.

When she'd ignored the menu, Damian had simply ordered for them both. Beluga caviar, green salads, roast duck glazed with Montmorency cherries and brandy and, for a grand finale, a chocolate soufflé garnished with whipped cream that looked as light as air.

Neither the waiter nor Damian seemed to notice her hunger strike. The one served each course, then cleared it away; the other ate, commented favorably on the meal, and kept up a light, pleasant conversation in which she refused to join.

"Coffee?" Damian said, when the soufflé had been served. "Or do you prefer tea?"

Even prisoners on hunger strikes drank liquids. Laurel looked across the table at him.

"Which are you having?"

"Coffee. As strong as possible, and black."

Coffee was what she always drank, and just that way. Laurel gave a mental sigh.

"In that case," she said, unsmiling, "I'll have tea."

Damian laughed as the waiter hurried off. "Is there anything I could do to make you less inclined to insult me?"

"Would you do it, if there were?"

"Why do I have the feeling your answer might prove lethal?"

"At least you got *that* right!"

He sighed and shook his head, though she could see amusement glinting in his eyes. "That's not a very ladylike answer."

"Since you're obviously not a gentleman, why should it be? And I'm truly delighted to have provided you with a laugh a minute today. First Haskell, then George and Susie, and now here I am, playing jester for the king while he dines."

"Is that what you think?" Damian waited until their coffee and tea were served. "That I brought you here to amuse me?"

"I think you get your kicks out of tossing your weight around."

"Sorry?"

"You like to see people dance to your tune."

He pushed aside his dessert plate, moved his cup and saucer in front of him and folded his hands around the cup.

"That is not why I asked you to join me this evening."

"Asked? Coerced, you mean."

"I had every intention of asking you politely, Laurel, but when you opened the door and I saw you with that man, Grey…"

"His name is George."

"George, Grey, what does it matter?" Damian's eyes darkened. "I saw him, half-dressed. And I saw you smiling at him. And I thought, very well, I have a choice to make. I can do as I intended, ask her to put aside the words that passed between us this morning and come out to dinner with me…''

''The answer would have been no.''

''Or,'' he said, his voice roughening, ''I can punch this son of a bitch in the jaw, sling her over my shoulder and carry her off.''

The air seemed to rush out of the space between them. Laurel felt as if she were fighting for breath.

''That—that's not the least bit amusing.''

''It wasn't meant to be.'' Damian reached across the table and took her hand. ''Something happened between us yesterday.''

''I don't know what you're talk—''

''Don't!'' His fingers almost crushed hers as she sought to tug free of his grasp. ''Don't lie. Not to me. Not to yourself.'' A fierce, predatory light blazed in his eyes. ''You know exactly what I'm talking about. I kissed you, and you kissed me back.''

Their eyes met. He wasn't a fool; lying would get her nowhere. Well, her years before the camera had taught her some things, at least.

''So what?'' she said coolly. She forced a faintly mocking smile to her lips. ''You caught me off guard but then, you know that. What more do you want, Damian? My admission that you kiss well? I'm sure you know that, too— or doesn't your blond friend offer enough plaudits to satisfy that ego of yours?''

''Is that what this is all about? Gabriella?'' Damian made an impatient gesture. ''That's over with.''

''She didn't like watching her lover flirt with another woman, you mean?'' Laurel wrenched her hand free of his. ''At least she's not a total idiot.''

''I broke things off last evening.''

''Last…? Not because of…?''

''It was over between us weeks ago. I just hadn't gotten around to admitting it.'' A smile curled across his mouth. ''It hadn't occurred to me that you'd be jealous.''

"Jealous? Of you and that woman? Your ego isn't big, it's enormous! I don't even know you."

"Get to know me, then."

"There's no point. I'm not interested in getting involved."

"I'm not asking you to marry me," he said bluntly. "We're consenting adults, you and I. And something happened between us the minute we saw each other."

"Uh-huh. And next, you're going to tell me that nothing like this has ever happened to you before."

Laurel put her napkin on the table and slid to the end of the banquette. She'd listened to all she was going to listen to, and it wasn't even interesting. His line was no different than a thousand others.

"Laurel."

He caught her wrist as she started to rise. His eyes had gone black; the bones in his handsome, arrogant face stood out.

"Come to bed with me. Let me make love to you until neither of us can think straight."

Color flooded her face. "Let go," she said fiercely, but his hand only tightened on hers.

"I dreamed of you last night," he whispered. "I imagined kissing your soft mouth until it was swollen, caressing your breasts with my tongue until you sobbed with pleasure. I dreamed of being deep inside you, of hearing you cry out my name as you came against my mouth."

She wanted to flee his soft words but she couldn't, even if he had let her. Her legs were weak; she could feel her pulse pounding in her ears.

"That is what I've wanted, what we've both wanted, from the minute we saw each other. Why do you try to deny it?"

The bluntness of his words, the heat in his eyes, the memory of what she'd felt in his arms, stole her breath away and, with it, all her hard-won denial.

Everything Damian had said was true. She couldn't pretend anymore. She didn't like him. He was everything she despised and more, but she wanted him as she'd never wanted any man, and with such desperate longing that it terrified her.

Her vision blurred. She saw herself in his arms, lying beneath him and returning kiss for kiss, wrapping her legs around his waist as she tilted her hips up to meet his possessive thrusts.

"Yes," he said fiercely, and she looked into his eyes and knew that the time for pretense was over.

Laurel gave a soft cry. She tore her hand from Damian's, shot to her feet and flew from the restaurant, but he caught up to her just outside the door, his fingers curling around her arm like a band of steel.

"Tell me I'm wrong," he said in a hoarse whisper, "and so help me God, I'll have my driver take you home and you'll never be bothered by me again."

Time seemed to stand still. They stood in the warmth and darkness of the spring night, looking at each other, both of them breathing hard, and then Laurel whispered Damian's name and moved into his arms with a hunger she could no longer deny.

CHAPTER FIVE

THEY WERE INSIDE the limousine, shut off from the driver and the world, moving swiftly through the late-night streets of the city. The car, and Damian, were all that existed in Laurel's universe.

His body was rock-hard; his arms crushed her to him. His mouth was hot and open against hers, and his tongue penetrated her in an act of intimacy so intense it made her tremble. She felt fragile and feminine, consumed by his masculinity. His kiss demanded her complete surrender and promised, in return, the fulfilment of her wildest fantasies.

There would be no holding back. Not tonight. Not with him.

Wrong, this is wrong. Those were the words that whispered inside her head, but the message beating in her blood was far louder. *Stop thinking*, it said. *Let yourself feel.*

And she could feel. Everything. The hardness of Damian's body. The wildness of his kisses. The heat of his hands as he touched her. It was all so new... and yet, it wasn't. They had just met, but Damian was not a stranger. Was this why some people believed they'd lived before? She felt as if she'd known him in another life, or maybe since the start of time.

Her head fell back against his shoulder as his hand swept over her, skimming the planes of her face, stroking the length of her throat, then cupping her breast. His thumb brushed across her nipple and she cried out against his mouth.

He said her name in a husky whisper, and then something more, words in Greek that she couldn't understand. But she understood this, the way his fingertips trailed fire over her skin, and this, the taste of his mouth, and yes, she understood when he clasped her hand and brought it to him so that she could feel the power and rigidity of his need.

"Yes," she said breathlessly, and he made a sound low in his throat, pushed up her skirt, slid his hand up her leg and cupped the molten heat he found between her thighs.

The shock of his touch, the raw sexuality of it, shot like lightning through Laurel's blood. A soft cry broke from her throat and she grabbed for his wrist. What she felt—what he was making her feel—was almost more than she could bear.

"Damian," she sobbed, "Damian, please."

"Tell me what you want," he said in a fierce whisper. "Say it."

You, she thought, I want you.

She did. Oh, she did. She wanted him in a way she'd never wanted any man, not just with her body but with something more, something she couldn't define...

The half-formed realization terrified her, and she twisted her face away from Damian's seeking mouth.

"Listen to me," she said urgently. Her fingers dug into his wrist. "I don't think—"

"Don't think," he said, "not tonight," and before she could respond, he thrust his hands into her hair, lifted her face to his and kissed her.

It was not the civilized thing to do.

Damian knew it, even as he took Laurel's mouth again.

The same wild need was beating in her blood as in his. He felt it in her every sigh, her caresses, her hungry response to his kisses. But she'd started to draw back, frightened, he suspected, of the passionate storm raging between them.

Hell, he couldn't blame her.

Something was happening here, something he didn't pretend to understand. The only thing he was sure of was that whatever this was, it was too powerful, too elemental, to deny. He'd sooner have given up breathing than give up this moment.

Minutes ago, when he'd touched her, when he'd felt the heat of her and she'd given that soft, keening cry of surrender, he'd damn near ripped off her panties, unzipped his fly and buried himself deep inside her.

That he hadn't done it had had little to do with propriety, or even with reason, though it would have been nice to tell himself so. The truth was simpler, and much more basic. What had stopped him was the burning need to undress her slowly, to savor her naked beauty with his eyes and hands and mouth.

He wanted to watch her face as he slowly caressed her, to see her pupils grow enormous with pleasure, to touch her and stroke her until she was wild for his possession. He wanted her in bed, his bed, naked in his arms, her skin hot against his, climbing toward a climax that would be more powerful than anything either of them had ever known, and though the intensity of his need was setting off warning bells, he didn't give a damn. Not now. His body was hot and hard; he wanted Laurel more than he'd ever wanted anything, or anyone, in this world.

She'd told him, in the restaurant, that he wasn't a gentleman but hell, he'd never been a gentleman, not from the moment of his birth. Now, as he cupped her face in his hands and whispered her name, as her eyes opened and met his, he knew that he'd sooner face the fires of hell than start pretending to be a gentleman tonight.

He lived in an apartment on Park Avenue.

It was a penthouse duplex, reached by a private elevator that opened onto a dimly lighted foyer that rose two stories into darkness. If he had servants, they were not visible.

The elevator doors slid shut, and they were alone.

Shadows, black-velvet soft and deep, wrapped around them. The night was so still that Laurel could hear the pounding beat of her heart.

There was still time. She could say, "This was a mistake," and demand to be taken home. Damian wouldn't like it, but what did that matter? She was neither a fool nor a tramp, and surely only a woman who was one or both would be on her way to bed with a man she'd met little more than twenty-four hours ago.

Damian's hands closed on her shoulders. He turned her toward him, and what she saw mirrored in his eyes drove every logical thought from her mind.

"Laurel," he said, and she went into his arms.

He kissed her hard, lifting her against him, his hands cupping her bottom so that she was pressed against his erection. His mouth teased hers open. He bit down on her bottom lip, then soothed the tiny wound with his tongue, until she was trembling and clutching his jacket for support.

"Say it now," he said in a savage whisper. "Tell me what you want."

The answer was in her eyes, but she gave it voice.

"You," she said in a broken whisper, "you, you—"

Damian's mouth dropped to hers. Heart surging with triumph, he lifted her into his arms and carried her up the stairs, into the darkness.

His bedroom was huge. The bed, bathed in ivory moonlight, faced onto a wall of glass below which the city glittered in the night like a castle from a fairy tale.

Slowly Damian lowered Laurel to her feet. For a long moment, he didn't touch her. Then he lifted his hand and stroked her cheek. Laurel closed her eyes and leaned into his caress.

Gently he ran his hand over her hair.

"Take it down," he said softly.

Her eyes flew open. She couldn't see his face clearly— he was standing in shadow—but there was an intensity in the way he held himself.

"My hair?" she whispered.

"Yes." He reached out and touched the silky curls that lay against her neck. "Take it down for me."

Laurel raised her hands to the back of her head. Her hair had already started coming loose of the tortoiseshell pins she'd used to put it up. Now, she removed the pins slowly, wishing she could see his face as she did. But he was still standing in shadow, and he didn't step forward until her hair tumbled around her shoulders.

"Beautiful," he whispered.

He caught a fistful of the shining auburn locks and brought them to his lips. Her hair felt like silk against his mouth and its fragrance reminded him of a garden after a gentle spring rain.

He let her hair drift from his fingers.

"Now your earrings," he said softly.

Her hands went to the tiny crystal beads that swayed on slender gold wires from her earlobes. He could see confusion in her eyes and he knew she'd expected something different, a quicker leap into the flames, but if that was what she wanted, he wouldn't, hell, he *couldn't,* oblige. His control was stretched almost to the breaking point. He couldn't touch her now; if he did, it would all be over before it began, and he didn't want that.

Nothing would be rushed. Not with her. Not tonight.

One earring, then the other, dropped into her palm. Damian held out his hand, and she gave them to him. Her hands went to the silver buttons on her silk jacket, and he nodded. Seconds later, the jacket fell to the floor.

He reached out and caught her wrists.

"Nothing more," he whispered, and brushed his mouth over hers. "I want to do all the rest."

She heard the soft urgency in his voice, the faint tone of command. His eyes glittered; there was a dark passion in his face, a taut pull of skin over bone that made her heart beat faster.

But his touch was gentle as he undressed her. And he did it slowly, so slowly that she thought she might die with the pleasure of it, first her blouse, then her skirt, her slip and her bra, until she stood before him wearing nothing but her high-heeled sandals, sheer stockings, a garter belt and panties that were a lacy wisp of white silk.

She heard his breath hitch in his throat. He stepped back and looked at her. She felt a flush rise over her skin and she started to cross her arms over her breasts, but he stopped her.

"Don't hide yourself from me," he said thickly. "Laurel, *mátya mou*, how exquisite you are."

She wanted to ask him what it meant, the name he'd called her; she wanted to tell him that no matter what he thought, this night was a first for her, that she'd never given herself to anyone this way, never wanted anyone this way.

There were a hundred things to say, but she couldn't bring herself to say anything but his name.

"Yes," he said, and he lifted her in his arms again, kissed her deeply and carried her to the bed.

He undid the garters, rolled down her stockings and dropped them to the floor. He lifted each of her feet and kissed the high, elegant arches; he sucked her toes into his mouth. Then he knelt beside her and undid the tiny hooks on the garter belt. His hands shook as he did, which was strange because while he'd never counted them, he'd surely undone a thousand such closures before. He had done all these things before, taken a woman to his bed, undressed her…and yet, when Laurel finally lay naked before him, he felt his heart kick against his ribs.

He whispered her name and then he put one arm beneath her shoulders and lifted her to him, kissed her mouth as she curled her hands into the folds of his jacket. There was a tightness growing deep within him, one that threatened to shatter what little remained of his control. He knew it was time to stop touching her. He needed to rip off his clothing and bury himself inside her or risk humiliating himself like an untried boy, but he couldn't.

Nothing could keep him from learning the taste and feel of her skin.

He kissed her breasts, drawing the beaded nipples deep into his mouth, and when she cried out his name and arced toward him, her excitement fueled his own. He ran his hand along her hip, his fingers barely stroking across the feathery curls that formed a sweet, inverted triangle between her thighs, and the tightness in his belly grew.

"Laurel," he said. "Look at me."

Her lashes fluttered open. Her eyes were huge, the blue irises all but consumed by the black pupils. She was breathing hard; her face, her rounded breasts, were stained with the crimson flush of passion.

He had done this to her, he thought fiercely, he had brought her this pleasure. He said her name again, his gaze holding hers as he moved his hand lower and when, at last, he touched her, she let out a cry so soft and wild that he thought he could feel it against his palm.

He rolled away from her and stripped off his clothing. His hands shook; it was as if he was entering into an unknown world where what awaited him could bring joy beyond imagining or the darkness of despair. He didn't know which right know, and he didn't give a damn.

All that mattered was this moment, and this woman.

Laurel. Beautiful Laurel.

Naked, he knelt on the bed beside her. She was watching him, her face pale but for the glow on her cheeks, and the urgency deep within him seemed to diminish. Just for a moment, he thought it might almost be enough to take her in his arms, kiss her, hold her close and listen to the beat of her heart against his the whole night through.

But then she whispered his name and held her arms up to him, and he knew that he needed more. He needed to penetrate her, to make her his in the way men have done since the dawn of time.

"Laurel," he said, and when her eyes met his, he gave up thinking, parted her thighs and sank deep into her heat.

* * *

Laurel rose carefully from the bed.

It was very late, and Damian was asleep. She was sure of it; she could hear the steady susurration of his breath.

Her clothing was scattered across the room. She gathered up the bits and pieces, moving quietly so as not to wake him, and she thought about how he had undressed her, how she'd let him undress her, how she'd wanted him to undress her.

A hot, sick feeling roiled in the pit of her stomach.

The apartment was silent as she slipped out of his bedroom, though the darkness had given way to a cheerless grey. It made it easier to see, at least; the last thing she wanted to do was put on a light and risk waking him.

What in heaven's name had she done?

Sex, she told herself coldly. An experience, a seduction, the kind other women whispered about, even joked about. That was what had happened to her, a mind-blowing night of passion in the arms of a man who obviously knew his way around the boudoir.

Laurel's hands trembled as she zipped up her skirt.

She had given up all the moral precepts she'd lived by. She'd humiliated herself. She'd…she'd…

A moan broke from her throat. She'd become someone else, that was what had happened, and the knowledge that such a woman even existed inside her would haunt her forever.

The things she'd done tonight, the things she'd let Damian do…

What had happened to her? Just the sight of him, kneeling between her thighs, had made her come apart. He was so magnificent, such a perfect male animal, his broad shoulders gleaming as if they'd been oiled, his hair dark and tumbling around his face. The tiny gold stud, glinting in his ear, had been all the adornment such a man would ever need.

And then he'd entered her. She'd felt her body stretching to welcome him, to contain him…and then he'd moved, and moved again, and a cry had burst from her throat and she'd shattered into a million shining pieces.

"Damian," she'd sobbed, "oh, Damian…"

"I know," he'd whispered, his mouth on hers, and then she'd felt him beginning to move again, and she'd realized he was still hard within her. The flames had ignited more slowly the second time, not because she'd wanted him less but because he'd made it happen that way, pulling back, then easing forward, filling her and filling her, taking her closer and closer to the edge until, once again, she'd felt herself soar into the night sky where she'd blazed as brightly as a comet before tumbling back to earth.

She'd found paradise, she'd thought dreamily, as Damian's arms closed around her. She'd blushed as he whispered soft words to her and when, at last, he'd kissed her forehead, and her mouth, and held her close against his heart, she'd drifted into dreamless sleep.

Hours later, something—a sound, a whisper of breeze from the window—had awakened her. For a moment, she'd been confused. This wasn't her bedroom…

And then she'd remembered. She was in Damian's arms, in his bed, with the scent of him and what they'd done on her skin, and suddenly, in the cold, sharp light of dawn, she'd seen the night for what it really had been.

Cheap. Tawdry. Ugly.

Paradise? Laurel's throat constricted. A one-night stand, was more like it. She'd gone to bed with a stranger, not just gone to bed with him but—but done things with him she'd never…

…*felt things she'd never…*

"Laurel?"

She gasped and spun around. The bedroom door had opened; Damian stood in a pool of golden light that spilled from a bedside lamp. Naked, unashamed, he was a Greek statue come to life, hewn not of cold marble but of warm flesh. There was a little smile on his lips, a sexy, sleepy one, but as he looked at her, it began to fade.

"You're all dressed."

"Yes." Laurel cleared her throat. "I—I'm sorry if I woke you, Damian. I tried to be quiet but—"

God, she was babbling! She'd never sneaked out of a man's apartment before, but she'd be damned if she'd let him know that. Anyway, there was a first time for everything. Hadn't she proved that tonight?

"I apologize if I disturbed you."

"Apologize?" he said, his eyes narrowing.

"Yes. Oh, and thank you for..." *For what? Are you crazy? What are you thanking him for?* "For everything," she said brightly.

"Laurel..."

"No, really, you needn't see me out. I'm sure I can find my way, just down the stairs and through the—"

"Dammit," he said sharply, "what is this?"

"What is what? It's late. Very late. Or early, I don't really know which. And I have to go home, and change, and—" The quick, brittle flow of words ended in a gasp as he reached out and brought her against him. "Damian, don't."

"Ah," he said softly, "I understand." He laughed softly, bent his head and took the tip of her earlobe gently between his teeth. "Morning-after jitters. Well, I know how to fix that."

"Don't," she said again. She could hear the faint rasp in her own voice; it said, more clearly than words, that though her head meant one thing, her traitorous body meant something very different. She could feel him stirring against her and a warm heaviness settled in her loins.

"Laurel." Damian spoke in a whisper. He wasn't laughing now; he was looking at her through eyes that had darkened to silvery ash. "Come back to bed."

"No," she said, "I just told you, I can't."

His smile was honeyed. Slowly he dipped his head and kissed her, parting her lips with his.

"You can. And you want to. You know that you do."

She closed her eyes as he kissed the hollow of her throat. He was right, that was the worst of it. She wanted to go with him into that wide bed, where the scent of their love-making still lingered.

Except that it hadn't been lovemaking. It had been... There was a word for what they'd done, a word so ugly, so alien, that even thinking it made her feel unclean.

His hands were at the top button of her blouse. In a moment, he'd have them all undone, and then he'd touch her, and she wouldn't want to stop him...

"Stop it!" Her hands wrapped around his wrists. His brows, as black as a crow's wings, drew together. She'd taken him by surprise, she saw, and she made the most of the advantage and pressed on. "We had—we had fun, I agree, but let's not spoil it. Really, we both knew it was just one of those things that happen. There's no need to say anything more."

His eyes narrowed. "I thought we might—"

"Might what? Work out an arrangement?" She forced a smile to her lips. "I'm sorry, Damian, but I'd rather leave it at this. You know what they say about too much of anything spoiling it."

He was angry, she could see that in the flush that swept over his high cheekbones. His ego had taken a hit but that was too damn bad. What had he expected? An if-it's-Tuesday-it-must-be-your-place kind of deal, the sort he'd no doubt had with the blonde?

She waited, not daring to move, knowing that if he took her in his arms and kissed her again, her pathetic show of bravado might collapse—but he didn't. He studied her in silence, a muscle bunching in his cheek, and then he gave a curt nod.

"As you wish, of course. Actually you're quite right. Too much of anything is never good." He smiled politely, though she suspected the effort cost him, and turned toward the bedroom. "Just give me a minute to dress and I'll see you home."

"No! No, I'll take a taxi."

Damian swung toward her. "Don't be ridiculous."

"I'm perfectly capable of seeing myself home."

"Perhaps." His voice had taken on a flinty edge, as had his gaze. He folded his arms over his chest and she thought, fleetingly, that even in the splendor of his nudity, he managed to look imposing. "But this is New York City, not some little town in Connecticut, and I am not a man to permit a woman to travel these streets, alone, at this hour."

"Permit? *Permit?*" Laurel drew herself up. "I don't need your permission."

"Hell," he muttered, and thrust a hand into his hair. "This is nothing to quarrel about."

"You're right, it isn't. Goodbye, Damian."

His hand fell on her shoulder as she spun away from him, his fingers biting harshly into her flesh.

"What's going on here, Laurel? Can you manage to tell me that?"

"I have told you. I said—"

"I heard what you said, and I don't believe you." His touch gentled; she felt the rough brush of his fingertips against her throat. "You know you want more than this."

"You've no idea what I want," she said sharply.

He smiled. "Tell me, then. Let me get dressed, we'll have coffee and we'll talk."

"How many times do I have to say I'm not interested before you believe me, Damian?"

His eyes darkened. Long seconds passed, and then his hand fell from her shoulder. He turned, strode into his bedroom, picked up the telephone and punched a button on the dial.

"Stevens? Miss Bennett is leaving. Bring the car around, please."

"Why did you do that? There was no need to wake your chauffeur!"

He looked at her, his lips curved in a parody of a smile as he hung up the phone.

"I'm sure Stevens would appreciate your thoughtfulness, but he's been with me for years. He's quite accustomed to being awakened to perform such errands. Can you find your own way to the lobby, or shall I ring for the doorman?"

"I'll find my own way," she said quickly.

"Fine. In that case, if you'll excuse me…?"

The door shut gently in her face.

She stood staring at it, feeling a rush of crimson flood her skin, hating herself and hating him, and then she spun away.

Would she ever forget the stupidity of what she'd done tonight? she wondered, as she rode to the lobby in his private elevator.

More to the point, would she ever forget that the only place she'd ever glimpsed heaven had been in Damian Skouras's arms?

In the foyer of the penthouse, Damian stood at the closed doors to the elevator, glaring at the tiny lights on the wall panel as they marked Laurel's passage to the lobby. He'd put on a pair of jeans and zipped them, but he hadn't bothered closing them and they hung low on his hips.

What the hell had happened, between the last time they'd made love and now? He'd fallen asleep holding a warm, satisfied woman in his arms and awakened to find a cold stranger getting dressed in the hallway.

No, not a stranger. Laurel had metamorphosed back into who she'd been when they'd met, a beautiful woman with a tongue like a razor and the disposition of a grizzly bear. And she'd done her damnedest to make it sound as if what had gone on between them tonight had no more importance than a one-night stand.

The light on the panel blinked out. She'd reached the lobby, and the doorman, alerted by the call Damian had made after he'd closed the bedroom door, would be waiting to hand her safely off to Stevens.

Still glowering, he made his way to the terrace in time

to see Laurel getting into the car. Stevens shut the door after her, climbed behind the wheel and that was that.

She was gone, and good riddance.

Who was he kidding? She wasn't gone, not that easily. Her fragrance still lingered on his skin, and in his bed. The sound of her voice, the way she'd sighed his name while they were making love, drifted like a half-remembered tune in his mind.

He had lied to her, when he'd said Stevens was accustomed to being roused at all hours of the night. Being at the beck-and-call of an employer was something he'd hated, in his youth; he'd vowed never to behave so imperiously with those who served him.

Besides, waking Stevens had never been necessary before.

No woman had ever risen and left his bed so eagerly, Damian thought grimly, as he strode into his bedroom. His problem was usually getting rid of them, not convincing them to stay.

Not that he really cared. It had been pleasant, this interlude; he'd have been happy to have gone on with it for a few more weeks, even for a couple of months, but there were other women. There were always other women.

Something glittered on the carpet. Damian frowned and scooped it up.

It was Laurel's earring.

His hand closed hard around it. He remembered the flushed, expectant look on her face when he'd taken the earrings from her, when he'd begun undressing her, when she'd raised her arms to him and he'd knelt between her thighs and thrust home...

"Home?" he said. He laughed, then tossed the earring onto the night table.

It was late, he was tired, and when you came right down to it, the only thing special about tonight had been the sheer effort it had taken to get Laurel Bennett into his bed.

Whistling, Damian headed for the shower.

CHAPTER SIX

SUSIE MORGAN sat at Laurel's kitchen table, her chin propped on her fist as she watched Laurel knead a lump of sourdough batter.

Actually, Susie thought with a lifted eyebrow, Laurel was closer to beating the life out of the stuff than she was to kneading it. Susie glanced at her watch and her brow rose another notch. Laurel had been at it for fifteen minutes, well, fifteen minutes that she knew of, anyway. Who knew how long that poor mound of dough had really been lying there? When she'd come by for Laurel's if-I'm-home-and-haven't-gained-any-weight-the-camera-might-notice Friday morning bread-baking session, there'd already been a dab of flour on Laurel's nose and a mean glint in her eye.

The flour was one thing, but the glint was another. Susie frowned as Laurel whipped the dough over and punched it hard enough to make her wince in sympathy. She'd never known her friend to look so angry, not in the three years they'd known each other, but that was the way she looked lately…though there were times when another expression chased across her face, one that hinted not so much of anger but of terrible unhappiness.

Laurel had alternated between those two looks for four weeks now, ever since the night she'd gone out with Damian Skouras, whose name she hadn't once mentioned since. He hadn't come by again, either, which didn't make sense. Susie had seen the way he'd looked at Laurel and, whether Laurel knew it or not, the way she'd looked at him. Any self-respecting scientist caught between the two of them would have had doubts about carbon emissions being the only thing heating up the atmosphere.

Susie had given it another try, just the other day.

"How's Adonis?" she'd said, trying to sound casual.

Laurel had tried to sound casual, too. "Who?"

"The Greek," Susie had replied, playing along, "you know, the one with the looks and the money."

"How should I know?"

"Aren't you seeing him anymore?"

"I saw him once, under protest."

"Yeah, but I figured—"

"You figured wrong," Laurel had answered, in a way that made it clear the topic was off limits.

"Well, if you say so," Susie had said, "but, you know, if anything's on your mind and you want to talk about it…"

"Thanks, but there's nothing worth talking about," Laurel had replied with a breezy smile, which, as Susie had tried to tell George that night, was definitely proof that there was.

"I don't follow you," George had said patiently. So she'd tried to explain but George, sweet as he was, was a man. It was too much to expect he'd see that if there truly was nothing worth talking about, Laurel would have said something like, "What *are* you talking about, Susie?" instead of just tossing off that meaningless response. She'd even tried to explain that she had this feeling, just a hunch, really, that something had happened between Laurel and the Skouras guy, but George's eyes had only glazed over while he said, "Really?" and "You don't say," until finally she'd given it up.

Susie's frown deepened. On the other hand, even George might sense there was a problem if he could see Laurel beating the life out of that poor sourdough. A couple of more belts like the last and the stuff would be too intimidated to rise.

Susie cleared her throat.

"Uh, Laurel?"

"Yeah?"

"Ah, don't you think that's about done?"

Laurel gave the dough a vicious punch and blew a curl off her forehead.

"Don't I think what's about done?"

"The bread," Susie said, wincing as Laurel slammed her fist into the yeasty mound again.

"Soon." She gave the stuff another whack that made the counter shudder. "But not just yet."

Susie's mouth twitched. She sat up straight, crossed her long, dancer's legs and linked her hands around her knee.

"Anybody I know?" she said casually.

"Huh?"

"Whoever it is you're beating to death this morning. I figure there's got to be a face in that flour that only you can see."

Laurel ran the back of her wrist across her forehead.

"Your imagination's working overtime. I'm making bread, not working out my frustrations."

"Ah," Susie said knowingly. She watched Laurel give the dough a few more turns and punches before dumping it into a bowl and covering it with a damp dish towel. "Because," she said, going with instinct, "it occurred to me, it might just be Damian Skouras you were punching out."

Laurel turned away and tore a piece of paper towel from the roll above the sink. She thought of saying, "Why would you think that?" and looking puzzled, but she'd barely gotten away clean the last time Susie had raised Damian's name. Susie knew her too well, that was the problem.

"I told you," she said flatly, "I'm making bread."

"That's it?"

"That's it."

Susie cleared her throat again. "So, have you heard from him?"

"Suze, you asked me that just the other day. And I said that I hadn't."

"And that you don't expect to. Or want to."

"Right again." Laurel took the coffeepot from the stove

and refilled Susie's cup. She started to refill hers, too, but when she saw the glint of oil that floated on what remained, her stomach gave a delicate lurch. Wonderful. She had definitely picked up some sort of bug. Just what she needed, she thought, as she hitched her hip onto a stool opposite Susie's. "So, where's that handsome hunk of yours this morning?"

"At the gym, toning up his abs so he can keep his devoted fans drooling. And don't try to change the subject. It's *your* handsome hunk we were talking about."

"My...?" Laurel rolled her eyes. "What does it take to convince you? Damian Skouras isn't 'my' anything. Don't you ever give up?"

"No," Susie said, with disarming honesty. She lifted her cup with both hands, blew on the coffee, then took a sip. "Not when something doesn't make any sense. You are the most logical, levelheaded female I've ever known."

"Thank you, I think."

"Which is the reason I keep saying to myself, how could a logical, levelheaded female turn her back on a zillionaire Apollo?"

"It was 'Adonis' the last time around," Laurel said coolly. "Although, as far as I'm concerned, it doesn't matter what you call him."

"You didn't like him?"

"Susie, for heaven's sake..."

"Okay, okay, maybe I'm nuts—"

"There's no 'maybe' about it."

"But I just don't understand."

"That's because there isn't anything *to* understand. I keep telling you that. Damian Skouras and I went to dinner and—"

"Do you know, you do that whenever you talk about him?"

Laurel sighed, shook her head and gazed up at the ceiling. "Do what?"

"Well, first you call him DamianSkouras. One word, no pause, as if you hardly know the guy."

As if I hadn't slept with him, Laurel thought, and she felt a blaze of color flood her cheeks.

"Aha," Susie said, in triumph. "You see?"

"See what?"

"The blush, that's what. And the look that goes with it. They always follow, right on the heels of DamianSkouras."

Laurel rose, went to the sink and turned on the water. "I love you dearly, Suze," she said, squeezing in a shot of Joy, "but you are the nosiest thing going, did you know that?"

"George says I am, but what does he know?" Susie smiled. "Men don't understand that women love to talk about stuff like this."

"Stuff like what? There's nothing to talk about."

"There must be, otherwise you wouldn't turn into a clam each time I mention Damian's name."

"I do not turn into a clam. There just isn't anything to say, that's all."

"Listen, my friend, I was here that night, remember? I saw the way you guys looked at each other. And then, that was it. No further contact, according to you."

"Hand me that spoon, would you?"

"You can't blame me for wondering. The guy's gorgeous, he's a zillionaire and he's charming."

"Charming?" Laurel spun around, her cheeks flushed. "He's a scoundrel, that's what he is!"

"Why?"

"Because—because…" Laurel frowned. It was a good question. Damian hadn't seduced and abandoned her. What had happened that night hadn't been a Victorian melodrama. She'd gone to his bed willingly and left it willingly. If the memory haunted her, humiliated her, she had no one to blame but herself. "Susie, do me a favor and let's drop this, okay?"

"If that's the way you want it…"

"I do."

"Okay, then. Consider the subject closed."

"Great. Thank you."

"It's just that I'm really puzzled," Susie said, after a moment's silence. Laurel groaned, but Susie ignored her. "I mean, he looked at you the way a starving man would look at a seven-course meal. Why, if Ben Franklin had come trotting through this place that night, he wouldn't have needed a kite and a key to discover that lightning bolts and electricity are the same thing!"

"That's good, Suze. Keep going like that, you can give up dancing and start writing scripts for George's soap."

"You make it sound as if you didn't like him."

"You clever soul." Laurel flashed a saccharine smile. "How'd you ever come up with an idea like that?"

"Yeah, well, I don't believe you."

"You don't believe me? What's that supposed to mean?"

Susie rose, went to the pantry cabinet and opened it. "It means," she said, taking out a box of Mallomars, "that lightning must have struck somewhere because I've never known you to come traipsing in at dawn." She peered into the box. "Goody. Two left. One for you, and one for me."

Laurel glanced at the chocolate-covered marshmallow cookie Susie held out to her. Her stomach lifted again, did a quick two-step, then settled in place.

"I'll pass."

"I can have both?"

"Consider this your lucky day. And how do you know what time I came in?"

Susie bit into a cookie. "I went running that morning," she said around a mouthful of crumbs, "so I was up at the crack of dawn. You know me. I like the streets to myself. Besides, these old floors squeak like crazy. I could hear you marching around up here. Pacing, it sounded like, for what seemed like forever."

Not forever. Just long enough to try to believe there was

*no point in hating myself for what I'd done because it was
already part of the past and I'd never, not in a million
years, do anything like it again.*

"Where'd he take you that night, anyway?"

"You know where he took me." Laurel plucked a cup
from the suds and scrubbed at it as if it were a burned
roasting pan. "To dinner."

"And?" Susie batted her lashes. "Where else, hmm?"

To paradise in his arms, Laurel thought suddenly, and
the feeling she'd worked so hard to suppress, the memory
of how it had been that night, almost overwhelmed her.

Maybe she'd been a fool to leave him. Maybe she should
have stayed. Maybe she should have taken up where the
blonde had left off...

The cup slipped from her hands and smashed against the
floor.

"Dammit," she said fiercely. Angry tears rose in her
eyes and she squatted and began picking up the pieces of
broken china. "You want to know what happened that
night?" She stood up, dumped the pieces in the garbage
and wiped her hands on the seat of her jeans. "Okay, I'll
tell you."

"Laurel, honey, I didn't mean—"

"I slept with Damian Skouras."

Susie took a deep breath. "Wow."

"I slept with a guy I didn't know all that well, didn't
like all that much and didn't ever want to see again, because—because—"

"I understand the because," Susie said softly.

Laurel spun toward her, her eyes glittering. "Don't pa-
tronize me, dammit! If *I* don't understand, how can you?"

"Because I slept with George, the first time we went out.
That's how."

Laurel sank down on the edge of a stool. "You did?"

"I did. And I'd never done anything like it before."

"Well, then, why did you, that time?"

Susie smiled. "Who knows? Hormones? Destiny? It happened, that's all."

Laurel's smile was wobbly. "See? I was right, you ought to be writing for the soaps."

"Mostly, though, I did it because my body and my heart knew what my brain hadn't yet figured out. George and I were soul mates."

"Yeah, well, I don't have any such excuse. Damian Skouras and I are definitely not soul mates. I did what I did, and now I have to live with it."

"The bastard!"

Laurel laughed. "A minute ago, he was Adonis. Or was it Apollo?"

"A minute ago, I didn't know he'd taken advantage of you and then done the male thing."

"Trust me, Suze," Laurel said wryly, "he didn't take advantage of me. I was willing."

Susie plucked the remaining Mallomar from the box. "That's beside the point. He did the male thing, anyway. 'Wham, bam, thank you, ma'am—and maybe I'll call you sometime.'"

Laurel stared at her friend. Then she rose, yanked a piece of paper towel from the roll, dampened it in the sink and began to rub briskly at the countertop.

"I told him not to call."

"What?"

"You heard me. He wanted to see me again. I told him it was out of the question, that I wasn't interested in that kind of relationship."

"You and Damian made love, it was great and you told him you never wanted to see him again?"

"I didn't say that."

"That it wasn't great? Or that you never wanted to see him again?"

Laurel stared at Susie, and then she dropped her gaze and turned to the sink.

"What's your point?" she said, plunging her hands into the water.

"It's *your* point I'm trying to figure out here, my friend. Why did you make love with the guy and then tell him to hit the road?"

"I didn't 'make love' with him," Laurel said sharply. "I slept with him."

"Semantics," Susie said with a shrug.

"No, it's more than that. Look, Susie, what you did with George was different. You loved him."

"Still do," Susie said, with a little smile.

"Well, I didn't love Damian. I can't imagine loving Damian. He's such an arrogant, egotistical, super-macho SOB…"

"Sigh," Susie said, rolling her eyes.

Laurel laughed. "The point is, he's not my type."

"Nobody's your type. Name one guy since that bastard, Kirk Soames, who you've given more than a quick hello and I'll eat whatever it is you think you're gonna make out of that poor overbeaten, overkneaded, overpounded sourdough."

"And I'm not his type," Laurel finished, refusing to rise to the bait. She shut off the water, dried her hands on a dish towel and turned around. "That's the sum, total and end of it, so—so…"

Susie had just taken a bite of the Mallomar. A smear of dark chocolate and marshmallow festooned her upper lip.

"You only think so, babe. I saw the way you guys looked at each other."

Laurel swallowed hard. "There's a—a smudge of chocolate on your mouth, Suze."

"Yeah?" Susie scrubbed a finger over her lip. "Did I get it?"

"Most of it. There's still a little bit…" Laurel's stomach rose slowly into her throat. "That's it," she said weakly. "You've got it now." She turned away and wrapped her hands around the rim of the sink, waiting until her stomach settled back where it belonged.

"Laurel? You all right?"

Laurel nodded. "Sure. I'm just—"

"Tired of me poking my nose where it doesn't belong," Susie said. She sighed. "Listen, let's drop the subject. You want to talk about it, I'm here. You don't...?" She gave an elaborate shrug. "Tell you what. How about having supper with us tonight? George is making *pirogi*. Remember his *pirogi*? You loved 'em, the last time."

"Yes, I did. They were—they were..."

Laurel thought of the little doughy envelopes filled with onion-studded ground beef. She *had* loved them, it was true, but now all she could think about was how they'd glistened with butter, how the butter had slid down her throat like oil...

"They were delicious," she said brightly, "but—but this bread is my last extravagance for a while. I'm going on a quick diet. You know how it is. I've got a layout coming up and I need to drop a couple of pounds. Give me a rain check, okay?"

Susie leaned back against the counter. "Well, have supper with us anyway." She patted her belly. "It wouldn't hurt me to lose some weight, and you know those close-ups they give George. Forget the *pirogi*. We'll go wild, take out a couple of Lean Cuisine Veggie Lasagnas and zap 'em in the microwave. How's that sound?"

Lasagna. Laurel imagined bright red tomato sauce, smelled its acidic aroma. Saliva filled her mouth, and she swallowed hard.

"Actually, I may just pass on supper altogether. I think I've got some kind of bug. I did a shoot in Bryant Park last week. Everybody was coughing and sneezing like crazy, and I've felt rotten ever since."

"Summer colds," Susie said philosophically, as she popped what remained of the Mallomar into her mouth.

"The worst kind to shake. A couple of aspirin and some hot chicken soup ought to…Laurel? What's the matter?"

A bead of jelly, glistening like blood at the corner of Susie's mouth, that was what was the matter.

Laurel's belly clenched.

"Nothing," she said, "noth—" *Oh hell.* Her eyes widened and she groaned, clamped her hand over her mouth and shot from the room.

When she emerged from the bathroom minutes later, pale and shaken, Susie was waiting in the bedroom, sitting cross-legged in the middle of Laurel's bed, a worried look on her face.

"Are you okay?"

"I'm fine," Laurel said with a shaky smile.

"Fine, my foot." Susie looked at her friend's face. Laurel's skin was waxen, her eyes were glassy and her forehead glistened with sweat. "You're sick."

"I told you, Suze, it's just some bug I picked up."

"The one that had everybody on that photo session coughing and sneezing?"

"Uh-huh."

Susie uncrossed her legs and stood up. "Except you're not."

"Not what?"

"Coughing. Or sneezing."

"Well, it hit me differently, that's all."

"Have you been out of the country or something?"

"Not in weeks."

"I mean, there's all kinds of nasties floating around this old planet. Weren't you in Ghana or someplace like that a couple of months ago?"

"It was Kenya and it was last year, and honestly, I'm okay. You know what the flu can be like."

"Uh-huh." There was a long silence and then Susie cleared her throat. "My sister had the same symptoms last year. Nausea in the mornings, tossing her cookies every time somebody so much as mentioned food and generally looking just about as awful as you do.''

"Thanks a lot." Laurel speared her hands into her hair and shoved it off her forehead. Her skin felt clammy, and even though her stomach was completely empty, it still felt like a storm-tossed ship at sea. "Listen, Susie—''

"So she went to the doctor."

"I'm not going to the doctor. All I need is to take it easy for a couple of days and—''

"Turns out she was pregnant," Susie said quietly, her eyes on Laurel's face.

"Pregnant!" Laurel laughed. "Don't be silly, I'm not…''

Oh God! The floor seemed to drop out from beneath her feet.

Pregnant? No. It wasn't possible. Or was it? When had she last had her period? She couldn't remember. Was it since she'd been with Damian?

No. No!

She sank down on the edge of the bed, feeling empty and boneless. Everything had happened so quickly that night. Had Damian used a condom? Not that she could remember. She certainly hadn't used anything. Why take the pill, when sex was hardly a major item in your life? She knew some women carried diaphragms in their handbags but she wasn't one of them. You needed a whole different mind set to do that. You had to be the sort of woman who might find herself tumbling into a man's bed at the drop of a hat and she had never—she had certainly never…

A little sound tore from her throat. She looked at Susie's questioning face and did what she could to turn the sound into a choked laugh.

"I can't be," she said. "How could I possibly have gotten pregnant?''

"The method hasn't changed much through the centuries.''

"Yes, but just one night…"

One night. One endless night.

"You need to make an appointment with your doctor," Susie said gently.

"No," Laurel whispered. She lifted her head and stared at Susie. "No," she said, more strongly. "It's ridiculous. I am not pregnant. I have the flu, that's all."

"I'm sure you're right," Susie said with a false smile. "But, what the heck, you want to make certain."

Laurel rose from the bed. "Look, how's this sound? I'll spend all day tomorrow in bed. I'll down aspirin and lots of liquids and if I'm not feeling better by Monday or Tuesday, I'll call my doctor."

"Your gynecologist."

"Really, Susie." Laurel looped her arm around the other woman's shoulders. Together, they headed for the foyer. "Give that imagination of yours a rest and I'll do the same for my flu-racked bones. And be sure and tell George I'm taking a rain check on dinner."

"I'm getting the brush-off, huh?"

"Well," Laurel said with forced gaiety, "if you want to hang around and listen to me upchuck again, you're welcome."

"Listen, if you need anything… Aspirin, Pepto-Bismol…" Susie flashed a quick smile. "Just someone to talk to, I'm here."

"Thanks, but I'm fine. Truly. You'll see. These bugs are all the same. You feel like dying for twenty-four hours and then you're as good as new."

"Didn't you say you'd been feeling shaky all week?"

"Twenty-four hours, forty-eight, what's the difference?" Laurel swung the door open. "It's flu, that's all. I'm not pregnant. Trust me."

"Uh-huh," Susie said, without conviction.

"I'm not," Laurel said firmly.

She held a smile until the door shut and she was safely

alone. Then the smile faded and she sank back against the wall, eyes tightly shut. "I'm not," she whispered.

But she was.

Four weeks gone, Dr. Glassman said, later that afternoon, as Laurel sat opposite her in the gynecologist's sunny, plant-filled Manhattan office.

"I'm glad we could fit you in at the last minute like this, Laurel." The doctor smiled. "And I'm glad I can make such a certain diagnosis. You are with child."

With child. Damian's child.

"Have you married, since I saw you last?" A smile lit Dr. Glassman's pleasant, sixtyish face again. "Or have you decided, as is becoming so common, to have a child and remain single?"

Laurel licked her lips. "I—I'm still single."

"Ah. Well, you'll forgive me if I put on my obstetrical hat for a while and urge that you include your baby's father in his—or her—life, to as great a degree as possible." The doctor chuckled softly. "I know there are those who would have me drawn and quartered for saying such a thing, but children need two parents, whenever it's possible. A mother and a father, both."

There was no arguing with that, Laurel thought, oh, there was no arguing with—

"Any questions?"

Laurel cleared her throat. "No. None that I can think of just now, anyway."

"Well, that's it for today, then." The doctor took a card from a holder on her desk, scribbled something on it and handed it to Laurel. "Phone me Tuesday and I'll give you your lab reports, but I'm sure nothing unforeseen will arise. You're in excellent health, my dear. I see no reason why your baby shouldn't be healthy and full-term."

Dr. Glassman rose from her chair. Laurel did, too, but when the doctor smiled at her, she couldn't quite manage a smile in return.

"Laurel?" The doctor settled back behind her desk and peered over the rims of her reading glasses. "Of course," she said gently, "if you wish to make other arrangements…"

"I'm four weeks pregnant, you say?"

"Just about."

"And—and everything seems fine?"

"Perfectly fine."

Laurel gazed down at her hands, which were linked carefully in her lap. "If I should decide… I mean, if I were to…"

The doctor's voice was even more gentle. "You've plenty of time to think things through, my dear."

Laurel nodded and rose to her feet. Suddenly she felt a thousand years old.

"Thank you, Doctor."

The gynecologist rose, too. She came around her desk and put her arm lightly around Laurel's shoulders.

"I know what an enormous decision this is," she said. "If you need someone to talk to, my service can always reach me."

A baby, Laurel thought as she rode down in the elevator to the building's lobby. A child of her flesh. Hers, and Damian's.

Babies were supposed to be conceived in love, not in the throes of a passion that made no sense, a passion so out of character that she'd tried to put it out of her mind all these weeks. Not that she'd managed. In the merciless glare of daylight, she'd suddenly think of what she'd done and hate herself for it.

But at night, with the moonlight softening the shadows, she dreamed about Damian and awakened in a tangle of sheets, with the memory of his kisses still hot on her lips.

Laurel gave herself a little shake. This wasn't the time for that kind of nonsense. There were decisions to be made, although the only practical one was self-evident. There was no room in her life for a baby. Her apartment wasn't big enough. Her life was too unsettled, what with her career winding down and an uncertain future ahead. And then there was the biggest consideration of all. Dr. Glassman was right; some people might think it old-fashioned but it was true. Children were entitled to at least begin life with two parents.

The elevator door slid open and she stepped out into the lobby. Her high heels clicked sharply against the marble floor as she made her way toward the exit.

A baby. A soft, sweet-smelling, innocent bundle of smiles and gurgles. A child, to lavish love upon. To warm her heart and give purpose to her existence. Her throat constricted. A part of Damian that would be hers forever.

She paused outside the building, while an unseasonable wind ruffled her hair. Gum wrappers and a torn page from the *New York Times* flapped at her feet in the throes of a mini-tornado.

What was the point in torturing herself? She wasn't about to have this baby. Hadn't she already decided that? Her reasoning was sound; it was logical. It was—

"Laurel?"

Her heart stumbled. She knew the voice instantly; she'd heard it in her dreams a thousand times during the past long, tortured weeks. Still, she tried to tell herself that it couldn't be Damian. He was the last person she ever wanted to set eyes on again, especially now.

"Laurel."

Oh God, she thought, and she turned toward the curb and saw him stepping out of the same black limousine that had a month ago transported her from sanity to delirium. All at once, the wind seemed to grow stronger. Her vision blurred and she began to sway unsteadily.

And then she was falling, falling, and only Damian's arms could bring her to safety.

CHAPTER SEVEN

WHAT KIND OF MAN wanted a woman who'd made it clear she didn't want him?

Only a man who was a damned fool, and Damian had never counted himself as such.

And yet, four weeks after Laurel Bennett had slept in his arms and then walked out of his life, he had not been able to forget her.

He dreamed of her—hot, erotic dreams of the sort he'd left behind in adolescence. He thought of her during the least expected moments during the day, and when he'd tried to purge his mind and his flesh by becoming involved with someone else, it hadn't worked. He had wined and dined half a dozen of New York's most beautiful women during the past month, and every one had ended her evening puzzled, disappointed and alone.

It was stupid, and it angered him. He was not a man to waste time mourning lost opportunities or dreams. It was the philosophy that had guided his life since childhood; why should it fail him now? Laurel was what his financial people would have termed a write-off. She was a gorgeous woman with a hot body and an icy heart. She'd used him the way he'd used women in the past.

So how come he couldn't get her out of his head?

It was a question without an answer, and it was gnawing at him as his car pulled to the curb before the skyscraper that housed his corporate headquarters…which was why, when he first saw her, he wondered if he'd gone completely over the edge. But this was no hallucination. Laurel was real, she was coming out of the adjacent building—and she was even more beautiful than he'd remembered.

He stepped onto the sidewalk and hesitated. What now? Should he wait for her to notice him? He had nothing to say to her, really; still, he wanted to talk to her. Hell, he wanted more than that. He wanted to go to her, take her in his arms, run his thumb along her bottom lip until her mouth opened to his…

Damian frowned. What was this? The feverish glow on her cheeks couldn't hide the fact that her face was pale. She seemed hesitant, just standing there while pedestrians flowed around her like a stream of water against an immutable rock.

Dammit, she was weeping!

He started toward her. "Laurel?"

She had to be ill. She'd never cry, otherwise; he knew it instinctively. His belly knotted.

"Laurel," he shouted, and she looked up and saw him.

For one wild, heart-stopping instant, he thought he saw her face light with joy but he knew it had only been his imagination because a second later her eyes widened, her pallor became waxy and she mouthed his name as if it were an obscenity.

His mouth thinned. To hell with her, then…

God, she was collapsing!

"Laurel," Damian roared, and he dove through the crowd and snatched her up in his arms just before she fell.

She made a little sound as he gathered her close to him.

"It's all right," he whispered, "I've got you, Laurel. It's okay."

Her lashes fluttered. She looked at him but he could tell she wasn't really focusing. His arms tightened around her and he pressed his lips to her hair while his heart thundered in his chest. What if he hadn't been here, to catch her? What if she'd fallen?

What if he'd never held her in his arms again?

"Damian?" she whispered.

There was a breathy little catch in her voice, and it tore at his heart. She sounded as fragile as Venetian glass. She felt that way, too. She was tall for a woman and he would never have thought of her as delicate yet now, in his arms, that was how she seemed.

"Damian? What happened?"

"How in hell should I know!" The words sounded uncaring. He hadn't meant them to be, it was just that a dozen emotions were warring inside him and he didn't understand a one of them. "I was just getting out of my car... You fainted."

"Fainted? Me?" He watched the tip of her tongue slick across her lips. "Don't be silly. I've never passed out in my..." Color flooded her face as she remembered. The doctor. The diagnosis. "Oh God," she whispered, and squeezed her eyes shut.

Damian frowned. "What is it? Are you going to pass out again?"

She took a deep breath and forced herself to open her eyes. Damian looked angry. Well, why not? He'd never expected to see her again and now here he was, standing on a crowded street with her in his arms, playing an unwilling Sir Galahad to her damsel in distress and, dammit, *he* was the reason for that distress. If she'd never laid eyes on him, never gone to dinner with him, never let herself be seduced by him...

It wasn't true. He hadn't seduced her. She'd gone to bed with him willingly. Eagerly. Even now, knowing that her world would never be the same again no matter what she decided, even now, lying in his arms, she felt—she felt—

She stiffened, and put her palms flat against his chest.

"I'm not going to pass out again, no. I'm fine, as a matter of fact. Please put me down."

"I don't think so."

"Don't be ridiculous!" People hurrying past were looking at them with open curiosity. Even in New York, a man standing in the middle of a crowded sidewalk with a woman in his arms was bound to attract attention. "Damian, I said—"

"I heard what you said." The crowd gave way, not much and not very gracefully, but Damian gave it no choice. "Coming through," he barked, and Laurel caught her breath as she realized he was carrying her back into the building she'd just left.

"What are you doing?"

"There must be a dozen doctors' offices in this building. We'll pick the first one and—"

"No!" Panic surged through her with the speed of adrenaline. "I don't need a doctor!"

"Of course you do. People don't pass out cold for no reason."

"But there was a reason. I—I've been dieting." It was the same lie she'd tried on Susie hours ago, but this time, she knew it would work. "Nothing but tomato juice and black coffee for breakfast, lunch and dinner," she said, rattling off the latest lose-weight-quick scheme that was floating through the fashion world. "You can drop five pounds in two days."

Five pounds? Damian couldn't imagine why she'd want to lose an ounce. She felt perfect to him, warm and lushly curved, just as she'd been in his dreams each night.

"You don't need to lose five pounds."

"The camera doesn't agree."

His smile was quick and dangerously sexy. "Maybe the camera hasn't had as intimate a view of you as I have."

Laurel stiffened in his arms. "How nice to know you're still the perfect gentleman. For the last time, Damian. Put me down!"

His eyes narrowed at the coldness of her voice. "My pleasure." He put her on her feet but he kept a hand clamped around her elbow. "Let's go."

"Go? Go where? Dammit, Damian…"

She sputtered with indignation as he hustled her through the door, across the sidewalk and toward the limousine. Stevens was already out of the front seat, standing beside the rear door and holding it open, his face a polite mask as if he were accustomed to seeing his employer snatch women off the street.

Laurel dug in her heels but it was useless. Damian was strong, and determined, and even when she called him a word that made his eyebrows lift, he didn't loosen his hold.

"Thank you, Stevens," he said smoothly. "Get into the car please, Laurel."

Get into the car, *please?* He made it sound like a polite request, but a request was something you could turn down. This was a command. Despite her struggles, her protests, her locked knees and gritted teeth, Damian was herding her onto the leather seat.

She swung toward him, eyes blazing, as he settled himself alongside her.

"How *dare* you? How dare you treat me this way? I am not some—some package to be dumped in a truck and—and shipped off."

"No," he said coldly, "you are not. You're a pigheaded female, apparently bent on seeing which you can manage first, starving yourself to death or giving yourself a concussion." The car nosed into the stream of traffic moving sluggishly up the avenue. "Well, I'm going to take you home. Then, for all I give a damn, you can gorge on tomato soup and black coffee while you practice swan dives on the living-room floor."

"It's tomato juice," Laurel said furiously, "not soup. And I was not doing swan dives." She glared at Damian. Her skirt was rucked up, her hair was hanging in her eyes, a button had popped off her knit dress and there he sat, as cool as ice, with a look on his face that said he was far superior to other human beings. How she hated this man!

"A perfect three-pointer," he said, "aimed right at the pavement."

"Will you stop that? I just—I felt a little light-headed, that's all."

"At the sight of me," he said, fixing her with a stony look.

Laurel flushed. "Don't flatter yourself."

"Tomato juice and black coffee," he growled. "It's a toss-up which you are, light-brained or light-headed."

Laurel glared at him. She blew a strand of hair off her forehead, folded her arms in unwitting parody of him and they rode through the streets in silence. When they reached her apartment house, she sprang for the door before Damian could move or Stevens could get out of the car.

"Thank you so much for the lift," she said, her words dripping with venom. "I wish I could say it's been a pleasure seeing you, but what's the sense in lying?"

"Such sweet words, Laurel. I'm touched." Damian looked up at her and a half smile curled over his mouth. "Remember what I said. You don't need to lose any weight."

"Advice from an expert," she said, with a poisonous smile.

"Try some real food for a change."

"What are you, a nutritionist?"

"Of course, you could always get back into the car."

"In your dreams," she said, swinging away from him.

"We could go back to the *Penthouse*. Maybe you'd like to see what you missed last time. The caviar, the duck, the soufflé…"

Caviar, oily and salty. Duck, with the fat melting under the skin. Chocolate soufflé, under a mantle of whipped cream…

Laurel's stomach lifted. No, she thought, oh please, no…

The little she had eaten since the morning bolted up her throat.

Dimly, over the sound of her retching, she heard Damian's soft curse. Then his hands were clasping her shoulders, supporting her as her belly sought to do the impossible and turn itself inside-out. When the spasms passed, he pulled her back against him. She went willingly, mortified by shame but weak in body and in spirit, desperately needing the comfort he offered.

"I'm so sorry," she whispered.

Damian turned her toward him. He took out his hand-kerchief and gently wiped her clammy forehead and her mouth. Then he swung her into his arms and carried her inside the house.

She was beyond protest. When he asked for her keys, she handed him her pocketbook. When he settled her on the living-room couch, she fell back against the cushions. He took off her shoes, undid the top buttons on her dress, tucked a pillow under her head and an afghan over her legs and warned her not to move.

Move? She'd have laughed, if she'd had the strength. As it was, she could barely nod her head.

Damian took off his jacket, tossed it over a chair and headed for the kitchen. She heard the fridge opening and she wondered what he'd think when he saw the contents. Her seesawing stomach had kept her from doing much shopping or cooking lately.

Laurel swallowed. Better not to think about food. With luck, there just might be some ginger ale on the shelf, or some Diet Coke.

"Ginger ale," Damian said. He squatted down beside her, put his arm around her shoulders and eased her head up. "It's flat, but that's just as well. Slowly, now. One sip at a time."

Another command, but she still didn't have the energy to argue. Anyway, it was good advice. She didn't want to be sick again, not with Damian here.

"There's a chemistry experiment in your kitchen," he said.

"A chem…?"

"Either that, or an alien presence has landed on the counter near the sink."

Laurel laughed weakly and lay back against the pillow. "It's sourdough."

"Ah. Well, I hope you don't mind, but I've disposed of

it. I had the uncomfortable feeling it was planning on taking over the apartment.''

''Thanks.''

''How do you feel now?''

''Better.'' She sighed deeply, yawned and found herself fighting to keep her eyes open. ''I must have eaten something that disagreed with me.''

''Close your eyes,'' he said. ''Rest for a while.''

''I'm not tired.''

''Yes, you are.''

''For heaven's sake, Damian, must you pretend you know every…''

Her eyes closed. She was asleep.

Damian rose to his feet. No, he thought grimly, he didn't know everything, but he knew enough to figure that a woman who claimed she'd been on a diet of tomato juice and black coffee wasn't very likely to have eaten something that made her sick…especially not when she was carrying around a little white card like the one that had fallen from her pocket when he'd put her on the couch.

He walked into the kitchen and took the card from the table, where he'd left it: Vivian Glassman, M.D., Gynecology and Obstetrics.

It probably didn't mean a thing. People tucked away cards and forgot about them, and even if that was where Laurel had been today, what did it prove? Women went for gynecological checkups regularly.

His fist clenched around the card. He thought of Laurel's face, when she'd seen him coming toward her a little while ago—and he thought of something else.

All these weeks that he'd dreamed of her, relived the night they'd spent in each other's arms. The heat, the sweetness—all of it had seemed permanently etched into his brain. Now, another memory vied for his attention, one that made his belly cramp.

In all that long, wild night, he'd never thought to use a condom.

It was so crazy, so irresponsible, so completely unlike him. It was as if he'd been intoxicated that night, drunk on the smell of Laurel's skin and the taste of her mouth.

He hadn't used a condom. She hadn't used a diaphragm. Now she was nauseous, and faint, and she was seeing a doctor whose specialty was obstetrics.

Maybe she was on the pill. Maybe his imagination was in overdrive.

Maybe it was time to get some answers.

He took a long, harsh breath. Then he reached for the phone.

Laurel awoke slowly.

She was lying on the living-room couch. Darkness had gathered outside the windows but someone had turned on the table lamp.

Someone?

Damian.

He was sitting in a chair a few feet away. There was a granitelike set to his jaw; above it, his mouth was set in a harsh line.

"How do you feel?"

She swallowed experimentally. Her stomach growled, but it stayed put.

"Much better." She sat up, pushed the afghan aside and swung her legs to the floor. "Thank you for everything, Damian, but there really wasn't any need for you to sit here while I slept." He said nothing, and the silence beat in her ears. Something was wrong, she could feel it. "What time is it, anyway?" she asked, trying for a light tone. "I must have slept for—"

"When did you plan on telling me?"

Her heart thumped, then lodged like a stone behind her breastbone.

"Plan on telling you what?" She rose to her feet and he did, too, and came toward her. Damn, where were her shoes? He was so tall. It put her at a disadvantage, to let him loom over her like this.

"Perhaps you didn't intend to tell me." His voice hummed with challenge; his accent thickened. "Was that your plan?"

"I don't know what you're talking about," she said, starting past him, "and I'm really not in the mood for games."

"And I," he said, clamping his hand down on her shoulder, "am not in the mood for lies."

Her eyes flashed fire as she swung toward him. "I think you'd better leave."

"You're pregnant," he said flatly.

Pregnant. Pregnant. The word seemed to echo through the room.

"I don't know what you're talking about."

"It will be easier if you tell me the truth."

She twisted free of his grasp and pointed at the door. "It will be easier if you get out of here."

"Is the child mine?"

"Is…?" Laurel stuffed her hands into her pockets. "There is no child. I don't know where you got this idea, but—"

"How many men were you with that week, aside from me?"

"Get out, damn you!"

"I ask you again, is the child mine?"

She stared at him, her lips trembling. No, she wanted to say, it is not. I was with a dozen men that week. A hundred. A thousand.

"Answer me!" His hands clamped around her shoulders and he shook her roughly. "Is it mine?"

In the end, it was too barbarous a lie to tell.

"Yes," she whispered, "it's yours."

He said nothing for a long moment. Then he jerked his head towards the sofa.

"Sit down, Laurel."

She looked up and their eyes met. A shudder raced through her. She stepped back, until she felt the edge of the sofa behind her, and then she collapsed onto the cushions like a rag doll.

"How—how did you find out?"

His mouth curled. He reached into his pocket, took out a small white card and tossed it into her lap. Laurel stared down at it. It was the card Dr. Glassman had given her.

She looked up at him. "She told you? Dr. Glassman *told* you? She had no right! She—"

"She told me nothing." His mouth twisted again. "And everything."

"I don't understand."

"The card fell from your pocket. I telephoned Glassman's office. The receptionist put me through when I said I was a 'friend' of yours and concerned about your health."

The twist he put on the word brought a rush of color to Laurel's face. Damian saw it and flashed a thin smile.

"Apparently your physician made the same interpretation. But she was very discreet. She acknowledged only that she knew you. She said I would have to discuss your medical condition with you, and she hung up."

Laurel's face whitened. "Then—then you didn't really know! You lied to me. You fooled me into—into—"

"I put two and two together, that's all, and then I asked a question, which you answered."

"It wasn't a question!" Laurel drew a shuddering breath. "You said you knew that I was—that I was—"

"I asked if it was my child." He moved suddenly, bending down and spearing his arms on either side of her, trapping her, pinning her with a look that threatened to turn her to ice. "My child, damn you! What were you planning, Laurel? To give it up for adoption? To have it aborted?"

"No!" The cry burst from her throat and, as it did, she knew that it was the truth. She would not give up the life within her. She wanted her baby, with all her heart and soul, had wanted it from the moment the doctor had confirmed that she was pregnant. "No," she whispered, her gaze steady on his. "I'm not going to do that. I'm going to have my baby, and keep it."

"Keep it?" Damian's mouth twisted. "This is not a puppy we speak of. How will you keep it? How will you raise a child alone?"

"You'd be amazed at how much progress women have made," Laurel said defiantly. "We're capable of rearing children as well as giving birth to them."

"A child will interfere with the self-indulgent life you lead."

"You don't know the first thing about my life!"

"I know that a woman who sleeps with strangers cannot possibly pretend to be a fit mother for my child."

Laurel slammed her fist into his shoulder. "What a hypocritical son of a bitch you are! Who are you to judge me? It took two of us to create this baby, Damian, two strangers in one bed that night!"

A thin smile touched his lips. "It is not the same."

"It is not the same," she said, cruelly mimicking his tone and his accent. She rose and shoved past him. "Do us both a favor, will you? Get out of here. Get out of my life. I don't ever want to see your face again!"

"I would do so, and gladly, but you forget that this life you carry belongs to me."

"It's a baby, Damian. You don't own a baby. I suppose that's hard for someone like you to comprehend, but a child's not a—a commodity. You can't own it, even if your name is Damian Skouras."

They glared at each other, and then he muttered something in Greek and stalked away from her.

Dammit, she was right! He was behaving like an ass. That self-righteous crap a minute ago, about a woman who slept with strangers not being a fit mother, was ridiculous. He was as responsible for what had happened as she was.

And now she was carrying a child. His child. A deep

warmth suffused his blood. He had always thought raising Nick would be the closest he'd come to fatherhood. Now, Fate and a woman who'd haunted his dreams had joined forces to show him another way.

Slowly, he turned and looked at Laurel.

"I want my child," he said softly.

Laurel went cold. "What do you mean, you want your child?"

"I mean exactly what I said. This child is mine, and I will not forfeit my claim to it."

His claim? She felt her legs turn to jelly. This kind of thing cropped up in the papers and on TV news shows, reports of fathers who demanded, and won, custody. Not many, it was true, but this was Damian Skouras, who had all the power and wealth in the world. He could take her baby from her with a snap of his fingers.

Be calm, she told herself, be calm, and don't let him see how frightened you are.

"Do you understand, Laurel?"

"Yes. I understand." She made her way toward him, her gaze locked on his face, assessing what to offer and what to hold back, wondering how you played poker with a man who owned all the chips. "Look, Damian, let's not discuss this now, when we're both upset."

"There is nothing to discuss. I'm telling you how it will be. I will be a father to my child."

"Well, I'm not—I'm not opposed to you having a role in this. In fact, Dr. Glassman and I talked a little bit about— about the value of a father, in a child's life. I'm sure we can work out some sort of agreement."

"Visiting rights?"

"Yes."

His smile was even more frightening the second time. "How generous of you, Laurel."

"I'm sure we can work out an arrangement that will suit us both."

"Did I ever tell you that my father played no part in my life?"

"Look, I don't know what the situation was between your parents, but—"

"I might as well have been a bastard."

"Damian—"

"I have no great confidence in marriage, I assure you, but when children are involved, I have even less in divorce."

"Well, this wouldn't be the same situation at all," she said, trying not to sound as desperate as she felt. "I mean, since we wouldn't be married, there'd be no divorce to worry ab—"

"My child deserves better. He—or she—is entitled to two parents, and to stability."

"I think so, too," she said quickly. "That's why I'd be willing to—to permit you a role."

"To permit me?" he said, so softly that she knew her choice of words had been an error.

"I didn't mean that the way it sounded. I won't keep you from my—from our—child. I swear it."

"You swear," he said, his tone mocking hers. "How touching. Am I to take comfort in the word of a woman who didn't even intend to tell me she was pregnant?"

"Dammit, what do you want? Just tell me!"

"I *am* telling you. I will not abandon my child, nor be a father in name only, and I have no intention of putting my faith in agreements reached by greedy lawyers."

"That's fine." She gave him a dazzling smile. "No lawyers, then. No judges. We'll sit down, like two civilized people, and work out an arrangement that will suit us both." She cried out sharply as his hands bit into her flesh. "Damian, you're hurting me!"

"Do you take me for a fool?" He leaned toward her, so that his face was only inches from hers. "I can imagine the sort of arrangement you would wish."

"You're wrong. I just agreed, didn't I, that a father has a place in a child's life?"

"Ten minutes ago, you were telling me you never wanted to see my face again."

"Yes, but that was before I understood how deeply you feel about this."

"You mean, it was before you were trapped into telling me you were pregnant." He laughed. "You're a bad liar, Laurel."

"Damn you, Damian! What do you want from me?"

There was a long, heavy silence. Then his arms wound around her and his hands slipped into her hair.

"Don't," she said, but already his mouth was dropping to hers, taking it in a kiss that threatened to steal her sanity. When, finally, he drew back, Laurel was trembling. With hatred, with rage—and with the shattering knowledge that, even now, his kiss could still make her want him.

"I have always believed," he said softly, "that a man should have children only within the sanctity of marriage. But that is a paradox, because I believe that marriage is a farce. Nonetheless, I see no choice here." His hand lifted, as if to touch her hair, then fell to his side. "We will marry within the week."

"We will...?" She felt the blood drain from her face. "Marry? Did you say, *marry*?"

"We will marry, and we will have our child, and we will raise him—or her—together."

"You're crazy! Me, marry you? Never! Do you hear me? Not in a million years would—"

"You've accused me of being arrogant, and egocentric. Well, I assure you, I can be those things, and more." A muscle beside his mouth tightened, and his eyes bored into hers. "I am Damian Skouras. I command resources you'll never dream of. Oppose me, and all you'll gain is ugly notoriety for yourself, your family and our child."

Laurel began to tremble. She stared back at him and then

she wrenched free. Angry tears blurred her eyes and she wiped them away with a slash of her hand.

"I hate you, Damian! I'll always hate you!"

He laughed softly, reached for his jacket and slung it over one shoulder.

"That's quite all right, dearest Laurel. From what I know of matrimony, that's the natural state of things."

Damian opened the door and walked out.

CHAPTER EIGHT

FIVE DAYS LATER, they stood as far apart as they could manage in the anteroom to a judge's chambers in a town just north of the city.

Judge Weiss was a friend of a friend, Damian had said. He'd begun to explain the connection, but Laurel had stopped him halfway through.

"It doesn't matter," she'd said stiffly.

And it didn't. For all she gave a damn, the man who was about to marry them could be an insurance salesman who was a justice of the peace in his spare time.

The only thing she wanted now was to get the thing over with.

She hadn't asked anyone to attend the ceremony. She hadn't told Susie or George or even Annie that she was getting married. Her sister had seemed preoccupied lately and anyway, what was there to tell? Surely not the truth, that she'd made the oldest, saddest female blunder in the world and that now she was paying the classic price for it by marrying a man she didn't love.

She'd decided it would be better to break the news when this was all over. She'd make it sound as if she and Damian had followed through on a romantic, spur-of-the-moment impulse. Susie might see through it but Annie, good-hearted soul that she was, would probably be thrilled.

She glanced over at Damian. He was standing with his back to her, staring out the window. He'd been doing that for the past ten minutes, as if the traffic passing by on the road outside was so fascinating that he couldn't tear his gaze from it.

She understood it, because she had been staring at a bad

oil painting of a man in judicial robes with mutton-chop whiskers for the same reason. It was a way of focusing on something other than the reality of what was about to happen.

Laurel took a deep breath. There was still time. Maybe she could convince him that his plan was crazy, that it was no good for him or her or even for their baby.

"Mr. Skouras? Miss Bennett?"

Laurel and Damian both looked around. The door to the judge's office had opened. A small, gray-haired woman smiled pleasantly at them.

"Judge Weiss is ready for you now," she said.

Laurel's hands tightened on her purse. It was like being told the dentist was ready for you. Your heart rate speeded up, your skin got clammy, you had to tell yourself to smile back and act as if that was exactly the wonderful news you'd been waiting for.

Except this wasn't the dentist's office, and she wasn't going to have a tooth drilled. She was going to hand her life over to Damian Skouras.

"Laurel."

She looked up. Damian was coming toward her, his expression grim.

"The judge is ready."

"I heard." She swallowed hard against a sudden rise of nausea, not from the pregnancy—that had ended, strangely enough, the day Damian had learned of her condition. This churning in her gut had to do with the step she was about to take.

I can't. God, I can't.

"Damian." She took a deep breath. "Damian, listen. I think we ought to talk."

His hand closed around hers, tightening in warning, and he smiled pleasantly at the clerk.

"Thank you. Please tell the judge we'll be along in a minute."

As soon as the door swung shut, Damian turned back to Laurel, his eyes cold.

"We have discussed this. There is nothing more to be said."

"We've discussed nothing! You've issued edicts and I've bowed my head in obedience. Well, now I'm telling you that it isn't going to work. I don't think—"

"I haven't asked you to think."

Color flew into her cheeks. "If *you'd* been thinking, we wouldn't be in this mess!"

It was an unfair attack, and she knew it. She was as responsible for what had happened as Damian, but why should she play fair when he didn't? Still, he didn't deny the accusation.

"Yes." A muscle tightened in his jaw. "You are correct. We are in, as you say, a mess, and since it is one of my own making, the solution is mine, as well. There is no other course to take."

"No other course that meets with your approval, you mean." She tried to shake off his hand, but he wouldn't let her. "If you'd be reasonable—"

"Meaning that I should permit you to do as you see fit?"

"Yes. No. Will you stop twisting everything I say? If you'd just think for a minute... We have nothing in common. We hardly know each other. We don't even like each other, and yet—and yet, you expect me to—to marry you, to become your wife."

"I expect exactly that."

Laurel yanked her hand from his. "Damn you," she whispered. She was trembling with rage, at Damian, at herself, at a situation that had gotten out of control and had brought this nightmare down on her head. "Damn you, Damian! You have an answer for everything and it's the same each time. You know best, you know what's right, you know how things have to be—"

Behind them, the door swung open.

"Mr. Skouras? The judge has a busy schedule this morning. If you and Miss Bennett wouldn't mind…?"

Miss Bennett minds, very much, Laurel thought…but Damian's hand had already closed around hers.

"Of course," he said, with a soft-as-butter smile that had nothing to do with the steely pressure of his fingers. "Darling? Are you ready?"

His smile was soft, too, but the warning in his eyes left no room for doubt. Make no mistake, he was telling her; do as I say or suffer the consequences.

Laurel gathered what remained of her self-composure, lifted her chin and nodded.

"As ready as I can be," she said coolly, and let him lead her into the judge's office.

It was a large, masculine room, furnished in heavy mahogany. The walls were paneled with some equally dark wood and hung with framed clippings and photos of politicos ranging from John F. Kennedy to Bill Clinton. Someone, perhaps the clerk, had tucked a bouquet of flowers into a coffee mug and placed it on the mantel above the fireplace, but the flowers weren't fresh and their drooping heads and faded colors only added a mournful touch to the room. An ancient air conditioner wheezed in the bottom half of a smeared window as it tried to breathe freshness into air redolent with the smell of old cigars.

"Mr. Skouras," the judge said, rising from behind his desk and smiling, "and Miss Bennett. What a fine day for a wedding."

It was, Laurel supposed. Outside, the sun was shining brightly; puffy white clouds sailed across a pale blue sky.

But weddings weren't supposed to be held in stuffy rooms like this one. A woman dreamed of being married in a place filled with light; she dreamed of flowers and friends around her, and of coming to her groom with a heart filled with joy and love.

If only this were real. If only Damian truly wanted her, and loved her…

A sound of distress burst from Laurel's throat. She took a quick step back. Instantly Damian's arm slid around her waist.

"Laurel?" he said softly.

She looked up at him, her eyes dark and glistening with unshed tears, and he felt as if a fist had clamped around his heart.

She didn't want this. He knew that, but it didn't matter. He'd told himself that a dozen times over. The child. That was the only thing that mattered. They had to marry, for the sake of the child. It was the right thing to do.

Now, looking down into the eyes of his bride, seeing the sorrow shimmering in their depths, Damian felt a twinge of uncertainty.

Was Laurel right? Was this a mistake?

She had offered to share the raising of their child with him, and he had scoffed. And with good cause. It didn't take a genius to see that what she really wanted was to get him out of her life forever. Still, a clever attorney could have made that an impossibility and he had a team of the best. A child should be raised by two parents; his belief in that would never change. But what good could come of being raised by a mother and father who lived in a state of armed truce?

Why, then, was he forcing this marriage?

Why was he taking as his wife a woman who hated him so much that she was on the verge of weeping? Damian's throat tightened. This wasn't the way it should be. A man wanted his bride to look up at him and smile; he wanted to see joy shining in her eyes as they were joined together.

If only, just for a little while, Laurel could look as if she wanted him. As if she remembered how it had been, that night...

"...always beautiful but you, my dear Miss Bennett, are a treat for an old man's eyes. And Mr. Skouras." The judge, a big man with a belly and a voice to match, clasped Damian's hand and shook it heartily. "I know you by reputation, of course. It is a pleasure to meet you, and to officiate at your wedding.''

Damian cleared his throat. ''Thank you for fitting us into your schedule, Your Honor. I know how difficult it must have been, but everything was so last minute…''

Judge Weiss laughed. ''Elopements generally are, my boy.'' He smiled, rubbed his hands together and reached for a small, battered black book. ''Well, shall we begin?''

''No!'' Laurel's cry was as sharp as broken glass. The judge's smile faded as he looked at her.

''I beg your pardon? Is there a problem, Miss Bennett?''

''There is no problem,'' Damian said smoothly. ''We made our decision so quickly…my fiancée is simply having a last-minute attack of nerves, Your Honor.'' Damian slid his arm around Laurel's waist. She looked up at him and he smiled. It was an affectionate smile, just as the way he was holding her seemed affectionate, but she knew better. ''I suppose,'' he said, flashing the judge a just-between-us-boys grin that made the older man chuckle, ''I suppose that no bride is calm on her wedding day.''

''Damian,'' Laurel said, ''it isn't too late—''

''Hush,'' he whispered, and before she could stop him, he tilted her chin up and kissed her.

It was a quick, gentle kiss, nothing more than the lightest brush of his mouth against hers, and she wondered, later, if that had been her undoing. Perhaps if he'd kissed her harder, if he'd tried, with silken tongue and teasing teeth, to remind her of the passion that had once consumed them, everything would have ended in that instant.

But he didn't. He kissed her the way a man kisses a woman he truly loves, with a sweet tenderness that numbed her senses.

''Everything will be fine, *kalí mou*,'' he murmured. He lifted her hand to his lips, pressed a kiss to the palm and sealed her fingers over it. ''Trust me.''

The judge cleared his throat. ''Well,'' he said briskly, ''are we ready now?''

"Ready," Damian said, and so it began.

The words were not as flowery, but neither were they very different from the ones that had been spoken in the little Connecticut church, barely more than four weeks before. The sentiments were surely the same; the judge had told Damian, over the phone, that he prided himself on offering a little ceremony of his own creation to each couple he wed.

He spoke of friendship, and of love. Of the importance of not taking vows lightly. Of commitment, and respect.

And, at last, he intoned the words Laurel had been dreading.

"Do you, Laurel Bennett, take Damian Skouras to be your lawfully wedded husband?"

A lump seemed to have lodged in her throat. She tried to swallow past it. The judge, and Damian, were looking at her.

"I'm sorry," she said, stalling for time, "I didn't—I didn't hear…"

The judge smiled. "I asked if you were prepared to take Damian Skouras as your lawfully wedded husband."

"Miss Bennett?"

Laurel shut her eyes. She thought of her baby, and of the power Damian held…and then, though it was stupid and pointless, because she didn't love him, didn't even like him, she thought of the way he'd kissed her only moments ago…

She took a shaky breath, opened her eyes and said, "Yes."

The car was waiting outside.

"Congratulations, sir," Stevens said, as he opened the door. He looked at Laurel and smiled. "And my best wishes to you, too, madam."

Best wishes? On an occasion such as this? Laurel felt like laughing. Or weeping. Or maybe both but then, the chauffeur was as much in the dark about this marriage as everybody else.

It wasn't easy, but she managed to summon up a smile.

"Thank you, Stevens."

Damian seemed to find that amusing.

"Nicely done," he said, as the car swung out into traffic. "I'd half expected you to assure Stevens that you were being carried off against your will."

Laurel folded her hands in her lap and stared straight ahead.

"Stevens was just being polite, and I responded in kind. I can hardly hold him responsible for the dilemma I'm in."

"The dilemma you're in?"

There was a soft note of warning in his voice, but Laurel chose to ignore it.

"We're alone now, Damian. The judge isn't here to watch our performance. If you expect me to pretend, you're in for an unpleasant surprise."

"I refer to your attitude toward my child. I will not have it thought of as a dilemma."

"You're twisting my words again. This travesty of a marriage is what I meant. I want this baby, and you damn well know it. Otherwise I wouldn't be sitting here, pretending that—that all that mumbo jumbo we just went through is real."

"Pretending?" His lips compressed into a tight smile. "There's no pretense in this. I have a document in my pocket that attests to the legitimacy of our union. You are my wife, Laurel, and I am your husband."

"Never!" The words she'd kept bottled inside tumbled from her lips. "Do you hear me, Damian? In my heart, where it matters, you'll never be my husband!"

"Such a sharp tongue, sweetheart." He shifted in his seat so that he was leaning toward her, his face only inches away. "And such empty threats."

"It isn't a threat." She could feel her pulse beating like a fist in her throat. "It's a statement of fact. You may have been able to force me into this marriage but you can't change what I feel.''

He touched the back of his hand to her cheek, then drew his fingers slowly into her hair. The pins that held it up worked loose and it started to come undone, but when she lifted her hand to fix it, he stopped her.

"Leave it," he said softly.

"It's—it's messy."

He smiled. "It's beautiful, and it's how I prefer it."

It was difficult to breathe, with him so close. She thought of putting her hands against his chest and pushing him away, but then she thought of that night, that fateful night, and how they'd ridden in this car and how she'd wound her arms tightly around his neck and kissed him...

...how she longed to kiss him, even now.

God. Oh God, what was happening to her?

"Really," she said, with a forced little laugh, "how I wear my hair is none of your business."

"You are my wife." He ran his hand the length of her throat. Her pulse fluttered under his fingers like a trapped bird, confirming what he already suspected, that though his bride seemed to have recovered her composure, she was not quite as calm as she wanted him to believe. "Is the thought so difficult to bear?"

"I learned something, when I was first starting in modeling. I never asked a question unless I was sure I wanted to hear the answer."

He stroked his thumb across the fullness of her bottom lip. A tremor went through her, and her eyes darkened.

"Don't," she whispered—but her lips parted and her breathing quickened.

His body quickened, too. She wanted him, despite everything she'd said. He could read it in the blurring of her eyes, in the softening of her mouth.

Now, he thought. He could have her now, in his arms, returning his kisses, sighing her acquiescence against his skin as he undressed her.

He bent his head, pressed his mouth to the slender column of her throat. She smelled of sunshine and flowers, summer and rain. He shut his eyes, nuzzled her collar aside and kissed her skin. It was softer than any silk, and as warm as fresh honey.

"Laurel," he whispered, and he drew back and looked into her face. Her eyes were wide with confusion and dark with desire, and a fierce sense of joy swept through him.

He ran his thumb over her mouth again. Again, her lips parted and this time, he dipped into the heat that awaited him. A soft moan broke from her throat and he felt the quick flutter of her tongue against his finger. Her hands lifted, pressed against his shoulders, then rose to encircle his neck. Damian groaned and pressed her back into the seat.

God, how he wanted her! And he could take her. She was his wife, and she wanted him. She was a sensual, sexual woman and now there would be no other men for her.

What choice did she have, but to want him?

He pulled away from her so quickly that she fell back against the leather seat.

"You see?" he said, and smiled coldly. "It will not be so bad, to be my wife."

Her face reddened. "I hope you go to hell," she said, in a voice that trembled, and as he turned his face and stared out the window at the landscape rushing by, he wondered what she would say if he told her that he was starting to think he was already there.

He had to give her credit.

He had told her they'd be leaving the country but she didn't ask any questions, not where they were going, or why, and she didn't blink an eye when they boarded a sleek private jet with Skouras International discreetly stenciled on the fuselage.

She settled into a seat, buckled her seat belt, plucked a magazine from the table beside her and buried her nose in it, never looking up or speaking except to decline, politely, when the steward asked if she'd like lunch.

But not even an actress as good as Laurel could keep up the deception forever. Four hours into the flight, she finally put the magazine down and stirred.

"Is it a matter of control?" she said. "Or did you just want to see how long it would take me to ask?"

He looked up from his laptop computer and the file he'd been pretending to read and smiled politely.

"Pardon?"

"Stop playing games, Damian. Where are we going?"

He took his time replying, signing off the file, shutting down the computer, stuffing it back into its leather case and laying it aside before he looked at her.

"Out of the country. I told you that yesterday."

"You told me you had business to attend to and to bring along my passport. But we've been flying for hours and—" *and I'm frightened* "—and now, I'm asking you where you're taking me."

"Greece," he said, almost lazily.

His answer shocked her. She'd been to Greece once; she remembered its stark beauty as well as the feeling that had come over her, as if she'd stumbled into another time when the old rules that governed behavior between the sexes were very different than they were now.

"Greece?" she said, trying not to let her growing apprehension show. "But why?"

"Why not?"

"I'm not in the mood for games, Damian. I asked a question, and I'd like an answer. Why are we going to Greece?"

There were half a dozen answers to give her, all of them reasonable and all of them true.

Because I own an island there, he could have said, and there was a storm last month and now I want to check on my property. Because I have business interests on Crete, and those, too, need checking. Because I like the hot sun and the sapphire water...

"Because it is where I was born," he said simply, and waited.

Her reaction was swift and not anything he'd expected.

"I do not want my child born in Greece," she said hotly. "He—or she—is going to be an American citizen."

Damian laughed softly. "As am I, dearest wife, I assure you."

"Then why...?"

"I thought it would be a place where we could be free of distraction while we get to know each other."

Catlike, he stretched. He'd taken off his jacket and tie, undone the top two buttons of his shirt and folded back the sleeves. His skin gleamed golden in the muted cabin light, his muscles flexed. Laurel felt a fine tremor dance down her spine. Whatever else she thought of him, there was no denying that he was a beautiful sight to behold.

And now, he was hers. He was her husband. The night she'd spent in his arms could be a night lived over again, on the sands beside a midnight sea or on a wild hilltop with the sun beating down on the both of them. She could kiss Damian's mouth and run her hands over his skin, whisper his name as he pleasured her...

Panic roughened her voice.

"I don't want to go to Greece, dammit! Didn't it ever occur to you to consult me before you made these plans?"

Damian looked at his wife's face. Her eyes glittered, with an emotion he could not define.

Fear. She was terrified, and of him.

God, why was he being such a mean son of a bitch? He had forced her into this marriage for the best of reasons but that didn't mean he had to treat her so badly. She was right, he should have consulted her. He should have told her, anyway, that he was taking her to Greece, to his island, Actos. He should have told her that for some reason he couldn't fathom, he wanted her to see where he had lost the boy he'd been and found the man he'd become.

He felt a tightening inside him, not just in his belly but in his heart.

"Laurel," he said, and touched her shoulder.

She flinched as if she'd been scalded.

"Don't touch me," she snarled, and he pulled back his hand, his face hardening, and thought that the place he was taking her was better than she deserved.

The plane landed on a small airstrip on Crete. A car met them and whisked them away, past hotels and streets crowded with vacationers, to the docks where sleek yachts bobbed at anchor.

Laurel smiled tightly. Of course. That was a Greek tradition, wasn't it? If you were what Susie had called a zillionaire Adonis, you owned a ship and, yes, Damian led her to one—but it was not a yacht. The *Circe* was a sailboat, large, well kept and handsome, but as different from the huge yachts moored all around her as a racehorse is from a Percheron.

"Damian," a male voice cried.

A man appeared on deck, opening his arms as they climbed the gangplank toward him. He was short and wiry; he had a dark beard and a bald head and he wore jeans and a striped T-shirt, and though he bowed over Laurel's hand and made a speech she sensed was flowery even though she couldn't understand a word, he greeted Damian with a slap on the back and a hug hard enough to break bones.

Damian reciprocated. Then, grinning, the two men turned to Laurel.

"This is Cristos. He takes care of *Circe* for me, when I am away."

"How nice for you," Laurel said, trying to look bored. Not that it was easy. Somehow, she hadn't expected such relaxed give and take between the urbane Damian Skouras and this seaman.

Cristos said something. Damian laughed.

"He bids you welcome, and says to tell you that you are Aphrodite come to life."

"Really?" Laurel smiled coolly. "I thought it was Helen who was carried off against her will."

If she'd thought to rile Damian, she hadn't succeeded. He grinned, told her to stay put, clattered below deck and disappeared.

Stay, she thought irritably, as if she were a well-trained puppy.

Well, she wasn't well trained. And the sooner he understood that, the better for them both.

She rose from the seat where he'd placed her and started forward. Instantly Cristos was at her side. He smiled, said something that sounded like a question and stepped in front of her. Laurel smiled back.

"I'm just going to take a look around."

"Ah. No, madam. Sorry. Is not permitted."

So, he spoke English. And he had his orders. What did Damian think, that she was going to dive overboard and swim for her freedom?

Actually it wasn't a bad idea.

Laurel sighed, wrapped her hands around the railing and gazed blindly out to sea.

It was too late for that.

She was trapped.

She didn't recognize Damian, when he reappeared.

Was this man dressed in cutoff denims, a white T-shirt and sneakers her urbane husband? And why the change of clothing? It was hot, yes, and the sun beat down mercilessly, but surely it would be cooler, once they set sail.

But Damian's change of clothes had nothing to do with the climate. Every captain needed a crew, and Cristos's crew was Damian.

Except she had it backward. In seconds, she realized that Damian was in charge here, not just in name but in fact.

There was a subtle change that took place between the two men as soon as Damian came up the ladder. Even she could sense it, though the men worked together easily. Still, there was no question about who was the leader.

It was Damian, and he led not by command but by example.

She watched him as he took the boat through the narrow channel that led to the open sea. His dark, wind-tossed hair curled around his face. Sunlight glinted on the tiny stud in his ear and when the sun grew too hot, he pulled off his T-shirt and tossed it aside.

Laurel felt her breath catch. She'd blocked the memory of how he'd looked, naked, during the night they'd spent together. Now, she was confronted with his perfect masculinity. He was the elemental male, this stranger she'd married, strong, and powerful, and beautiful to see.

The breeze caught at her hair and whipped it free of the pins she'd carefully replaced during the drive from the airport. She put her hand up to catch the wild curls and suddenly Damian was there, beside her.

"Are you all right?"

Laurel nodded. He was so close to her that she could smell the sun and salt on his skin, and the musky aroma of his sweat. She imagined pressing her lips to his throat, tasting him with the tip of her tongue.

"Yes," she said, "yes, I'm fine."

His hand fell on her shoulder. "You'd tell me if you felt ill, wouldn't you?"

"Damian, really, I'm okay. The nausea is all gone, and you know that Dr. Glassman gave me a clean bill of health."

"And the name of a physician on Crete," he said, and smiled at Laurel's look of surprise. "I told her where I was taking you, and she approved."

He wouldn't have taken her on this trip otherwise. Still, out here on the sea, with the wind blowing and the waves rising to slap against the hull, he was struck again by his bride's fine-boned delicacy.

"Go on," she said, with a little smile that might almost have been real, "Sail your boat. I don't need watching."

His lips curved in a smile. He bent his head and put his lips to her ear, and she shuddered as she felt the soft warmth of his breath.

"Ah," he whispered, "you are wrong, my beautiful wife. Watching is exactly what you need, if a man is to feed his soul."

She tilted her head back and looked at him and when she did, he wrapped his hand around the back of her neck, bent his head and kissed her, hard, on the mouth.

"Leave your hair loose for me," he said, and then he kissed her again before scrambling lithely back to the helm.

Laurel waited until her heartbeat steadied, then raised her head and found Damian looking at her. This was the way a flower must feel, she thought dazedly, as its tightly closed petals unfurl beneath the kiss of the sun.

His final words whispered through her head. Leave your hair loose, he'd said, just like the night they'd made love, just before he'd undressed her, with such slow, sweet care that her heart had almost stopped beating.

But that night was far behind them, and it had no meaning.

Her shoulders stiffened. Defiantly she raised her arms and began to pin up her hair again.

And then the wind gusted, and before she could prevent it, the pins sailed from her hand and disappeared into the sea.

CHAPTER NINE

THE ISLAND ROSE before them an hour later.

"Actos," Damian said, coming up beside Laurel. She knew, from the way he said it that this was their destination.

She shaded her eyes with her hand and gazed over the narrowing strip of blue water that separated the *Circe* from a small, crescent-shaped harbor. No yachts bobbed at anchor here; the few boats moored were small, sturdy-looking fishing vessels. Square, whitewashed houses topped with red tile roofs stood clustered in the shadow of the sunbaked, rocky cliffs that rose behind them. Overhead, seabirds wheeled against the pale blue sky, their shrill cries echoing over the water.

All at once, Laurel thought of how she had wept last night, as she'd thought of the unknown days and years that lay ahead, and she shuddered.

Damian put his arm around her and drew her against his side.

"What is it? Are you ill?"

"No. No, I told you, I'm fine."

He stepped in front of her, leaned back against the rail of the boat and drew her between his legs. His body felt hard and hot, and the faint male smell of his skin rose to her nostrils. Another tremor went through her. This man was her husband.

Her husband.

"You *are* ill! You're as white as a sheet." His mouth twisted. "I should have realized. The motion of the boat…"

"Damian, really, I'm okay. It's just—too much sun,

maybe.'' She smiled brightly. ''I'm used to the concrete canyons of New York, remember?''

''I wasn't thinking. We should have made this trip in two days instead of one.'' The wind ruffled her hair and he caught a strand of it in his fingers. It felt silky, and warm, and he fought to keep from bringing it to his lips. ''I should have considered your condition when I made these plans.''

His hand dropped to the curve of her shoulder and he stroked his thumb lightly against her neck. She had the sudden desire to close her eyes, lean into the gentle caress and give herself up to his touch.

The realization frightened her, and she gave herself up, instead, to a sharp response.

''You should have considered a lot of things, Damian, but you didn't, and here we are.''

His hand fell away from her. ''Yes,'' he said, ''and here we are.''

When Laurel had come to Greece before, it had been to do a cover for *Femme*. They'd shot it on a tiny island that had stunned her with its natural beauty.

Actos was not such a place.

If the island was beautiful, she was hard-pressed to see it. A rusted Ford station wagon was waiting for them at the dock, its mustachioed driver as ancient and gnarled as an olive tree. He and Damian greeted each other quietly, though she noticed that when they clasped hands, the men looked deep into each other's eyes and smiled.

The old man turned to her and took off his cap. He smiled, bowed and said something to Damian.

''Spiro says he is happy to meet you.''

''Tell Spiro I am glad to meet him, too.''

''He says you are more lovely than Aphrodite, and that I am a very fortunate man to have won you.''

''Tell him Aphrodite's an overworked image but that I thank him anyway for being such a charming liar, and that you are not fortunate, you are a scheming tyrant who black-mailed me into marriage.''

Damian laughed. ''That would not upset Spiro. He still remembers the old days, when every man was a king who could as easily take a woman as ask for her.''

The old man leaned toward Damian and said something. Both men chuckled.

Laurel looked from one to the other. ''What did he say now?''

''He said that your eyes are cool.''

''It is more than my eyes that are cool, Damian. And I fail to see why that should make the two of you smile.''

''Because,'' he said, his smile tilting, ''Spiro tells me there is a saying in the village of his birth. A woman who is cold in the day fills the night with heat.''

A flush rose in her cheeks. ''It's amazing, how wrong an old saying can be.''

''Is it, my sweet wife?''

''Absolutely, my unwanted husband.''

Spiro muttered again and Laurel rolled her eyes.

''I feel like the straight man in a comedy act,'' she snapped. ''Now what?''

Damian moved closer to her. ''He thinks there is more than coolness in your eyes,'' he said softly. ''He says you do not look like a happy woman.''

''A clever man, this Spiro.''

''It is, he says, my responsibility to make you happy.''

''Did you tell him you could have done that by leaving me alone?''

Damian's slow smile was a warning, but it came too late. His fingers threaded in her hair and he bent his head and kissed her.

''Kissing me to impress the old man is pathetic,'' Laurel said, when he drew back. She spoke calmly and told herself that the erratic beat of her pulse was the result of weariness, and the sun.

Damian kissed her again, as gently as he had when she'd said 'No' at their wedding."

"I kiss you because I want to kiss you," he said, very softly, and then he turned away and helped Spiro load their luggage into the old station wagon, while Laurel fought to still her racing heart.

A narrow dirt road wound its way up the cliffs, through groves of dark cypresses and between outcroppings of gray rock. They passed small houses that grew further and further apart as they climbed. After a while, there were no houses at all, only an occasional shepherd's hut. The heat was unrelenting, and a chorus of cicadas filled the air with sound.

The road grew even more narrow. Just when it seemed as if it would end among the clouds, a house came into view. It was made of white stone with a blue tile roof, and it stood on a rocky promontory overlooking the sea.

The house, and the setting, were starkly simple and wildly beautiful, and Laurel knew instantly that this was Damian's home.

A heavy silence, made more pronounced by the shrill of the cicadas and the distant pound of the surf, filled the car as Damian shut off the engine. Behind them, the car door creaked as Spiro got out. He spoke to Damian, who shook his head. The old man muttered in annoyance, doffed his cap to Laurel and set off briskly toward the house.

"What was that all about?"

Damian sighed. "He will be eighty-five soon, or perhaps even older. He's rather mysterious about his age." He got out of the car, came around to Laurel's door and opened it. "Still, he pretends he is a young man. He wanted to take our luggage to the house. I told him not to be such an old fool."

Laurel ignored Damian's outstretched hand and stepped onto the gravel driveway.

"So you told him to send someone else to get our things?"

Damian looked at her. "There is no one else at the house, except for Eleni."

"Eleni?"

"My housekeeper." He reached into the back of the wagon, picked up their suitcases and tossed them onto the grass, his muscles shifting and bunching under the thin cotton T-shirt. "Besides, why would I need anyone to do such a simple job as this?"

Her thoughts flashed back to Kirk, and the staff of ten who'd run his home. She'd never seen him carry anything heavier than his attaché case, and sometimes not even that.

"Well?" Damian's voice was rough. "What do you think? Can you survive a week alone with me, in this place?"

A week? Alone, here, with Damian? She didn't dare tell him what she really thought, that if he had set out to separate her from everything safe and familiar, he had succeeded.

"Well," she said coolly, "it's not Southampton. But I suppose there's hot water, and electricity, at least."

Out of the corner of her eye, she saw Damian's jaw tighten. Good, she thought with bitter satisfaction. What had he expected? Tears? Pleas? A fervent demand he take her somewhere civilized? If that was what he'd hoped for, he'd made an error. She wasn't going to beg, or grovel.

"I know it would please you if I said no." His smile was curt as he stepped past her, hoisted their suitcases and set off for the house. "But we have all the amenities you wish for, my dear wife. I know it spoils things for you, but I am not quite the savage you imagine."

The house was almost glacial, after the heat of the sun-baked hillside. White marble floors stretched to meet white painted walls. Ceiling fans whirred lazily overhead.

Damian dumped the suitcases on the floor and put his hands on his hips.

"Eleni," he roared.

A door slammed in the distance and a slender, middle-aged woman with eyes as dark as her hair came hurrying toward them. She was smiling broadly, but her smile vanished when she saw Damian's stern face. He said a few words to her, in Greek, and then he looked at Laurel.

"Eleni speaks no English, so don't waste your time trying to win her to your cause. She will show you to your room and tend to your needs."

The housekeeper, and not Damian. It was another small victory, Laurel thought, as he strode past her.

Eleni led the way up the stairs to a large, handsome bedroom with an adjoining bath.

Laurel nodded.

"Thank you," she said, "*efcharistó*."

It was the only word of Greek she remembered from her prior trip. Eleni smiled her appreciation and Laurel smiled back at her, but when the door had shut and she was, at last, alone, her smile faded.

She had set out to irritate Damian and somehow, she'd ended up wounding him. It was more of a victory than she'd ever have hoped.

Why, then, did it feel so hollow?

The cypresses were casting long shadows over the hillside. Soon, it would be night.

Damian stood on the brick terrace and gazed at the sea. He knew he ought to feel exhausted. It had been a long day. An endless day, following hard on the heels of an endless week—a week that had begun with him thinking he'd never see Laurel again and ending with his taking her as his wife.

His wife.

His jaw knotted, and he lifted the glass of chilled *ouzo* to his lips and drank. The anise-flavored liquid slipped easily down his throat, one of the few pleasurable experiences in the entire damned day.

It still didn't seem possible. A little while ago, his life had been set on a fixed course with his business empire as its center. Now, in the blink of an eye, he had a wife, and a child on the way—a wife who treated him, and everything that was his, with such frigid distaste that it made his blood pressure rumble like the volcanos that were at the heart of these islands.

So she didn't like this house. Hell, why should she? He knew what it was, an isolated aerie on the edge of nowhere, and that he'd been less than forthright about its amenities, which began, and just about ended, with little more than electricity and hot water. She was a woman accustomed to luxury, and to the city. Her idea of paradise wasn't likely to include a house on top of a rocky hill overlooking the Aegean, where she was about to spend seven of the longest days of her life trapped with the fool who'd forced her into marriage.

Damian frowned and tossed back the rest of the *ouzo*.

What the hell had he been thinking, bringing her here? God knew this wasn't the setting for a honeymoon—not that this was going to be one. Spiro, that sly old fox, had slapped him on the back and said that it was about time he'd married. Damian had told him to mind his own business.

This wasn't a marriage, it was an arrangement…and maybe that was the best way to think about it. Marriage, under the best of circumstances, was never about love, not once you scratched the surface. It was about lust, or loneliness, or procreation. Well, in that sense, he and Laurel were ahead of the game. There was no pretense in their relationship, no pretending that anything but necessity had brought them to this point in the road.

Damian refilled his glass and took a sip. Viewed reasonably, he really had no cause to complain. Not about having a child, at least. The more he'd thought about it the past week, the more pleased he'd been at the prospect of fatherhood. He'd enjoyed raising Nicholas, but the boy had come into his life almost full-grown. There'd be a special pleasure in holding an infant in his arms, knowing that it carried his name and his genes, that it would be his to mold and nurture.

His mouth twisted in a wry smile. And, despite all the advances of modern science, you still needed a woman to have a baby. A wife, if you wanted to do it right, and as wives went, Laurel would be eminently suitable.

She was beautiful, bright and sophisticated. She'd spent her life rubbing elbows with the rich and famous; to some degree, she was one of them herself. She'd be at ease as the hostess of the parties and dinners his work demanded, and he had no doubt that she'd be a good mother to their child.

As for the rest…as for the rest, he thought, the heat pooling in his loins, what would happen between them in bed would keep them both satisfied. She would not deny him forever. She wouldn't want to. Despite her protestations, Laurel wanted him. She was a passionate woman with a taste for sex, but she was his now. If she ever thought to slake her thirst with another man, he'd—he'd…

The glass splintered in his hand. Damian hissed with pain as the shards fell to the terrace floor.

"Dammit to hell!"

Blood welled in his palm. He cursed again, dug in his pocket for a handkerchief—and just then, a small, cool hand closed around his.

"Let me see that," Laurel said.

He looked up, angry at himself for losing control, angry at her for catching him, and the breath caught in his throat.

How beautiful his wife was!

She was wearing something long, white and filmy; he thought of what Spiro had said, that she looked like Aphrodite, but the old man was wrong for surely the goddess had never been this lovely.

Laurel must have showered and washed her hair. It hung

loose in a wild cloud of dark auburn curls that tumbled over her shoulders as she bent over his cut hand.

"It isn't as bad as it probably feels," she said, dabbing at the wound with his handkerchief.

He felt a fist close around his heart. Yes, it was, he thought suddenly, it was every bit as bad, and maybe worse.

"Come inside and let me wash it."

He didn't want to move. The moment was too perfect. Laurel's body, brushing his. Her hair, tickling his palm. Her breath, warm on his fingers...

"Damian?" She looked up at him. "The cut should be— it should be..."

Why was he looking at her that way? His eyes were as dark as the night that waited on the rim of the sea. There was a tension in his face, in the set of his shoulders...

His wide shoulders, encased in a dark cotton shirt. She could see the golden column of his throat at the open neck of the shirt; the pulse beating in the hollow just below his Adam's apple; the shadow of dark, silky hair she knew covered his hard-muscled chest.

A chasm seemed to open before her, one that terrified her with its uncharted depth.

"This cut should be washed," she said briskly, "and disinfected."

"It is not necessary." His voice was low and throaty; it made her pulse quicken. "Laurel..."

"Really, Damian. You shouldn't ignore it."

"I agree. A thing like this must not be ignored."

Her eyes met his and a soft sound escaped her throat. "Damian," she whispered, "please..."

"What?" he said thickly. He lifted his uncut hand and pushed her hair back from her face. "What do you want of me, *kalí mou*? Tell me, and I will do it."

Kiss me, she thought, and touch me, and let me admit the truth to myself, that I don't hate you, don't despise you, that I—that I...

She let go of his hand and stepped back.

"I want you to let me clean this cut, and bandage it," she said briskly. "You've seen to it that we're a million miles from everything. If you developed an infection, I wouldn't even know how to get help."

Damian's mouth twisted.

"You are right." He wound the handkerchief around his hand and smiled politely. "You would be stranded, not just with an unwanted husband but with a disabled one. How selfish of me, Laurel. Please, serve yourself some lemonade. Eleni prepared it especially for you. I will tend to this cut, and then we shall have our dinner. You will excuse me?"

Laurel nodded. "Of course," she said, just as politely, and she turned and stared out over the sea, watching as a million stars fired the black velvet sky, and blinking back tears that had risen, inexplicably, in her eyes.

She woke early the next morning.

The same insect chorus was singing, accompanied now by the soaring alto of a songbird. It wasn't the same as awakening to an alarm clock, she thought with a smile, or to the honking of horns and the sound of Mr. Lieberman's footsteps overhead.

Dressed in a yellow sundress, she wandered through the house to the kitchen. Eleni greeted her with a smile, a cup of strong black coffee and a questioning lift of the eyebrows that seemed to be the equivalent of, "What would you like for breakfast?"

A bit of sign language, some miscommunication that resulted in shared laughter, and Laurel sat down at the marble-topped counter to a bowl of fresh yogurt and sliced strawberries. She ate hungrily—the doors leading out to the terrace were open, and the air, fragrant with the mingled scents of flowers and of the sea, had piqued her appetite. She poured herself a second cup of coffee and sipped it outdoors, on the terrace, and then she wandered down the steps and onto the grass.

It was strange, how a night's sleep and the clear light of morning changed things. Yesterday, the house had seemed disturbingly austere but now she could see that it blended perfectly with its surroundings. The location didn't seem as forbidding, either. There was something to be said for being on the very top of a mountain, with the world laid out before you.

Impulsively she kicked off her sandals and looped the straps over her fingers. Then she set off toward the rear of the house, where she could hear someone—Spiro, perhaps—beating something with what sounded like a hammer.

But it wasn't the old man. It was Damian, wearing denim cutoffs, leather work gloves, beat-up sneakers and absolutely nothing else. He was wielding what she assumed was a sledgehammer, swinging it over and over against a huge gray boulder.

His swings were rhythmic; his attention was completely focused on the boulder. She knew he had no idea she was there and a part of her whispered that it was wrong to stand in the shadow of a cypress and watch him this way…but nothing in the world could have made her turn away or take her eyes off her husband.

How magnificent he was! The sun blazed down on his naked shoulders; she could almost see his skin toasting to a darker gold as he worked. His body glistened under a fine layer of sweat that delineated its muscled power. He grunted softly each time he swung the hammer and she found herself catching her breath at each swing, holding it until he brought the hammer down to smash against the rock.

Her thoughts flashed two years back, to Kirk, and to the hours he'd spent working out in the elaborate gym in the basement of his Long Island home. Two hours a day, seven days a week, and he'd still not looked as beautifully male as Damian did right now.

She thought of how strong Damian's arms had felt

around her the night they'd made love, of how his muscles had rippled under her hands…

"Laurel."

She blinked. Damian had turned around. He smiled, put down the hammer and wiped his face and throat with a towel that had been lying in the grass.

"Sorry," he said, tossing the towel aside and coming toward her. "I didn't mean to wake you."

"You didn't. I've always been an early riser."

He stripped off his gloves and tucked them into a rear pocket.

"I am, too. It's an old habit. If you want to get any work done in the summer here, you have to start before the sun is too high in the sky or you end up broiled to a crisp. Did you sleep well?"

Laurel nodded. "Fine. And you?"

"I always sleep well, when I am home."

It was usually true, though not this time. He'd lain awake half the night, thinking about Laurel, lying in a bed just down the hall from his. When he'd finally dozed off, it was only to tumble into dreams that had left him feeling frustrated. He'd figured on working that off this morning through some honest sweat, but just the sight of his wife, standing like a barefoot Venus with the wind tugging at her hair and fluttering the hem of her sundress, had undone all his efforts.

Laurel cleared her throat. "What are you doing, anyway?"

"Being an idiot," he said, and grinned at her. "Or so Spiro says. I thought it would be nice to plant a flower garden here."

"And Spiro doesn't approve?"

"Oh, he approves. It's just that he's convinced that I will never defeat the boulder, no matter how I try." He bent down, picked up a handful of earth and let it drift through his fingers. "He's probably right but I'll be damned if I'll give in without a fight."

She couldn't imagine Damian giving in to anything without a fight. Wasn't that the reason she was here, as his wife?

"Besides, I've gotten soft lately."

He didn't look soft. He looked hard, and fit, and wonderful.

"Too many days behind a desk, too many fancy lunches." He smiled. "I can always find ways to work off a few pounds, when I come home to Actos."

"You grew up here, in this house?"

Damian laughed. "No, not quite. Here." He plucked her sandals from her hand and knelt down before her. "Let me help you with these."

"No," she said quickly, "that's all right. I can…" He lifted her foot, his fingers long and tan against the paleness of her skin. Her heart did another of those stutter-steps, the foolish ones that were coming more often, and for no good reason. "Damian, really." Irritation, not with him but with herself, put an edge on her words. "I'm not an invalid. I'm just—"

"Pregnant," he said softly, as he rose to his feet. His eyes met hers, and he put his hand gently on her flat stomach. "And with my child."

Their eyes met. It was hard to know which burned stronger, the flame in his eyes or the heat in his touch. Deep within her, something uncoiled lazily and seemed to slither through her blood.

"Come." He held out his hand.

"No, really, I didn't mean to disturb you. You've work to do."

"The boulder and I are old enemies. We'll call a truce, for now." He smiled and reached for her hand. "Come with me, Laurel. This is your home, too. Let me show it to you."

It wasn't; it never would be. She wanted to tell him that but he'd already entwined his fingers with hers and anyway, what harm could there be in letting him walk her around?

"All right," she said, and fell in beside him.

He showed her everything, and she could tell from the way he spoke that he took a special pride in it all. The old stone barns, the pastures, the white specks in a lower valley that he said were sheep, even the squawking chickens that fluttered out of their way…it all mattered to him, and she could see in the faces of the men who worked for him, tilling the land and caring for the animals, that they knew it, and respected him for it.

At last he led her over the grass, down a gentle slope and into a grove of trees that looked as if they'd been shaped by the wind blowing in from the sea.

"Here," he said softly, "is the true heart of Actos."

"Are these olive trees? Did you plant them?"

"No," he said, with a little smile, "I can't take any credit for the grove. The trees are very old. Hundreds of years old, some of them. I'm only their caretaker, though I admit that it took years to restore them to health. This property had been left unattended for a long time, before I bought it."

"It wasn't in your family, then?"

"You think this house, this land, was my inheritance?" He laughed, as if she'd made a wonderful joke. "Believe me, it was not." His smile twisted; he tucked his hands into his back pockets and looked at her, his gaze steady. "The only thing I inherited from my parents was my name—and sometimes, I even wonder about that."

"I'm sorry," Laurel said quickly. "I didn't mean to pry."

"No, don't apologize. You have the right to know these things about me." A muscled knotted in his jaw. "My father was a seaman. He made my mother pregnant, married her only because she threatened to go to the police with a tale of rape, and left her as soon as I was born."

"How terrible for her!"

"Don't waste your pity." He began walking and Laurel hurried to catch up. Ahead, a low stone wall rose marked the edge of the cliff, and the bright sea below. "I doubt it

happened as she described it. She was a tavern whore.''
His voice was cold, without inflection; they reached the
wall and he leaned against it and stared out over the water.
''She told me as much, when she'd had too much to drink.''

''Oh, Damian,'' Laurel said softly, ''I'm so sorry.''

''For what? It is reality, and I tell it to you not to elicit
your pity but only because you're entitled to know the
worst about the man you've married.''

''And the best.'' She drew a deep breath and made the
acknowledgment she'd refused to make until this moment.
''Your decision about this baby—our baby—wasn't one
every man would choose.''

''Still, it was not a decision to your liking.''

''I don't like having my decisions made for me.''

A faint smile curved over his mouth. ''Are you suggesting that I am sometimes overbearing?''

Laurel laughed. ''Why do I suspect you've heard that
charge before?''

The wind lifted his dark hair and he brushed it back off
his forehead. It was a boyish gesture, one that suited his
quick smile.

''Ah, now I see how things are to be. You and Spiro
will combine forces to keep me humble.''

''You? Humble?'' She smiled. ''Not unless that old man
is more of a miracle worker than I am. Who is he, anyhow?
I got the feeling he's more than someone who works for
you.''

Damian leaned back, elbows on the wall, and smiled.

''What would you call a man who saves not only your
life, but your soul?'' A breeze blew a curl across her lips.
He reached out and captured the strand, smoothing it gently
with his fingers. ''Spiro found me, on the streets of Athens.
I was ten, and I'd been on my own for two years.''

''But what happened to your mother?''

He shrugged. It was a careless gesture but it couldn't
mask the pain in his words.

''I woke up one morning, and she was gone. She left me

a note, and some money... It didn't matter. I had been living by my wits for a long time by then.''

"How?'' Laurel said softly, while she tried to imagine what it must have been like to be ten, and wake up and find yourself alone in the world.

"Oh, it wasn't difficult. I was small, and quick. It was easy to swipe a handful of fruit or a couple of tomatoes from the outdoor markets, and a clever lad could always con the tourists out of a few drachma.'' The wind tugged at her hair again, and he smoothed it back from her cheek and smiled. ''I was quite an accomplished little pickpocket, until one winter day when Spiro came into my life.''

"You stole from him, and he caught you?''

Damian nodded. ''He was old as Methuselah, even then, but strong as an olive tree. He gave me a choice. The police—or I could go with him.'' He smiled. ''I went with him.''

"Damian, I'm lost here. Didn't you have a sister? Nicholas—the boy who married my niece—is your nephew, isn't he?''

"It's how his mother and I thought of each other, as brother and sister, but, in truth, we weren't related. You see, Spiro brought me here, to Actos, where he lived. The summer I was thirteen, an American couple—Greeks, but generations removed—came to the island, searching for their roots. Spiro decided I needed a better future than he could provide and, since I'd learned some English in Athens when I'd conned tourists, he convinced the Americans to take me to the States.''

"And they agreed?''

"They were good people and Spiro played on all their Greek loyalties. They took me home with them, to New York, and enrolled me in school. I studied hard, won a scholarship to Yale...'' He shrugged. ''I was lucky.''

"Lucky,'' she said softly, thinking of the boy he'd been and the man he'd become.

"Luck, hard work...who knows where one begins and

the other ends? The only certainty is that if it hadn't been for Spiro, I would be living a very different life.''

She smiled. ''I'll have to remember to thank him.''

''Will you?'' His dark, thick lashes drooped over his eyes, so that she couldn't quite see them. ''If he'd left me on the streets, I'd never have stormed into your life and turned it upside down.''

''I know.''

The words, said so softly that they were little more than a whisper, hung in the air between them. Damian framed Laurel's face in his hands. Her eyes gave nothing away, but he could see the sudden, urgent beat of her pulse in the hollow of her throat.

''*Mátya mou*,'' he whispered.

''What does that mean? *Mátya mou*?''

Damian bent his head and brushed his mouth gently over hers. ''It means, my dearest.''

She smiled tremulously. ''I like the sound of the words. Would it be difficult, to learn Greek?''

''I'll teach you.'' His thumb rubbed lightly over her bottom lip. ''I'll do whatever makes you happy, if you tell me what's in your heart.''

A lie would have been self-protective, but how could she lie to this man, who had just opened himself to her?

''I—I can't,'' she said. ''I don't know what's in my heart, Damian. I only know that when I'm with you, I feel—I feel…''

His mouth dropped to hers in a deep, passionate kiss. For one time-wrenching moment, Laurel resisted. Then she sighed her husband's name, put her arms around his neck and kissed him back.

CHAPTER TEN

LAUREL'S KISS almost undid him.

It was not so much the heated passion of it; it was the taste of surrender he drank from her lips.

She had been his, but only temporarily on that night in New York. Now, holding his wife in his arms on a wind-swept hill above the Aegean, Damian made a silent vow. This time, when he made love to her, she would be his forever.

Was he holding her too closely? Kissing her too hard? He knew he might be and he told himself to hold back—but he couldn't, not when Laurel's mouth was so soft and giving beneath his, not when he could feel her heart racing, and he knew that her desire burned as brightly as his. Desire, and something more.

He couldn't think. All he could do was feel, and savor, and when she moaned softly and pressed herself against him, so that he could feel her body molded to his, he almost went out of his head with need.

"Damian," she whispered. Her voice broke. "Damian, please…"

He thrust his hands into her hair, his thumbs tracing the delicate arch of her cheeks, and lifted her face to his. Her eyes were dark with desire; color stained her cheeks.

"Tell me," he murmured, just as he had that first time, and he moved against her so that she caught her breath at the feel of him. "Say it, *o kalí mou.*"

Laurel brushed her lips against his. "Make love to me," she sighed, and he caught her up in his arms and carried her to a stone watchtower that was a part of the wall.

The tower was ancient, older, even, than the wall. A

thousand years before, it had been a place from which warriors safeguarded the island against pirates. Now, as Damian lay his wife down gently on a floor mounded with clean, sweet-smelling hay, he knew that the battle that would be fought here today was one in which there would be no way to tell who was the conqueror and who the conquered.

He told himself to undress her slowly, despite the hunger that beat within him. But when she moved her hands down his chest, down and down until she cupped his straining arousal, the last semblance of his control slipped away.

"Now," he said fiercely, and he tore away her sundress.

Beneath, she was all lace and silk, perfumed flesh and heat. He tried again to slow what was happening but Laurel wouldn't let him. She lifted her head, strained to kiss his mouth; she stroked his muscled shoulders and chest, drew her hand down his hard belly, and then her fingers slid under the waistband of his shorts. Damian groaned; his hands closed over hers and together, they stripped the shorts away.

At last, they lay skin against skin, heat against heat, alone together in the universe.

"Damian," Laurel said brokenly, and he bent his head to hers and kissed her.

"Yes, sweetheart, yes, *o kalóz mou.*"

And then he was inside her, thrusting into the heart of her, and in that last instant before she shattered in her husband's arms, Laurel, at last, admitted the truth to herself.

She was in love, completely in love, with Damian Skouras.

A long time later, in the white-hot blaze of midday, they made their way to the house.

Someone—Eleni, probably—had closed the thin-slatted blinds at all the windows so that the foyer was shadowed and cool. Everything was silent, except for the soft drone of the fan blades rotating slowly overhead.

Laurel looked around warily. "Where's Eleni?"

"Why? Do you need something?" Damian pulled her close and kissed her, lingeringly, on the mouth. "Let me get whatever it is. I've no wish to share you with anyone else just now."

"I don't need anything, Damian. I was just thinking…" She blushed. "If she sees us, she'll know that we—that you and I—"

Damian smiled. Bits of hay were tangled in his wife's hair, and there was a glow to her skin that he knew came from the hours she'd spent in his arms.

"What will she know, *keería mou*, except that we have made love?"

"What does that mean? Keerya moo?"

"It means that you are my wife." He pressed a kiss into her hair. "And a husband may make love to his wife whenever he chooses." He put his hand under her chin and gently lifted her face to his. "On Actos, in New York…anywhere at all, so long as she is willing. Do you agree?"

"Only if the same rules apply for the wife."

Damian's eyes darkened. "Has no one ever told you that democracy was invented here, in these islands?"

Laurel smiled. "In that case…"

She rose on her toes, put her mouth to her husband's ear and whispered.

Damian laughed. "I couldn't have put it better myself," he said, and he lifted her into his arms, carried her up the stairs and into his bedroom.

The days, and the nights, flew past. And each was a revelation.

Damian, the man who could do anything from saving a dying corporation to making an endless assault against a boulder, turned out to have a failing.

A grave one, Laurel said, with a solemnity she almost managed to pull off.

He didn't know how to play gin rummy.

He was, he assured her, an expert at baccarat and chemin de fer, and he admitted he'd even been known to win a dollar or two at a game of poker.

Laurel wasn't impressed. How could he have reached the age of forty without knowing how to play gin?

"Thirty-eight," he said, with only a glint in his eye, and then he said, well, if she really wanted to teach him the game, he supposed he'd let her.

He lost six hands out of six.

"I don't know," he said, with a sigh. "Gin just doesn't seem terribly interesting."

"Well, we could try playing for points. I'll keep score, or I can show you…what's the matter?"

"Nothing. It's just… I don't know. Points, scoring…it seems dull."

"Okay, how about playing for money?"

"A bet, you mean? Yes, that would be better."

"A nickel a hand."

Damian's brows lifted. "You call that interesting?"

"Maybe I should tell you that I'm the unofficial behind-the-runways-from-Milan-to-Paris gin rummy champion."

"So? What's the matter? Afraid of losing your title?"

Laurel blew her hair back out of her eyes. "Okay, killer, don't say I didn't warn you. We'll play big time. A dime a hand."

Damian's smile was slow and sexy. "I've got a better idea. Why don't we play for an article of clothing a hand?"

Laurel's eyes narrowed. "You sure you never played gin before?"

"Never," he said solemnly, and dealt out the cards.

Half an hour later, Laurel was down to a pair of jeans and a silk teddy. Her sandals, belt, shirt, even the ribbon she'd used to tie back her hair, lay on the white living-room carpet.

"No fair," she grumbled. "You *have* played gin before."

Damian gave her a heart-stopping smile and fanned out another winning hand. He leaned back against the cushions they'd tossed on the floor and folded his arms across his chest. "Well?"

Laurel smiled primly and took off an earring.

"Since when is an earring an article of clothing, *keería mou*? An article of clothing for each losing hand, remember?"

Her heart gave a little kick. "You wouldn't really expect me to—"

He reached out a lazy hand, drew his fingertip lightly over her breasts, then down to the waistband of her jeans. "Your game and your rules," he said huskily. "Take something off, sweetheart."

Laurel's eyes met his. She rose to her feet, undid the jeans and slid them off.

"Your turn is coming," she said, "just you wait and see."

He smiled and dealt the cards. It pleased her to see that his hands were unsteady. Surely he would lose now.

"Gin."

Laurel ran the tip of her tongue over her lips, and Damian's eyes followed the gesture. Heat began pooling in her belly.

"Damian, you're not going to make me..."

Their eyes met again. She swallowed dryly, then got to her knees. Slowly she hooked a finger under one shoulder strap and slid it off. She slid off the second. There were three satin ties on the teddy, just between her breasts, and she reached for them.

Damian's breathing quickened, but his eyes never left hers.

"One," she said softly. "Two. Three..."

With a throaty growl, he tumbled her to the carpet. And then, for a long, long time, the only sounds in the room were the sighs and whispers of love.

*   *   *

He refused to believe that she could cook.

They discussed it, one afternoon, as Laurel sat in a field of daisies with Damian's head in her lap.

She reminded him, indignantly, of the bread he'd found rising in her kitchen. He reminded her, not very gallantly, that it had resembled a science experiment gone bad.

Laurel plucked a handful of daisies and scattered them over his chest.

"I'll have you know that I make the most terrific sourdough bread in the world."

"Uh-huh."

"What do you mean, 'uh huh'? I do. Ask George. He loves my bread."

"George," Damian scoffed. "The man's besotted. He'd say it was great even if it tasted like wet cardboard."

Laurel dumped more daisies over him. "He is not besotted with anyone but his own wife."

Damian sat up, reached for her hand and laced his fingers through hers. There was something he had to tell her, something he should have told her sooner. It meant nothing to him, but she had the right to know.

"It's good, for a man to be besotted with his wife," he said softly.

She smiled and brushed a daisy petal from his hair. "Is it?"

"Did I ever tell you," he asked, catching her hand and raising it to his mouth, "that I was married before?"

Laurel's teasing smile vanished. "No. No, you didn't."

"Well, I was. For a grand total of three weeks."

"What happened?" She tried another smile and hoped this one worked. "Don't tell me. The lady served you a slice of wet cardboard, called it sourdough bread and you sent her packing."

"Nothing so simple. It turned out we had nothing in common. She wanted my name and my money, and I..."

"And you? What did you want?"

"Out," he said, with a little laugh, "almost from the

beginning. The marriage was a complete mistake. I think we both knew it.''

''Why did you marry her, then?'' A chill crept into Laurel's heart, and she gave him a stiff smile. ''Was she pregnant, too?''

She regretted the ugly words as soon as she'd said them, but it was too late to call them back. Damian sat up, his face cold and hard.

''No. She was not pregnant. Had she been, I can assure you, I would still be married to her.''

''Because it would have been your duty.'' Laurel stood up and dusted the grass from her shorts. ''Of course,'' she said, and started briskly toward the house, ''I almost forgot how noble you are, Damian. Sorry.''

''*Theé mou!*'' Angrily he clasped her shoulders and spun her around. ''What is the matter with you, Laurel? Are you angry with me for having divorced a woman I did not love? Or for admitting that I would have done the right thing by her, if I'd had to?''

''I'm not angry with you at all.'' Her smile was brittle. ''I'm just—you can't blame me for being curious, Damian. After all, I only just found out you have an ex-wife.''

''I told you, the relationship was meaningless. We met, we thought we were in love, we got married. By the time we realized what we'd done, it was too late.''

''Yes, well, that's what happens, when a person marries impetuously.''

''Dammit, don't give me that look!''

''What look? It's the only one I've got—but how would you know that?''

''Don't be a little fool!'' Damian glared at her, his face dark with anger. ''There is no comparison between this marriage and the other. I married you because—be-cause…''

''Because I was pregnant.''

''Yes. No. I mean…'' What did he mean? Of course he'd married her because she was pregnant; why deny it? What other reason could possibly have made him ask Laurel to be his wife?

"You needn't explain." Laurel's voice was frosty, a perfect match to her smile. "We both know what an honorable man you are. You married me for the sake of our child, and you'll stay married to me for the same reason. Isn't that right?"

Damian's jaw knotted. "You're damned right," he growled. "I'm going to stay married to you, and you to me, until as the man said, 'Death do us part.'"

He pulled her into his arms and kissed her just as he had the day he'd announced he was going to make her his wife. For the first time since they'd made love in the tower overlooking the sea, Laurel didn't respond. She felt nothing, not desire, not even anger.

"You are my wife," Damian said. Stone-faced, he held her at arm's length and looked down into her face. "And nothing more needs to be said about it."

Laurel wrenched free of his grasp. "How could I possibly forget that, when you'll always be there to remind me?"

She swung away and strode up the hill, toward the house. Damian's hands knotted at his sides. Dammit, what was wrong with her? He thought they'd gotten past this, that Laurel had made peace with the circumstances of their marriage, but it was clear that she hadn't.

Had she been pretending, all those times they'd made love? Had she lain in his arms, touching him, kissing him, and wishing all the while that he'd never forced her into becoming his wife? Because he had. Hell, there was no denying it. He'd given her about as much choice in the matter as the rocks below gave to the ships they'd claimed, over the centuries.

His mouth twisted. So what? They were man and wife. She had to accept that. As for this afternoon's pointless quarrel…she'd get over it when he took her to bed, tonight.

He took a deep breath, stuck his hands into his pockets and stood staring out to sea.

She hadn't been pretending, when they made love. He would have known if those sweet sighs, those exciting whispers, had been false.

Of course, he would... Wouldn't he?

Laurel sat at the dressing table in the bedroom where she'd spent her first night as Mrs. Damian Skouras, staring at her reflection in the mirror.

She hadn't been back in this room since then. Every night—and a lot of long, wonderful mornings and afternoons—had been spent in Damian's bed.

Her hand trembled as she picked up a silver-backed brush and ran it over her hair.

What had gotten into her today? Damian had been married before. Well, so what? She'd had a relationship before, too, and even if Kirk hadn't treated it as a marriage, she had. She'd been faithful, and loving, and when she'd found out that he'd deceived her, her heart couldn't have been more broken than if she had been Mrs. Kirk Soames. She'd loved Kirk every bit as much as if—as if—

A choked cry burst from her lips and she dropped the brush and buried her face in her hands.

It wasn't true. She'd never really loved Kirk, she knew that now. What she felt for Damian made her feelings for Kirk seem insignificant.

And that was what this afternoon's performance had been all about, wasn't it?

"Wasn't it?" she whispered, lifting her head and staring at her pale face and tear-swollen eyes in the mirror.

Damian had told her he'd been married before, that it had been an impetuous marriage and hadn't worked out, and all she'd been able to think was that he'd married her the same way, impetuously, because it had been the right thing to do.

How she'd longed for him to deny it!

I married you because I love you, she'd wanted him to say, because I'll always love you.

But he hadn't. He'd married her because he wanted his child to have a father, and even though part of her knew how right, how decent, that was, another part of her longed to hear him say he'd married her for love.

She picked up the hairbrush again and stared at her reflection.

But he hadn't. She was Damian's wife, but not his love. She had his name, and his interest in bed, but if she made many more scenes like the one she'd made today, she probably wouldn't even have that, and never mind the Until death do us part promise. Her mouth turned down with bitterness. She knew all about men like Damian, and promises of fidelity. Oh, yes, she knew all about—

"Laurel?"

Her gaze flew to the mirror just as the bedroom door opened. Damian stood in the doorway, wearing a terry cloth robe. She knew from the experience of the past week that he had nothing on beneath it. His hair was tousled, his eyes were dark and she wanted nothing so much as to jump up and hurl herself into his arms.

Pride and pain kept her rooted in place.

"Yes, Damian," she said. She smiled politely, put down the brush and turned around.

"Are you feeling better?"

She'd missed dinner, pleading a headache. It would never have done to have told him the truth, that what ached was her heart.

"Much better, thank you. Eleni brought me some tea, and aspirin."

He nodded and stepped further into the room. "It's late."

"Is it? I hadn't noticed."

He paused beside her and lifted his hand. She thought, for a moment, he was going to touch her hair and if he had, that would have been her undoing. She'd have sighed under his hand like a kitten—but he didn't. He only reached out, straightened the dressing table mirror, then put his hand into his pocket.

"Are you coming to bed?"

Laurel turned away and looked into the mirror again. He'd asked the question so casually but then, why wouldn't he? So far as he was concerned, her place was in his bed. Not only was she his wife, but she'd made it clear she wanted to be there. Her throat constricted as she remembered the things they'd done together in that bed.

Why was it that loving a man who didn't love you, knowing he'd *never* love you, could suddenly make those things seem cheap?

"Actually," she said, picking up the brush again, "I thought I'd sleep in here tonight."

"In here?" he repeated, as if she'd suggested she was going to spend the night on an ice floe in the North Sea.

"Yes." Briskly, she drew the brush through her hair. "I still have a bit of a headache."

"Shall I phone the doctor Glassman recommended on Crete?"

"No. No, I don't need a doctor."

"Are you sure? Laurel, if you're ill—"

"I'm fine. The baby's fine." She smiled tightly at him in the mirror. "It's just an old habit of mine, Damian. Sometimes, I need a night to myself. Kirk used to say—"

"Kirk?" he said, and the way he said it made her heart stop.

Don't, she told herself, oh, don't do this...

"A man I used to live with. Well, actually, a man I thought about marrying. Didn't I ever tell you about him?"

"No," he said coldly, "you did not."

She looked into the mirror again and what she saw in his face terrified her. The brush clattered to the mirrored top of the dressing table and she swung toward him.

"Damian," she said quickly, but it was too late. He was already at the door.

"You're right," he said, "a night apart might be an excellent idea for the both of us. I'll see you in the morning."

"Damian, wait…"

Wait? He stepped into the hall and slammed the door after him. She wouldn't want him to wait, if she knew how close he was to smashing his fist into the wall. He stormed into his bedroom, kicked the door shut, then flung open the french doors that let out onto the terrace. The black heat of the Agean night curled around him like a choking fog.

All right, so she'd lived with a man. So what? It didn't matter a damn. She'd married him, not Kirk, whoever in hell Kirk might be.

Married him under protest. Under the threat of losing her child to him. Under the worst kind of blackmail.

Damian spun around and slammed his fist against the wall. It hurt like hell, and he winced and put his knuckles to his mouth, tasted the faint tang of blood, and wished to God it was Kirk's blood instead of only his own. What sort of name was that, anyway? A stupid name, befitting a man foolish enough to have let Laurel go.

Any man would want her. Would desire her. Would fall in love with her.

And, just that simply, Damian saw the truth.

He loved Laurel. He loved his wife.

"I love her," he said to the night, and then he laughed out loud.

What a fool he'd been, not to realize it sooner.

And maybe, just maybe, she loved him, too.

He lifted his face to the moonless sky, as if the answer might be there, in the blazing light of a million stars that dotted the heavens.

It would explain so much, if she did.

The softness of her, in his arms. The passion she could never hide when he touched her. Even her reaction earlier today, when he'd so clumsily told her that he'd been married before.

His heart filled with hope. Maybe what had seemed like

anger had really been pain. Maybe she'd felt the same jealousy at his mention of a former lover that he'd felt at the mention of Kirk.

But if she loved him, would she have chosen to sleep alone tonight? Would she have taken such relish in telling him she'd lived with another man and almost married him?

Damian took a deep breath. He'd always prided himself on knowing how to chart a direct path from A to B, but tonight he felt as if he were going in circles.

There was only one thing to do, by God, go back into Laurel's room, confront her, drag her from that bed if he had to, shake her silly or kiss her senseless until she told him what she felt for him...

The telephone rang. Damian cursed and snatched it up.

"Whoever you are," he snapped, "you'd better have a damned good reason for calling."

It was Hastings, his personal attorney, phoning from New York.

Damian sat down on the edge of the bed. Hastings was not a man given to running the risk of waking his most important client in the middle of the night.

"I'm afraid we have a problem, Mr. Skouras."

Damian listened and, as he did, the look on his face went from dark to thunderous.

"Gabriella is suing me for breach of promise? Is she crazy? She hasn't got a case. What do you mean, she's going to sell her story to 'The Gossip Line' unless I meet her demands? Who'd give a crap about...? What's my marriage got to do with...?" His face went white. "If she drags my wife down into the mud, so help me God, I'll—"

Hastings spoke again. According to Gabriella, Damian had made promises. He'd said he'd marry her. He'd been not just her only lover but her first lover, since her divorce, and her last.

Damian took a stranglehold on the telephone cord. "All right," he said abruptly, rising to his feet and shrugging off his robe. "Here's what I want you to do." He rattled off a string of commands. Hastings repeated them, then asked a question, and Damian glared at the phone as if he could see the attorney's face in it. "How the hell do I know who to contact? That's why you're on retainer, Hastings, because you're the legal eagle, remember? Just get the information by tomorrow. That's right, man. Tomorrow. I'll see you in New York."

Rage and determination propelled him through the next few minutes. He phoned Spiro on the intercom, called his pilot on Crete—and then he hesitated.

Should he wake Laurel, to tell her he was leaving? No. Hell, no. The last thing he needed right now was to explain to his wife that his vindictive former mistress was trying to stir up trouble by selling a story to some TV gossip show featuring herself as an abandoned lover—and Laurel as a scheming, pregnant fortune hunter.

Spiro could deal with it. The old man could tell her he'd been called to New York on urgent business. She wouldn't like it, but how long would he be gone? A day? Two, at the most. Then he'd be back, on Actos, and he'd take his wife in his arms, tell her he loved her and pray to the gods that she would say she loved him, too. And if she didn't— if she didn't, he'd make her love him, dammit, he'd kiss her mouth until all memory of Kirk whoever-he-was had been wiped from her mind and her soul, and then they'd begin their lives together, all over again.

He just had to see her once, before he left. The house was quiet, as he left his room; no light spilled from beneath Laurel's closed door. Damian opened it and slipped inside.

She lay on her back, fast asleep.

How lovely she was. And how he adored her.

"*Kalí mou*," he murmured, "my beloved."

He bent and brushed his mouth gently over hers. She stirred and breathed a soft sigh, and it was all he could do to keep from lying down beside her and gathering her into his arms.

First, though, there was Gabriella to deal with.

Damian's jaw hardened as he left his wife's room and quietly shut the door after him.

And deal with the bitch, he would.

CHAPTER ELEVEN

LAUREL AWAKENED to bright sunlight and a memory as ethereal as a wisp of cloud.

Was it a dream, or had Damian really entered her room in the middle of the night, kissed her and called her his beloved?

It seemed so real…but it couldn't have been. They'd quarreled, and even though he'd held out a tentative olive branch, she'd rejected it.

She sat up, pushed aside the light sheet that covered her and scrubbed her hands over her face.

Rejected his peace offering? That was putting it mildly. She'd damn near slapped his face, then rubbed his nose in her relationship with Kirk for good measure.

Laurel puffed out her breath. What on earth had possessed her? The man she loved—the only man she'd ever loved—was Damian.

She dressed quickly, with little care for how she looked. All that mattered was finding a way to rectify the damage she'd caused last night. Damian didn't love her, not yet, but she knew that he cared for her—at least, he had, until she'd instigated that ugly scene.

Well, there was only one way to fix things.

She had to tell Damian the truth. To hell with pride, and the pain that would come of admitting she loved him without hearing that he loved her, too. She'd go to him, tell him that Kirk had never meant a damn to her, that no one had or ever would, except him.

Her heart was racing, as much with apprehension as with anticipation. After Kirk, she'd promised she'd never leave herself so vulnerable to any man again. But Damian wasn't *any* man. He was her husband, her lover—he was the man she would always love.

Laurel squared her shoulders and stepped out into the hall.

He wasn't in his bedroom. Well, why would he be? It was past eight o'clock, late by his standards, and there'd been nothing to make him linger in bed today. She hadn't been lying in the curve of his arm, her head pillowed on his shoulder; he hadn't whispered a soft, sexy "good morning" and she hadn't given him a slow, equally sexy smile in return.

He wasn't in the kitchen, either, nor on the terrace, sipping a second cup of coffee while he and Spiro conferred on what might need doing today.

Eleni was there, though, out on the terrace, busily watering the urns filled with pansies and fuchsias and impatiens.

"*Kaliméra sas.*"

Laurel smiled as she stepped outside. "*Kaliméra sas*, Eleni. Where is Mr. Skouras, do you know?"

Eleni's brows lifted. "Madam?"

"My husband," Laurel said. "Have you any idea where…" She sighed, smiled and shook her head. "Never mind. I'll find him, I'm sure."

But she didn't. He wasn't at the barns, or strolling along the wall, or hammering at the boulder.

"*Kaliméra sas.*"

It was Spiro. He had come up behind her, as quietly as a shadow.

"*Kaliméra sas,*" Laurel said, and hesitated. The old man spoke no English and she spoke no Greek beyond the few words she'd picked up during the week. Still, it was worth a try. Damian had to be here somewhere. "Spiro, do you know where Mr. Skouras is?"

The old man's bushy brows lifted questioningly.

"I'm trying to find Damian. Damian," she repeated,

pointing at the platinum wedding band on her left hand, "you know, my husband."

"Ah. Damian. *Né.* Yes, I understand."

"You *do* speak English, then?"

"A little bit only."

"Believe me, your English is a thousand times better than my Greek. So, where is he?"

"Madam?"

"Damian, Spiro. Where is he?"

The old man cleared his throat. "He leave island, madam."

"Left Actos? For Crete, you mean?"

"He is for New York."

Laurel stared at him. "What do you mean, he's… No, Spiro, you must be mistaken. He wouldn't have gone to New York without me."

"He is for New York, madam. Business."

"Business," she repeated and then, without warning, she began to weep. She cried without sound, which somehow only made her tears all the more agonizing for Spiro to watch.

"Madam," he said unhappily, "please, do not cry."

"It's my fault," she whispered. "It's all my fault. We quarreled, and I hurt him terribly, and—and I never told him—he doesn't know how much I—"

She sank down on a bench and buried her face in her hands. Spiro stood over her, watching, feeling the same helplessness he'd felt years ago, when he'd come across a lamb who'd gotten itself caught on a wire fence.

He put out his hand, as if to touch her head, then reached into his pocket instead, pulled out an enormous white handkerchief, and shoved it into her hands.

"Madam," he said, "you will see. All will be well."

"No." Laurel blew her nose, hard, and rose to her feet. "No, it won't be. You don't understand, Spiro. I told Damian a lie. An awful lie. I said cruel things…"

"You love him," the old man said gently.

"Yes. Oh, yes, I love him with all my heart. If only I'd gone to him last night. If only I hadn't been so damn proud. If only I could go to him now…"

Spiro nodded. It was as he'd thought. Something had gone wrong between Damian and his bride; it was why he had left her in the middle of the night.

"Where are you going at such an hour?" Spiro had asked.

Damian's reply had been sharp. "New York," he'd said, "and before you ask, old man, no, Laurel does not know I'm going, and no, I am not going to tell her."

"But what shall I tell her, when she asks?"

"Tell her whatever seems appropriate," Damian had said impatiently, and then he'd motioned Spiro to cast off the line.

The old man frowned. Damian and this woman loved each other deeply, any fool could see that, but for reasons that were beyond him to comprehend, they could not admit it.

"Spiro."

He looked at the woman standing beside him. Her eyes were clear now, and fierce with determination.

"I know that you love Damian," she said. "Well, I love him, too. I have to tell him that, Spiro, I have to make him understand that there's never been anyone but him, that there never could be."

Tell her whatever seems appropriate…

The old man straightened his shoulders. "Yes," he said. He put his gnarled hand on Laurel's shoulder. "Yes, madam. You must tell him—and I will help you to do it."

New York City was baking in brutal, midsummer heat.

It had been hot on Actos, too, but there the bright yellow sun, blue sea and pale sky had given a strange beauty to the land.

Here, in Manhattan, the sun was obscured by a sullen sky. The air was thick and unpleasant. And, Damian thought as the doors of the penthouse elevator whispered open, it had been one hell of a long day.

He stripped off his jacket and tie, dumped them on a chair and turned up the air conditioner. A current of coolness hissed gently into the silent foyer. Stevens and his housekeeper were both on vacation; he had the place to himself. And that was just as well.

Damian closed his eyes and let the chill envelope him as he undid the top buttons of his shirt, then rolled back his cuffs. He was in no mood to pretend civility tonight, not after dealing with Gabriella. The hour he'd spent closeted with her and their attorneys had felt like an eternity. Even the cloying stink of her perfume was still in his nostrils.

"Are you certain you're up to a face-to-face meeting?" Hastings had asked him.

Damian had felt more up to putting his hands around Gabriella's throat, but he'd known this was the only thing that would work. She had to be confronted with the information he'd ordered gathered but, more than that, she had to see for herself that he would follow through.

For the next sixty minutes, while Gabriella wept crocodile tears into her lace handkerchief and cast him tragic looks, he'd tried to figure out what he'd ever imagined he'd seen in her.

The bleached hair. The artful but heavy makeup. The clinking jewelry—jewelry he'd paid for, from what he could tell—all of it offended him. The sole thing that kept him calm was the picture he held in his mind, of Laurel as he'd last seen her, asleep at Actos, in all her soft, unselfconscious beauty.

Finally he'd grown weary of the legal back-and-forth, and of Gabriella's posturing.

"Enough," he'd said.

All eyes had turned to him. In a voice that bore the chill of winter, he'd told Gabriella what she faced if she took him on and then, almost as an afterthought, he'd shoved the file folder across the conference table toward her.

"What is this, darling?" she'd said.

For the first time, he'd smiled. "Your past, *darling*, catching up to you."

She'd paled, opened the folder...and it was all over. Gabriella had called him names, many that were quite inventive; she'd hurled threats, too, but when her attorney peered over her shoulder at the contents of the folder, the list of names of the men she'd been involved with, the photos culled from the files of several private investigators including one of her, topless, sitting between the thighs of a naked man on a palm tree lined beach, he'd blanched and walked out.

Damian smiled, went to the bar and poured himself a shot of vodka over a couple of ice cubes.

"To private investigators," he said softly, and tossed back half his drink.

Glass in hand, he made his way up the stairs to his bedroom, the room where he'd first made love to his wife. And it *had* been love; he knew that now. It was illogical, it was almost embarrassingly romantic, but there wasn't a doubt in his mind that he'd fallen in love with Laurel at first sight.

He couldn't wait to tell her that.

As soon as he got back to Actos, he was going to take her in his arms and tell her what had been in his heart all the time, that he loved her and would always love her, that it didn't matter what faceless man she'd loved in the past because he, Damian Skouras, was her future, and the future was all that mattered.

He put down his drink, stripped off the rest of his clothes and stepped into the bathroom. His plane was waiting at the airport. Just another few hours, and he'd be home.

He showered quickly. There wasn't a minute to waste. The sooner he left here, the sooner he'd be in Laurel's arms.

But there was one stop to make first.

He knotted a bath sheet around his waist, ran his fingers carelessly through his damp hair and retrieved his drink from the bedroom.

He was going to go to Tiffany's. He'd never given his wife an engagement ring. Well, he was going to remedy that failing right away. What would suit her best? Diamonds and emeralds? Diamonds and sapphires? Hell, maybe he'd solve the problem by buying her a whole bucketful of rings.

He grinned as he headed down the stairs. Another drink—ginger ale, because he wanted a clear head for this—and then he'd phone Tiffany's, see if they were open. If they weren't…what was the name of that guy he'd met last year? He was a Tiffany Veep, or maybe he was with Cartier or Harry Winston. Damian laughed out loud as he set his glass down on the bar. It didn't matter. Laurel wouldn't care where the ring was from, she wouldn't give a damn if it came from Sear's, not if she loved him, and he was closer and closer to being damned sure that she—

What was that?

Damian frowned. He could hear the soft hum of the elevator, see the lighted panel blinking as the car rose.

What the hell? He certainly wasn't expecting anyone, and the doorman would not send someone up without…

Unless it was Laurel.

His heart thudded.

That was impossible. She was on Actos. Or was she? Spiro hadn't approved of his hasty departure. In the old days, the old man had never hesitated to do what he thought best, even if it meant overriding Damian's wishes. Of course, a lot of years had gone by since then.

On the other hand, Spiro could still be stubborn. If he thought it wise to take matters into his own hands…

The elevator stopped, and Damian held his breath. The doors opened—and Gabriella stepped out of the car.

"Surprise," she said in a smoky contralto.

The sight of her, draped in hot pink that left nothing to

the imagination and with a crimson smile painted on her lips, twisted his gut with such savage rage that it left him mute for long seconds. Then he drew a deep, painful breath and managed to find his voice.

"I'm not going to bother asking how you talked your way past the doorman," he said carefully. "I'm just going to tell you to turn around, get back into that elevator and get the hell out."

"Damian, darling, what sort of greeting is that?" Gabriella smiled and strolled past him, to the bar. "What are you drinking, hmm? Vodka rocks, it looks like. Well, I'll just have a tiny one, to keep you company."

"Did you hear me? Get out."

"Now, darling, let's not be hasty." She lifted her glass, took a sip, then put it down. "I know you were upset this morning, but it's my fault. I shouldn't have tried to convince you to come back to me the way I did."

"Convince me to…?" Damian put his fists on his hips. "Let's not play games, okay? What you tried was blackmail, and it didn't work. Now, do us both a favor and get out of here before it gets nasty."

Gabriella licked her lips. "Damian," she purred, "look, I understand. You married this woman. Well, you had no choice, did you? I mean, the word is out, darling, that your little Laurel got herself pregnant."

He came toward her so quickly that she stumbled backward. "I'll give you to the count of five," he snarled, "and then I'm going to take you by the scruff of your neck and toss you out the door. One. Two. Three…"

"Dammit," she said shrilly, "you cannot treat me like this! You made promises."

"You're a liar," he said flatly. "The only promise you've ever heard from me is this one. Go through that door on your own, or so help me…"

"Don't be a fool, Damian. You'll tire of her soon enough." Gabriella's hand went to the sash at her waist and pulled it. The hot pink silk fell open, revealing her naked body. "You'll want this. You'll want me."

Later, Damian would wonder why he hadn't heard the elevator as it made its return trip but then, how could he have heard anything, with each thud of his heart beating such dark fury through his blood?

"Cover yourself," he said, with disgust—and then he heard the sound of the elevator doors opening.

He saw Gabriella's quick, delighted smile and somehow, he knew, God, he knew...

He spun around and there was Laurel, standing in the open doors of the elevator.

"Laurel," he said, and when he started toward her, she threw up her hands and the look in her face went from shock to bone-deep pain.

"No," she whispered, and before he could reach her, she stabbed the button and the doors closed in his face.

And Damian knew, in that instant, that his last chance, his only chance, at love and happiness was gone from his life, forever.

CHAPTER TWELVE

RAIN POUNDED at the windows; late summer lightning split the low, gray sky as thunder rolled across the city.

Inside Laurel's kitchen, three women sat around the table. Two of them—Susie and Annie—were trying to look anywhere but at each other; the third—Laurel—was too busy glaring at her cup of decaf to notice.

"I *hate* decaffeinated coffee," Laurel said. "What is the point of drinking coffee if you're going to take out all the caffeine?"

Susie's gaze connected with Annie's. "Here we go again," her eyes said.

"It's better for you," she said mildly. "With the baby and all."

"I know that. For heaven's sakes, I'm the one who decided to give up coffee, aren't I? It's just that it's stupid to drink stuff that smells like coffee, looks like coffee, but tastes like—"

"Okay," Annie said, getting to her feet. She smiled brightly, whisked the coffee out from under Laurel's nose and dumped it into the sink. "Let's see…" She opened the cabinet and peered inside. "You've got a choice of herbal tea, cocoa, regular tea—"

"Regular tea's got as much caffeine as coffee. A big help you are, Annie."

Annie's brows shot skyward. "Right," she said briskly. She shut the cabinet and opened the refrigerator. "How about a nice glass of milk?"

"Yuck."

"Well, then, there's ginger ale. Orange juice." Her voice

grew muffled as she leaned into the fridge. "There's even a little jar of something that might be tomato juice."

"It isn't."

"V8?"

"No."

"Well, then, maybe it's spaghetti sauce."

"I don't remember the last time I had pasta."

Annie frowned and plucked the jar from the shelf. "It's not a good idea to keep chemistry experiments in the—"

Laurel shot to her feet. "Why did you say that?"

"Say what?" Annie and Susie exchanged another look. "Laurel, honey, if you'd just—"

"Just because a person finds something strange in another person's kitchen is no reason to say it looks like a— it looks like a…" Laurel took a deep breath. "Sorry," she said brightly. She looked from her big sister to her best friend. "Well," she said, in that same phony voice, "I know the two of you have things to do, so—"

"Not me," Susie said quickly. "George is downstairs, glued to the TV. I'm free as a bird."

"Not me, either," Annie said. "You know how it is. My life is dull, dull, dull."

"Dull? With your ex hovering in the background?" Laurel eyed her sister. "What's that all about, anyway? You're not seriously thinking of going down that road again, are you?"

For one wild minute, Annie considered telling Laurel the whole story…but Laurel's life was complicated enough. The last thing she needed was to hear someone else's troubles.

"Of course not," she said, with a quick smile. "Why on earth would I do that?"

"Good question." Laurel shoved back her chair, rose from the table and stalked to the sink. "If there's one truth in this world," she said, as she turned on the water, "it's that men stink. Oh, not George, Suze. I mean, he's not a man…"

Susie laughed.

"Come on, you know what I'm saying. George is so sweet. He's one in a million."

"I agree," Susie said. She sighed. "And I'd have bet my life your husband was, too."

Laurel swung around, eyes flashing. "I told you, I do not wish to discuss Damian Skouras."

"Well, I know, but you said—"

"Besides, he is not my husband!"

"Well, no, he won't be, after the divorce comes through, but—"

"To hell with that! A man who—who forces a woman into marriage isn't a husband, he's a—a—"

"A no-good, miserable, super-macho stinking son of a bitch, that's what he is!" Annie glared at her sister, as if defying her to disagree. "And don't you tell me you don't want to talk about it, Laurel, because Susie and I have both had just about enough of this nonsense."

"What nonsense? I don't know what you're talk—"

"You damn well *do* know what we're talking about! It's two months now, two whole months since I got that insane call from you, telling me you'd married that—that Greek super-stud and that you'd found him in the arms of his bubble-brained mistress a week later, and in all that time, I'm not supposed to ask any questions or so much as mention his name." Annie folded her arms and lifted her chin. "That is a load of crap, and you know it."

"It isn't." Laurel shut off the water and folded her arms, too. "There's nothing to talk about, Annie."

"Nothing to talk about." Annie snorted. "You got yourself knocked up and let the guy who did it strong-arm you into marrying him!"

Laurel stiffened. "Must you say it like that?"

"It's the truth, isn't it?"

After a minute, Laurel nodded. "I guess it is. God, I almost wish I'd never gone to Dawn's wedding!"

Susie sighed dramatically. "That must have been some

wedding.'' Annie and Laurel spun toward her and she flushed. ''Speaking metaphorically, I mean. Hey, come on, guys, don't look at me that way. It must have been one heck of a day. Annie's ex, coming on to her...''

''For all the good it's going to do him,'' Annie said coldly.

''And didn't you say that friend of yours, Bethany, met some guy there and ended up having a mad affair?''

''Her name's Stephanie, and at the risk of sounding cynical, I don't think very much of mad affairs, not anymore.'' Annie jerked her chin toward Laurel. ''Just look where it got my sister.''

''I know.'' Susie shook her head. ''And Damian seemed so perfect. Handsome, rich—''

''Are you two all done discussing me?'' Laurel asked. ''Because if you aren't, you'll have to continue this conversation elsewhere. I told you, I will not talk about Damian Skouras. That chapter's over and done with.''

''Not quite,'' Annie said, and looked at Laurel's gently rounded belly.

Laurel flushed. ''Very amusing.''

''Can we at least talk about how you're going to raise this baby all by yourself?''

''I'll manage.''

''There are financial implications, dammit. You said yourself you're at the end of your career.''

''Thank you for reminding me.''

''Laurel, sweetie—''

''Don't 'Laurel sweetie' me. I am a grown woman, and I made a lot of money over the years. Trust me, Annie, I saved quite a bit of it.''

''Yes, but children cost. You don't realize—''

''Dammit,'' Laurel said fiercely, ''now you sound just like him!''

''Who?''

''Damian, that's who. Well, you sound like his attorney, anyway. 'Raising a child is an expensive proposition,' she said in a voice that mimicked the rounded tones of John Hastings. "'Mr. Skouras is fully prepared to support his child properly.'"

Susie and Annie exchanged looks. "You never told me that," Susie said.

"Me, neither," Annie added.

Laurel glared at the two women. "It doesn't matter, does it? I'm not about to take a penny from that bastard."

"Yes, but I thought... I mean, I just figured..." Susie cleared her throat. "Not that being willing to support his kid makes me change what I think of the man. Running off that way, going back to his mistress after a week of marriage... It makes me sick just to think about it"

Annie nodded. "You're right. How he could want that idiotic blonde instead of my beautiful sister..."

"He didn't." Susie and Annie looked at Laurel, and she flushed. "I never said that, did I?"

"You said he left you, for the blonde."

"I said he went back to New York and that I found him with her. I never said—"

"So, he didn't want to take up where they'd left off?"

"I don't know what he wanted." Laurel plucked a sponge from the sink, squeezed it dry and began wiping down the counter with a vengeance. "I never gave him the chance to tell me."

"What do you mean, you never...?"

"Look, when you find your husband with a naked blonde, it's not hard to figure what's going on. I just turned around and walked out. Don't look at me like that, Annie. You would have, too."

Annie sighed. "I suppose. What could he possibly have said that would have made things better? Besides, if he'd really wanted to explain, he'd have called you or come to see you—"

"He did come here."

Annie and Susie looked at each other. "He did? When?"

"That same night."

Susie looked shocked. "You see what happens when George and I take a few days off? Laurel, you never said—"

"I wouldn't let him in. What for? We had nothing to say to each other."

"And that was it?" Annie asked. "He gave up, that easily?"

Silence fell on the kitchen and then Laurel cleared her throat.

"He phoned. He left a message on my machine. He said what had happened—what I'd seen—hadn't been what it appeared to be."

"Oh, right," Annie said, "I'll just bet it—"

"What did he say it had been?" Susie asked, shooting Annie a warning look.

"I don't remember," Laurel lied. She remembered every word; she'd listened to Damian's voice a dozen times before erasing it, not just the lying words but the huskiness, hating herself for the memories it stirred in her heart. "Some nonsense about his bimbo threatening to drag my name through the mud unless he paid her off. Oh, what does it matter? He'd have said anything, to get his own way. I told you, he was determined to take my baby."

"Well, it's his baby, too." Susie swallowed hard when both women glared at her. "Well, it is," she said defiantly. "That's just a simple biological fact." She frowned. "Which brings up an interesting point. How come he's backed off?"

Annie frowned, too. "Good question. He has backed off, hasn't he?"

Laurel nodded. She pulled a chair out from the table and sank into it. "Uh-huh. He has."

"How come? Not that I'm not delighted, but why back off now, after first all but dragging you into marriage?"

Laurel folded her hands on the tabletop.

"He—he called and left another message."

"The telephone company's best pal," Susie said brightly.

"He said—he said that he had no right to force me into living with him. That he understood that I could never feel about him as I had about Kirk—"

"Kirk?" Annie's brows arched. "How'd that piece of sewer slime get into the picture?"

"He said he'd been wrong to make me marry him in the first place, that a marriage without love could never work."

"The plot thickens." Susie leaned forward over the table. "I know you guys are liable to tar and feather me for this, but Damian Skouras isn't sounding like quite the scuzzball I'd figured him for."

Annie reached out and clasped her sister's hand. "Maybe you should have taken one of those phone calls, hmm?"

"What for?" Laurel snatched back her hand. "Don't be ridiculous, both of you. I called him and left him a message of my own. I said it didn't matter what had been going on or not going on with the blonde because I agreed completely. Not only could a loveless marriage never work, a marriage in which a wife hated the husband was doomed. And I hated him, I said. I said that I always had, that he had to accept the fact that it had been nothing but sex all along... Don't look at me that way, Annie! What was I supposed to believe? That that woman appeared at his door, uninvited, and stripped off her clothes?"

"Is that what he claimed?"

"Yes!"

Annie smiled gently. "It's possible, isn't it? The lady didn't strike me as the sort given to subtle gestures."

Laurel shot up from her chair. "I don't believe what's going on here! The two of you, asking me to deny what I saw with my own eyes! My God, it was bad enough to be deceived by Kirk, a man I'd thought I loved, but to be deceived by Damian, by my own husband, the only man I've ever really loved, is—is..." Her voice broke. "Oh God, I *do* love him! I'll never stop loving him." She looked from Susie to Annie, and her mouth began to tremble. "Go away," she whispered. "Just go away, and leave me alone."

They didn't, not until Laurel was calmer, not until she was undressed and asleep in her bed.

Then they left because, really, when you came right down to it, what else was there to do?

What else was there to do? Damian thought, as he attacked the boulder outside his house overlooking the Aegean with the sledgehammer.

Nothing. Nothing but beat at this miserable rock and work himself to exhaustion from sunup to sundown in hopes he'd fall into bed at night and not dream of Laurel.

It was a fine plan. Unfortunately it didn't work.

He had not seen Laurel, or heard her voice, in two months—but she was with him every minute of the day, just the same. The nights were even worse. Alone in the darkness, in the bed where he'd once held his wife in his arms, he tossed and turned for hours before falling into restless, dream-filled sleep.

He had considered returning to New York, but he could not imagine himself sitting behind a desk, in the same city where Laurel lived. And so he stayed on Actos, and worked, and sweated, and oversaw his business interests by computer, phone and fax. He told himself that the ache inside him would go away.

It hadn't. If anything, it had grown worse.

He knew that Eleni and Spiro were almost frantic with worry.

"Is he trying to kill himself?" he'd heard Eleni mutter just that morning, as he'd gone out the door. "You must speak to him, Spiro," she'd said.

Damian's mouth thinned as he swung the sledgehammer. If the old man knew what was good for him, he'd keep his mouth shut. He'd interfered enough already. Damian had told him so, on his return to Greece.

"Was it you who permitted my wife to leave the island and follow me to New York?" he'd demanded.

Spiro had stiffened. "*Né*," he'd said, "yes, it was I."

Damian's hands had balled into fists. "On whose authority did you do this thing, old man?"

"On my own," Spiro had replied quietly. "The woman was not a prisoner here."

A muscle had knotted in Damian's cheek. "No," he'd said, "she was not."

Spiro had waited before speaking again.

"She said that she had something of great importance to tell you," he'd said, his eyes on Damian's. "Did she find you, and deliver her message?"

Damian's mouth had twisted. "She did, indeed," he'd replied, and when Spiro had tried to say more, he'd held up his hand. "There is nothing to discuss. The woman is not to be mentioned again."

She had not been, to this day. But that didn't mean he didn't think about her, and dream about her. Did she dream of him? Did she ever long for the feel of his arms and the sweetness of his kisses, as he longed for hers?

Did she ever think of how close they'd come to happiness?

Damian's throat constricted. He swung the hammer hard, but his aim wasn't true. His vision was blurred—by sweat, for what else could it be?—and the hammer hit the rock a glancing blow.

"Dammit," he growled, and swung again.

"Damian," Spiro's voice was soft. "The rock is not your enemy."

"And you are not a philosopher," Damian snapped, and swung again.

"What you battle is not the boulder, my son, it is yourself."

Damian straightened up. "Listen here," he said, but his anger faded when he looked at the old man. Spiro looked exhausted. Sweat stained his dark trousers and shirt; his weathered face was bright red and there was a tremor in his hands.

Why was the old fool so stubborn? The heat was too much for a man his age. Damian sighed, set the sledgehammer aside and stripped off his work gloves.

"It is hot," he said. "I need something to drink."

"There is a bottle of *retsina* in my jacket, under the tree."

Damian plucked his discarded T-shirt from the ground and slipped it on.

"I know the sort of *retsina* you drink, old man. The sun will rot our brains quickly enough, without its help. We will go up to the house. Perhaps we can convince Eleni to give us some cold beer."

"*Né.*" Spiro smiled. "For once, you have an excellent idea."

It took no convincing at all. Eleni took one look at them, rolled her eyes and brought cold beer and glasses out to the terrace. Damian ignored the glasses, handed one bottle to the old man and took the other for himself. He leaned back against the railing and took a long drink. Spiro drank, too, then wiped his mustache with the back of his hand.

"When do you return to New York?" he said.

Damian's brows lifted. "Are you in such a rush to get rid of me?"

"You cannot avoid reality forever, Damian."

"Spiro." Damian's voice was chill. "I warn you, do not say anything more. It is hot, I am in a bad mood—"

"As if that were anything new."

Damian tilted the beer bottle to his lips. He drank, then set the bottle down. "I am going back to work. I suggest you go inside, where it is cooler."

"I suggest you stop pretending you do not have a wife."

"I told you, we will not discuss her."

"And now I tell you that we must."

"Dammit, old man—"

"I saw how happy she made you, Damian, and how happy you made her."

"Are you deaf? I said that we would not—"

"You loved her. And you love her still."

"No! No, I do not love her. What is love anyway, but a thing to make men idiots?"

Spiro chuckled and folded his arms. "Are you saying I was an idiot to put up with you, after I found you on the streets of Athens? Be careful, or I will have to take a switch to your backside, as I did when you were a boy."

"You know what I mean," Damian said, stubbornly refusing to be taken in. "I'm talking of male and female love, and I tell you that I did not *love* her. All right? Are you satisfied now? Can I get back to work?"

"She loved you."

"Never." Damian's voice roughened. "She did not love me, old man. She despised me for everything I am and especially for forcing her into a marriage she did not want."

"She loved you," Spiro repeated. "I know this, for a fact."

"She loved another, you sentimental old fool."

"It is not sentiment or foolishness that makes me say this, Damian, it is the knowledge of what she told me."

Damian's face went pale beneath its tan. "What the hell are you talking about?"

"It is the reason I sent her after you. She said she loved you deeply."

For one sweet instant, Damian felt his heart might burst from his chest. But then he remembered the reality of what had happened: the swiftness with which Laurel had accepted the ugly scene orchestrated by Gabriella, the way she'd refused even to listen to his explanation…and the message he'd found on his answering machine, Laurel's cool voice saying that she'd never stopped hating him, that what they'd shared had been nothing but sex…

"You misunderstood her, old man. You speak English almost as badly as she spoke Greek."

"I know what she told me, Damian."

"Then she lied," Damian said coldly. He picked up the bottle and drained it dry. "She lied, because it was the only way she could get you to agree to let her leave the island, and you fell for it. Now, I am going to work and you are going to stay out of the sun before it bakes your brain completely. Is that clear?"

"What is clear," the old man said quietly, "is that I raised a coward."

Damian spun toward him, his eyes gone hard and chill. "If any other man but you dared say such a thing to me," he said softly, "I would beat him within an inch of his life."

"You are a coward in your heart, afraid to face the truth. You love this woman but because she hurt you in some fashion, you would rather live your life without her than risk going after her."

"Damn you to hell," Damian roared, and thrust his face into the old man's. "Listen, Spiro, and listen well, for I will say this only once. Yes, I love her. But she does not love me."

"How do you know this?"

"How? How?" Damian's teeth glinted in a hollow laugh. "She told me so, all right? Does that satisfy you?"

"Did you ever tell her that you loved her?"

"Did I ever...?" Damian threw his arms skyward. "By all the gods that be, I cannot believe this! No, I never told her. She never gave me the chance. She came bursting into my apartment in New York, found me with another woman and damned me without even giving me an opportunity to explain."

Spiro's weather-beaten face gave nothing away. "And what were you doing with this woman, my son? Arranging flowers, perhaps?"

Damian colored. "I admit, it did not look good..."

"You were not arranging flowers?"

"What is this? An interrogation? I had just come out of the shower, okay? And the woman—the woman was trying to seduce me. I just admitted, it did not look good." He took a deep breath. "But Laurel is my wife. She should have trusted me."

"Certainly she should have trusted you. After all, what had you ever done to make her distrustful, except to impregnate her and force her into a marriage she did not want?"

"How did you—"

"Eleni says that there is a look to a woman's face, when she is carrying a child. Any fool could see it, just as any fool could see that when you first brought her here, neither of you was happy." Spiro smiled. "But that changed, Damian. I do not know how it happened, but you both finally admitted what had been in your hearts from the beginning."

"All right. Yes, I fell in love with her. But nothing is that simple."

"Love is never simple."

Damian turned and clasped the railing. He could feel his anger seeping away and a terrible despair replacing it.

"Spiro, you are the father I never knew and I trust your advice, you know that, but in this matter—"

"In this matter, Damian," the old man said, "trust your heart. Go to her, tell her that you love her. Give her the chance to tell you the same thing."

Damian's throat felt tight. He blinked his eyes, which seemed suddenly damp.

"And if she does not?" he said gruffly. "What then?"

"Then you will return here and swing that hammer until your arms ache with the effort—but you will return knowing that you tried to win the woman you love instead of letting her slip away." Spiro put his hand on Damian's shoulder. "There is always hope, my son. It is that which gives us the will to go on, *né*?"

Out in the bay, a tiny sailboat heeled under the wind. The sea reached up for it with greedy, white-tipped fingers. Surely it would be swallowed whole…

The wind subsided as quickly as it had begun. The boat bobbed upright.

There is always hope.

Quickly, before he could lose his courage, Damian turned and embraced the old man. Then he headed into the house.

They were wrong. Dead wrong.

Laurel pounded furiously at the lump of sourdough.

What did Annie and Susie know, anyway? Annie was divorced and Susie was married to a marshmallow. Neither of them had ever had the misfortune to deal with a macho maniac like Damian Skouras.

Damn, but it was hot! Too hot for making bread but what else was she going to do with all this pent-up energy? Laurel blew a strand of hair out of her eyes, wiped her hand over her nose and began beating the dough again.

They were driving her crazy, her sister and her friend. Ever since yesterday, when she'd been dumb enough to break down in front of them and admit she'd loved Damian, they hadn't left her alone. If it wasn't Annie phoning, it was Susie.

Well, let 'em phone. She'd given up answering. Let the machine deal with the cheery "hi"'s and the even cheerier "Laurel? Are you there, honey?"'s.

This morning, in a fit of pique, she'd snatched up the phone, snarled, "No, I'm not there, *honey*," and slammed it down again before Annie or Susie, whichever it was, could say a word. Why listen to either of them, when she knew what they were going to say? They'd both said it already, that maybe she'd misjudged Damian, that maybe what he'd told her about the blonde was the truth.

"I didn't," Laurel muttered, picking up the dough and then slamming it down again. "And it wasn't."

And anyway, what did it matter? So what, if maybe, just maybe, Blondie had set him up? He'd left her, damn him, in the middle of the honeymoon, he'd gone off without a word.

Because you hurt him, Laurel, have you forgotten that?

No, she thought grimly, no, she had not forgotten. So she'd hurt him. Big deal. He'd hurt her a heck of a lot more, not telling her where he was going or even that he was going, not saying goodbye...

Not loving her, when she loved him so terribly that she couldn't shut her eyes without seeing his face or hearing his voice or—

"Laurel?"

Like that. Exactly like that. She could hear him say her name, as if he were right here, in the room with her...

"Laurel, *mátya mou*..."

Laurel spun around, and her heart leaped into her throat. "Damian?"

Damian cursed as her knees buckled. He rushed forward, caught her in his arms and carried her into the living room. "Take a deep breath," he ordered, as he sat down on the sofa with her still in his arms. "You're not going to pass out on me, are you?"

"Of course not," she said, when the mist before her eyes cleared away. "I never pass out."

"No," he said wryly, "you never do—except at the sight of me."

"What are you going here, Damian? And how did you get in?"

"That George," he said, smoothing the hair back from her face with his hand. "What a splendid fellow he is."

"George gave you my spare key? Dammit, he had no right! *You* had no—"

"And I see that I got here just in time." A smile tilted at the corner of his mouth. "You've been doing experiments in the kitchen again."

"I've been making bread. And don't try to change the

subject. You had absolutely no right to unlock the door and—''

''I know, and I apologize. But I was afraid that you'd leave me standing in the hall again, if I asked you to let me in.''

''You're right, I would have done exactly that.'' Laurel put her hands on his shoulders. ''Let me up, please.''

''I love you, Laurel.''

Hope flickered in her heart, but fear snuffed it out.

''You just want your child,'' she said.

''I want *our* child, my darling wife, but more than that, I want you. I love you, Laurel.'' He took her face in his hands. ''I adore you,'' he said softly. ''You're the only woman I have ever loved, the only woman I will ever love, and if you don't come back to me, I will be lost forever.''

Tears roses in Laurel's eyes. ''Oh, Damian. Do you mean it?''

He kissed her. It was a long, sweet, wonderful kiss, and when it ended, she was trembling.

''With all my heart. I should have awakened you that night and told you I had to leave, but you were so angry and I—I was angry, too, and wounded by the knowledge that you'd once loved another.''

Laurel shook her head. ''I didn't love him. I only talked about Kirk to hurt you. I've never loved anyone, until you.''

''Tell me again,'' he whispered.

She smiled. ''I love you, Damian. I've never loved anyone else. I never will. There's only you, only you, only—''

He kissed her again, then leaned his forehead against hers.

''What I told you about Gabriella was the truth. I didn't ask her to my apartment. She—''

Laurel kissed him to silence. A long time later, Damian drew back.

''We'll fly to Actos,'' he said, ''and ask that interfering old man to drink champagne with us.''

Laurel linked her arms around her husband's neck and smiled into his eyes.

"Did anybody ever tell you that you can sound awfully arrogant at times?"

Damian grinned as he got to his feet with his wife in his arms.

"Someone might have mentioned it, once or twice," he said, as he shouldered open the bedroom door.

Laurel's pulse quickened as he slowly lowered her to the bed.

"I thought we were going to Actos," she whispered.

"We are." Damian gave her a slow, sexy kiss. "But first," he said, as he began to undo her buttons, "first, we've got to get reacquainted."

Laurel sighed as he slipped off her blouse. "And how long do you think that's going to take, husband?"

Damian smiled. "All the rest of our lives, wife."

Slowly he gathered her into his arms.

EPILOGUE

NO ONE ON THE ISLAND of Actos had ever seen anything quite like it.

There were always weddings, of course, young people and life being as they are, but even the old women at the fish market, who usually argued about everything, agreed on this.

There had never been a wedding the equal of Damian and Laurel's.

Of course, as the old women were quick to point out, the Skourases were already married. But the ceremony that had joined them meant nothing. It had been performed all the way across the sea, in America, and—can you imagine?—a judge had said the words that had made them man and wife, not a priest.

No wonder they had chosen to be wed all over again, and in the proper way.

The day was perfect: a clear blue sky, a peaceful sea, and though the sun shone brightly, it was not too hot.

The bride, the old ladies said, was beautiful in her lacy white gown. And oh, her smile. So radiant, so filled with love for her handsome groom.

Handsome, indeed, one of the crones said, and she added something else behind her wrinkled hand that made them all cackle with delight.

It was just too bad the bride wasn't Greek...but she was the next best thing. Beautiful, with shining eyes and a bright smile, and Eleni had told them that she was learning to think like one of them, enough so that when her groom had teasingly warned her that marriage in a Greek church

185

was forever, she'd smiled and put her arms around him and said that was the only kind of marriage she'd ever wanted.

And so, in a little church made of whitewashed stone, with the sun streaming through the windows and baskets of flowers banked along the aisle and at the altar, and with friends and relatives from faraway America flown over for this most special of days, Laurel Bennett and Damian Skouras were wed.

"Yes," Laurel said clearly, when the priest asked—in English, at Damian's request—if she would take the man beside her as her husband, to love and honor and cherish for the rest of her days. And when Damian offered the same pledge, he broke with tradition by looking deep into his wife's eyes and saying that he would cherish forever the woman he had waited all his life to find.

The old ladies in black wept, as did the two stylishly dressed American women in the front pew. Even old Spiro wiped his eyes, though he said later that it was only because a speck had gotten into one.

Retsina and *ouzo* flowed, and bubbly champagne flown in from France. Everyone danced, and sang; they ate lobster and red snapper and roast lamb, and the men toasted the bride and groom until none could think of another reason to raise his glass.

It was, everyone said, an absolutely wonderful wedding—but if you'd asked the bride and the groom what part was the most wonderful, they'd have said it came late that night, when the crickets were singing and the air was heavy with the scent of flowers and they were alone, at last, on their hilltop overlooking the sea.

The groom took his bride in his arms.

"You are my heart," he said, looking deep into her eyes, and she smiled so radiantly that his heart almost shattered with joy.

"As you are mine," she whispered, and as the ivory moon climbed into the black velvet sky, Damian swept Laurel into his arms and carried her up to their bedroom.

*   *   *

The next morning, Laurel awoke to the ring of the sledge-hammer.

She dressed quickly and went outside, to where the boulder stood.

"Damian," she called, and her husband turned and smiled at her.

"Watch," he said.

He swung the hammer against the boulder. The sound rang like a bell across the hilltop, and the rock crumbled into a thousand tiny pieces.

AN ENTICING PROPOSAL

MEREDITH WEBBER

CHAPTER ONE

'I CAN arrange for Dougal to see Dr Barclay this afternoon, Mrs Dean, but I know he won't prescribe antibiotics for Dougal's cold so it would be a waste of your time, coming back again.'

Paige sighed inwardly, wondering why she bothered to waste breath in an argument she was certain to lose.

'All I want is some more of the pink medicine,' Mrs Dean whined. 'Dr Graham let me have some and it fixed Darryl's nose so why can't I have the same for Dougal?'

Forcing back the urge to scream and rant and rave at the woman, Paige explained, for the fourth time in ten minutes, the difference between sinusitis and the common cold, pointed out that the viruses causing the cold would be unaffected by the pink medicine and tried to convince Mrs Dean that rest and a diet including plenty of fluids would soon have young Dougal on the mend.

Young Dougal in the meantime, bored with the conversation, had hooked his thumbs into the corners of his mouth, set his forefingers against his temples and was now contorting his face into various gargoyle shapes which he directed at Paige. If anything, she decided as she listened to Mrs Dean's praise for pink medicine, it improved the looks of a child with a white pudgy face and small raisin eyes, liberally decorated at the moment with the inevitable nasal effusion of the so-called 'common' cold.

A commotion in the waiting room beyond her door suggested restlessness among the natives, so she turned her attention from Dougal's antics and tried once again to prevent an incursion into Ken Barclay's freely given but limited time.

'Look, Mrs Dean, you can ask Carole if Dr Barclay has an appointment available this afternoon, but, believe me, Dougal's cold will run its course and he's better off without unnecessary antibiotics.'

The 'noises off', as script writers might describe the raised voices outside, were increasing so Paige, with a final smile of appreciation for Dougal's facial contortions, stood up to show the visit was at an end. Mrs Dean took the hint, rising laboriously to her feet, grumbling under her breath about no-good nurses and services that were supposed to help the needy, not send them away empty handed.

Having heard it all before, Paige ignored the barbed comments, holding out her hand to offer support to the hugely pregnant woman, wondering idly what the Deans would call the new baby, should it be a girl. Darlene? Dorothy? Diana? After Darryl, Denzil, David, Dennis and Dougal, maybe they would change the initial letter.

'And by the sound of things you've got men in the place.' The grumbling became audible and Paige realised her patient was right. There was at least one man in the waiting room—and not a very happy man at that, if his tone of voice was any indication.

'Supposed to be for women, Tuesdays!' Mrs Dean griped, resisting Paige's attempts to hustle her out the door and calmly rearranging multitudinous layers of clothes around her bulk.

Paige opened the door, more anxious now to discover what was going on than to be free of Mrs Dean. The waiting room was in its usual state of chaos. Children crawled around the floor or fought over the small collection of toys and books she'd managed to accumulate. Their mothers sat on hard plastic chairs, exchanging news and gossip in a desultory fashion, their attention focussed on the confrontation taking place at the reception desk. Some were waiting to see her, but others would have appointments with Sue Chalmers, an occupational therapist who volunteered her time on Tuesday mornings to run a small toy library.

Carole Benn, the community service's receptionist, was in place behind the high counter, which provided her with little protection from the man who was leaning across it, waggling his finger in her face and growling threateningly at her.

A second man stood slightly behind this aggressive type, looking remote and disinterested, seemingly oblivious to the noise and activity all around him. His colour was bad—olive overlaid with grey. An illness perhaps. Had the pair strayed in here, thinking it was a medical practice? She studied the silent man covertly—from a female not a nursing point of view this time. Bad colour did little to diminish the magnetism of a face which could have been carved from mountain rock—like the heads of presidents somewhere in the United States.

The wayward thought flitted through Paige's mind as she ushered Mrs Dean towards the counter and raised her eyebrows at Carole. Carole lifted one hand and made an almost imperceptible shooing movement with her fingers but the irate man observed the motion and spun immediately towards Paige.

'So you are Paige Morgan!' he said in accusatory tones. 'This woman tries to tell me you are not available. I am Benelli and this is Prince Alessandro Francesco Marcus Alberici.'

To the astonishment of Paige, and all the occupants of

the waiting room, the younger man came to attention and all but clicked his heels together as he indicated the second man with a wild flourish of one hand and a movement of his body that suggested obeisance.

'Ah, at last my prince has come.' Paige clasped her hands theatrically in front of her chest and raised her eyes to the ceiling. Then she grinned at Carole. 'Wouldn't you know he'd arrive on a Tuesday when I'm too busy for a coronation.'

Inside, she wasn't quite so light-hearted as bits of her fizzed and squished in a most unseemly manner—the result of another quick appraisal of the second man's bone structure.

Lust at first sight?

With a determined effort, she turned away, concentrating on the underling, hoping to surprise a smile in his eyes, some confirmation he wasn't serious.

'Am I supposed to guess something—or answer a question and get a prize?' she hazarded. 'Is it a joke of some kind, or a new form of fund-raising? I'm afraid my sense of humour's a bit dulled this morning and, as for money, this place takes every penny I can scrounge up.'

Mr Benelli turned an unattractive shade of puce—now she had two bad-complexioned strangers in her waiting room! He jumped up and down—or rose on his toes to give that impression—and began waggling his forefinger at her.

'This is no joke! He is a prince, a real prince, and he does not want money.'

'Well, that's a change,' Paige replied, risking a swift glance towards the 'real prince' and catching what appeared to be a glint of humour in his black eyes. Black eyes? Did eyes come in black? Not that she could see them closely enough to judge eye colour accurately. 'What *does* he want?'

She shook her head as she heard her own question. Why the hell was she carrying on this conversation through an intermediary?

'He wishes to speak with you on a matter of extreme urgency,' Mr Benelli informed her, and for the first time Paige caught the hint of a foreign accent in his properly worded and pronounced English and realised that he, too, had the dark hair and olive complexion of his companion, a colouring she associated with Mediterranean origins.

Surely it couldn't be… Her heart skittered at the half-formed thought.

'I'll be free at twelve,' she said crisply, hoping her rising anxiety wasn't apparent in the words. 'Perhaps you could both come back then.' She glanced again towards the second man, realised the grey colour was probably fatigue and added, 'Or you could wait here if you prefer.'

The offer failed to please Benelli, who all but exploded on the spot as he poured out his indignation.

'This is urgent, he must see you now. The car waits outside to drive him back to Sydney. He is busy man. Important. Not to be—'

Paige missed the end of the sentence, too intent on trying to settle the new upheaval within her—one that had nothing to do with lust. Perhaps it *was* a joke, she hoped desperately. Hadn't she glimpsed a gleam of humour in the dark eyes? And why didn't the second man speak if it was his errand—his urgency?

He answered the second question almost as she thought it.

'We will wait, Benelli,' he said, in a voice that vibrated across Paige's skin like a bow drawn across violin strings.

Shivering at the effect, she pulled a file from the holder on her office door and called the name of the next patient, seeing Benelli offer the newly vacated chair to the 'prince', the man refusing it and propping himself on the window-ledge as her father had done during her childhood when this had been their living room, not a place for those who could not afford other services to wait—and hope.

Her father had been a tall man—a little over six feet—and the window-ledge had been comfortable for him. But she'd never found it anything but awkward to perch there, although at five feet eight she wasn't a short woman.

And why you're thinking about how tall you are is beyond me, she admonished herself silently, leading Mabel Kruger into the room, then closing the door firmly on the unwelcome visitors.

''Andsome enough to be a prince,' Mabel remarked, settling into the visitor's chair and lifting her leg onto the stool Paige had pulled towards her.

'Why should we expect princes to be handsomer than ordinary mortals?' she asked crossly, peeling dressings off Mabel's ulcer as gently and carefully as she could.

'They are in books,' Mabel pointed out. 'And, apart from that Charles, the Queen's lads are good-looking.'

'Well, I'm sure she'd be pleased to hear you say so,' Paige responded, talking to distract Mabel's attention as she debrided dead tissue, cleaning out the gaping hole and wondering if a skin graft might eventually be necessary or if they were winning the battle against infection. 'Though I think I prefer blond men. Why are princes always depicted as dark?'

They chatted on, and she knew she was diverting herself as well as Mabel. Not wanting to think about the phone call she'd made, about betrayal—and being caught out. No, the two couldn't be connected. A simple phone call in return was all she'd expected—wanted.

So why did she feel sick with apprehension? Why was she harbouring a grim foreknowledge that the strangers in her waiting room were connected with Lucia?

She set aside unanswerable questions. Mabel was explaining, with minimal use of the letter 'h', about the beauty of the princes she'd encountered in the fairytale books of her youth. She then moved on to wonder about the reliability or otherwise of princes, given the unreliability of men in general. Paige let her talk and concentrated all her attention on her task, peeling the protective backing off the new dressing, then pressing it firmly in place.

'Now, leave it there all week unless your leg swells or you notice any unusual redness or feel extra pain,' she told her patient. 'And rest with your leg up whenever you can—'

'So I don't 'ave to go to 'ospital and get a graft!'

Mabel repeated the usual ending to this warning, then she patted Paige—who was still kneeling on the floor, pulling Mabel's sock up over the dressing—on the head and said, 'Not that you don't deserve a prince, girl.'

Paige looked up at her and smiled.

'Don't wish that on me. I don't want any man—let alone a princely one,' she teased, using the back of Mabel's chair to lever herself up to her feet.

'You mightn't want one,' Mabel argued, 'but you're the kind of girl as needs a man about the place—well, not needs, maybe, but should 'ave. I see your eyes when you look at those kids sometimes, and the babies. That fancy doctor did you no favour, getting you all interested in things like marriage then taking off with that floozy.'

Well, that's a different take on my break-up with

James, Paige thought as she helped Mabel to her feet. Was that how all her patients viewed the nine-day wonder of it all? How her friends saw it?

'Not all men are the same,' Mabel declared with as much authority as if she'd made that notable discovery herself.

Paige grinned at the pronouncement. She walked the elderly woman to the door and saw her out, her eyes going immediately to the man framed in the window embrasure. No, all men were not the same, she admitted silently, then trembled as if a draught had brushed across her neck.

Calling for the next patient, she turned back inside so she didn't have to look at the stranger in their midst.

Well, you mightn't have to look at him, but you'll have to think about him some time soon, she reminded herself, grabbing the chubby two-year-old who'd scampered through the door ahead of her mother, intent on climbing onto Paige's desk and creating as much havoc as she could.

'Not today, Josephine,' she murmured as she swung the child into her arms and gave her a quick hug. 'Is she any calmer on the Effilix?' she asked, turning to the young woman who'd followed them into the room and settled into the chair with a tired sigh.

Yes, she had more to worry about than princes—or men either—at the moment, she reminded herself, watching Debbie and wondering how she juggled her studies and motherhood.

'I suppose it depends on your definition of calmer,' Debbie Palmer replied with a wry grin that told Paige no miracle cure had been effected by the natural therapy. 'But Susie's been giving her massages every second day and that seems to have a good effect on her, and the other mothers at playgroup feel she's interacting much better with their kids.'

'Well, that's something,' Paige said in her most encouraging voice, setting Josie back on her feet and handing her a small bright top, demonstrating how it spun, then watching as the little hands tried to duplicate the action. In her opinion, Josephine was a very bright child with an active, enquiring mind, but too many people had muttered 'hyperactive' to Debbie, and the young single mother now feared a diagnosis of ADD—the attention deficit disorder—which was the popular label for behavioural problems used among parents and school teachers at the moment.

Debbie was ambivalent about the drugs used to treat the disorder—some days determined to keep Josie off medication, while on others wanting the relief she imagined they might bring. Paige had come down on the side of a drug-free life for the child and pressed this point of view whenever possible, although at times she wondered how she would feel in a similar situation.

'I've arranged for a paediatrician to see Josie next month,' she said. 'It's a Dr Kerr, and he's agreed to meet you here so she's in familiar territory. But as I've said before, Deb, there's no guarantee he'll come up with anything. It's very difficult to pin a label on so young a child.'

Debbie looked at her without answering, then she shrugged and grinned.

'Seems a little unfair, doesn't it? You get a prince and I get a paediatrician!'

'I can't imagine he's really a prince,' Paige retorted. 'And, even if he is, what would I want with one?'

'Well, he's decorative for a start,' Debbie pointed out. 'And he oozes that magnetic kind of sex appeal only some men have, in case you're too old to remember what sex appeal is.'

Paige chuckled in spite of the worry Debbie's conversation had regenerated.

'Am I walking around looking jaded and depressed? Or like someone gnawing at her bones with frustration?' she said. 'Mabel's just told me I need a man and now you're here offering me good-looking sex.'

'Oh, he's beyond good-looking,' Debbie argued, taking the top from her daughter before it could be hurled across the room. She leaned forward and demonstrated its action once more, then smiled as she watched the little figure squat down on the floor and try again.

Paige watched the interaction of mother and child, saw Debbie's smile, so full of love for this difficult little mortal she'd conceived by accident, and felt the tug of envious longing which told her Mabel was right.

But the prince, if prince he was and her assumptions were correct, had come to reclaim his wife, not carry a tired community nurse off into some fabled distance on his shining white charger.

She sighed.

'Sighing's usually my line, not yours,' Debbie told her. 'Are you OK?'

'A bit tired,' Paige explained, not untruthfully. The problem of what to do with her uninvited house guest had been keeping her awake at night for the last month.

'That's why you need a change—a holiday,' Debbie reminded her. 'You've been working for what…four years without a break. You deserve a bit of time to yourself.'

To do what? Paige thought, but she didn't say it. She *did* need a break, needed to get right away somewhere so she wouldn't be tempted to step in if things went

wrong at the service, answer calls at night which someone else should take.

But with Lucia?

She sighed again.

'OK, OK, I get the message,' Debbie said. 'I won't
keep you. I brought back the library toys and Sue chose
some new ones for Josie, so all I need is a time for Dr
Kerr's appointment and I'm out of here.' She grinned
cheekily at Paige. 'Leaving you with only one patient to
go before the prince!'

'Lucky me! Who is it? Do you know?'

'I think it's Mrs Epstein. I noticed her in the corner,
huddling into that black wool coat of hers and trying to
look invisible.'

'Poor thing. She's not at all well, and hasn't had a
proper medical check since Sally Carruthers left town.
She refuses to see a male doctor. I guess eventually
someone will have to drive her down to Tamworth to see
one of the women in practice down there. Would you
send her in, to save me going to the door? Just lift her
file out of the slot and give it to her to bring in.'

Paige gave Josie a hug and said goodbye to Debbie,
then sat down at her desk and buried her head in her
hands. One more patient then the prince to confront. He
had to have come about Lucia, so what did she tell him?
She could hardly reveal Lucia's presence in the house
without at least consulting her—explaining about the
phone call and why she'd made it.

And she couldn't leave this room to go upstairs and
talk to Lucia without being seen by her two unwelcome
visitors.

Unless…

She glanced towards the windows, stood up and
walked across to open the one closer to her desk. To poke

her head out and look up. As a child she'd climbed both up and down the Virginia creeper innumerable times, but would it hold an adult's weight?

And was she seriously considering climbing up there?

'Seeking an escape route?'

The deep voice made her spin around, and she knew from the flash of heat in her cheeks that her stupid pale skin was flushing guiltily.

'The room was warm,' she sputtered, compounding her stupidity with the lie. She took control. 'Anyway, I've another patient to see before you.'

'Your patient has departed,' he responded coolly.

'Or been intimidated into leaving by your presence,' Paige retorted, curbing an urge to add a scorching remark about princely arrogance. 'What's happened to your side-kick?'

'Sidekick?' The man looked bemused.

'Mr Benelli. The guy who bowed you in.'

'Ah, you took offence at his behaviour. I can under-stand that reaction, but to check him, tell him this cere-mony was not what I wanted or desired, would have been to humiliate him in front of your patients.'

Paige stared at him, though why his compassion for a fellow man should startle her she didn't know. Unless she'd assumed princes were above such things! Which reminded her—

'Are you really a prince?'

He shrugged, moved further into the room and smiled.

Bad move, that—making him smile. The rearrange-ment of his features made him even more devastatingly attractive—and, coming closer, it had brought his eyes into view. Not black but darkest blue, almost navy.

'I am Francesco Alberici. The title "prince" is a hang-over from bygone days—something I do not use myself.

Benelli is an official at our consulate in Sydney. It is he who sees honour in a useless appellation, not myself.'

He'd held out his hand as he'd said his name, and politeness had decreed she take it. But to let it rest in his as he finished speaking? Another mistake.

She took control, stuck her still-warm but nonetheless offending hand into the pocket of her blazer and looked—confidently, she hoped—into his eyes.

'So, now we've cleared up the prince business, how can I help you?'

As if I don't know, an inner voice quailed, and she regretted not escaping through the window, even if she hadn't climbed the creeper.

'You phoned me—left a message.'

Marco watched the colour fluctuate beneath her cheeks—no doubt she was considering what lie to tell him—and wondered about her background. With that pale skin, cornsilk-coloured hair falling in a straight drop to chin level and the smatter of freckles across her nose, she certainly didn't fit his image of a bronzed Australian. But, then, this New England city in the northern tableland area of New South Wales had the feel of an English market town, in spite of the lush sheep country which surrounded it.

'You're Marco?'

Her question, when it came, held surprise—and, he suspected, dread. Or guilt?

'Who else?' he said harshly, surprised to find an inner anger surging into the reply. He could usually control his emotions better than that. Tiredness? The long flight? Or the months of gut-wrenching, muscle-straining, heart-breaking worry over Lucia?

He curbed the anger as wide spaced green eyes, flecked

with the gold of the sunlight outside, stared warily into his.

'Why didn't you phone?'

'I came instead.'

'Why?'

The question gave him momentary pause, then the anger churned again, rising, threatening to erupt.

'To take Lucia home,' he said bluntly.

Paige had seen him stiffen earlier, guessed at anger, saw the tension in his body, controlled now but ready to explode. She wondered about violence. Was that why Lucia had fled? She had to forget her own reaction to the man—that strange and almost instant attraction. Right now she needed to stall, to buy time. With time maybe she could persuade Lucia to talk about her flight, before revealing her whereabouts to anyone. Or this man's presence in town to Lucia!

She tried for innocence in her expression—in her voice.

'Lucia?' she repeated in dulcet tones.

Wrong move! His body language told her she'd unwittingly lit the fuse to set him off. He stepped closer, spoke more softly, but there was no escaping the rage emanating from his body and trembling in his words.

'Yes, Lucia, Miss Morgan. And don't act the innocent with me. You phoned my private work number, a new number only a handful of people know, you asked for Marco—a name only Lucia and my family use to address me. You left a message—said you wanted to speak to me. I haven't come halfway around the world to play games with you, so speak to me, Miss Morgan. Or tell me where she is and let her explain her behaviour.'

Paige shivered under the onslaught of his words—and the emotion accompanying them. No way could she inflict him on her ill and unhappy house guest. But how to tell an enraged husband—however handsome and sexy he might be—you won't let him see his wife, without risking bodily harm to yourself? She gulped in some replenishing air, waited for the oxygen to fire into her blood, then squared up to him.

'I will speak to her, ask her if she wishes to see you.'

'You will…'

Well, at least she'd rendered him speechless!

She raised her hands as if to show helplessness. 'I can't do any more than that.'

He glared at her, his eyes sparkling with the fierceness of his anger.

'Then why did you contact me? To tease me? Torture me even more? Was it her idea? Did she say, "Let's upset Marco in this new way"?'

The agony in his voice pierced through to her heart and she found herself wanting to put her arms around him, comfort him—for all her doubts about his behaviour towards his wife.

'She doesn't know I contacted you,' she said softly—feeling the guilt again. Wondering how to explain.

He was waiting, the fire dying from his eyes, the grey colour taking over again.

'Please, sit down. Do you want a drink—something hot—tea, coffee?'

No reply, but he did slump into the chair. He ran the fingers of his right hand through his dark hair, then stared at her. Still waiting.

'She came to me—off a backpackers' coach. Do you know about backpackers?'

He shrugged and managed to look both disbelieving and affronted at the same time. 'Young tourists travelling on the cheap. But a coach? Lucia? Backpacking? And why would she come here?'

Well, the last question was easy. If you took it literally.

'The bus company has a number of coaches which follow the same route through the country towns of New South Wales. People buy a six-month ticket and can get on and off wherever they like—staying a few days in some places, longer in others. This is a very popular stopping-off place and the company recommends the health service as a number of the professionals here speak more than one language.'

'Parla italiano?'

The words sounded soft and mellifluous in Paige's ears and again she felt a pang of sorrow—a sense of loss for something she'd never had.

'If you're asking if I speak Italian, the answer's no. I used a phrase book to leave a message on your answerphone. I studied Japanese and Indonesian and can get by in German. Many of the European tourists also speak or understand it, so I communicate to a certain extent.'

'Which is a credit to you but isn't diverting me from the subject of Lucia, Miss Morgan.'

Mellifluous? Steely, more like!

'Or your phone call,' he added, in a no-less-determined voice.

'She wasn't well, and I sensed...'

How to explain her conviction that Lucia was in trouble—ill, lost and vulnerable—so alone that to take her in and care for her had been automatic.

She looked at the man from whom the young woman had fled and wondered how to tell him why she'd been compelled to phone him.

'She wasn't like the usual backpackers I see. Mostly they're competent young people, clued up, able to take care of themselves, if you know what I mean. Lucia struck me as someone so far out of her depth she was in danger of drowning.' She met his eyes now, challenging him yet willing him to understand. 'But I also felt she'd been very much loved and cherished all her life,' she admitted, 'and from the little she told me, I guessed someone, somewhere, would be frantically worried about her whereabouts.'

He said nothing, simply stared at her as if weighing her words, wondering whether to believe them.

'She doesn't know I made that call,' Paige admitted, feeling heat flood her cheeks again. 'I looked through her passport one day and found the number pencilled in the back of it. I felt you—her family—someone some-where—might need to know she was alive.'

He bowed his head, letting his chin rest against his chest, and she saw his chest rise and fall as be breathed deeply.

'Yes,' he said, after a long pause. 'I—we all—did need to know she was alive.'

She studied him. Saw tiredness in the way his body was slumped in the chair. But when he raised his head and looked into her eyes there was no sign of fatigue— and the anger which she'd seen earlier still lit his from within.

'Did she tell you why she ran away?' he demanded.

Paige shrugged.

'She told me very little,' she said bluntly. 'All I've done is guess.'

'Abominable girl!' the man declared, straightening in his chair and flinging his arms into the air in a gesture of frustration. 'She's been spoiled all her life, that's her trouble. Cherished is right! Of course she was cherished. And how does she repay that love and affection? How does she treat those who love her? By taking off! Running away! Leaving without a word to anyone, a note from Rome to her mother, saying she will be all right! Then nothing for months. We all assume she's dead! *Dio Madonna!*'

Perhaps it was as well she didn't speak Italian. The intonation of the words told her it was a phrase unlikely to be repeatable in polite company. Not that the man didn't look magnificent in his rage, on his feet now and prowling the room like a sleek black animal, still muttering foreign imprecations under his breath and moving his hands as if to conduct his voice. But watching him perform, that wasn't getting them anywhere, and no matter how magnificent and full of sex appeal he was, he'd be out of her life by tomorrow so the sooner she got rid of him now, the sooner she could tackle Lucia.

And the thought of *her* reaction to this latest development wasn't all that appealing! Paige stood, drew herself up to her full height and assumed her most businesslike expression. The one she used when asking for government funding from petty officials put on earth to frustrate her plans for the community centre.

'If you rant and rave at her like that, I can understand why she ran off,' she said crisply. 'Now, if you tell me where you're staying, I'll have a talk to her and get back to you.'

'Staying?' He sounded as shocked as if she'd suggested he strip naked in the main street. 'I am not staying! I have work to do. I must get back to Italy. I am—in fact, we, Lucia and I, are booked on a flight out of Sydney tomorrow morning.'

Paige stared at him in astonishment.

'You flew out from Italy to Australia for a day? You thought you could arrive here, drive up, wrest Lucia forcibly into the car, then career back down the highway and be out of the country within twenty-four hours?'

Maybe her amazement caught his attention for he stopped his pacing and faced her.

'I did not know where this town was—how far away from the capital,' he said stiffly. 'I gave the telephone number to a person at the embassy. He found the address—this address—and arranged to bring me here. It was not until I was in the car I learned she was at a far-off place—a regional centre I think Benelli called it.' He paused, then added, 'He said it was still possible to be back in Sydney late this evening and make the flight to-morrow.'

As that pause was the first hint of weakness she'd seen in the man—apart from the fatigue—she took it as an opening and pounced.

'Well, I suggest you see Mr Benelli again and ask him to arrange accommodation for you, and rearrange your flight home. Apart from anything else, I doubt Lucia is well enough to travel.'

She watched the colour drain from his face.

'What is wrong with her?' he demanded, and a hoarseness in his voice told her of his love for Lucia.

CHAPTER TWO

How to answer? Tell a man his wife had gestational diabetes mellitus when he didn't know she was pregnant? And Marco wouldn't know because Lucia hadn't known herself—hadn't even guessed what might be wrong with her. The diabetes was an added complication, one not usually occurring until late into the second trimester of pregnancy when the foetus was extracting more nutrients from the maternal source, but the trauma of leaving home could have triggered a possible predisposition to it, bringing it on earlier than usual.

The thoughts rushed through Paige's head and she studied him as she decided what to say. He didn't look like a man who'd give in easily and telling him Lucia was carrying his child, that would hand him an added incentive to force her to return to him. It would also betray Lucia's trust. Again!

Hide behind professional discretion?

She didn't think this man would take too kindly to this ethical solution to her dilemma but what the hell.

'I need to speak to her before I can give you any information about her health or where she's staying,' Paige replied, already feeling the waves of his anger as it built again. 'Give me an hour—or maybe two—and I'll contact you, or, better still, you could phone me here.'

She opened a desk drawer to get a card for him then realised it would show this building as her home address as well as that of the health service. Bring him closer than she wanted at the moment. Pulling out a scrap of

24

paper instead, she jotted down her number and pushed it across the desk.

He was standing opposite her, staring at her with an unnerving intensity.

'I already have your phone number, Miss Morgan,' he said softly. 'What I don't know is Lucia's whereabouts. Now, are you going to tell me where she is or do I call in your police force?'

She did her straightening-up thing again, hoping to look more in control.

'Lucia is an adult—able to make her own decisions. No police force in the world can compel a woman to return to a situation from which she's fled.'

She wasn't absolutely certain about the truth of this statement but he wasn't to know that. Not that he seemed to be taking much notice. In fact he was laughing at her.

Derisively!

'Fled, Miss Morgan? Aren't you overdramatising the situation?'

Damn her cheeks—just when she wanted to appear super-cool they were heating up again.

'You said yourself she ran away,' she countered hotly. 'And now you've arrived, like some vengeful gaoler, to take her back—threatening me with the police force! No, I think if anyone's overdramatising, it's you, Prince Highfaluting-whatever. Sweeping in here, making demands. I'm the one who's being reasonable about this!'

OK, so she didn't sound very reasonable right now, but he'd made her mad. And that superior expression on his carved-rock face made her even madder.

He ignored her rudeness, nodded once, stepped back a pace from his position near the desk and said, 'I will give you an hour, Miss Morgan, but that is all. For some reason you are under the impression Lucia will not wish to see me. You are wrong. She will be glad and grateful that I have arrived to take care of her.'

'Oh yeah?' Paige muttered with as much cynicism as she could muster, though why his sudden switch to politeness was aggravating her more than his anger had she didn't know. 'Well, we'll let her be the judge of that. Will you phone?'

His eyes scanned her face, as if he wanted to imprint it on his mind, and when he finally replied—saying, 'No, I will return to this house,'—Paige felt a tremor of apprehension flutter down her spine.

And dealing with Lucia wasn't any easier. When Paige confessed she'd found the number in the passport and had phoned it, her guest had pouted and turned her face to the wall, prepared to sulk.

'I had to let someone know you were alive,' Paige said desperately. 'It wasn't fair that all your friends and family should have been worrying themselves to death—imagining the worst of fates for you. I just didn't expect him to come.'

The slim figure shot upright, delight and apprehension illuminating her usually pale face, giving her a radiant beauty.

'He's here? Marco's here? Oh, why did you not tell me straight away? Where is he? Bring him to me! Now, Paige, now!'

One of the few things she had told Paige was that she'd only been married two months before she'd left. It hadn't taken her long to learn imperious ways!

'Are you sure you want to see him?' Paige asked, mistrusting this swift change of mood. 'He's here to take you home.'

The beauty faded, leaving her visitor pale again.

'Of course! He *would* have come for that reason. Trust

him to do such a thing, thinking he would persuade me.'
She pouted again, then tossed the cloud of soft dark hair
and added defiantly, 'Well, I won't go!'

There was another pause, and Paige could almost read
the expressions that washed across Lucia's face—hope,
longing, doubt and confusion.

'But I'd like to see Marco,' Lucia continued tremulously. 'Will you stay with me while he visits? Not let
him bully me or talk me into going home?'

Paige sighed. The very last thing she wanted to do was
play gooseberry between a man and his wife—particularly, for some reason, between the man in question and
this young woman she'd come to like.

'I think you should talk to him on your own,' she said.
'Don't you think you owe him that?'

Huge brown eyes gazed piteously into hers.

'But he'll talk me into going back,' Lucia wailed. 'Into
doing whatever he wants. Marco *always* gets his way.'

I can believe that, Paige thought, picturing the man
who'd invaded her office, but the idea of acting as a
chaperone at this forthcoming meeting was making her
feel quite ill. She patted Lucia's arm and suggested she
get up and have a shower before her visitor arrived.

'I don't know about staying with you while you talk
to him, but I'll be right outside the door if you need me.'
She watched Lucia stand and saw her slender frame silhouetted against the light from the window, a neat bulge
showing the eighteenth week of her pregnancy but still
far too thin to be healthy, and another idea occurred to
her.

'If he does want to take you home and you decide
you'd prefer to stay, we can use your health as an excuse.
In my opinion, you're not yet stable enough, even on the

insulin, to be undertaking an arduous flight and I'm sure your obstetrician would agree with me.'

From the new expressions on Lucia's face, this suggestion was receiving a mixed reception. Paige came closer and put her arms around the woman's narrow shoulders.

'You're not happy here,' she said gently. 'Are you sure you wouldn't be better off at home? Perhaps not with your husband, but with family or friends? People you know and love? People who would care for you?'

Lucia shrugged away from her.

'My family would say my place is with my husband,' she said bitterly. 'I can hear them now. My mother especially—and my sisters. It was their idea I marry, their fault, all of this.'

Paige hesitated. Lucia was emotional, but the words had more petulance than fear and, thinking of the handsome man with the dark blue eyes—remembering his genuine pain when he'd talked of Lucia's flight—she pressed a little further.

'Didn't you want the marriage? Did you love someone else?'

Lucia shook her head and began to cry, silent tears sliding down her cheeks.

'Love someone else?' She sobbed out the words. 'How could I when he was all I knew, the man I was destined to marry? I loved him, and only him—but he… He had different ideas about love—ideas Italian men of position held many centuries ago, not now, although I know many men cheat on their wives. When I told him I would not allow it, he laughed and said he would take a mistress if he wished for who was I to stop him?' She sniffed, then finished with a tilt of her head, 'So I ran away!'

Paige stared at her, unable to believe what she was

hearing. Well, she could believe the arrogant man she'd met downstairs might have such antediluvian views, but that a vague and possibly teasing threat about some future indiscretion had made Lucia flee? She'd imagined assault—either physical or emotional—shuddered over her mental images of what the gentle, trusting soul might have endured. But to run away because he'd said he might take a mistress one day?

'Go take a shower and get dressed,' she said abruptly. 'And while you're in there make up your mind whether you want to see him or not. I'll have lunch ready when you come out, then you'll have time to see him before we do the next blood glucose test.'

Lucia grimaced but she left the sunny sitting room where she spent most of each day—lying on the couch watching soaps on TV—and turned towards the bathroom. Paige watched her go and wondered, not for the first time, what on earth had prompted her to take the girl-woman in.

Instinct.

Ironic that the same inbuilt warning system had sent up flares when she'd first seen Lucia's husband! Only then they'd signalled 'danger' instead of 'help'.

'I will see him,' Lucia announced when she returned, dressed in loose-fitting tan trousers and a golden yellow mohair sweater—looking stunning for all her poor health. 'I will see him here and tell him I cannot go home.'

Paige sighed but didn't argue, going downstairs to the kitchen and fixing a sandwich for the two of them, counting off the calories in Lucia's meal and writing them down so she knew how many her patient-guest had eaten. In the beginning she'd tried to persuade Lucia to undertake this task for herself, but had finally given up, deciding it was more important to teach her to do her own injections and blood glucose tests.

Huh!

'OK, your turn to do the injection.' She said this every time and every time Lucia came up with some excuse for not taking the responsibility. Paige fitted a needle to the syringe, lifted the insulin out of the refrigerator and set it on the table. 'Just try filling the syringe, Lucia. Pull down to the mark, stick the needle through the rubber top on the bottle and press the plunger in to release the air.'

'I cannot touch that needle, I might injure myself!'

It was the usual argument—one they had four times a day—so both knew their part in it.

'You can't injure yourself if you hold it properly. Do you want to be dependent on someone else all through your pregnancy?' Paige grinned to herself as she realised why this argument had had little effect on Lucia in the past. Given the princely husband, the younger woman had probably had swarms of servants catering to her every whim—being dependent on someone was a habit rather than a concern.

'You do it, Paige, just today?'

The voice cajoled and the brown eyes begged.

Paige grumbled about her weakness in always giving in, and filled the syringe with the fast-acting insulin Lucia would need for her body to handle the meal she was about to eat.

'But I'm not staying with you while you talk to him,' Paige warned, determined to win one argument today. 'You've got to see him on your own.'

Lucia didn't argue. In fact, she smiled and looked excited, flushed with a soft and youthful radiance which made Paige feel older than her twenty-five years and unaccountably depressed as she tackled her own lunch with far less gusto than her guest.

And the depression wasn't lifted by the stern expression on her next visitor's face. She had sent Lucia upstairs to the sitting room and was waiting outside the house when the long black car with the consular plates drew up. Although the autumn sun was warm, she found herself shivering as he alighted. A fact that didn't escape him.

'You should be wearing a jacket,' he chided, and moved towards her as if to wrap his arm around her shoulders. The cold was replaced by warmth and she dodged ahead, leading him towards the side door which led directly into her flat.

'No wonder she ran away,' she muttered, more to herself than him. 'If you tell a *stranger* what to wear…'

'Pardon?'

'It was nothing.' She reached the door and paused, then turned to face him, looking into his eyes—hoping to read his reaction to what she had to say. 'Lucia has agreed to see you, but I'd like to say…' The words petered out under the intensity of that blue gaze. Pull yourself together! Think of Lucia, not eyes that seem to drill into your soul. 'She's in a very fragile state, easily upset, both physically and emotionally. Will you remember that? Treat her gently?'

Or eyes that darken dangerously!

'And what do you imagine I intend to do to her? Throw her over my shoulder and force her to return with me? Is that how an Australian man would behave, Miss Morgan? How you would like a man to act with you?'

Damn him—and her give-away cheeks! The image had made her go hot all over. Battling to regain control, she tried an imperious look of her own.

'Australia has as many gentlemen as any other country, though they may not carry fancy titles, and, no, I wouldn't expect any man to ride roughshod over a woman, but men can exert more than physical power.'

'And women can't?' he countered, fixing her with a look so quizzical she wondered how she'd come to be arguing with him.

'Just treat her gently,' Paige said, turning abruptly away before her face betrayed even more of her inner chaos. She'd never felt such a physical reaction to another human being. For the first time in her life, she was beginning to understand what people meant when they talked about instant attraction. And sex appeal! Not only could she now accept its existence, but she had to acknowledge that this man had it by the bucket-load.

Yet his wife had run away from him.

The thought occurred to her as she walked up the stairs ahead of him, hearing his firm tread behind her, feeling his presence in the nerves down her spine, aware even of a faint whiff of some sophisticated cologne or after-shave—not a pungent or overpowering odour, but more a tantalising hint of something smooth and sleek but very masculine.

Help! Now it seemed her thoughts were doing the running away—straight into a fantasy land.

'Lucia is inside.'

She knocked and was about to grasp the doorknob when the door flew open and a vision of loveliness in a bright mohair sweater flung herself into the waiting arms of the prince.

Which is how all good fairytales should end, Paige reminded herself as she returned to the kitchen to play Cinderella-before-the-ball, washing the lunch dishes, working out a dinner menu, wondering what she could do about arranging nutritious meals for Lucia to take on the plane if her prince insisted she return home immediately.

By the time footsteps sounded on the stairs, she'd not only organised what they'd have for dinner but had cleaned the kitchen thoroughly, written out a shopping list, contemplated polishing the silver and settled for washing the floor instead—anything to keep her mind off what might be happening upstairs.

And, no, she wouldn't take that thought any further either!

She straightened up as the heavy footfall hesitated only fractionally at the bottom of the steps then turned unerringly towards the kitchen. One glance at the dark scowl on Marco's face told her the reunion hadn't gone quite the way he'd planned.

'Lucia tells me you will explain her medical condition. She pleaded tiredness, a need to rest and, in fact, she does not look well. Is this a new game of hers or is she indeed ill?'

Paige felt the words jar against her brain.

'She didn't tell you?'

The scowl deepened.

'Tell me what?'

Drat the girl? What was Paige supposed to do? Blurt out to the man that his wife was not only pregnant but suffering a complication which required a strict medical and personal regimen of care?

Marco watched the slim, pale-skinned woman pace up and down beside the kitchen table, leaving a trail of shoe prints on the floor she'd evidently just washed, and wondered what he'd said to cause so much agitation. Not that having Lucia as a house guest wasn't enough to drive anyone to distraction. Spoilt, that's what she was.

But this woman had seemed so sensible—so 'together' as he'd heard it described in English. And she'd taken Lucia in and cared for her, been kind enough to feel concern for her relatives—something which still wasn't worrying Lucia over-much.

'If you prefer to walk and talk, I would be glad to be outside for a while. I was cooped up in the plane, then the car journey and a hotel.'

She glanced up at him, as if surprised to hear his voice. Had she forgotten he was there—that he was waiting for an answer? Now she looked at her watch and frowned as if calculating something. How much time she could waste perhaps? How long she could procrastinate?

'Actually, I have to be outside fairly soon anyway. I have some house calls to make, and as they're close I usually walk.' She smiled at him, and he caught an echo of it in her eyes and knew he'd misjudged the frown. That was a real smile, not the plastic version most women he knew could flash at will—trained by years of practice at society functions where a camera could catch any unwary facial grimace and reveal it in the daily papers.

He found himself hoping she'd smile some more during the short time they would have together.

'I will walk with you,' he announced, and saw her frown again, sigh, then shrug her shoulders as if she wasn't happy about his presence but would accept it.

'Most women would be happy to walk with me,' he growled, riled by the reaction, but she appeared not to have heard his piqued comment. She slipped past him to the door, turning to say, 'I'd better check on Lucia before we go.' Then she disappeared into the passageway.

It was because he was tired that her patent lack of interest in him niggled. Although he'd had his share of attractive women as friends and lovers, he certainly didn't expect every woman he met to fall at his feet. He glared at the empty doorway, then realised the futility of such an act and chuckled, turning his attention instead to the room where he waited.

It was attractive in a homely way—a big practical kitchen with tiled floors and stained timber cupboards and benches. A long wooden table was scarred by use, and the two comfortable armchairs pulled up close to the fuel stove hinted that this room was the real heart of the dwelling. It seemed to hold the faint echoes of happy family gatherings and the accumulated aroma of good hearty meals. Almost an Italian kitchen in its ambience, he decided, sniffing the air and touching the leaves of the herbs which flourished in pots along the windowsill.

Did this flat at the back of the health service come with Miss Morgan's job? Did she live here alone—when she wasn't bringing home stray runaways like Lucia?

He felt the now-familiar clutch of fear Lucia's disappearance had caused, then said a silent prayer of thanks that she had fallen into such safe and apparently sensible hands.

'OK, let's go!'

The soft, slightly husky voice summoned him from the doorway. She'd pulled a padded jacket over her cream sweater and trousers and the dark green colour deepened the colour in her eyes, making them more green than gold. He'd read on the flight that green and gold were the colours of Australia, but she still didn't match his mental image of an Australian any more than the streets she led him down, lined with trees bright with autumn leaves, fitted his notions of the land they called the sunburnt country.

He took from her the small bag she was carrying and

matched her pace, walking silently, unwilling to prompt her again, thinking his own thoughts.

Paige said, 'She's pregnant.'

He stopped dead, forcing her to turn back to him as he stumbled into a mess of incoherent, half-formed questions.

'She's what? *Madonna mia!* How—? When—?'

Paige stared at him, unable to believe the man's shock and disbelief.

'How the hell do you think she got pregnant?' she stormed. 'And as for when, I presume it was shortly after you were married. One thing I did get out of her was the wedding date. How any man could be so insensitive as to speak of taking a mistress before he'd been married less than three months is beyond me.'

Now he looked plain bewildered.

'Who spoke of taking a mistress?' he asked, rubbing at his temples as if to massage his brain into working order.

'You did—or you intimated as much!' Paige retorted, then she looked at him again and wondered, having second thoughts. 'Or Lucia understood that's what you said,' she amended.

Her explanation didn't seem to help his confusion.

'What, in the name of all that's holy, have my mistresses to do with Lucia?'

It was Paige's turn for bewilderment—only that was too weak a word. 'Flabbergasted' fitted better. She stared at him, carefully controlling a lower jaw which seemed inclined to drop to an open-mouthed gape of disbelief. She wanted to shake him—pummel him—felt her fingers tingle with an itch to belt some sense into him, but it was none of her business how he ran his life.

'I've got patients to see,' she muttered, turning away

from him and striding down the road. He caught up in two paces, so she let him have a short blast of the anger churning inside her. 'And if you don't understand how a young sensitive woman like Lucia would view your behaviour—would suffer enormous anguish over it—then I'm certainly not wasting my breath telling you.'

They walked in silence for a few minutes, then he said, 'OK, so she's pregnant. Let's forget the other nonsense and proceed from there. I know I reacted badly to that news. Anyone would.'

Another mind-boggling concept—and one she had to refute.

'Not in Australia!' Again she stopped and faced him, wondering how a man who looked so good could be so shallow and fickle and downright stupid. 'Over here, prospective fathers are usually delighted to receive the news that their wives are pregnant. Most even put on a show of concern for them.'

His frown drew his eyebrows together in a slightly satanic manner.

'Prospective fathers? What does the reaction of prospective fathers have to do with me?'

Paige shook her head. First a fairytale prince, now fantasy land! Did this man know nothing about the process of reproduction? Or was he assuming the child wasn't his?

'Lucia is eighteen weeks pregnant,' she said carefully, wondering if, in spite of his beautifully correct use of English, he didn't understand it as well as she'd assumed. 'Given the date of your wedding, I would say she became pregnant in the early days of your honeymoon.'

It was his turn to do the flabbergasted act.

'My wedding? My honeymoon? You think Lucia is my wife? That it was me she ran away from?'

Only he wasn't flabbergasted at all. He was laughing, his head thrown back and the deep rumbles of sound echoing up into the trees.

'Well, if you're not her husband, who are you?' Paige asked the question crossly, cutting across his mirth, shaken by this turn of events and by the effect of his glee on her already stretched nerves.

'I am Marco,' he said, with a funny little bow. 'Lucia's loving and long-suffering brother. And knowing that, Miss Morgan, shall we start again?'

He held out his hand in a formal gesture and, reluctantly, she took it.

'It's Paige, not Miss Morgan,' she said, wondering where her voice had gone, leaving the words to falter out in a breathless undertone.

'Now we are friends,' he announced with complete assurance. He tucked her hand into the crook of his arm. 'Already I've delayed you so first we visit your patients, then we talk about Lucia, her marriage, her husband, her pregnancy and her flight. For the moment, it is enough to have seen her and know she is safe.'

Paige tried to think of some objection, considered removing her hand from the warm place where it lay— asserting her independence—but her mind had fled back to the fantasy land and it was only with a strenuous effort of will that she managed to dredge up one weak objection to his plan.

'You can walk with me but you can't visit my patients.'

He cocked his head to one side as he looked down at her.

'They would not like a visit from a prince?'

His lips teased into a smile, and she shook her head, although she knew the three women she was about to see would all revel in a visit from a prince, no matter how ancient or meaningless his title was. All three were housebound and anything out of the usual could provide them with something to think and talk about for weeks to come.

'These are medical visits,' she said primly, not wanting to say no outright, but aware of the ethical considerations of taking strangers into her patients' homes.

'So a doctor could accompany you?' he asked. 'Even a visiting doctor?'

Her hand was feeling increasingly comfortable, and the close proximity of his body was creating havoc with her senses, so she didn't place any importance on his questions, assuming he was making conversation. She struggled to keep her end of it going so he wouldn't guess at her thoughts and feelings.

'Of course, if the patients agreed to see him.'

'Well, that is arranged,' he said, satisfaction purring in the deep tones of his voice. 'You will say I wish to see Australian medicine while in your country and ask if they will allow me in.'

She pulled her hand away and tucked it out of temptation's reach in the pocket of her jacket.

'I can't pretend you're a doctor just to get you inside a few Australian homes, however interested you may be. And why should you be interested anyway? The health service clients are poor people, not only poor financially but some are lacking the skills necessary to survive without help. This is not typical Australia you'd be seeing, and I don't know that it's right to put them…on display, I suppose, for you or anyone else.'

He didn't reply immediately, but frowned off into the distance as if trying to work out his answer. Or perhaps thinking in Italian and translating into English. She looked at the strong profile, the dark hair brushed back but with one lock escaping control to fall across his temple.

She was glad he wasn't married to Lucia!

Stupid thought!

'We have poor people in Italy as well,' he said, cutting into her self-castigation. 'And those who are inadequately equipped in living skills as well. I would not judge your country on what I see, but, with that said, shouldn't a country be judged on how it treats these very people? How it provides support so they can live fulfilling and worthwhile lives?'

She had to smile, having used the same argument so often herself.

'I agree,' she conceded, 'but it still doesn't make you a doctor.'

She walked on, because smiling at him—and having him smile back—had turned out to be a very bad idea.

'But I *am* a doctor,' he announced, catching up with her in three long strides and falling into step again.

Marco a doctor?

She glanced at him, at the erect carriage, the aristocratic head, and said, 'Rubbish! You're a prince. Mr Benelli said so, and even a girl from the back blocks of New South Wales can recognise royalty when she sees it!'

She spoke lightly, jokingly, although she half meant every word.

'The "prince" is a an old title handed down through my family—inescapable if one is the eldest son—but it isn't a job description, Paige Morgan, any more than "Miss" describes the work you do.'

'You *are* a doctor?'

Disbelief ran riot through the question, but again he bowed just slightly in reply.

'I am,' he said. 'Now, should we continue this delightful chat here on the street or walk on to visit your patients?'

She walked on, remembering Lucia's words... 'Marco always gets his way.'

CHAPTER THREE

'MY FIRST patient lives in here,' Paige said, stopping in front of a small bungalow tucked well back from the road and almost hidden behind huge cotoneaster bushes which had been allowed to run wild.

'Sleeping Beauty, presumably,' Marco remarked, and Paige glanced swiftly at him, recalling how often she'd had that thought herself.

'Almost,' she said. 'Mrs Bevan was fine up until five years ago when her husband fell ill. She then began to feel all the classic symptoms of panic attacks—accelerated heart rate, flushing, faintness, perspiring heavily—usually when the doctor called. By the time Mr Bevan died a year later, she was unable to leave the house without being overcome by these sensations—often fainting before she reached the gate.'

Paige pushed through the same gate as she spoke and looked around as she walked up the path. Time to get the Scouts here again to do some subtle trimming of the trees.

'Was she diagnosed as agoraphobic?' Marco asked. 'If so, she may not wish to see me. I will understand.'

Paige was still coming to terms with his apparent interest. This was the same man who'd arrogantly demanded access to his sister earlier—who'd wanted nothing more than to be out of this town and on his way back to his home country. Now he was walking the back streets of the town with Paige—*and* offering to wait outside.

'She hasn't seen a psychiatrist if you feel that's required for official diagnosis. And I don't think she'll object to your visit. She's more secure in her own home these days and even welcomes company—it's going beyond the garden gate which induces the anxiety.'

'And her treatment?' Marco pursued as Paige lifted her hand to ring the bell.

She shrugged one shoulder, uncomfortable with admitting that in this respect she'd failed.

'She's not receiving any—' The explanation was cut short by the door opening as far as the safety chain would allow.

'Hi, Mrs Bevan. It's Paige and I've someone with me, a visiting doctor from Italy. Would you like him to come in or shall I ask him to wait outside?'

'Not the prince?' Mrs Bevan responded in a breathless voice. 'Oh, my, oh, my!'

Paige could hear her fingers scrabbling against the wood, fiddling with the chain as she hurried to unlatch it—apparently anxious to provide a royal welcome.

'Yes, yes, bring him in. Mabel called on her way back from the centre and told me he was visiting you.' Mrs Bevan must have freed the chain at last for she flung open the door and all but bowed Marco into the hall. 'Said he came in such a lovely car and with a courtier and all, she said.'

Marco seemed to accept this evidence of grandeur with equanimity, standing back and indicating that Paige should go ahead, but she was rooted to the top step, praying Mrs Bevan wouldn't repeat any of the other things Mabel had told her—particularly about Paige being in need of a man.

A light touch on her shoulder propelled her forward—out of touching range—gabbling explanations and excuses no one in their right mind would understand. Not that Mrs Bevan had noticed. Oh, no, she was far too busy gazing in awe at her visitor, standing, her hands clasped in front of her apron, and staring at him as if he'd arrived clad in ermine robes—or whatever princes traditionally clad themselves in—complete with crown and sceptre.

Paige took control of herself and Mrs Bevan. She guided her patient to a chair, indicating to the visitor to take another, then looked around, wondering what she'd done with her bag. Perhaps not quite in control!

Marco guessed what she was seeking and held up the bag he'd carried, amused by her confusion and surprised by the older woman's reaction to his title. Not that he hadn't experienced it before. Even at home, where old titles were common, the older people—those who knew—still treated him as something special. But here in egalitarian Australia?

He introduced himself to their hostess and watched as Paige took out a small sphygmomanometer from the bag and wrapped a blood-pressure cuff around Mrs Bevan's arm.

'You have a problem with your blood pressure?' he asked the patient.

'It's old age,' she responded. 'Everything breaking down, and what does work usually hurts. I guess it will happen even to princes when they get old.'

'That's telling you,' Paige whispered to him, jotting down her findings on a card and tucking the equipment back into the bag. She smiled at her patient. 'Your blood pressure is fine today, Mrs B. You've obviously been taking the tablets. Now, what about exercise? Are you walking in the garden each day?'

Mrs Bevan beamed, first at Paige, then at Marco and said, as proudly as a child revealing a good mark at school, 'Ten times in the morning and another ten in the afternoon.'

'That's grand,' Paige responded, while Marco considered the bungalow's size and wondered if twenty might not have been a better target. 'Perhaps you could build it up to twelve this week. Or do a few quick turns after dinner as well.'

He nodded his head in acknowledgment that their thoughts were in tandem, realising that the nurse was treading very carefully with this particular patient.

While he chatted to Mrs Bevan, Paige checked some small bottles which were lined up on a bench at the end of the room, then turned back to announce they should be on their way.

'You've enough tablets to last until next week, but if you think of anything you need, give me a call,' she said as she tucked some slips of paper into her pocket. 'I'll see you tomorrow.'

Then, to Marco's astonishment, she bent and kissed the wrinkled cheek, before heading towards the door. He followed, so many questions flung up by this routine visit that he hoped the next patient lived a long way down the road.

'Is she on some form of anti-anxiety medication?' he asked as they made their way to the gate. 'Under a psychiatrist? Do you encourage her to go out? Have you used behaviour therapies at all to get her over the initial shock of being out of her own environment? What treatment is considered appropriate over here?'

She must have been surprised by his interest for she stopped abruptly and he ran into her—felt the softness of her body against his chest.

He put a hand on her shoulder to steady them both, told himself it was the softness of her jacket he'd felt,

and why should he notice anyway? All women had soft
bodies. She dodged away from his hand and half turned
to face him.

'The answer to all but the last of your questions is no.
Yes, all of those treatments are used here, but you have
to remember that most people suffering from anxiety dis-
orders are young, with the mean onset in the early twen-
ties. The seriousness of the disorder necessitates drugs
for many people and psychiatrists use the often harsh
treatment judged necessary to alter behaviour because of
a patient's youth and the fact that he or she should have
a long and productive life ahead of them. Even then many
refuse treatment, being unable to admit to illness by taking drugs or visiting a specialist.'

He considered this and shook his head.

'So Mrs Bevan's age means you don't bother treating
her?' he demanded, angry for the gentle old woman
who'd reminded him of his grandmother.

Paige waved a hand, indicating they should walk and
talk, and he wondered if she, like he, thought better when
her body was in motion. Following a pace behind her
through the gate, his mind clipped the two words together
in a different frame and decided her body in motion was
a most attractive sight. In fact, the impression of slimness
was misleading as she undoubtedly had curves in all the
right places. Plump curve of hips tapering into a tiny
waist he could perhaps span with his hands—not that he
could see her waist under the bulky jacket, but he'd noticed earlier—

'Pardon?'

She turned her head and smiled at him—that warm and
genuine smile he'd observed and admired earlier.

'I've just produced a perfect explanation for not treating Mrs Bevan—or at least treating her in a way that's

beyond the parameters of so-called normal therapy—and you haven't heard a word of it. Are you worrying about Lucia?'

. Her brows, a darker gold than her hair, twitched together, and when he answered with a slight negative movement of his head she provided him with another excuse for his inattention.

'You must be tired,' she said. 'And here I am dragging you all over town, visiting the elderly.'

He shook his head again, denying tiredness but glad he didn't have to explain the real cause of his distraction.

She walked on and he caught up with her.

'I was saying we've tackled Mrs Bevan differently, encouraging her to have people in, to accept visitors. At first it was difficult as her husband's illness had isolated her, but as you saw today even a stranger didn't upset her unduly. And I've got her exercising in the yard. She's keen on birds, and always knows where the nests are in her garden. I live in hope that one day a bird will tempt her beyond the gate, and when she's done it once, it might become easier.'

'And have you constructed the nest of the bird beyond her boundary yet and trained the bird to fly above her towards the gate?'

He saw her shoulders move and heard the soft chuckle which escaped her.

'Don't think I haven't considered it,' she told him. 'But, like so many people with psychological problems, I have to move very slowly with her. Another friend, knowing of her interest in birds, gave her a canary in a cage, thinking it would be company for her. Mrs Bevan was horrified and made me find a good home for it. She couldn't bear the thought of a living creature being imprisoned like that, yet it's how she lives herself.'

'Perhaps that's why she was upset by it. Perhaps she has more insight into her self-imposed bars than you credit her with.'

He spoke gently, for he was moved by the compassion of this woman towards this particular patient. True, most nurses had compassion by the bucket-load, but Paige Morgan seemed to go an extra step. Which reminded him…

'And how does she exist? Who shops for her? She has sons, daughters, family?'

There was no answer from his guide, and he remembered the pieces of paper she'd tucked into her pocket.

'You?'

She glared at him.

'Well, someone has to and it's no bother for me to get her things when I'm shopping for myself,' she said defiantly.

'So someone else has told you you're stepping beyond professional duty,' he teased, enjoying the colour temper brought to her cheeks.

'You can't draw lines and boundaries in community care,' she retorted, pausing with her hand on another gate—this one leading into the yard of what looked like a block of apartments. 'What should I do? Starve her out of her house? Refuse to let people shop for her until she's desperate and has to overcome her fears in order to eat? Perhaps that's some people's way, but it isn't mine. The poor darling had no children, her husband was everything to her, then he died and left her so ill-prepared for life it's not surprising she began to panic.'

'And has been panicking ever since,' he said softly. 'I am not judging or condemning you. In fact, it is admiration I feel—for your understanding, and your willingness to take that extra step so many professionals, myself included, sometimes fail to realise needs taking! We tend to hope some safety net spread by someone else will catch these people, but all too often there is no net.'

Paige forgot about old Miss Wilde who would be peering through the lace curtains of the lower floor apartment, waiting anxiously for her to arrive.

'You sound as if you've experienced the "no net" phenomenon.' She probed cautiously for there'd been emotion in his voice.

'Had experience of it—seen the effects of it—fought with government officials about the implications of not having one—or not having it spread far enough,' he admitted, his voice abrasive with remembered anger.

'Someone close to you?' she asked. She couldn't have hidden her surprise very well for his reply was first a bark of laughter, then a gruff, 'You're surprised I should know such people? Being born with a title doesn't necessarily mean being born with wealth and, although my family was—is—well off thanks to my father's and grandfather's business acumen, not all our friends and associates are as fortunate. Yes, I've known people who have slipped through the welfare system and not been fortunate enough to have a Paige Morgan there to hold out a hand in friendship and support.'

He spoke stiffly, as if unused to speaking of such personal matters, and Paige guessed the person who had suffered had been close to him. A relative perhaps? Too proud to ask for help?

Embarrassed by his words, she walked towards the front door of the apartment building, thinking about the contradictions she'd seen in this man who strode beside her.

You only had to look at his face to know he'd be the

same as the person of whom he spoke, should bad times ever descend upon his shoulders.

'Well, Miss Wilde isn't afraid to speak out when she needs something, but she's hearing impaired and, although she's tried a variety of hearing-aids, she's too sensitive to the noise they make to persevere with wearing them.'

'So she stays at home? Does this make sense to you as well as her? Is it only I who cannot understand it?'

Paige grinned at his confusion.

'She isn't a permanent stay-at-home,' she explained. 'Actually, she has a better social life than I do, but she's laid up with gout at the moment so I said I'd drop in a new bottle of tablets for her. Be careful what you say to her. She'll get on to Henry the Eighth if you give her the slightest encouragement and regale you with tales of other royal gout sufferers.'

'Henry the Eighth? The English king of many wives?'

Paige watched the way his brow wrinkled in puzzlement and realised all his facial expressions were of interest to her. Probably because he was so impossibly good-looking, she had to keep watching in case one made him look ordinary.

She nodded. 'He was also known for his fits of temper when enduring the pain caused by his overindulgence in good food and even better wine,' she explained, but the frown deepened on his forehead and she guessed he was thinking of something far removed from gout.

'Alex said he'd take a mistress? *That's* why Lucia ran away? I can't believe it!'

Sorry she'd pressed the button that would light a globe inside Miss Wilde's apartment and let her know they were there, Paige faced him. She could follow Marco's mental leap from King Henry to Lucia's indiscreet husband, but to discuss it here and now?

'Well, he must have, or she wouldn't have been so upset.'

Blue eyes stared fixedly into hers.

'No man would do such a thing!' he declared, as if his conviction should wipe the whole scenario from both their minds.

'Say it, or take a mistress?' Paige asked, smiling at his delayed reaction to something she'd explained some hours ago.

'Both!' he said firmly, then actually had the grace to look embarrassed when she laughed.

'Well, not consider taking a mistress while still, more or less, on his honeymoon,' he amended, but before Paige could pursue the subject Miss Wilde arrived at the door, seated in a wheelchair, her left leg, with its grossly swollen foot and ankle, propped on a box-like contraption in front of her.

'Is this the prince?' she asked Paige in a voice which could have been heard four blocks away.

'What did you do, alert the town crier?' Marco demanded in an undertone.

'It was your fault for coming into the clinic,' she told him, before introducing him to Miss Wilde, being careful to speak slowly and face the woman as she formed the words.

'Come in, come in.'

As Miss Wilde began to turn in the direction of her front door, it was Marco who took control, swinging her carefully around and pushing her towards the open door on the far side of the foyer.

'In there?' He threw the words over his shoulder to

Paige, who had to stop admiring his straight back and broad shoulders and work out what he was talking about.

'Oh, yes, just through that door,' she floundered.

They were the last words she said for forty minutes. It turned out that Miss Wilde, ex-history teacher at the local high school, had a fascination with Italian history, so royal gout was passed over in favour of Italian royal lineage. She had Marco write down his full name and lineage then dissected it, pointing out the different dynastic families who had contributed to his gene pool and regaling them both with risqué tales of the more notorious members.

'We have to go,' Paige said at last, interrupting the flow when she realised it was getting late and she had another visit before she could return home.

Miss Wilde protested, but Marco must have sensed Paige's anxiety and he politely but firmly said his farewells then guided her towards the door.

'You are concerned about time? Is it Lucia who worries you? Do you not like leaving her alone? Would you wish me to return to the house to be with her?'

'I'm more concerned about her meal,' she explained. 'I try to keep them as regular as possible.' The words were no sooner out than she realised she hadn't explained the added complication of Lucia's pregnancy. And couldn't now, with one more visit to make. 'But, no, we still have time to visit Mrs Grantley. She's not much of a talker and has Mr Grantley for company. Actually, it's him I visit. I shower him and dress him ready for bed.'

'Perhaps I could do the task for you,' Marco offered, and Paige looked at him in surprise. Whether he'd worn a three-piece suit, made, she suspected, out of the finest quality wool, for the long flight to Australia, she didn't know, but she could hardly see him showering the easily agitated Mr Grantley in it.

'I'll manage,' she said dryly. 'Mr Grantley and I have a system. Here's the house. I'll introduce you to Mrs Grantley and you can chat to her while I fix her husband.'

Marco was smiling as they left the house half an hour later.

'And what's the system?' he enquired with exaggerated politeness. 'You get under the shower with him?'

Damn! She'd huddled quickly back into her jacket when the job was done, hoping he wouldn't notice how wet her clothes were.

She tilted her chin and assumed what she hoped was an expression of great dignity. 'Some days I don't get wet at all.'

Dignity got her nowhere for he continued to smile as he loped along beside her.

'Not that wet clothes don't do something for a woman,' he remarked, making her hug the jacket even closer. 'Although you shouldn't be wandering out in the cold night air in such dampness. Is there no kind of protection you could wear? A raincoat, for instance?'

Paige sighed, knowing that what he said made sense and that the regular community nurses always wore protection.

'I don't want to make it look as if I'm someone come in to bathe him,' she muttered, although she knew the words probably wouldn't make any sense to him. 'He seems to react better with me—usually—because he sees me as a friend, and although his mind is affected by dementia he has good days and good moments. On a good day, he'd be appalled to think I had to wear a raincoat to help him in the shower.'

She received no answer. Perhaps Marco had been

thinking of something else and hadn't heard her limp explanation.

Well, she wasn't going to repeat it, she decided, as she quickened her pace to keep up with his long strides.

'You like to make sure Lucia has regular meals?' He stopped walking and turned to face her. 'You must excuse me for catching up with your information so slowly. I can only suppose it is fatigue from the flight—a delayed reaction that is slowing my thought processes. Lucia has been ill during this pregnancy? Yes, she looked ill. She has been nauseous, vomiting, unable to retain food? Is she seeing a specialist? How is he treating her? Not with drugs, I assume?'

He sounded so anxious—so annoyed with himself for not asking more questions earlier—that Paige laid a hand on his arm and said, 'She's certainly under specialist care and she's so much better now you needn't be overly concerned.' She paused, not wanting to shock him further yet knowing she couldn't protect him from the truth.

'She's suffering from gestational diabetes mellitus.' There, it was out. She watched his face as he absorbed this information and ran it through his mind, probably dredging up half-forgotten facts from his student days— unless he had specialised in either obstetrics or illnesses such as diabetes.

'But it's too early to know that,' he protested. 'You said what? Eighteen weeks?'

Paige nodded then walked on.

'Yes, but apparently it can come on earlier than the usual twenty-four- to twenty-eight-week onset.' She hesitated, wanting to make the explanation as concise as possible but not wanting to alarm him too much.

'She's only been with me a month,' she began. 'I'm not certain when she arrived in Australia but I do know she spent some time in Melbourne and later in Sydney with a lass she met on the plane. Then, when a group of young people decided to take the outback coach, she joined them. Unfortunately, within ten days of travelling with them, she was feeling ill enough for these friends to be concerned about her health and to tell the coach captain, who brought her to the health service.'

'Where you took her in!'

He shook his head as if this was the least understandable aspect of the saga.

'She was desperately ill. Not eating properly, having fainting spells. In fact, if the group hadn't carried a constant supply of sweets and offered them to her whenever she was strong enough to suck something, she might have been worse off. Or perhaps the condition didn't surface until just before she arrived here. A form of morning sickness, which I gather went on all day and was aggravated by and mistaken for motion sickness, would have depleted her body of nutrients even without the drain of foetal needs.'

'And now?' he demanded. 'Is she able to balance her blood glucose by diet alone? Is she exercising?' He struck his forehead with the heel of his hand. 'Stupid question! When did Lucia ever exert a milligram more energy than she need?'

'Well, she is exercising, as it happens,' Paige told him, hurrying the pace now they were back in sight of her home. 'I explained how important it was.'

'And she took notice of you?' Marco demanded, disbelief ringing in the deep register of his voice.

'Well, actually, no, but when I talked about losing her figure after the baby is born, she did agree to follow some simple routines. I hired a walking machine as I've been reluctant to let her walk the streets on her own. I'm not

sure how much experience you've had of pregnant dia-
betic patients but, unfortunately, by keeping the blood
sugar under control you get an added risk of hypoglycaemia—dizzy spells, loss of consciousness—if not
treated quickly.'

'You hired a walking machine?'

This time the disbelief was tinged with mirth and he'd
totally ignored all her medical explanations.

'Well, it was all I could think of for her,' Paige muttered defensively. 'And I might add that although you
seem to be finding this amusing none of it's been very
funny from my side of the fence.'

He immediately looked chastened, and rested a hand
on her shoulder as if in apology.

'I can understand your position, and I do not laugh at
you,' he said, that fascinating voice now as deep and soft
and smooth as the most expensive chocolate. 'I and my
family will be eternally grateful to you for taking care of
Lucia. It is simply that you keep surprising me with
your—your resourcefulness! Are all Australians as practical and filled with common sense?'

Night had fallen swiftly but they had halted where the
streetlight threw a buttery wedge of light around them,
casting the darkness beyond its reach into darker shadows. But not as dark as those which hid his eyes.

Paige stared at him, wondering why the question
should make her feel so downhearted. Was it because
common sense didn't usually feature as a prerequisite for
the heroines in fairytales? Because she'd rather he
thought her ravishingly beautiful than sensible?

Not that she *was* ravishingly beautiful, of course.

'Well?' he prompted, looking down at her, seeing more
of her than she could of him because the light fell on her

face. 'Can you not answer or are you too modest to explain you are one among few?'

She shrugged the question away and said lightly, 'I don't think kindness is defined by nationality. Faced with an ill young woman, anyone would have done the same thing.' She thought of the weirdos who infected every society and amended the sentence. 'Almost anyone!'

That made him laugh again, attracting the attention of Lucia who must have been waiting for their return. A window above them opened and her head appeared in the aperture.

'Marco. Paige. Hello to you. I was worrying. I slept then woke and feel very well indeed.' She was bubbling with excitement, not even waiting for an answer to her greeting before continuing. 'I have had a so wonderful idea. Because you have been so kind to me, Paige, Marco will take us both to dinner. You said you knew an Italian restaurant you would take me to when I was well—and now I am well, so we shall go. See...'

She leaned even further out, making Paige yell a warning to be careful lest she fall, but her words went unheeded as Lucia flung her arms wide.

'I am already dressed!'

'It's no good arguing with her,' Marco told Paige with enough gloom to convince her a dinner at the local Italian restaurant was the last thing he wanted. He ushered her towards the side door they'd used earlier. 'Much better just to go along. Has she a diet sheet? Does she know what she can and can't eat?'

Paige chuckled.

'You may know her well enough not to argue, but if you think either her specialist or myself could convince her of the importance of taking control of her own health requirements, then you're wrong. Your sister Lucia is far too used to being cared for to be even vaguely interested in dietary needs, nor have I persuaded her—so far—to do her own injections—even her own blood glucose tests.'

'But that's a simple matter—a prick of the finger.' Marco pointed out the obvious. 'I've known six-year-olds do it.'

'Not Lucia!' Paige corrected him, unlocking the door and letting them both into the downstairs hallway. 'But that's something you can rectify, I'm sure. After all, while you might think Lucia always gets her own way, she's equally convinced of your powers of persuasion. "Marco *always* gets his way," she told me.'

She heard the words echo in the open space and regretted them, wishing she'd resisted the urge to tease him. He was too close—too masculine—too threatening in some undefined way. Paige shivered and felt his hands settle on her shoulders. She tried to pull away but her willpower had deserted her.

'Not always,' he said in a husky voice that felt like velvet in her ears.

'No?' The word squeaked out, betraying her agitation, although she was sure he could also hear her erratic heartbeat and feel the nerves jumping in her skin.

'No!' he whispered. 'Because right now Marco has an almost uncontrollable urge to kiss your lips—to see if they taste as sweet as they look. Of course, he would pretend it was a thank-you for caring for his sister—a casual salute. But he was brought up to treat a woman with respect so he won't do it, but it's proof—no? Proof that Marco doesn't always get his way.'

And on that most unexpected note he let her go, and stepped back out through the door.

'I shall return in half an hour. It is not too late for my sister to eat?'

Paige shook her head, completely bemused by the events of the entire day—shocked into silence by those of the last few minutes.

'Half an hour is fine,' she managed to mumble, but when he'd disappeared from sight she realised how little time she had to shower and change and yelled after him, 'And thanks for asking if it suited me as well!' Then she stomped crossly up the stairs, smiling at Lucia's excitement but inside annoyed with the woman for arranging that they go out, and with herself for letting a man she'd never see again get under her skin, and most of all with him, for...

Well, just with him!

CHAPTER FOUR

THERE was nothing in Paige's wardrobe she could remotely consider to be 'going out with a prince' gear so she settled on a tartan miniskirt she'd paid too much for at the fashion parades during the recent Wool Week, teaming it with a fine knit sweater in her favourite forest green.

The dark colour made her skin seem paler, but reflected more green into her eyes so they didn't look quite so much like stagnant creek water. Eschewing make-up, apart from mascara and lipstick, she took extra time to brush her hair. It mightn't curl and froth attractively around her shoulders, as Lucia's did, but with a bit of extra effort in the brush strokes at least it shone.

'You are ready, Paige?' Lucia called. 'Marco will be here any minute. He is never late.'

'Well, good for him,' Paige muttered to herself, wondering how she was going to face this paragon of punctuality again after that odd conversation in the downstairs hall.

Put it down to his tiredness, common sense told her, but no amount of common sense could quite extinguish the tiny flicker of warmth his words had fanned to life inside her.

'It's the reaction of any woman who's told she's seen as desirable,' she reminded herself. 'Don't make a big thing of it.'

But as she left the bathroom and walked with Lucia down the stairs, she could feel the heat from the flicker creeping upwards through her body—heading for her cheeks no doubt, where it would make it clear to even the most insensitive of men that she was uneasy—to put it mildly—in his presence.

Not that Marco seemed to notice. His arrival coincided with their descent and Lucia ran ahead to let him in. Politeness decreed that she offer him a drink, but he refused, saying he had the driver waiting in the car.

'Benelli has relations in the area and has arranged for both he and the driver to visit them this evening,' he added.

'Then we could take my car and I'll drop you back at your hotel later,' Paige suggested. 'That would save interrupting their evening.'

Marco seemed to find this suggestion unusual but when Paige pressed further, explaining that Lucia tired easily and would not be wanting a late night, he gave in and went out to speak to his 'courtiers' while Paige found her car keys.

'He's not used to being driven by a woman,' Lucia said gleefully as they set off on the short distance to the centre of the town. 'In fact, he refused to let me drive his car for practice when I was having lessons because he said women weren't meant to be drivers—they have too many things on their minds all the time to be able to concentrate.'

Paige glanced at her front-seat passenger, wondering how he was taking this apparently verbatim recital of his words. She saw a smile twitch at his lips and remembered the sound of his laughter. So, he liked a joke, even if it was against him, she decided, and smiled herself.

She pulled up in front of the restaurant and was flattered to find princely good manners extended to him first opening the rear door for his sister, then walking around to hold hers as she alighted.

'Thank you,' she said, wondering how long it had been since someone performed this probably meaningless courtesy for her. She had usually driven when she and James had gone out, as he'd considered a few drinks part of his relaxation routine, but he'd have wondered why she'd been taking so long getting out of the car if she'd waited for him to open the door.

In fact, he'd probably have assumed she'd lost something—and seen it as yet another example of her failure to conform to his expectations of her.

'May we sit in the courtyard out the back?' Lucia asked, peering in through the door and spying the open area beyond the main restaurant.

'Miss Morgan may prefer warmth to a draughty courtyard,' Marco replied, while Paige wondered why he'd reverted to formality.

Well, it explained him opening the car door—formality, nothing more. And why? No doubt tiredness and relief to be reunited with his sister had prompted that strange exchange, and in hindsight he'd retreated behind a wall of good manners.

'The courtyard is only open in summer,' she told Lucia, playing peacemaker before an argument began. 'Hello, Mrs Ryan. These are friends of mine—Marco and Lucia. Do you have a table for three?'

'Mrs Ryan? Now there's a good Italian name,' Marco whispered as the short, square-built woman with elaborately coiffed white hair led them to a small table at the rear of the room, and dropped three menus into the centre of it.

'She was Theresa Agnelli before she married Tom Ryan,' Paige explained. 'Although Tom does the cooking, she's the guiding force and, with her mother, taught him most of what he knows. In fact, her mother helped out in the restaurant until last year.'

'Last year? Her mother? Your Mrs Ryan looks well into her sixties.'

Paige grinned at him. He might have reverted to formality but he seemed genuinely interested in the little details of lives which touched his—even remotely.

'Mrs Ryan's sixty-eight, and still as spry and active as most forty-year-olds. She's organised a number of local people into growing vegetables for her and every morning drives around to visit them and select what she wants for the day's meals.'

Marco's brow creased.

'Small farms? Benelli showed me grazing land for sheep and cattle, but when I asked he said there are no smallholdings in this area.'

'It's not farmers Mrs Ryan visits, but ordinary householders who have vegetable plots in their backyards.' OK, so it wasn't riveting conversation, but at least talking distracted her thoughts from his blue eyes. 'In fact, we have two houses built to cater for the needs of young people with disabilities, and their gardens produce all the herbs and many of the rarer vegetables Mrs Ryan wants. Things like okra, which isn't widely grown here.'

'This is not the talk I wish to hear,' Lucia said, breaking into a conversation which didn't centre on her needs before Marco could answer. 'I want to talk of food and what we shall all eat now I'm finally out in the real world again. I shall have salad and then cake,' she announced, dropping her menu on the table and glancing at Paige, as if expecting her to argue, then at Marco, seeking an ally when it happened.

Paige pushed the menu back towards her.

'You will have a proper meal first—then perhaps Mr Ryan's diet zabaglione,' she said firmly. 'I know he makes it with an aspartame sweetener.'

'Seems my headstrong young sister has finally met her match,' Marco said, and received a glare from Lucia in reply.

'Not at all,' Paige replied. 'Lucia understands that to stay well she must watch what she eats, balance her calorie intake, restrict her fats and cut out simple sugars. That's the only way the insulin will be effective in controlling her blood glucose levels.'

Marco realised Paige was repeating this for Lucia's sake, not his, and wondered what battles had been fought to bring his sister to even this level of reluctant compliance. As Paige slipped a sheet of paper he guessed might be a diet substitution chart from her pocket and placed it unobtrusively beside her menu, he knew she'd taken on a bigger job than he'd imagined—especially given Lucia's partiality for sweets and chocolates.

'And what do you recommend for me?' he asked Paige, closing his menu and letting her decide his food intake as well.

'Let's ask Mrs Ryan what the speciality is tonight,' she suggested. 'Maybe we could all have that.'

'No, I'll have pasta,' Lucia argued. 'With broccoli, sun-dried tomatoes and pine nuts.' She poked out her tongue at Paige as if to say 'so there' then added with a long-suffering sigh, 'And the zabaglione!'

Used to his sister's behaviour when thwarted, Marco was more interested in Paige's reaction to what amounted to rudeness no matter how teasing the gesture had been. But the nurse—well, he assumed she was a trained nurse—took no notice but checked the menu once more, comparing it to the list she carried, then turning as Mrs

Ryan approached the table to consult with her about the specials for the evening.

A supremely unflappable young woman—or one who'd summed up Lucia very quickly and had learned that the best way to deal with his sister's behaviour was to ignore it. She intrigued him—this Paige Morgan. Even her name—Paige. Plain, yet soft—serene. He liked serenity—perhaps all the more because his family, himself included, were inclined to be excitable.

'It's a kind of stew,' she said, and he had to give himself a mental shake to remember what they were discussing. 'The special tonight. Like osso bucco but without the bones is how Mrs Ryan explained it.'

He nodded, catching up on the conversation before he made a fool of himself and letting Paige order for all of them. But after that she seemed to withdraw, allowing Lucia to take over, asking him questions about the family and their friends.

'I shouldn't answer you,' Marco replied, keeping his face stern but unable to stop smiling inside—so glad was he to see this irresponsible but much-loved sister. 'You've shown you didn't care about any of them, going off like that and not letting anyone know where you were.'

'I phoned Mama,' she answered sulkily. 'And asked a friend who was going to back to Italy to phone her as well.'

He must be tireder than he thought. He glanced at Paige and received a slight lift of her shoulders—a signal that said, 'I don't know about that.'

Nice shoulders but he had to follow through on Lucia's words, not be distracted by the shapely body parts of a woman he would never see again.

'You phoned Mama?' he repeated. 'When?'

'All the time. I told her not to tell a soul. I said I wouldn't phone again if she told you or anyone else and she knew I meant it. And I didn't tell her I was in Australia. The phone calls go straight through so I let her think I was travelling in Europe with some friends, but we didn't talk much about where I was and I couldn't tell her about the baby or she'd have got hysterical. She was already very angry with me.'

'Don't strangle her here in public,' Paige murmured. 'If you leave it until we get back to my place I'll say it was justifiable homicide. In fact, I may even help. I imagine it's my phone bill she's been running up with these clandestine calls.'

'Por amor di Dio.' He bit back a second, even worse oath and frowned at Paige, then turned his attention back to Lucia who at least had the grace to look embarrassed. He couldn't decide which crime was worse—his mother's deceit about this contact, although she had kept assuring him Lucia would be all right and he had wondered that she hadn't been more distressed, or Lucia calmly using someone else's phone, especially when that someone had already rescued her from who knew what kind of fate.

'If Mama had told you, you would have told Alex, or at least insisted I go home.'

'Which I shall,' he said grimly, then sat back as Mrs Ryan arrived with a plate of antipasto.

'Paige says I am too ill to travel,' Lucia snapped, ignoring the woman serving them and glaring her defiance across the table. 'I will stay here.'

'Dependent on a stranger's kindness for all your needs?'

Paige heard the disbelief in Marco's voice and turned her attention to the food, carefully considering the delights offered before selecting a piece of melon wrapped in prosciutto. The longer she could stay out of this sibling argument the better.

'Paige enjoys having me!'

With reservations, she thought, and heard Marco growl his rebuttal.

'Enjoys having to work out your menu every day, weigh your food, test your blood, probably give you your injections? Perhaps if you were self-sufficient and offered help to her she might just tolerate your company, but enjoy?'

She didn't have to glance towards Lucia to know that tears would be gathering in her eyes. Time to cut it short. She'd experienced her guest's emotional outbursts before and was too tense to cope with the dramatics of one to-night.

'Arguing won't achieve much. And Lucia is right when she says it would be unwise to travel right now. In a week or so perhaps, when we've more idea of the correct insulin levels she needs to keep in balance, but even then the journey would have to be strictly supervised to prevent either hyper- or hypoglycaemia.'

She looked at Marco, and wondered if she would be mad to voice her next thought—to encourage him to stay when he was disrupting her usually controllable body after half a day in town. She did it anyway!

'I know you spoke of having to get back to Italy, but could you delay a week? I can give you details of her regimen, and by then you'd know how it all works. I think she'll need qualified support on hand to undertake the long flight safely whenever she goes.'

'I will not go back with Marco, like a child dragged home by her big brother,' Lucia stormed. 'It is none of his business. It is not Marco who should take me back, but Alex! After all, it was his fault I had to go!'

'And a great lot of help he'd be,' Marco growled, his frustration so apparent Paige wondered they couldn't see it like a huge red cloud hovering above his head. 'He's as infantile as you are, Lucia. Does nothing but sit around and weep that you are gone. Day in and day out, phoning me to weep across the airwaves when no one else will listen to him.'

Paige pulled a face at Marco's description of this limp behaviour of the deserted groom but Lucia seemed delighted at the image, clapping her hands and uttering, 'Oh, does he really weep?' It was said in such melodramatic tones that Paige had to wonder if they might not deserve each other.

'All the time!' Marco assured her, although his voice suggested he found the behaviour more repugnant than delightful.

'Perhaps I *shall* go back to him!' Lucia announced. 'But he must come for me, and then something must be arranged. I think you are right about him helping me, though. He would not be so good with diets or tests or injections because he would not wish to hurt me.'

'More fool he,' Marco told her darkly. 'If you were my wife, I'd ring your neck for all the trouble you've caused in a fit of pique. And don't tell me about what he said or did, because I don't believe anything short of whipping you could have been enough justification to excuse your behaviour. And even that might not have been such a bad idea.'

The thought made Paige shiver, not entirely from discomfort. She waited for Lucia to erupt in her own defence, but the young woman remained silent, suspiciously so, toying with an olive, piercing it with her fork and rolling it around the plate, her gaze abstracted.

'I know!' she said at last. 'I have the most wonderful idea. Tonight you will phone Alex, Marco, and tell him where I am so he can begin his journey to rescue me, and Paige, who has months and months of holidays coming soon—beginning in one week, I think she said—will fly to Italy with us to make me eat the right things and do my finger-pricks and injections.' She clapped her hands at this example of her own cleverness and beamed at both of them. 'Is not that a grand idea?'

'No!'

'No!'

If anything, Paige decided, her no had marginally beaten Marco's, but unfortunately she couldn't think of anything to back it up. She was too stunned by Lucia's proposal and her apparent belief that both the erring Alex and the patient Paige would unquestioningly fall in with her plans.

'You cannot ask this of a woman who has already given so much of her time and patience to care for you.' Apparently Marco wasn't having trouble finding words. 'Which reminds me. Have you contributed to her housekeeping for your food? Have you even offered to pay board?'

'I took Lucia in as a guest,' Paige protested.

Lucia said furiously, drowning Paige's words, 'She asked me to stay.'

'That's getting off the subject,' Paige persisted. 'I need no repayment for a simple kindness. In fact, I've enjoyed Lucia's company.'

She ignored the dark eyebrows which flew upwards at this declaration—and the quizzical gleam in the eyes beneath them. Telling herself that good looks and smiling eyes weren't everything in a man, she went on, 'There are services which would provide a trained nurse to travel with Lucia if you can't change your plans to accompany her home.'

'May I ask one more kindness?' Marco asked, the smile she'd seen in his eyes playing about his lips. 'That you furnish me with the address or contact number of such a service so I may speak with them before I leave.'

He glanced at Lucia, sighed, then rubbed his fingers through his hair, disturbing the smoothness of it and causing that wayward lock to fall forward again. But when he spoke again it was to Paige, not his sister.

'I have to attend a conference in Switzerland at which I am speaking. That is the reason why I cannot further delay my return. I have no doubt that Alex, being as foolish as Lucia, is already making plans to come out here. I phoned him this afternoon. Can you put up with her until she is able to travel? And handle things once a decidedly damp groom arrives to offer his apologies?

'I don't envy you the job and wouldn't blame you if you moved her immediately into a hotel with a nurse-carer to look after her. Her husband's tears won't stop simply because he knows she is safe. If my phone call to him this afternoon was any indication, he will weep more than ever at the fond reunion.'

Lucia slapped at him, but she was smiling at the same time, as if the thought of a weeping husband pleased her.

'She can stay with me as long as she wishes,' Paige promised, and received a rapturous smile from Lucia and another sardonic lift of eyebrows from her brother.

'I wouldn't allow her too much leeway,' he warned, then deftly turned the conversation, as if afraid she might change her mind. He asked about the health service, the extent of its operations and the source of its funding.

'It began as a drop-in centre for the people in the area—somewhere they could meet. A few new mothers organised a playgroup for their little ones, meeting four mornings a week in the room we use as a waiting room now.'

'There was nowhere else for them—no regular facility?'

His eyes told her he was interested, not just making idle conversation, so she explained.

'They could have used one of the local church halls, I suppose—in fact, there's another playgroup in town which does use church premises, but for a small group the hall is so large, and when attendance is irregular sometimes the person rostered to tidy up is away and it doesn't get done.'

He smiled suddenly, as if his mind had made the leap across all she hadn't said.

'So the church asked them to leave?'

'Got it in one,' she said, acknowledging his perception with a dip of her head. 'At the house, if it was a mess it wasn't a big mess, and more often than not whoever arrived first the next morning cleaned it up.'

His interest must have geared up a notch, for he leaned forward.

'Or whoever was living in your flat cleaned it up. Was the house always divided? Is it owned by your government or a local authority?'

He's only asking for the sake of conversation, she told herself, but 'the house' had become such a large part of her disagreements with James that she didn't want to discuss it.

'*Vitellone all cacciatore.*' Mrs Ryan saved her from answering, arriving at the table and setting an earthenware casserole down in the middle. 'I'll get the pasta

now, but the child should eat some vitellone as well.'
She patted her own solidly rounded stomach. 'Good for
baby.'

An even greater diversion!

Lucia turned on Paige. 'How could you tell her? Talk
about me like that behind my back? It was our secret,
Paige. Only you and me were to know. You promised
me!'

Paige reached out to touch her hand, but Lucia
snatched it away.

'I've told no one,' Paige told her. 'Some women seem
to be able to sense these things. I wouldn't break my
word.'

The explanation was plainly disbelieved by Lucia who
made small grunting noises and proceeded to sulk.

'We were talking about the house,' Marco persisted.
'Take no notice of that tantrum—she's behaving like the
child Mrs Ryan called her. Tell me how the arrangement
works.'

But the mood had shifted, Lucia's small outburst reminding Paige how little she knew of these people—and
how transient their contact was likely to be. Far from
pleasing her, the thought made her feel profoundly depressed, but she tried to sound cheerful as she responded.

'I think Lucia has reason to be upset. We're out for a
dinner to celebrate the two of you being reunited and you
and I are talking shop.' She turned to Lucia, asking about
the home to which she'd return, getting on to someone
else's house instead.

It wasn't until much later, when the meal was finished
and Lucia, exhausted by the excitement of the day, had
been taken home, had had her blood tested and had received her final longer-acting insulin injection which
would see her through the night, that Paige realised the

subject hadn't been dropped at all, merely shelved by this virtual stranger who was not only disrupting her hormones but seemed intent on delving into too many other aspects of her life.

She'd suggested dropping Marco back at the hotel on their way home, but, no, he had to see Lucia's routine, he'd said, in case Paige tossed her out into the street and he was left to handle it.

Lucia had pouted again, but as they'd walked to the car she'd clung to Paige's arm, and intuition had told Paige there was more to Lucia's behaviour than petulance. The young woman had probably been thrust into too many new situations too quickly in the last few months and was suffering from an emotional overload on top of her medical condition.

'Don't be too harsh on her,' she said to Marco when Lucia had finally retired and they were walking back down the stairs. She wondered if she should offer him coffee before driving him home. They'd said no at the restaurant but that had been because Lucia had been wilting.

The woman in her wanted him to stay—only because she enjoyed his company and his arrival had made her realise she missed male company—but the nurse could see the tiredness in the lines cut more deeply into his cheeks and the shadowy darkness beneath his eyes.

'I couldn't be harsh to Lucia no matter how much she deserved it,' he answered after a pause that made her wonder what he'd been thinking. They had reached the bottom of the stairs and stood in the wide hall, the area softly lit by wall sconces. 'And there's no need for you to drive me back to the hotel. I can walk—it isn't far and I've been this way often enough to know the direction.'

So much for wanting coffee! an inner voice jeered as Paige's chest tightened slightly with disappointment.

'What time are you going back to Sydney? When is your flight?'

He took her hand in his and bent his head as if to study her fingers.

'You are anxious to be rid of at least one Alberici? I do not blame you. I must leave your town by mid-morning and will catch an evening flight home, going via Athens. I will visit Lucia again in the morning, but...'

The hesitation seemed out of character but Paige refused to prompt him. Let him come out with whatever it was himself.

She did, however, extract her hand, thinking what a strange habit this handholding was, wondering if it was typically Italian.

He stepped back, looked down at her and smiled.

'Already we have imposed on you far too much, but if I could have a little more time. Perhaps a cup of coffee? Would you like to return to the restaurant to have it?'

Of course! she decided. He needs to know more of Lucia's condition, of the regimen we've been following—that's why he wants to stay.

'I could make you coffee,' she offered. 'Real coffee, not instant, but I'm not sure if it's the type you'd prefer.'

His reply was a devastating smile. 'You ask that question of a fellow professional who has endured untold cups of the liquid hospitals call coffee? I have often considered doing a paper on it—how so many medical institutions in all parts of the globe have developed the same recipe for ruining what is such a simple drink to make.' The smile twinkled in his eyes in a way that made her stomach go into spasms and her heart begin to jitterbug.

'I'll make you coffee,' she muttered, almost running

from him, into the kitchen, busying herself, anything to prevent him guessing at her agitation.

'You want to know more about Lucia's health,' she said, when he followed her and seemed intent on helping, standing too close—getting in her way, affecting the air in some way that made it difficult for her to breathe. 'I can contact Jim Edgar, her obstetrician, and see if he can see you before he begins his rounds in the morning.'

Her companion nodded casually.

'That was to be my first question—I would appreciate you making arrangements—but it is not my main interest, for other doctors than I will be treating Lucia.'

He paused, and she waited, unable to guess what might be coming, knowing only that the sooner he was out of her house—and her life—the sooner she could return to normal. She grinned to herself, wondering if Cinderella had felt the same way as she'd fled from the ball—too far out of her league to be comfortable.

He moved away, circling the kitchen like a dog did its territory, then he selected one of the armchairs in front of the stove, shifting about until he'd comfortably disposed of his length in its depths. But all the time he watched her, and she felt his interest—not personal man-woman stuff, but interest nonetheless.

She put the two cups of coffee on the small table between the armchairs and sat down herself.

'My interest is in this house,' he told her.

'This house?' She couldn't have been more startled if he'd expressed an interest in Abyssinian ants—if such things existed. 'It's just a house—typical of many built about a hundred years ago when the town was first established. Merchants, doctors, lawyers—all the more financially successful people in town—went in for sturdy brick construction and, because they generally had large families, they built big.'

He was smiling at her in a way that made the blood sing in her veins, but she wasn't going to be diverted by musical blood and was about to explain her great-grandfather's design when he interrupted her.

'It isn't the actual building that draws my attention, but the services it offers to the community. You began to tell me of this playgroup. What is that?'

Easy question! She explained the system which enabled mothers of young and very young children to meet, providing interaction for their children, some guided play activities and an informal support group for the mothers.

'Older women pass on their experience, the women share solutions to common problems, tell what works for them in things that range from mastitis to infant colic to where to buy baby clothes made with natural fibres. The conversation ranges far and wide, and the children learn some socialising skills. It's not as formal as a kindergarten situation, and provides a sense of security for the children, allowing them to move beyond their normal boundaries because their mothers—or sometimes fathers—are present.'

'So, it began with a playgroup. Did the owner of the house simply say, ''I have a house with too many rooms—you may use one of them for this purpose''?'

She felt a frown pluck at her eyebrows. It *was* the house that was interesting him. But why?

'Yes, more or less,' she told him, then she picked up her coffee and sipped at it, determined to ignore the invisible undercurrents zapping her body. They were so strong she wondered if it was possible he couldn't feel them—but then, he had the kind of body which would zap unwary females every minute of every day, so why should he be aware of her reaction?

'Then the owner said, "Please, use another room for a nurse to see people"?' The smile accompanying the words did strange things to her toes.

But why the questions?

Paige considered how best to answer. How to reply at all when tingling toes were demanding her attention.

'More or less,' she replied, then guessed he wasn't going to leave it there. 'The town had, and still has, regular community health services—nurses who visit bedridden patients, meals-on-wheels for the elderly or those who find preparing meals difficult for other reasons. We have an outpatients service at the hospital which provides free medical attention, but...'

'But?'

His deep voice seemed to her disordered sense to caress the word.

'But it lacked cohesion.' She blurted out the words. 'No one knew what anyone else was doing—the safety net we spoke about earlier was strung so loosely there were huge gaps. The playgroup mothers began referring each other to different people and places.

'For instance, they talked about toys which helped their children's development, then someone realised that not all the families attending had the money to provide what are often very expensive age-oriented toys. And what did families whose children had passed that age group do with the old toys? The idea of a toy library came from that. It needed housing so they took over another room for that.'

She stopped abruptly, actually remembering those times when it had seemed new ideas were floated every day and everyone involved had been fired with so much enthusiasm the place had tingled with its energy.

'Go on,' he prompted, pushing his empty coffee cup away and settling back in his chair as if he had all night to listen to her prattle on about something that couldn't possibly interest him.

'We had a child with cerebral palsy, others lagging behind in their fine motor development. One of the occupational therapists at the hospital offered to come one morning a week to work with these children and select the best toys for them to take home.'

He chuckled. 'Now I am beginning to understand—I can see it spreading out like honey spilled from a jar. What other services are offered here? Do all the professionals volunteer? And who pays for the house—its rent, upkeep?'

Easy stuff this. In fact, the conversation would have been enjoyable, for she was proud of what her ad hoc group had achieved, if her mind hadn't been constantly diverted by her physical responses to this man.

'We have an aromatherapist, a physio, two other people who do therapeutic massage, one qualified doctor who also practices acupuncture and four other doctors who volunteer one afternoon a week to see patients who find the waiting time at the hospital too difficult to handle or who don't wish to go there for some other reason. And, yes, they all work for nothing.'

'And you, Paige Morgan? What is your place in all of this?'

Another smile, even more devastating than the first. Paige steeled herself against it.

'I try to draw it all together,' she explained. 'I do normal nurse stuff like dressings or injections, inoculation of the infants, that kind of thing. I also talk to people, screen those who wish to see a doctor, direct others to whatever service might prove most helpful to them. I'm officially the co-ordinator but I'm more a go-between.'

'And pay? You obviously work full time here. Is it for wages? Do the patients contribute? Does your government provide?'

She was bemused by his interest but answered anyway. Talking kept her mind off the way his fingers were intertwined, the way his hands lay so still on his knees—kept it off thinking of the warmth she'd felt when he'd held her hand in his.

'At first it was voluntary but now the government funds the co-ordinator's and the receptionist's positions and many of the patients contribute. We don't ask for money, but there's a coin box on the front counter and people drop what they can afford into it.'

'And it works?' he demanded.

She was surprised by his tone but nodded.

He sighed, then shook his head.

'It is amazing that something which has grown with so little forethought and organisation should succeed when so often similar initiatives provided by the government, in Italy anyway, have failed.'

'You know that for a fact?' she asked, startled by his statement. 'You've been involved in such a failure?'

Surely not. Studying him again, she found it impossible to link the word 'failure' with him.

'Involved in the theoretical exercise that preceded setting it up, not in its implementation,' he admitted, and sighed again.

'So Marco doesn't always get his way,' Paige said softly, but her guest didn't reply, and when she looked at him she realised his head had dropped forward onto his chest. She wasn't going to get a reply. He was asleep.

CHAPTER FIVE

PAIGE knew she should wake Marco and drive him to his hotel so he could get a proper night's rest, but she hesitated, wanting to look at him, to think about his sudden—and very temporary—advent into her life. And her reaction to it.

It's a sign I'm over James. Perhaps ready to socialise more, mix and mingle, go out with men.

She shuddered, amended the word to the singular and looked at her guest again. Prince or no prince, most men would pale into insignificance beside him, although now she studied it more closely she could see his face was too strongly defined for classical beauty and possibly too rugged for a lot of women to find handsome.

So where did the sex appeal—the magnetism—stem from? Good looks? A great body? Well, she didn't know anything about his body apart from the fact that it filled a well-tailored three-piece suit very nicely. A combination of physical attributes and some inner fire?

'I'm sorry. Did I fall asleep on you? How rude of me. It's something I trained myself to do in boring university lectures and I've kept the practice going as it's useful from time to time in hospital meetings.'

He smiled disarmingly—and tiredly—at her.

'And when women prattle on about their work,' she added, returning his smile but cautiously. 'Come along, I'll drop you back at your hotel.'

She stood up as she spoke and watched him rise, then stretch some stiffness out of his back.

It was a homely picture, a man stretching tiredly in her kitchen. Her father had often done it, before walking up the stairs to bed.

Shutting the thought of men and beds away, she led him into the hall, towards the outer door, not the stairway.

'I could walk,' he said, catching up with her, moving with her so their bodies all but brushed together.

'I'll drive you,' she said firmly, 'then phone you in the morning to tell you what I've arranged with the obstetrician. I'll also follow up on the agencies who could provide support for Lucia's journey home.'

He hesitated at that, then thanked her, again opening her car door, holding it while she got in and shutting it with firmness but no bang.

'Was Lucia right about you having time off in the near future?' he asked. 'Would it be so impossible for you to accompany her home? We would pay your fare and for your time, of course.'

The questions were so unexpected it took a moment for Paige to absorb them.

'You said yourself, or intimated, that it will be a hellish journey,' she pointed out. 'The pair of them either weeping—or—worse still, I suspect—smooching for the entire journey.'

'Smooching? I don't know the word.'

She was glad of the darkness within her small sedan for her cheeks had scorched again.

'Kissing and cuddling,' she said stiffly. 'It's probably a slang expression.'

'Ah!'

He seemed to ponder it for a moment, then returned to his original question.

'But you do have holidays? You would have the time to undertake the journey?'

'You're a persistent cuss!' she muttered at him. 'And before you ask what a cuss is, I'll tell you. It's a slang word for a person, nothing derogatory.'

'I am glad of that,' he said gravely but she didn't need to see his lips to know his smile was back in place. 'Well?'

'I suppose the answer is yes as far as time is concerned,' she admitted slowly, trying to ignore an excited voice that was yelling at her to stop arguing. No need to tell him that she'd already considered taking Lucia home—would possibly have offered if he'd phoned instead of coming so unexpectedly. Once she'd returned Lucia to the bosom of her family, she could explore Italy, perhaps go across to France, visit Paris, see something of the world as she'd intended doing before James had come along.

So why wasn't she responding more positively now he'd suggested it? Because he'd suggested it?

She pulled up in front of the hotel and turned to the visitor.

'But I don't think I want the job. In fact, I couldn't do it as a job. Lucia is a friend. If I went, I would pay my own fare.'

He shifted slightly in his seat, turning to face her.

'I would like you to consider it, Paige Morgan,' he said, ignoring her proviso, 'if only for Lucia's sake. You must have learned how volatile she is. If a nurse she did not like were to accompany her, do you think she would obey her?'

'That's moral blackmail. I can arrange for her to meet the nurse before she's due to travel—to meet several and make the choice herself.'

He smiled as if he'd won which was strange considering she thought her own argument had been the winning one, then he opened the car door and swung his legs out, turning back to say, 'Thank you for everything, from taking such care of Lucia to your company this evening and the tasks you are still undertaking for us. I shall look forward to speaking with you in the morning.'

The words were formally delivered, and the hand he offered to her was for a shake goodnight, nothing more. Paige took it, shook it and this time withdrew her own before it could be enticed to linger.

'Goodnight,' she responded, an echo in her mind, something from schooldays, adding a silent 'sweet prince'.

But there was nothing 'sweet' about the princely tactics, she realised a few days later. The humbled and repentant groom had arrived and, as Marco had predicted, had wept all over his errant bride. He'd cried for joy about the pregnancy and groaned for Lucia's pain every time Paige tested her blood or injected insulin.

'You should be learning to do this for her or insisting she do it herself,' Paige told him crossly late one afternoon when her patience had worn thin and she'd decided she had to get rid of them, even if it meant driving them to Sydney and putting them on the plane herself.

'Marco's getting a nurse for me when I go home so Alex does not need to know,' Lucia told her with a sly smile. 'Marco promised me before he left. But I think you will have to come home with me, Paige, for the nurses you are finding are not good, not—what is your word, compatible?'

'You don't have to be compatible with someone who checks your diet, tests your blood and injects insulin,'

Paige stormed. 'Whether you like the person or not, all you have to do is grin and bear it!'

The pretty lips moved into pout position.

'I will not have people near me who upset me. Dr Edgar told me that being emotional is bad for me and the baby, and how can I not be emotional if some stranger I do not like is pricking me?'

Paige sighed and shook her head, wishing Dr Edgar had told Marco the same thing. This disapproval of the available nurses was the thin edge of the wedge—a move she should have seen coming from the moment his highness had agreed to her agency suggestion with such docility. He probably knew his sister well enough to guess her reaction to being thwarted.

His phone call followed so promptly on their conversation that she wondered if Lucia had sent some message winging through space. Not that he didn't call regularly—usually speaking to her as well as to Lucia, often talking for an hour or more as if they were friends, not casual acquaintances.

'Lucia mentioned again that you have time off from your work,' he began when they'd exchanged the usual civilities and established he wanted to speak to her, not Lucia. 'Are you not well that you need a long break? Or do you have family affairs to settle? Some personal reason for taking this time off from a job you obviously enjoy?'

He sounded concerned for her, which was nice even if there was no need, but how could she explain why she was leaving a job that had come to mean so much to her. It was something she found hard to explain even to herself. She pretended it was partly because she'd worked without a break for four years, right through her relationship with James and its traumatic conclusion, determined not to let down the people she'd committed herself to serve, but deep down she knew it was more than that.

'It's more for business reasons,' she began, then wondered why she was explaining anything to this man. It was certainly nothing to do with him.

'Personal business?' he probed.

'No, it's connected to the running of the service.' He'd irritated her and she snapped the words at him.

He said in a sympathetic voice, 'Ah, it became too much for you.'

She realised she'd have to take it further, although she'd never voiced the inner uncertainties which had prompted her to make this move.

'It did not become too much for me,' she retorted, then weakened enough to admit, 'although I do need some time off. But I began to realise that it was wrong for such a diverse service to rely so heavily on the knowledge and experience of just one person.'

She hesitated, not sure if he would understand what she was trying to say, not sure why she wanted him to!

'It was probably limiting its growth as well because all it had was my vision of it. Anyway, we'd already formed a committee which now administers the government-allocated funds, and when I spoke to the committee members about my reservations they agreed and have appointed two women to take my place. It's a trial of sorts—for a few months to begin with. It's job-sharing for the appointees, but for the service it means two new people coming to it with fresh ideas.'

There was no need to add that if the trial did work she'd be unemployed. Footloose and fancy-free. Which she *thought* was what she wanted.

'It might also benefit the people who use it because it

is not good for anyone to become too reliant on any one particular person.'

His comment told her he did understand and she smiled.

'That's what I keep telling Lucia.'

'Ah, but that is different, for you would be doing her and her family a very great favour if you accompanied her to Italy. And, with the service in good hands, you could be our guest for some time. It would be my pleasure to show you something of my country.'

'I thought you worked!' she replied. '"Prince" is a title, not a job description, you said. No doctor I know has enough free time to be running a tourist around the place.'

He didn't argue but she heard a ripple of laughter echo through the phone, felt her body respond to it and reminded herself how foolish it would be to expose her hormones to him again. The phone calls were bad enough—especially as she now looked forward to them and felt flat and disappointed when he didn't phone.

Not that they spoke of personal matters or exchanged confidences. Conversations tended to be more work—or Lucia—oriented. Like tonight, when his next question was about Mrs Bevan.

'Her sister has come to live with her,' Paige told him. 'I'm so pleased for both of them as it's an ideal arrangement.'

'One you could not have organised better yourself?' he teased, and again she felt a rush of warmth, as if the conversation *was* more personal.

They said goodbye with no more mention of Lucia or the logistics of her journey home, but as Paige put down the receiver and began to prepare their evening meal she could hear the sound of his amusement lingering in her ears and imagine how his face had looked when he'd laughed.

It wasn't until she'd peeled the same carrot four times that she realised her mind wasn't on the job—and what was left of the carrot was inedible!

Without a doubt, the man had a most unsettling influence on her, and no matter how much part of her wanted to give in to Lucia's wiles, she knew she was better off with many thousands of kilometres and an ocean between herself and Marco Alberici.

It was a distance which was growing smaller with every second they spent on the plane, the ocean crossed so effortlessly it might as well not have existed. Although just how she came to be sitting in the first-class section of the huge jetliner—just *when* she'd given in—she wasn't entirely certain.

'Only one more hour and we will be in Rome!' Lucia said, her face radiant as she slipped into the empty seat beside Paige and snuggled down next to her. 'Silly Alex is asleep, but I am too excited. You are excited, Paige?'

'I suppose so,' Paige agreed, not adding that she was even more relieved. The task of keeping Lucia stable had been more difficult than she'd imagined, and she'd be thankful to get her patient back down to earth and delivered into the hands of whoever would monitor the rest of her pregnancy.

'Do you think my mother will come to Rome to meet us, or will Marco arrange a car and driver to collect us and make Mama wait at home?'

'I've no idea,' Paige told, pleased that Marco meeting them in person wasn't listed as a possibility. She began to wonder if she could hand Lucia over and leave immediately—well, she'd have to run through the regimen Lucia was on, but as soon as she'd done that...

However, it was Marco she saw as she wheeled her suitcase out of customs, although Lucia hadn't spotted him, running instead to a slight attractive woman who stood a little to the right of him.

'We will travel north in two cars,' he announced, after shaking Paige's hand in welcome and taking her case from her suddenly nerveless fingers. 'Lucia will wish to chatter to her mother and Alex will doubtless want to stay with her, so I will take you.'

'But Lucia—she's still my patient, I assume. Shouldn't I stay with her?'

He smiled, ignored her objection and introduced her to his mother who was voluble in her praise—and as fluent in English as her son and daughter.

'You will go with Marco in his car.' The older woman repeated Marco's plans. 'And worry no more about Lucia for we have a niece of mine, a nurse, who will care for Lucia. She is older than Lucia—with two nearly grown-up sons—but she had the same problem in her pregnancies so knows exactly what to do for Lucia. She is in the car, awaiting us, and as the journey is only a short few hours she can watch Lucia as we travel while you begin a holiday. You will see something of our country as Lucia was seeing yours before she became ill.'

It seemed a strange way of looking at the runaway bride scenario, Paige thought, smiling to herself as Lucia's mother proceeded to bustle them out of the airport and into cars.

'She amuses you, my mother?' Marco asked as he lifted her suitcase into the boot.

'No, of course not but, seeing her in action, it's obvious where you and Lucia get your organising ability.'

He stepped towards her, grave, not smiling.

'We have organised you too much? Persuaded you against your will?'

Paige shrugged. Now she was actually here, within range of whatever it was that attracted her to him, she remembered why she hadn't wanted to come. But, to be honest, since she'd said finally given in to the combined pleas of Marco, Lucia and Alex, a very real excitement had been building within her.

And she should admit it. She sniffed the air—kerosene fumes, like any other airport—but couldn't she smell a hint of Rome as well?

'No, I'm happy to be here,' she told him. 'It's just strange to be transported to a place that's been a familiar name for as long as I can remember.'

'Roma! Rome, as you call it.' His eyes looked deep into hers for a moment. 'It will be my privilege to show it to you, but first we go to my home. Lucia has told you about it? It is a small place beyond Spoleto in Umbria, more a village that has grown too big to be a village yet not big enough to be a town in the real sense. In Umbria we have cheap power from the rivers so industry has grown up in the valleys near them. This has provided jobs, brought new people to the area.'

He hesitated and Paige had the impression that he'd been about to say something else—about either the people or the town—but he turned the conversation sideways, asking, 'Has Lucia talked much about it?'

'About Spoleto, which, I gather, is Alex's home,' Paige said. 'I looked it up in the atlas. It's up the Via Flamina, a town strategically placed to protect one of the great Roman ways.'

Marco seemed pleased but said nothing, merely opened the car door for her and waited until she was comfortable before closing it. The car smelt rich—leather seats, no doubt—and the wood panelling on the dash-board shone with a deep lustre. All of which distracted her from watching him as he walked around the bonnet, but when he slid in behind the wheel the car lost its sensory appeal, all her receptors being too occupied with the driver.

'It is not a great Roman way but a motorway on which we begin our journey. Like all cities, getting in and out is difficult. You will talk while I concentrate on the traffic. Tell me how the flight progressed, how Lucia's health is now.'

Paige should have objected to the peremptory tone but talking was probably a good idea. And looking around, even if it was only at an Italian motorway and Italian traffic, was an even better idea as Marco's body was like a magnet to her eyes and if she wasn't careful she'd be sitting and staring at him for the 'few short hours' it took to reach his home.

'The flight went better than I thought it would,' she admitted. 'I took a good supply of food in case we were delayed anywhere and I waited until Lucia's meals were served before giving her the quick-acting insulin. Funny things were different, though. Because of the pressuris-ation in the plane, you have to inject less air into the vials than usual before withdrawing the insulin. Small adaptations to be made.'

'But you handled them.' He sounded pleased by her competence, though he must have assumed it to entrust his sister to her care.

'I did—and even managed to persuade both Alex, who has no great taste for exercise either, and Lucia to walk around the interior of the airports where we had short fuel stops. That was another difference in the plane.

Although she did agree to do half an hour of walking around the cabin every six hours, the exercise had less effect on her glucose levels than a similar walk did at home.'

He glanced her way again and she could read his interest on his face.

'Something to do with different atmospheric conditions perhaps?'

He smiled and Paige's heart teetered on the brink of chaos, though there was no leap of imagination which could make talk of atmospheric conditions at all seductive!

'I guess so,' she managed. 'Or perhaps she needs more exercise at this stage. I've tried to tell her about the possibility of having a large baby and the importance of watching the weight she puts on, but exercise and Lucia?'

'A tough task,' he agreed, 'although now she is home perhaps she will swim. Nicolette, my cousin, will see she does whatever is necessary. Is Lucia aware she might need to have a Caesarean birth?'

That was better—medical matters could distract more of her attention from the company.

'Dr Edgar realised he wouldn't be treating her all through her confinement so I doubt he mentioned it. Mind you, with Lucia's obsession about not inflicting injury on her body, it might not be a bad idea to tell her of the possibility. It might make exercise seem more enticing.'

Marco chuckled, echoing the word 'enticing' in equally enticing tones, tilting Paige's mind back towards his physical appeal.

'And her blood glucose? It's holding down at reasonable levels?'

That told her where his mind was centred, and that any

physical sensations she might be experiencing were definitely one-sided. Yet when they'd spoken on the phone those nights his interest had often veered towards the personal, his desire for her to undertake the journey seemingly centred on more than concern for Lucia's health.

Or had she read more into his words than he'd intended? Allowed herself to drift into a fairytale again...

She sighed inwardly, and tried to dredge up some enthusiasm for this technical discussion of Lucia's health.

'Between four and eight—though more often close to eight. I've been afraid to raise the insulin level too quickly in case she began to suffer hypos. In the beginning she was very unstable, but by the time we left Dr Edgar seemed content with the way the pregnancy is progressing and the scans show no sign of distress in, or damage to, the foetus.'

A car shot past her window, frightening her with its speed and sudden appearance. Of course, she'd have to rethink the traffic conditions in view of the left-hand driving—would she drive her herself, perhaps hire a car? What plans had the family made? And should she go along with them or obey the dictates of common sense and remove herself from his home as fast as possible?

She glanced at Marco who was concentrating on the road, his long slender fingers resting lightly on the steering wheel. Get out, her head replied to the unasked question. A.S.A.P. But the yearning inside her heart suggested a different answer. She looked away before her eyes could be tempted to study his face in more detail, determine why the combination of his features provided such potency, and stared out the window where another feeder lane was pouring more traffic onto the concrete ribbon of road.

'Does your cousin speak English or should I write down the routine I've been following with Lucia and get you to translate it for her?'

She felt his movement and turned as he looked towards her—and smiled.

'The perfect nurse,' he teased. 'Always thinking of the patient.'

She held her body very still as she dealt with the shock waves of that smile.

'Yes, she speaks English. My grandmother—and hers—was English so we all visited England often and learned from her when we were children. In fact, we had an English nanny for a while who also taught us at home until my father decided we should attend the local school. My older sisters and I, that is. Lucia was a late baby—which might explain why she has been perhaps more pampered than the rest of us and is now not so independent.'

'Not so independent?' Paige repeated. 'That's the understatement of the year!'

'She has been a trial to you,' he said, those deep dark tones of empathy reverberating in his voice and crawling across her already exacerbated nerves. 'I am sorry.'

'She hasn't been that bad,' Paige responded and she knew the words sounded weak enough for him to disbelieve them where, in truth, the weakness had another source. Himself!

They were off the motorway now, travelling through country so green it seemed to shimmer in the warmth of the sun. A mountain range rose to one side of them, snow sprinkled like talcum powder on the topmost peaks. Every hill, it seemed, had either the battlements of an old fortified castle on the top of it or a village clinging to its slopes. In her mind Umbria had been the colour so close to it in name, a sandy brown, taupe, golden even—sun-burnt, like parts of Australia. But this land was green—grey-green where olive trees marched up the slopes, lush emerald in the meadows where poppies and some yellow flower she couldn't identify grew wild.

And the stones of the old buildings were white or pink, the colours muted by age but warm, inviting—welcom-ing. Marco was forgotten—well, almost forgotten—as she relaxed back into the seat and let these first visual impressions of this foreign land flood her senses.

Marco smiled to himself as he glanced at his guest. So, the magic was working on her. He'd often wondered how other people saw his country—whether they felt the physical renewal which came over him as he drove through the countryside after even a short absence. Today he'd deliberately chosen the longer way home, taken a smaller road which led through villages and wound along the valley beneath the Sibilline range.

Originally, he'd thought it would give him time to broach the subject of the job he wanted her to do, but now she was here he was uncertain about it. Not so much about the task he wished her to undertake for him, but about having this woman in his home for any length of time. She intrigued him, fascinated him—attracted him, if the truth be told—but instinct told him she wasn't a woman with whom one could carry on a light-hearted affair then say goodbye without regrets.

This was a love-and-marriage type of woman, and his own family history had proved that marrying outside one's own nationality—even province, his mother said—was fraught with danger.

'Oh, Marco, it is beautiful!'

She turned towards him, her cheeks flushed and her eyes bright with pleasure, breathing the words in a tone of such wonder he was tempted to forget the danger, stop the car and cover those soft lips with his.

'Not what you expected?' he asked instead, absurdly pleased by her pleasure.

'Not at all,' she said, smiling at him, the rose colour deepening in her cheeks and the green of her eyes matching the grass beyond the windows.

He breathed deeply, reminded himself that driving along narrow winding roads required all of his attention and began to play the host.

'That high peak is Mt Sibillini, the cluster of mountains called the Sibillini range although they are part of the Apennine range which forms the backbone of Italy.'

Did he sound like a tour guide? Most likely, but that was too bad. It was better than sounding like a lover!

'The river is the Tessino and we follow its valley to Spoleto and beyond that town to my home. Spoleto is a very old town. It was very conscious of its importance in Roman times, and people from Spoleto thought themselves immensely superior to those of Perugia and Assisi.'

He glanced towards his guest and saw a smile make tiny creases in her cheeks. He guessed what she was thinking!

'I am not of Spoleto but a village beyond it,' he reminded her. 'Different situation altogether.'

She turned towards him and he saw the whole smile instead of just a part of it.

'Oh, I'm sure of that,' she replied with mocking gravity, although the glint of gold in her eyes told of silent laughter.

'Well, it is!' he said, a little piqued but pleased as well that they could enjoy a joke together.

'See that red tiled building beyond the grove of olive

trees?' he said as they drew closer to the new village. 'That is the factory, the *fabbrica*, my grandfather built after the Second World War. He was careful to site it so it did not stand out too much and design it so it looked like a farm complex, not a factory.'

'It certainly doesn't yell ''industrial area'' as you drive past, which so many of our factory complexes do,' Paige agreed, studying the area as they travelled slowly by, then turning her head towards him. 'Lucia told me your father died some years ago. Are you involved with the running of the factory?'

'Not in any administrative capacity, although all the family members are on the board. One of my sisters runs the place now, and does an excellent job. It was she who inherited the family's business acumen and we all acknowledge how fortunate we are to have her.'

Paige chuckled, a sound that reminded him of the sound of a spring on the hill above his home.

'That doesn't sound at all like my preconceived notion of an Italian man speaking. For some reason, the image is always of the ''bed and kitchen'' breed.'

'Bed and kitchen?' he teased, wanting to see the colour deepen in her cheeks. 'A woman's place is in the home— that kind of thing? Yes, we do tend to think in stereotypes of different nationalities. You weren't my idea of a sun-bronzed Aussie.'

She laughed again, and the colour did chase across her cheeks. Alluring. Intoxicating.

Dangerous!

'So we're even,' she declared. 'Tell me about the factory your sister runs so well.'

He talked about it, about the footwear they manufactured, mostly school shoes and children's shoes, about the competition from the American-style 'labels' and keeping abreast of current trends. He could feel his body relaxing now they were close to home, now his guest was less tense and more aware of her surroundings—admiring them, excited by the beauty.

Perhaps he should let his little corner of Italy work its magic before mentioning the project. Yes, he could spare an extra few days to show her around, take her to Assisi and Norcia, perhaps up the mountains for a night, then broach the subject when she was hooked on Italy—hooked enough to want to stay a while.

CHAPTER SIX

'YOUR house?'

Paige whispered the words, awed by the beauty of the surroundings and by the sight of the modern house built to blend with the natural landscape yet take advantage of the views of the mountains and deep cleft of the valley.

'You're surprised?'

She glanced at Marco, saw the smile on his lips and read his love for his home in the way he looked ahead.

'Well, we've driven past enough old castles for me to wonder if perhaps they were all inhabited by princes, dukes, counts and other titled gents, but this, it's breath-taking—the view, the way the house nestles into the hill as if it's part of it.'

'Much of it is,' he told her, stopping the car on a wide sweep of gravelled drive in front of shallow stone steps which led up to a long, sun-washed terrace. 'The structure of the old house was weakened in an earthquake, and our local engineers and architects now tie the houses more firmly to the ground, although still allowing for flexibility so walls will sway rather than crack. We have used more timber than many Italian houses for that same reason, but tried to keep the ambience of our old home.'

He fell silent after this explanation but remained in the car, and she sensed he wanted her to take it all in—to like his house, in fact.

'The view helps,' she said, turning once again towards the range of mountains, yet knowing that from the terrace she would see down the valley over which the house stood guard and the village they'd passed only minutes earlier, a tumble of old houses, the mountain road widening to a piazza between the shops and cafés, then narrowing again, twisting once more before reaching this point. And beyond that, the newer village near the factory. Or would it be invisible from up here?

'It *is* special,' he agreed, and now he did get out, walking around the car to open her door then leading her up the steps and along the terrace to the far end, where she could see not only down the valley but higher up to where water tumbled down the rocky cleft, the sound of it reaching her ears like the distant notes of a familiar melody.

'Welcome to my home,' he said with great formality, and she sensed that was how it was to be between them and was thankful. Well, she told herself she was thankful because 'formal' would provide a mask behind which she could safely hide her attraction to him. But there was disappointment present as well, like the momentary sense of regret on waking from a pleasant dream, an illusion pricked as easily as a bright-coloured bubble.

'Thank you,' she said, shutting the book on the fairy-tale and deciding to make the most of the short stay she would have in this magical place. She walked back towards the car, knowing he'd flipped a switch which had released the lock on the boot before getting out. She'd get her case, show him she didn't need his little courtesies—didn't want them as they confused her already overreacting body into thinking things it shouldn't.

'I will see to your case, but first you must come inside, walk through the house with me so you know your way around and feel at home in it.'

Which is the very last thing I want to feel, she mused.

But she couldn't argue with her host who was only being polite—and formal!

He took her elbow and steered her towards a wooden door which was already open as if to welcome its master. The ochre-coloured tiles which paved the terrace continued inside, leading into a massive front hall. In the very centre was a square carpet, brightly woven in green and blue, and on it a table which held, beside an arrangement of wild poppies interspersed with what looked like grass and wheat, a jumble of mail, a woman's hat and a child's ragged doll.

It was homely, she realised, in spite of the formidable size—the little bits of untidiness not detracting from the perfection of the entry but adding warmth to it.

'This is the vestibule.' Marco pointed out the obvious, then waved his hand to indicate direction. 'On the right we have the living room, then dining room, all open space because the old house had small rooms and my mother wanted space around her. These rooms lead onto the terrace, while on the left my study and the kitchen open out to the garden and pool area.'

They looked into all the rooms, before crossing the entry to stairs which gave the appearance of being suspended in space.

'Upstairs are bedrooms and bathrooms and beyond them, on that level, one of my sisters has an apartment, then above that on the next level there are rooms for guests where Lucia and Alex will stay while Nicolette learns from you about Lucia's care.'

Paige shook her head.

'You've lost me. Do all these people come in and out through here?'

He smiled at the question and led her up the stairs.

'You will understand the levels when you see them.

All are connected through hallways and the outer terraces but within themselves they are private and self-contained. They are also accessible from the road which goes beyond where we stopped—in fact, to the very top of the mountain.'

'So, it's three houses in one,' she said, hoping she wasn't showing open-mouthed astonishment at the bedroom Marco had entered.

'Four, actually, because my mother's quarters, beyond the kitchen, are also self-contained, although she and I share one cook and gardener and usually eat together in the main dining room. Tonight you will meet us all for, with Lucia's return, the family will gather. This room will suit you?'

She looked at the solid four-poster bed with its net of brilliant white, its snowy embroidered quilt and lace-trimmed pillows. She bit back a comment that it looked too bridal, flushed at the thought and turned hurriedly towards the windows.

'It's unbelievable,' she murmured, forcing out the words through lips which had become uncomfortably dry. It was the bed, and errant images superimposed on it which had caused the trouble. And Marco standing there—so at ease in his own territory it added an extra dimension to his attraction.

'I'm glad you are pleased,' he said, coming closer to peer over her shoulder as if to check the view was still where it should be. 'I would like you to be happy here.'

The sentence jarred—or was it something in his voice which put her senses on alert? Yet there'd been sincerity in the remark as well, and that deserved a truthful answer.

'It would be hard not to be,' she said. 'Such comfort and such beauty. But I won't stay long. Your family has had enough disruption recently with Lucia's disappearance, then coping with the knowledge of her condition. Once I've explained things to Nicolette I'll be on my way. I've made some plans to travel now that I'm over here.'

It wasn't quite a lie, as she did plan to travel, although where and when and for how long she'd been unable to decide—her mind refusing to tackle the multitude of choices Europe offered the first-time visitor.

When he didn't reply she turned and looked at him, catching a slight frown, quickly erased, between his eyebrows.

'Of course, it is up to you, but I have free time now the conference is over. I was hoping to show you what this area has to offer. It is not as well known to tourists as Tuscany, although in my mind it has as much beauty and antiquity.'

Another warning sounded inside her head, but all the man was offering was simple kindness born of a desire that others might appreciate the attractions of the country he loved. She'd done the same herself, driving Lucia on weekends to the national parks near her home town, showing her the rugged beauty of the landscape, the chasms down which wild waters plunged and roared.

'That's very kind,' Paige answered, trying for a formality to match his earlier behaviour. 'Now, perhaps I should unpack then see if the other car has arrived. The sooner I can talk to Nicolette, the sooner we can get Lucia settled between us.'

'You should rest, not concern yourself about Lucia,' he chided, standing far too close and showing no inclination to take the hint and fetch her suitcase from the car.

'I'm far too hyped-up to rest, although a shower would be nice.' She'd get the case herself—after all, it was what she'd intended doing. But even when she walked towards the door Marco remained where he was by the window, staring, not at the view but at her, as if confused by who she was or what she was doing in his house.

'I'm sorry.' He came to with an almost visible start. 'Aldo should by now have brought your case inside. No doubt it is in the hall.' He was all business again, but the look she'd seen in his eyes a second earlier had been personal—almost sexual in its appraisal—as if his thoughts had strayed a long way from formality.

He'd have to stop thinking about her as a woman— consider her as a colleague, nothing more. Or perhaps a friend of Lucia's. He'd handled dozens of the pretty young things honing their flirting skills on a safe 'big brother' figure. Not that Paige Morgan could be classed as a 'pretty young thing'—she was attractive more than pretty, but it was her colouring that fascinated him—the pale rose of her lips, the way a darker shade of that same colour washed her cheeks, the gold-flecked green eyes and shiny, silken hair.

Nor had she had done any flirting. Had that added to his interest in her physical charms—the casual indifference with which she treated him?

He found her suitcase outside the door and carried it into the room, lifting it onto the low table at the end of the bed. And he'd better keep out of this room, for the vision he'd had earlier of corn-coloured hair spread across those white pillows had seriously threatened his intention to treat her formally.

'I will be downstairs. A light luncheon will be served at one, but if you are tired and wish to sleep, Mirelle will fix you something to eat later in the afternoon.'

She smiled at him, which made him forget the formality decision once again.

'I understand the rule with international travel is to try to get into step with the new time zone as soon as possible so, inviting though that bed looks, I won't sleep until later.'

'Perhaps after lunch,' he replied. 'That would be falling into the natural rhythms of this country for we still follow the custom of the long lunch.'

'You sleep after lunch?' she challenged, her eyes glinting with a teasing mischief.

'I rest and read, perhaps do book-work. You will find all business stops here, even doctoring.'

'And surgery? Are patients scheduled around this long lunch?'

Her interest was apparent in her voice, and he hoped she would stay for he'd like to show her around the private hospital in Terni where he had worked for many years. Still could work in the future, if everything else fell into place.

'Like travellers avoiding jet lag, we try to keep our hospital routines as much as possible in keeping with the patients' natural way of life, although, like all such places, they are woken early by the business of the day. So, yes, in many hospitals we take two or even three hours off at lunchtime, although when the theatres are busy patients are scheduled right through this time to maximise use of the facilities.'

Paige listened to his voice—heard the words and stored away the information—but it was the lilting cadences which held her, the slightly different intonations and phrasing, like music that is unfamiliar yet intensely pleasing to the ear.

'I'd like to see an Italian hospital,' she heard herself say, and knew immediately it was a tactical error because it was committing her to stay beyond the strict limit of the time needed for handing over Lucia's supervision, prolonging her stay within the range of the spell this man could so effortlessly cast about her body. 'I might do that later when I'm in Rome,' she added in a desperate attempt to regroup.

'Are you in such a hurry you must rush away from here?' Marco replied. 'Is there someone awaiting your return? A lover perhaps?'

Surprise made her flick her eyes to his. She saw a confusion there which equalled her own. He hadn't meant to say that. Looked remorseful. Perhaps Lucia had told him of James and he was sorry for her. Well, she didn't want his sympathy.

Just his body, a teasing voice whispered in her head.

She hid a rueful smile and turned her attention to her suitcase, unzipping it, pretending she wasn't perturbed at all.

'I'm in no hurry,' she said airily, 'but I won't trespass on your family's good nature for too long.' Now she looked at him and let him see the smile. 'I may not be a sun-bronzed Aussie, but I'm an independent one.'

He returned her smile with a devastating one of his own.

'That's offering me a challenge, Paige Morgan. I shall have to see what I can do to change your mind.'

And on that cryptic note he walked from the room, leaving Paige to stare after him, her mind telling her body he hadn't meant it the way he'd made it sound—or the way she'd wanted it to sound.

She showered and debated what one wore to a family lunch in Italy. Not jeans, she decided, selecting a long, button-through linen skirt the colour of ripe wheat and teaming it with a paler yellow blouse. At lunch she would sit beside Nicolette and explain Lucia's routine, after which she would no longer feel obliged to stay.

Politeness decreed she remain at least one night—possibly two—but no more.

'You will sit here, by Marco, as you are our honoured guest.' His mother took up the decreeing, less than an hour later. Knowing Lucia needed insulin before the meal, Paige had gone down to the big room early and had found the cousin waiting for her there. They had talked of Lucia's case and of Nicolette's own experiences with pregnancy and diabetes.

'You'll be far better qualified to help than I was,' Paige had told her, and the older woman had smiled as if pleased by the remark.

'Although I doubt she will mind me as well as she must have minded you,' she'd said, which had made Paige laugh.

'Lucia minding anyone would be a sight to see,' she'd answered. 'I found the only thing that worked was threats about losing her figure.'

'Marco told me you tried that. Yes, I can see it would work.'

The talk had become more technical, Nicolette explaining that her aunt had already arranged for an obstetrician to see Lucia and asking Paige to accompany them on their first visit the following day.

'I have read the letter Lucia brought from her doctor, and Lucia has talked of her routine. I have insulin here, but if you have brought some with you...'

She paused, as if uncertain where to draw the line between her tasks and Paige's, and Paige hastened to assure her that she could take over immediately.

'Although I'm happy to discuss anything with you if you feel at all concerned.' She held up the small case she'd carried with her on the plane. 'This is my supply of drugs. I should transfer it to the refrigerator.'

Nicolette showed her to the kitchen, where they continued their conversation, although it was carried on with difficulty as the woman preparing the meal in the kitchen, introduced as Mirelle, asked questions of Nicolette and tutted over the answers she was given, throwing up her hands and evidently praising God for either Lucia's return to the family or the news that a new baby was on the way.

The next interruption was Lucia herself, who submitted to hugs and what seemed like loud recriminations of her behaviour from Mirelle, who promptly burst into tears when Paige slid the injection under the skin of Lucia's abdomen.

'We'll talk later,' Nicolette suggested. 'Far too much commotion going on here.'

At that stage Signora Alberici had arrived on the scene, sweeping them all out of the kitchen and into the dining room.

'Nicolette, you will sit by Lucia, with Alex between you and Miss Morgan.' Signora Alberici continued her arrangements. 'I shall take my place on Marco's left and there will be no talk of Lucia's illness or condition at this table. After we have rested, Nicolette and Miss Morgan can confer again.'

Paige hid a smile—well, it was hidden until she glanced at Marco and he winked at her.

'Miss Morgan thinks Lucia and I get our organising ability from you,' he teased his mother.

'Miss Morgan is too formal,' Paige protested, trying to cover what might seem like rudeness to the older woman. 'Please, call me by my first name, Paige.'

'It is an attractive name. It is often used in your family?'

It was an innocent query, but somehow, as lunch progressed, Paige realised that Marco's mother was not only a good organiser but was also adept at wheedling information out of her guests. The family now knew of her mother's early death, her upbringing by her adored father, the reasons for her decision to nurse rather than practise medicine as he had—most of the details of her life, in fact, apart from James!

'You will want to lie down, tired from all that questioning?' Marco asked as they left the dining room after a lunch which had offered an array of meats, salads, breads and luscious cheeses.

'I need exercise more than a rest,' Paige told him. 'I've eaten more than I do in a week and, to top it off, had wine at lunchtime! May I walk on up the road to the top of the hill?'

He smiled at her.

'You may do whatever you wish, Paige, for we would like you to treat this house as your own.' Once again he hesitated, then he smiled, triggering the sweep of sensory responses Paige had hoped she'd had under control. 'But the road is a dull walk on such a nice day. I know a better one through the fields if you could bear my company.'

'Typical Alberici way of putting something,' Paige scolded. 'If I say no, it will sound as if your company is insupportable. Lucia would do the same thing to me. You're all too good at painting people into corners.'

His smile widened, lit his eyes and twinkled down at her, sending heat coursing through her blood.

'So you do not find my company insupportable?'

'Not *all* the time,' she told him, wondering why she'd

let herself be drawn into this conversation. She should
have said she was going to rest, or that she wanted to be
on her own while she walked. But neither answer would
have been true. The part of her which advocated half a
loaf was better than no bread was clamouring to walk the
mountain fields with him—though she guessed he
wouldn't take kindly to being compared to bread.

'Shall we go?'

She shrugged, trying for casual and missing by a mile,
especially when he led her to a hat stand in the front hall
and chose a wide-brimmed raffia hat.

'It is a new one—my mother keeps a couple here for
guests such as yourself, a gift from Casa Alberici.' He
came towards her and set the hat on her head, standing
so close she could see the rise and fall of his chest
through the grey silky-knit shirt he was wearing. She felt
the hat settle on her head, then the warmth of his fingers
brushing her cheek as he tucked away a stray strand of
hair.

'You improve the hat's beauty,' he said softly, and her
body forgot all her mind's warnings about this man and
went through a melting routine so unfamiliar she wondered if she might be sickening for something.

Or perhaps jet lag had symptoms like this. She *should*
have rested!

'Come!'

He spoke softly, took her hand—that handholding
thing again—and led her out the front door, taking the
road for about twenty yards then heading off it to the
right along a path towards a small stream which gurgled
over satiny rocks.

'I must be back to speak to Nicolette when Lucia's
blood test is due,' she said, forcing her mind from hand-

holding and hot blood. She told herself it was a local custom and meant nothing to him.

'I shall have you back in time,' Marco promised, then he pointed to a peak and gave its name, taking his role as a guide seriously.

They crossed the stream, his hand providing support, but ahead the path narrowed and she was relieved to find they had to walk in single file—and, in order to do that, not hold hands.

But the thankfulness didn't last long for now she walked behind him, her eyes drawn to the way he moved, to shoulders wide enough to hold the world—although that was Greek legend, wasn't it—not fairytales?

'So, from my mother's probing, I gather the house I thought was owned perhaps by the government or some agency is, in fact, yours,' he said, when the ground flattened out and they could once again walk abreast.

Again that interest in her house. Well, it was far safer for her mind to puzzle over that than to think about his back and shoulders.

'Yes. It was too big for one person, and at the time I didn't want to sell it so I let the health service gradually take over most of the downstairs area.'

'Did you never think you'd have a family and need all those rooms?' he asked, and she hoped he hadn't seen her shiver.

'There's plenty of space for a family in the rest of the house. A formal living room and a conservatory which could be used as a dining room downstairs, plus four bedrooms and the small sitting room upstairs.'

He smiled at her.

'You sound defensive, Paige. Has someone, in the past, criticised your generosity in letting the service use the house, or do you sometimes wonder why you made such a splendid gesture? Do the people who fill your home aggravate you from time to time?'

She half smiled as she heard the echoes of James's outrage when she'd said she wanted to allow the community service to continue to operate there.

'But how can we entertain—have guests up from the city for weekends and functions—if your rabble is inhabiting half our house?' he'd said, and at that moment, well before she'd known about Gayle Sweeney, she'd wondered if marriage to James was really what she wanted.

'No, the people could never aggravate me,' she answered, tucking the memory back where it belonged—in the past.

'I thought not,' he said, and she caught a note of satisfaction in his voice, as if she'd confirmed some judgement he didn't mean to share with her.

They walked on again, the talk turning once again from work to the beauty of the countryside through which they strolled, although every now and then some comment made her realise that he was still thinking of the service—or the house from which it operated. In fact, the comments were so entwined she wondered if perhaps her brain was misbehaving—that she was imagining the double layering of the conversation.

'The Apennines run down the centre of Italy like a spine.' That was one example, for he followed it with a question unrelated to the view. 'Do you think people come because it *is* a house? Did you consider this in the early days, that, like the church hall proved too big for your playgroup, an office somewhere might have intimidated them and stopped the work before it began?'

Definitely not her imagination! She made the leap with

him, but *her* mind was on the beauty of the mountains which shed a kind of calm across her agitated soul.

'Yes, I think the house does make a difference. It's less formal so people feel more as if they're dropping in on a friend rather than consulting, in inverted commas. It's also geographically central to the poorer area of the town which was another plus. If it was too much effort to get there, a large number of our clients wouldn't come.'

He seemed to consider this for a while, then nodded as if satisfied by the tenor of his thoughts—but kept them private, not speaking again until the full glory of the view was revealed.

'So, now we are on top of the world, as you see,' he said. They had reached the summit and serried rows of mountains marched across in front of them rising ever higher and higher towards the Alps, while below them, the valley lay spread like a multi-patterned and layered cloth beneath their feet.

'It's beautiful,' Paige breathed, turning slowly around through three hundred and sixty degrees to appreciate every angle of the magical view.

'Yes,' Marco responded, but his eyes were on her, not the view, and a huskiness in his voice made her heart flutter wildly. More jet lag—or perhaps altitude this time?

To cover her confusion, she bent and plucked a poppy, then another. With a small handful she straightened up to admire their fragile petals, and released them from suddenly nerveless fingers when Marco reached out for them.

She should walk away, look again at the mountains, start back down the track, but she couldn't move, held by some strange magic the place—or perhaps the company—had woven around her. He stepped closer, and she saw him lift his hand, felt the pressure as he tucked a poppy in her hat, then another and another.

'Very pretty,' he said, as if satisfied at what he'd done, but he didn't step away from her and her taut nerves screamed for release. She should have moved, but didn't. Instead she watched his hand rise again—one poppy left—and felt his fingers gently touch her skin as he tucked it, as red as blood, as bright as a flag of danger, into the opening of her shirt, the stem tickling at the cleft between her breasts, her body growing heavy with an aching need for more caresses.

'Beautiful,' he whispered, and this time she did move—stepping back, away from him, before he felt the tension of her need, the tightness of her nerves and flesh and sinews, the clammy heat which flooded through her body.

'Yes, it is,' she managed to say, pretending it was the view all the time which had interested him.

And perhaps it was. Perhaps to think anything else was to believe in fairytales.

CHAPTER SEVEN

WHICH could come true, Paige started to believe as the few days she'd intended staying slowly slipped into a week. She'd met Marco's other sisters, their husbands and the three small grandchildren that first evening. The chatter at the table, mostly in English for her benefit but with lapses into the musical beauty of Italian, had fascinated her. An only child of only children, she'd seen little of the interaction of an extended family, the warmth, support and security it offered, even when they were teasing each other or arguing volubly over their differences.

'And how you stayed sane with Lucia in your home for a whole month is beyond us all,' Paola exclaimed, when Paige had been drawn into telling how she'd met their sister.

The others agreed despite Lucia's protests and Alex's strong defence of his wife.

'I enjoyed having her stay with me,' Paige explained, but this, too, was howled down in disbelief and mirth.

'Unless you are a saint,' Anna, the younger, quieter sister suggested.

'Or a very special person,' Marco put in, and a certain huskiness in his voice made her shiver.

Thinking about that dinner party now, seven days later, Paige realised how often those words had repeated themselves in her head. Not that he'd meant them to be memorable, any more than he'd intended the glance he'd sent her way to carry a special message. But her silly heart had leapt with hope—only she hadn't realised it was hope until she'd analysed her feelings later. She'd assumed it was the same physical reaction he'd been causing since their first meeting.

Now, after a week spent mostly in his company, tasting wine in cellars tunnelled deep into the ground, climbing to the tops of peaks to breathe in the sharp cold air and dazzle the eyes with the beauty of the mountains, walking down the narrow, cobbled streets of tiny hill villages and standing on the ramparts of castles built as fortresses to withstand sieges in harsh and bloodier times, the hope had died, for there'd been no hint that the attraction she felt might be returned.

Although that wasn't entirely true. As they'd walked a wooded path at Monteluco, she'd seen a bird and had stopped suddenly, not wanting to frighten it away, and Marco had walked into her, taken her shoulders to steady himself and held her close for a moment. The tension in his body had communicated itself to her, and she'd half turned her head to see if she could guess what he was thinking and had caught a blaze of what had looked like desire flaring in his eyes.

Her breath held, Paige had waited, wanting the kiss his eyes were signalling, her body trembling with a need to be spun around and held against him so their shapes fitted and their bodies could feed each other's hunger.

But the blaze had died.

Quenched?

Or never there at all? A figment of her overactive imagination? Another fantasy?

Then at Assisi, late in the afternoon after the tourists had departed, they'd knelt in the tiny chapel where the gentlest of saints had died, and Marco had put his arm around her shoulders, a silent pledge of something she couldn't understand. Friendship perhaps, although her heart had whispered love, for in that sacred place there'd been no physical awareness—lust at bay for those precious moments.

However, apart from those two incidents, he'd become less personal in his attention, less likely to take her hand in his or slip flowers between her breasts.

Which made things worse for her, not better, for she, too, had stood apart and studied him—a prince who wasn't a prince—mixing and mingling with the local villagers, friends not subjects, all of whom treated him with both respect and camaraderie. He appeared to be an admirable man in every way, a pity when what she needed was something to dislike about him—a flaw to mar the image of perfection—at least one foot of clay!

'Today we will "do", as the tourists say, the new village and then enjoy a lunch in Spoleto,' he announced, meeting her at breakfast on the eighth day of her visit and bestowing on her a smile which made her mouth water.

'Surely you should be returning to work,' she argued. 'You've been very kind, but I'm beginning to feel guilty about taking up so much of your time. Not that I haven't enjoyed it, but I can't go on accepting your hospitality, doing nothing in return except disrupting your life.'

His smile slid off his face, then returned, a rueful version this time.

'Ah,' he said gravely, 'there's that, of course. But this morning it will be work for me. There are some people I must see in the new village and I thought it might interest you to accompany me. It is a situation not unlike the health service which operates from your home.'

She'd been standing by a laden sideboard, choosing fruit and crisp rolls for her breakfast—avoiding his smile, in fact—but something in his voice made her turn towards him. He sounded uncertain—which in Marco was extremely rare.

'It's a community service?'

He nodded and busied himself spreading honey on his roll. Avoiding an answer?

Intrigued, she crossed to the table and sat opposite him, nodded acceptance as he lifted the coffeepot and indicated her cup. She watched him pour her coffee, set the pot back on its heated pad in the centre of the table, then return his attention to his breakfast.

'And?'

He glanced up as if surprised by her question.

'And what?'

His face was still, his blue eyes deliberately masking any emotion.

'There's more, isn't there?' she persisted, and saw the eyes give way first, a gleam appearing fractionally before the smile.

'It doesn't work as we—or I—had hoped. I thought perhaps…' Not only uncertain but practically stuttering! Dithering!

Several pennies not only dropped but clanged, then echoed with reverberating force in her head, plunging her into such despair and uncertainty that she dropped her napkin on the table, stood up and left the room, crossing the big entry hall, heading for the terrace where the view of the mountain and the chuckle of the stream might offer solace to her wounded spirits.

Some hope! She paced the length of it, spun around to retrace her steps, trying to sort out the maelstrom of emotions bubbling and churning inside her. Marco had appeared by the door but he stopped there, not approaching, waiting for her to come to him. Which she didn't, turning short and pacing away from him.

'You are upset?' He put the obvious into words when she drew close a second time—near enough to hear his voice.

'Of course I'm upset!' she raged, flinging up her arms in a gesture which would do credit to any one of his volatile family. 'Why wouldn't I be upset?'

He approached her now, caution in every step he took, concern written clearly on his strong features.

'It is because I suggested you might like to see the health service?'

Now he sounded tentative, which *had* to be a con job. Tentative didn't feature in this man's genetic structure! Princes didn't come in tentative. Well, not the only one she knew!

She stared at him, thinking perhaps he was joking— that he must know how she was feeling.

'Because I said it wasn't running well?' he prompted, and as anger surged she felt her arms lift again.

'I don't give a damn about your service,' she stormed, 'or whether it's running well or not!' She about turned, pacing again, hoping the release of energy might loosen the knots in her intestines. Finding it didn't work as he caught up and paced beside her.

'But that was your intention all the time, wasn't it? And I should have known. Should have guessed when every second conversation was about my house and the way we'd set up our community service. I always found it strange, but did it click? Of course not. I'm too stupid!

'Not that I thought you'd phoned and talked to me, persuaded me to come for the sake of my flashing green eyes or outstanding beauty, but I thought it might be friendship! I let myself to think you were shunting me around the countryside because this imaginary friendship and your princely politeness decreed it, but you weren't, were you? You were softening me up—hoping I'd like the place, might be willing to stay a while and perhaps suggest something to help your ailing service. Was that the plot?'

She had read his thoughts—well, most of them—so accurately, Marco realised that whatever he wanted to say would now be tainted by her conclusions.

'I showed you my country with pride and love,' he said stiffly. 'I felt you would appreciate its special beauty and feel something of the pull it has for me.' He paused, feeling as shaken as if a layer of his soul had been stripped away. 'More than that, I did it in the hope that, in some small way, it might go towards a debt we can never repay—your loving care for, and attention to, Lucia. So gratitude played a part, but you are not the kind of person who accepts gratitude easily. You shrug our thanks aside, diminish what you did, which might make you feel comfortable but leaves us at a loss.'

'So, it's my fault now!' Paige retorted, reaching the end of the terrace and spinning around. He kept pace with her and as they turned he thought he read confusion in her lovely eyes. Instinct told Marco to take her in his arms until the confusion cleared, but fortunately his brain was still in partial working order and suggested he'd be compounding his mistake.

'No, there is no fault, I am simply talking. And, yes, even with so little experience of your service, I *was* impressed and I did wonder, if you agreed to accompany Lucia home, if you might have time to take a look at what we do and how we do it. I considered, with your experience, you might pick up on what we are doing wrong. Some things, I suspect, I have already learned, but fresh eyes could bring a new approach.'

She stopped pacing suddenly so he overshot her and

had to turn back to face her. Face eyes alive with anger and—disgust?

'Is the Machiavellian principle of weaving convoluted plans bred into all Italians?' she demanded. 'Did you have to do it this way? Why couldn't you have said, "Paige, I have a similar service in my home town and it isn't working. Would you be willing to take a look at it?" Would that have been so hard? Or would it have dented your pride to admit it wasn't working? You had to set me up like this? Hell's teeth, Prince Manipulator, if you'd asked I'd probably have said yes. *And* I could have claimed the cost of the trip off my tax!'

She stormed away from him again, leaving him wondering, not why he hadn't asked her outright but what on earth she meant by 'the cost of her trip'.

He asked when he caught up with her.

'I told you at the time that, if I were to take Lucia home it would be as a friend, not an employee—I *said* I would pay my own fare.'

It made no sense. Her anger must be making her irrational—and more attractive than he'd ever seen her, with the fire of her emotion flaming in her cheeks and sparkling in her eyes. Not that he would ever be able to admit that the green eyes might have played a part in all of this. Would he have worked so hard to persuade a woman less attractive to him to accompany Lucia?

'I could not countenance you undertaking a first-class journey at your own expense.' He managed to drag his disordered senses together enough to refute her foolish statement. 'I paid for all those tickets.'

'Checked your Visa account lately?' she shot back at him. 'Noticed a credit of one return first-class fare from Sydney to Rome?'

'You changed the tickets! Paid yourself! *Madonna*

mia!' He roared the accusation, the oath, at her, so hot with anger now himself he wondered he hadn't inflicted physical violence on her person.

Except to touch her—even in anger—was to invite trouble, for she affected his senses as no one ever had before, and he had to keep reminding himself that an affair wouldn't do for Paige Morgan. And anything more than an affair was so fraught with problems as to be impossible.

'Why shouldn't I?' she said pertly, and smiled because she knew, in forcing him to lose his temper, she'd won that duel.

'Because it is my responsibility to look after my family,' he pointed out, each word clipped and curt. 'Lucia is my responsibility and that was extended to you. I will not have you out of pocket because of the behaviour of my sister.'

Now she had to hide her smile.

'Can't do much about it, can you?' she sniped, then her smile faded as she added, 'And perhaps all this responsibility stuff has gone too far. Can't you see that's what has made Lucia the way she is? She's an adult. OK, a young adult at nineteen. But she's old enough to be taking responsibility for her own actions. Did you fuss over Anna and Paola in the same way, protect them from the world then thrust them into marriage with someone you'd chosen so that another dominant male could take responsibility for them?'

'I did not choose Alex for Lucia. It was not "arranged" so much as, my mother and his mother being friends, the two of them had grown to know each other.'

'Not good enough,' Paige struck back at him. 'You allowed the marriage to go ahead, knowing he was just as foolish as she was—and don't deny that because you told me so yourself!'

Her eyes challenged him but he could think of nothing in his own defence—except where his other sisters were concerned.

'Paola and Anna both chose their own husbands. They are women as independent as you yourself, university educated—which Lucia would have been if she hadn't gone her own headstrong way and insisted on marrying Alex the moment she was out of school.'

'Well, no one's going to change Lucia overnight, but you could start by stepping back and letting her and Alex make their own decisions. And, in future, think of me as one of your independent sisters, Marco, and don't take on responsibility for me, OK?'

She walked away, her pace now slowed, the movements of her body less stressed.

Enticing.

No, he could not be enticed by Paige! He'd listened to her talk about Australia, and had heard so much love in her voice at times he'd lost track of their conversation, distracted by the realisation that she felt as strongly about her homeland—even about her house—as he did about his. However much she exclaimed at or praised the beauty of his country, Australia would be tugging at her heart—as cool and misty England had beckoned to his grandmother.

It was a strange thought to be having at that moment, as most of his sexual thoughts concerning Paige Morgan had been halted by his certainty that she wasn't the type of woman to join him in a light-hearted but non-permanent affair. Permanent hadn't been an option before this morning.

Marco stared out towards the mountains and waited

for the beauty to work its magic and pacify his soul. Once upon a time that magic had worked on his body also, but since this woman with the hair like golden silk had come to stay, filling the empty corners of his house with her presence, his body had become immune to pacification, controlled only by the forceful exertions of his will-power, a lot of walking and the occasional cold shower.

Hardly appropriate at the moment!

What mattered now was to mend the rift between them. How?

What to say? To do?

How to repair the situation?

The mountains told him nothing. No oracles there to guide his way with cryptic comments.

He waited until Paige's path brought her close enough to hear his words, then said, 'You do not need to visit the service that concerns me. Or even visit Spoleto with me today. Anna is free and she has been wanting to take you to Gubbio, a favourite place of hers. Would you enjoy that?'

He'd almost added, Or would you prefer me to make arrangements for you to leave us? But the thought of her departure had become increasingly unsettling over the week she'd been with them, and he couldn't ask a question he didn't want her to answer.

'I haven't said I wouldn't see your service.'

The words flicked as sharp as stones against his already battered flesh.

'In fact, I'd be interested in it, *and* only too happy to make suggestions which might be worth a try, although I can't imagine I will be much help as an outsider, looking in. Perhaps Anna could take me there instead.'

It was the cruellest cut of all!

'You do not wish to see it with me?' The question

seemed to fly from his lips without forethought—instantly regretted as it sounded pathetic, like the cry of a child deprived of a treat.

She stared at him, her eyes assessing him as if weighing up his future trustworthiness.

'I'm still angry with you,' she warned, then she lifted her shoulders in a little gesture he'd come to know and watch for. 'But I suppose you'd be the best person to show me around.'

It was a truce of sorts—the best he could hope for at the moment.

'You should have something to eat,' he suggested, and a sidelong glance caught a smile flickering at the corner of her mouth.

'Is that damaging to your independence also?' he asked. 'Me taking responsibility again?'

She stopped and turned to him and although the words, when they came, were gravely spoken, the smile still danced in her eyes.

'I think I could accept it as the action of a concerned host,' she told him. 'Good thing I'm used to drinking cold coffee.'

Had that sounded casual enough? Paige wondered as she preceded him back to the dining room.

And why had she been so upset when she'd realised he had an ulterior motive in inviting her to accompany Lucia to Italy?

Because her stupid heart had fallen in love with the man, and love offers up any number of impossible scenarios where dreams *can* come true. But they *are* dreams, she reminded herself—doomed to that moment of waking when the magic lingers for an instant, before being lost in the reality of everyday life.

'Y-yes, thank you,' she stuttered when she realised

Marco was offering her fresh coffee before passing her a basket of warm, crusty rolls.

For a moment she was tempted to let the dream return, to imagine them as husband and wife, sharing a breakfast of coffee and rolls, at ease with each other, not tense and tetchy, their bodies perhaps filled with the warmth and satisfaction of the aftermath of lovemaking, one hunger satisfied, another tempting them to eat…

'Does a good fight before breakfast always make you hungry?'

Hungry? Had he heard her thoughts? Could she have spoken them aloud?

She looked up at Marco and then, puzzled by the amusement in his eyes, back down at her plate. She had four rolls lined up there, obviously selected by her fingers while her mind had been elsewhere.

'I was thinking of something else,' she said lamely, confused and embarrassed. She could hardly put three back when she'd already handled them.

'Keep them for the pigeons in the square,' he suggested, the laughter reaching his lips now, escaping in a low, incredibly sexy chuckle.

Stop thinking sex! she ordered herself. Think work.

'Why don't you think the service is working?' she asked, then frowned and added, 'Or should that be, why do you think the service is not working?'

'I take the point, whichever way it's phrased,' he told her, cupping his hands around his coffee cup as if to warm them and leaning towards her. 'But, if you don't mind, I would prefer you see it for yourself so you would not be swayed by my views.'

She grinned at him and said in tones of mocking wonder, 'Oh, do you think it possible people *could* be swayed by your views, Marco?'

'You are a tease, Paige Morgan. And, on top of that, a source of great annoyance to me. You have said that you are angry. Well, I, too, am angry. Paying for your own ticket was a foolish extravagance on your part.'

He didn't sound angry—more put out.

'Wounded pride, that's all you're feeling,' she retorted. 'I would probably have come to Europe even if Lucia's destiny hadn't dropped her in my lap, so I would have been paying my fare anyway.'

She'd watched him as she'd answered and both saw and sensed him biting back a cynical, 'First class?'

Just as well, for it would have started another argument—if only in defence of her own pride. Now she waited, because the conversational ball was in his court and she didn't want to argue about the travel arrangements again.

'Do you believe in destiny?'

The question was so unexpected, so far wide of the line she'd been following, she couldn't reply.

'I've never given it much thought,' Paige admitted eventually. 'I don't know if it's destiny as such which guides our lives or if we simply stumble along the path we happen to be on until something bobs up which forces us to take another track, or to detour and return later where the path is different. Then, from time to time, events erupt in our lives, making us hurry over bits which are rough, or linger longer where the track winds through nice grassy meadows.'

She could feel the heat of her own embarrassment climbing into her cheeks, couldn't look up and meet his eyes. How could she have babbled on like that?

She finished her coffee in one long draught, and pulled her handkerchief out of her pocket to wrap the bread rolls for the pigeons. The silence was growing heavier by the second.

'I suppose we should be talking about your service,' she muttered, anxious to lighten it—to clear the memory of her words from the air around them.

'Here,' Marco said, which wasn't really a reply so she had to look up from the impossible task of securing three rolls in her minuscule wrapping.

He was handing her his handkerchief, an immaculate square of white linen.

She took it, feeling more foolish by the minute, growing angry with him now for not answering her and so relieving the terrible tension.

'The public health system in Italy is always under strain so most businesses arrange private health cover for their employees.'

Release at last!

She sighed, stood up and shoved the now-wrapped rolls in her pocket, signalling she was ready to leave.

'So employees can be treated in private hospitals?'

'Exactly, but that is the easy part. The cover is also tied in with pension funds and other benefits, but in rural areas, because the family and the church have traditionally played the supportive and caring roles, such ancillary services like your meals-on-wheels and domiciliary care do not always exist.'

'Then how do you provide help for people where family support isn't available?' Damn, she was becoming interested now in spite of herself.

'That was our problem. It is all very well having the funds to provide these services to the workers who have retired or to their families, but who is to do the work where there are no generic organisations?'

'You set up something yourself?'

He shrugged.

'That is what we have tried. My father started the pension scheme but died before the use or uselessness of it became apparent. Our workforce was still young, made up in the most part of men and women from the village, but as the business grew and we had to import labour—'

'Import labour as in immigrants from other countries?' Paige asked, wondering if there were ethnic considerations to take into account.

He came around the table and stood beside her, smiling slightly as if amused by her sudden switch from prickly and defensive guest to interested professional. She could hardly explain it was a defence mechanism on her part— an attempt to wrest her mind from fairytales.

'No, but people from other regions of Italy, particularly in the south where unemployment is much higher. When these people came they needed housing. Spoleto is too far away, the old village already overcrowded because now there was employment in the area the young people were not moving away. So a new village grew around the factory, first houses for the workers, then shops, a school. There was a school in the old village as well, but it was cramped and dark so when the new school came along children from the old village also travelled to it and the edges of the new settlement and the old village became blurred.'

'Which school did you and your sisters attend?' Paige found herself asking, although it had no bearing on his story.

He smiled as if pleased she'd remembered his words, the glint in his eyes playing havoc with her resolution to stick with reality.

'The old village school. The factory was much smaller then, and most of the workers still lived here on the hill

It was to provide employment for these local people when the farming ways declined that the factory was built.'

Paige understood, remembering his talk of the 'old' system where farmers leased their land from the big land-holders, paying rent with a portion of their crops. Like sharefarming at home.

'Then, as the factory workers earned more money—or perhaps realised they would have a regular income, which was something new for people raised on the land—they wanted more comfort.'

'So some entrepreneurial type saw an opportunity, bought up land and began to build smart, new houses for them?'

Marco scowled and she wondered if she'd inadvertently insulted him. Had his grandfather or father built the houses?

'Exactly,' he said crisply. 'Bought land cheap, closer to the factory, which seemed like a good idea to the workers at the time, they could walk to work—and built just as cheaply.'

No, not his father or grandfather! Marco was an honourable man for all he'd manipulated her visit to his home, and she couldn't conceive him being bred by rogues. But she could pursue the shoddy real-estate deal some other time.

'And now?'

He sighed and shook his head at her.

'I should have explained all this earlier,' he said, and she chuckled.

'Exactly my sentiments,' she reminded him, 'although I may have expressed them more heatedly.'

He smiled again and she felt her body relax, spun helplessly into the vortex of his charm.

But it wasn't charm he was wanting her to see—it was his problem. A fact which became only too obvious when he said, 'Let's continue this in the car.'

The route to the village was familiar to her now, so, although her eyes were on the scenery which never failed to fascinate her, she gave her attention to his words.

'Originally, villages grew with need—spreading in the easiest and most logical geographical direction. The church was always the centre point as the priest not only looked after the community's spiritual wellbeing but many of the practical aspects of its existence. People went to him for advice, for help, and, as you do in your service, he referred them on.'

'Does the new village have a church?'

He glanced at her as if pleased by her perception.

'Blind Freddy would have seen that coming,' she assured him, which led into a diversion over colloquial expressions before Paige brought them back on track.

'So the lack of a church meant a lack of a central focus?' she suggested.

'More than that because, although the men could walk to work, the women now had a much longer and uphill walk to the shops and the market, and the older women—mothers and mother-in-laws who would normally attend mass each day—found it increasingly hard to reach the church. Even the older men suffered because the bars and cafés were too far away.'

'So, did everyone move back to the old village?' Paige asked, interested in the logistics of the situation but unable to see where community health came in.

'Many did,' Marco answered, slowing down as they drove through the square, then speeding up again as the road wound lower until the old houses of the original village were all behind them. 'Times have changed and fewer young people are happy to remain in the home of their parents or parents-in-law, so the young families like to move into the new houses close to the factory. After all, the school is there for their children and observance of the sabbath is no longer so rigid, so not having a church close by does not bother them.'

'And as we've now passed through the old village, do I assume your service is based in the new village? Is that your problem?'

He sighed, then shot a quick glance her way and a smile which tempted her to think of fairytales again.

'We have regular buses which run between the two areas so it shouldn't be a problem,' he explained. 'But it's as if an "us and them" culture has sprung up in the area, and if a service is used by one group the other group will shun it.'

He swung the car to the right, leaving the main road and entering a tree-lined avenue which eventually opened onto playing fields.

'Look,' Marco said, disgust edging his voice. 'It's end of shift for about one hundred men and how many are there, playing soccer? Four!'

Paige laughed and shook her head.

'OK, you've got me,' she admitted. 'What's the connection between a health service which isn't working and only four men kicking a ball around a paddock?'

'Kicking a ball around a paddock? You laugh at a game which is practically sacred to our nation?'

His shocked accents made her laugh even more, drawing more fire.

'What is wrong with you?' he demanded.

'Oh, Marco,' she said, swiping happy tears from her eyes with the back of her hand. 'You should have heard yourself.'

He made a strangled noise, as if swallowing an oath, then smiled, reluctantly, himself.

'I suppose I see it as a symptom,' he explained. 'In other times, at end of shift all the men would have a game. Back then the factory's bus brought the workers down to the factory and took them back to the village, and the bus would wait because everyone knew that men coming off night duty would rest better after they had had some exercise. Our factory soccer team was one of the best in the area for many, many years.'

'I agree with the exercise idea because it's good for both their mental and physical health. But you said there's still a bus,' Paige protested. 'What I can't understand is how the split in the housing arrangements of the workers has affected the football games.'

'Now the bus is owned by a bus company which runs regular hours—by timetable. If the workers have a kick of the football they must wait two hours for the next service. Our bus was stopped because it was deemed to be against competitive trade practice, although it was free for the workers. You have this trade practice in Australia?'

He sounded so affronted that Paige had to curb an urge to laugh.

'We do indeed,' she assured him, 'and it's not all bad, but bureaucracy can be too cumbersome when it's dealing with individuals, which is why our health service was set up.'

'Exactly!' Marco exclaimed, his hand slapping the steering wheel in what seemed like triumph. 'I knew you would understand it all completely!'

Oh, yeah? Paige thought, totally bemused by what she was supposedly understanding.

And as for completely...

CHAPTER EIGHT

THEY drove on and Paige looked around her. The new houses, for all Marco's denigration of the workmanship, looked bright and cheerful, and not too unlike the ancient village ones to jar *her* sensibilities. Then he pulled off and parked in a bay of tarred area beside a tall, stolid-looking building which seemed to shriek public offices.

She remembered why she was here and glanced towards her host. Even if she didn't understand as completely as he thought she did, she may as well speak out about what struck her.

'If this is where your health service is located, that's a problem for a start,' she said.

'I'd begun to realise that,' he said gloomily. 'It doesn't look welcoming, like your house does.'

'Forget the welcoming and think practical. It has no ramp access.' Paige pointed out the obvious. 'It's not only older people who have trouble with steps but mothers of young families who are struggling with a pram or stroller and probably a toddler as well.'

He led her up the steps and pushed open a heavy glass door.

'Do I keep going?' she asked, wondering where advice ended and criticism began.

'Door no good?' he asked.

'It should be left open or changed to automatic and slide open. Same reason as the steps.'

'That is easily fixed,' he agreed, 'but I think it is more than steps and doors keeping people away.'

133

Inside the door was a wide foyer, with corridors leading off it to the right and left and a bank of lifts directly opposite the entrance. Signs in Italian evidently pointed to the various services to be found in the building.

'This way.' Marco indicated the passage to the right but Paige hesitated.

'I don't think this is the best way for me to see it,' she said. 'If your family was involved in setting it up, how many people will risk upsetting you by saying truthfully what they think is wrong?'

'Risk upsetting me? I have no power over their lives. You take this prince thing too literally. I am nothing special in this town.'

So his temper was as uncertain as her own still felt.

'Oh no?'

'Well, there is respect.'

'There's more than that,' she told him bluntly. 'Many of these people are dependent on your family's factory for their livelihood.'

'So they won't speak the truth? That's what you're saying?'

'It's what I'm assuming.' She stared at him, wondering how to convince him. 'What have you already done to try to solve it? Surely you've spoken with staff, with patients, perhaps had a meeting of all those involved?'

He nodded, then answered grudgingly. 'I have done those things and been told things were working as well as in any other service.'

'Yet you know that's not true.'

His fingers tangled in his hair, leaving it in slight— and very attractive—disarray, then he sighed and muttered, 'An old man, a former tenant of my father who was very close to our family, died in his home in the village. It was three days before his body was discovered.

That should not happen if a community service is working. Someone should have known he was to be alone at that time and seen to regular contact, but one party thought another would do it and he fell through the net we spoke of at your home.'

And you're carrying the blame for it, Paige thought, seeing real pain in his eyes.

'Let's get out of here,' she said. 'No, better still, is there someone in the consulting rooms who speaks enough English to understand me if I ask questions?'

'Lisette, the co-ordinator, speaks it well. She is French, but married to a local man.'

'Then how about you leave me with her for a few days while you go off and do your own thing?'

He smiled, and the combination of unruly hair and teasing lips made her heart throb.

'My own thing, as you call it, is here today. Today I am the doctor. But I understand what you are saying— that we should not be too closely connected. I will go in and send Lisette out to you.' The smile disappeared. 'Not that it will work,' he added gloomily. 'By now the entire village must know a foreigner is staying at my home, and the news has probably spread to this lower village as well. They will put two and two together.'

He sounded so put out that she patted his arm.

'Don't worry, I'll do more watching than questioning. And listening too,' she added, grinning at him, 'because I'm beginning to pick up on bits of conversation so be warned.'

'Ah, now I must watch my words,' he said gravely, then he smiled again, so warmly that Paige wondered if there was a hotel down here where she could stay while doing her 'research'. It was definitely time she got away from him—time she got her body back under control.

As he walked away from her, she studied him. Was it because he was so unlike anyone she'd ever known that she'd fallen under his spell? James, for all his stated belief in women working, had seen her job as demeaning—her work with less fortunate people as some kind of social disgrace. In Marco she sensed admiration, and for all his inbred sense of family responsibility he was the first to admit his sister made a better manager of the factory than he ever could.

She was still pondering the make-up of the man when a young woman appeared.

'Oh great!' she greeted Paige in idiomatic English. 'Another blonde in town. I'll stop being a nine-day wonder. I'm Lisette. Francesco sent me to rescue you.'

Paige introduced herself and shook Lisette's hand. She was used, now, to people outside the family addressing Marco by his given name—and pleased by the sense of privilege that he didn't insist she use it.

'He says you're here to take a look at how we run. Please, ask anything you like. I know the service should work better, but we're all at our wits' end, trying to work out how.'

'Nine-day wonder? Wits' end? You have to be English!'

Lisette smiled.

'I grew up just outside London,' she explained. 'My father was employed by IBM. He took a holiday job there when he was at university and somehow he stayed on, pausing only briefly to go home to France and persuade my mother she would like living in England. She never did, which is why they returned home some years ago.'

They had walked together down the corridor as she'd explained, and they now reached a door which Lisette pushed open.

Another difficult door for potential clients.

The waiting room could not have been more unlike the one at home. With horrible anatomical drawings and quit-smoking posters adorning all the walls, it shrieked medical surgery, not community service.

'Is this the only place you have where people can come to talk to you?' she asked Lisette.

'Awful, isn't it? This is Vitti, our receptionist.' Lisette rattled off an introduction, then explained, 'Her name's Vittoria but she hates it, hence Vitti. Now, I have this room on the left and the doctors' room is on the right. Come with me, and we can sit down while I explain things. As you see, there's no one waiting for my attention although Francesco has a patient at the moment and several booked in for later in the morning.'

'Does he come in every day?' Paige asked, although she should have been thinking of the service, not Marco. And hadn't he mentioned Terni in connection to his work?

Lisette looked shocked.

'Oh, no! He has to earn a proper living like the rest of us. He's a surgeon at a big hospital in Terni but he tries to do one morning a week here to keep up his general practice skills. We need a full-time doctor but each time we get one he leaves so usually we have locums. The present locum is an older man. You will meet him this afternoon.'

The locum business was another obvious problem, and one Paige understood. All too often, community health centres couldn't afford to pay the wages permanent doctors required. At home she managed with volunteers, but that was in a town large enough to have a good supply of general practitioners. From the way Marco had spoken, this was the only service in the two villages. Perhaps in Spoleto there'd be someone...

The phone rang and as Lisette fielded the call Paige let her mind wander.

'I have a visit to make. Do you want to remain here or come with me?' Lisette asked.

'Stay here,' Paige said promptly. 'If you don't mind. I'll sit out in the waiting room for a while and pretend to read a magazine, see if I can get a feel for things— have a think.'

Lisette seemed to understand, which was just as well because Paige couldn't have explained it any more clearly but, sitting in the waiting room, it did give her a feel for things. People came and went, shown by Vitti into the room Lisette had indicated was Marco's.

As far as she could see, this part of the service was entirely medically oriented, but she didn't want to jump to conclusions.

'Well?'

She was alone in the waiting room when Marco appeared in the doorway of his office, and looked expectantly at her.

'Oh, I've been here all of three hours and solved the whole thing,' she snapped at him, mainly because he'd upset her equilibrium, not to mention her pulse rate.

'Yes, of course, but that wasn't what I meant. I was wondering if you were ready for lunch.'

Ready for lunch when her stomach was doing somersaults—perhaps the result of no contact with him for a few hours.

'Not with a stranger,' she said firmly. 'I may not have come up with any solutions, but I do think that the less we see of each other around here the better if this crazy idea of yours is to have any chance of working.'

'You didn't seem to think it such a crazy idea earlier,' he grumbled. 'You yelled about not being asked properly, but you didn't mention crazy.'

'I did not yell,' Paige argued, but he ignored her injured dignity and smiled.

'Well, raged,' he amended, propping himself against the jamb. 'What will you do for lunch?'

'The same as the locals, I suppose. I'll go down to the porchetta stand and eat some delicious hot roasted pork in fresh crusty bread.'

His smile broadened.

'Ha, I knew you'd develop a taste for it.'

She remembered the first time she'd eaten it, the juice running over her fingers, probably dribbling down her chin. He'd laughed when she'd complained about the mess and had handed her a handkerchief, his fingers brushing hers in the exchange, warming bits of her which had been cold for too long.

She sighed and wondered if she was being silly not to eat with him today, denying herself the pleasure of his company.

No, said her head. Not in the circumstances. This 'job' has given you the perfect excuse to draw back and get your emotions under control.

'Then I will leave now to go down to Terni, but I've arranged for Lisette to phone Anna who will collect you when you are ready to go home.'

Ready to go home! The little phrase sneaked into her heart and she had to remind herself that his house was not her home.

'No need to bother Anna,' she said crisply. 'Lisette can show me where to catch the bus—it's better that way as I'll get the feel of the local transport. I can walk up to the house from the village.'

'You do not need to do that,' he argued, and she grinned at him, and knew from the flash of challenge in his eyes he'd remembered her teasing remarks about his overdeveloped sense of responsibility.

'No, I don't need to,' she agreed, 'but as the patients who visit the centre catch the bus, I will have to include the experience in my research.'

'So you win again!' he said, but he was smiling, accepting her decision even though it overrode his plans.

'Was it an argument?' she tempted, wanting to see that light in his eyes again.

'Isn't it always?' he responded, but so gravely that the fun went out of the conversation.

'I will see you at home later,' he said. Once again the phrase snagged in her heart, but her ears had caught another message. A hesitation? Why? Was he likely not to return home this evening? Any evening?

She realised how little she knew of him and that, in the week they'd spent together, he'd rarely mentioned his work.

'Do you always commute or do you stay in the city during the week?'

'I commute,' he said, so abruptly she wondered if that was a problem. For him? Or for someone else?

'OK, I'll see you later.'

She tried for lightness, but the thought of someone else—a female someone else, perhaps—had rattled her.

Marco remained where he was in the doorway, going neither in nor out, and again she sensed uncertainty. Not a word she'd have associated with his prince-ship before this! Did he not want to leave her to lunch alone?

But when he spoke any hope that his thoughts might be personal was dashed.

'I am grateful to you,' he said, then he shifted, came

through the door and walked towards her, holding out his hand. 'And I will see you this evening.'

She took the offered hand for she'd caught onto the European habit of handshaking, but even a 'habit' hand-shake with this man affected her body and sent her mind back to fantasy land.

Where it remained long after he'd departed.

'Come, we will lunch!'

Lisette's reappearance brought her out of her dream, and she followed her new acquaintance out of the build-ing and down the road to the square at the centre of the 'new' village.

As they lingered over coffee, knowing the office was closed until three, Paige half listened to Lisette talk while another part of her mind absorbed the atmosphere. Yes, the square lacked the antiquity of many she'd sat in with Marco, but it was still a place where people congregated, talking, eating, laughing, drinking—arguing as well, if the raised voices were any indication.

'The new village works on this level,' she said to Lisette. 'The square has the right feel to it.'

Lisette nodded.

'Yes, the new village is growing into itself, developing its own traditions, but the division still exists. For in-stance, although the doctors' patients come from both villages, all the clients I have spoken with this morning were from here, not the old village, and that's one of the problems.'

'Transport?'

Lisette smiled. 'I wish! No, it's that the service is seen as "theirs" by the people in the old village, yet it is the elderly people in the old village who are most in need of services. I should know, I live there.'

They talked around the subject, straying from it into more personal conversation but usually returning to it.

'Is there accommodation I could rent down here?' Paige asked a little later—surprising herself almost as much as she'd shocked Lisette, if her expression was any guide.

'But you're a guest of the Albericis,' she objected. 'Why would you want to rent something down here?'

'I'm interested in your problem,' she said, although an honest answer would have been 'to get away from Marco' or 'I like this place, this area. I'd like to spend more time here, but without the distraction of his presence'.

Realising that what she *had* said wasn't quite enough, she added, 'I thought I might stay on for a while, but I don't want the Alberici family to feel obligated to keep me.'

Lisette lifted her hands in a 'well, I don't understand but it's your life' gesture, then replied, 'There's a guest house which supplies meals. Many of the single men who work at the factory have lodgings there. Or there are a number of apartment buildings and, given that so many people moved back to the old village, I'm sure you'd find an owner willing to let one on a short-term basis. I'll make some phone calls when we return to the office.'

'That's great!' Paige said, excitement building within her as she contemplated her immediate future. Perhaps she'd get a car, revisit some of the beautiful places Marco had taken her and explore some new ones on her own.

They returned early to the office, and by six that evening Paige had not only checked out several furnished apartments but had chosen one and signed a month's lease.

*   *   *

'You cannot do this,' Marco decreed, much later. He was standing in the doorway of her bedroom where she'd retired to pack, after telling his mother of her plans over a dinner which he'd missed—held up at work. He looked tired, but as attractive as ever, setting her hormones into their usual frenzy of delight.

'Of course I can,' she countered, the words more casual than she felt. 'I'd like to get the feel of living in a village and I can't do that from here. Also, I'm interested in your problem but, as I pointed out earlier, it's much better that I'm not too closely connected with your family. This way, the villagers will find it easier to accept that I was employed to accompany Lucia home, and am now staying on to learn something of the health service.'

'You weren't paid to accompany Lucia home.' He ground out the words as if the non-payment was another bone of contention—one he still found difficult to swallow.

'No, but the villagers don't know that. Now, don't argue, Marco, because I'm going, and, unless you want to play the heavy-handed head of the health service board and forbid me to visit it, I don't think you can stop me.'

'Do you delight in putting me in the wrong, Paige Morgan?' he growled. 'Does it satisfy some feminine instinct in you to be always throwing what you see as my position in my face?'

She was surprised by the emotion in his voice, and by how he saw her actions, but she didn't let it show, smiling at him and saying lightly, 'No, to both your questions, but perhaps you see it that way because you're not used to women standing up to you. You must admit, you run a household where a number of women do say "yes, Marco" more often than they argue.'

'The day my sister Paola says "yes, Marco" without

an argument, I'll be surprised. You've just seen less of her and more of Anna. And as for Lucia!' He threw up his hands in a gesture of despair. 'She might say "yes, Marco" but she then goes ahead and does exactly what she wants.'

He was arguing but his tone had softened, as it always did when he spoke of his family. And he seemed more relaxed about, even resigned to, her imminent departure from his house. Perhaps relieved?

As she was—in one way.

He said goodnight, not asking about the arrangements for her departure. Perhaps his mother had already told him that Aldo was to drive her, with her luggage, to the lower village in the morning.

Nor did he visit her new abode that first week, although Anna dropped in regularly, Paola called on her way home from the factory and Signora Alberici visited, bringing two potted plants to give the place a more homely look. Friday evening brought Lucia and Alex, dropping in on their way home for the weekend, but no Marco.

'He's probably sulking because you moved out,' Lucia stated after she'd enquired about her brother's reaction to the move. 'Didn't ask him first and let him arrange everything for you. Although why you'd want to leave the Casa for such a small apartment...'

Paige hid a smile. Marco might not consider himself a prince, but his little sister had 'princess' in her blood!

When she saw him at the health centre the following week he was polite but distant, and she was glad when Lisette suggested they do some home visits. Anything to keep away from him.

Which worked for one morning at the health centre, but not when he finally arrived on her doorstep, two days later, holding a bunch of yellow roses in one hand. Apart from shutting the door in his face, there was little she could do to avoid him.

'Are you going to ask me in? The flowers could do with some water. I bought them in Terni, so they'll probably start wilting shortly.'

'Flowers?' she repeated, still too shocked to get her act together.

'These things.' He waved the roses helpfully in her face. 'House-warming gift. That is traditional in Australia as well?'

Of course! A house-warming gift. Not flowers for her at all! Except they were, but not in the way her silly heart had hoped.

'Do come in,' she managed to mutter. 'And thank you for the flowers. I'm not sure the apartment runs to more vases, but there's a large jug that will do the trick.'

She turned away, letting him follow her into the one room which was living room and kitchen, then bedroom when she unfolded the bed from the settee. The usual squeal of protest from the large armchair told her he'd not only followed her in but had sat down as well. Was he preparing to stay?

'Well, what do you think?' she asked, when she'd unwrapped the roses, put them in a jug of water and placed them, in the centre of the her small table, beside the flowers Lucia had brought.

'A typical soulless apartment, but if you prefer it to remaining in my home…'

His shoulders lifted in an expressive shrug.

'Did you come here because you can't stir up a decent fight at your place?' Paige demanded. 'Or did you have some other reason?'

Another shrug, but different this time—slow enough

for her to notice fatigue in his face and the lethargy of the movement. He was tired and she wasn't helping matters, trying to provoke an argument.

'Have you eaten? I was about to have supper. Lazy Aussie pizza—tomato, olives, ham and cheese spread on bread then toasted. And you could have some Colli Perugini to wash it down. Alex presented me with a case of Umbrian wines.'

He didn't reply immediately, instead looking around once again, his gaze lingering on the potted plants, the bright floor rug which Paola had lent her. Would he recognise them, remember having seen the kitchen items, the hanging rack of assorted implements Mirelle had insisted she would need adorning his own kitchen wall?

'So, all the family has visited, bar me,' he said gravely. 'Do you always feed them?'

'If they come at mealtimes,' she said, trying for calm although her mind was squirming with questions about his presence, her body in revolt for different reasons. 'Are you staying?'

He looked up at that.

'Would you like me to?'

The question was so unexpected she couldn't answer, then she realised, like the flowers, it hadn't been meant as she'd first thought.

'You would always be welcome in my home,' she said, with formal politeness.

'Ah!' he responded, as if some other question had been answered, but he did stay, sitting opposite her at the small table, eating the simple meal she'd prepared, talking of the wine and other Umbrian wines which had won international acclaim. Of the standards now imposed to ensure quality, then later, as they sipped their coffee, of his work at the hospital.

'You enjoy surgery?' Paige asked. 'I did some work in Theatres during my training but knew it wasn't ever going to be something I could handle. Too impersonal somehow.'

'You found it impersonal yet for the time the patient is in the theatre his life is in your hands? And those of the anaesthetist?'

Marco was so close she could see the muscles moving in his jaw and cheek as he spoke, watch the way his lips formed words.

Form some yourself or he'll think you've gone to sleep! her brain warned.

'It wasn't the actual operation that was impersonal, although the patient isn't a whole person in a theatre—just a shrouded form with a hole revealing a carefully prepped piece of flesh. It's the before and after stuff. You don't get to know the patients as people.'

'And you do in general nursing on a ward?' he argued. 'In Australia, perhaps, but here in Italy our hospital bed numbers have been so reduced by cost-cutting and other expediencies that the beds barely get cold between patients. And the nursing staff, though excellent, are too busy to be providing much care beyond what is necessary.'

'It's the same at home,' she agreed. 'Not enough time for patient-nurse relationships to develop. Although there, the length of stay has been greatly reduced as well. I think the powers that be use the excuse that research has shown a patient recovers far more quickly in familiar surroundings.'

He nodded, his eyes alight as if was enjoying the conversation—or was about to shoot her down in flames.

'You are right, but also wrong.' Shoot her down in flames! 'Because it spoils your argument about personal and impersonal.' He smiled, lifted his glass towards her in a kind of salute, then asked, 'Is it for that reason, lack of patient-nurse relationship, you chose community nursing?'

'I suppose so,' she admitted. 'Or perhaps it chose me. My father became ill four years ago and I came home to nurse him. There wasn't enough to keep me occupied all the time so everything grew from there.'

He sipped his drink then set the glass back on the table.

'Ah!' he said, his gaze catching hers, holding it, making the air tangle in her lungs.

'Ah, what?' she asked, trying to behave as if her pulse rate were normal, not galloping so fast she thought he could probably see it beating in the hollow beneath her chin or throbbing at her temple.

'It explains your talk of paths through life and rough patches where you hurry past. You were very close to your father?'

'Very close,' Paige admitted, then determinedly changed the subject. 'But we've talked enough about other things. Didn't you call in to see how things were going at the centre—to ask me what I thought?'

His smile teased its way into her heart, doing nothing to steady her still-racing blood.

'No, I did not,' he replied. 'I came, belatedly I will admit, to see that you were comfortable. I was put out by you spurning my hospitality, but that does not excuse my neglect of you.'

Paige chuckled, aware of the effort it would have taken for him to apologise.

'Very handsomely put,' she said, wondering if she should have added 'do come again', although that would have placed her inner self in more jeopardy. She resisted the politeness, although it pleased her that he seemed at ease. And that the fatigue had given way to relaxation, so much so that when she suggested they move to more comfortable chairs he stood up and smiled.

'If I get any more comfortable I will fall asleep. I must go on home.' He held out his hand, and as she took it, shook it and released it as quickly as politeness would allow, he added, 'May I call again?'

She nodded, so discomfited by the words she hadn't said herself—or perhaps that fleeting touch of his skin, his warmth—she couldn't speak.

By the time she reached the door, she'd recovered sufficiently to say, 'Perhaps next time we should discuss the health service.'

'Do you think so?' he asked, and on that enigmatic note he left, walking away without a backward glance.

CHAPTER NINE

MARCO did come again, calling in so often that Paige began to buy extra food, to cook for two instead of one. The formality they'd established on that first visit set the pattern. He would arrive, shrug off his suit coat, unknot his tie, roll up his sleeves then relax into her one comfortable chair, sometimes sipping a glass of wine from the bottle he now brought as his contribution to the meal. She would alternate between fussing in her 'kitchen'—the bench which held a sink and small electric stove—and sitting opposite him on the settee, her legs curled under her, pretending a relaxation she was far from feeling.

They would then move to the table which seemed to shrink in his presence, and Paige would watch his movements, note silly things like the way the silky, dark hairs lay flat against the lightly tanned skin on his forearms—tell herself she shouldn't while her eyes recorded every fleeting image of the man, her heart hoarding them against the time she wouldn't have him there in person.

Each time he left she told herself she wouldn't ask him in next time because the tension was too great while he was with her, the sense of loss when he departed even worse. Yet she listened for the bell to ring each evening, summoning her to the door.

Until the final week, when he didn't come on Monday, or on Tuesday. She saw him at the office on the Wednesday, but he was back to Prince Impersonal, nodding formally when she handed him a written account of her impressions of the service. So, when the bell rang on the Thursday, it was hard to believe it could be him, and when he invited her to eat with him at a bar in the square she became flustered, muttering about lamb—which she'd had in the small refrigerator for three days and which was now in the oven because she'd decided it *had* to be cooked whether the awaited guest turned up or not—and eventually inviting him to eat with her instead.

'I have no duty this weekend. Would you like to visit Rome?'

He asked the question as they sipped wine before dinner, and Paige, who'd been expecting more talk of the things they usually discussed—his work, the service, Lucia's health—took a moment to register what he'd said.

Rome! Would she like to visit Rome? With Marco?

Do birds fly? Fish swim? Babies cry?

'No, thank you,' she said politely, although her heart was breaking as she spoke the words. 'It's my last weekend here and I've so much to do.'

He nodded, as if it didn't matter to him—which it wouldn't, of course—and began to talk instead about the service, thanking her for the report, asking for recommendations.

'Don't run it from a building,' she told him. 'The more I've thought about it, the more obvious that becomes. OK, the doctor's there, but what you're trying to provide isn't medical. Leave him where he is—or, better still, shift him to somewhere accessible—but don't include him in the services you're offering.'

He studied her in silence for a moment, his eyes remote, then with a slight shake of his head he seemed to refocus.

'Well, truthfully speaking, he isn't part of the service,

but it seemed convenient to tie the two together as he could suggest to Lisette what was needed for the patients. And, if it's not based there, what do we do with Lisette? Are you saying dispense with her entirely?'

'That might have worked if the doctor was a permanent fixture and knew all the people who were on his list. But—'

'But that's another problem,' Marco admitted with a deep sigh.

'And not one easily solved, according to Lisette,' Paige agreed, then turned to what could be fixed. 'I'd make her more mobile. She already has a cellphone with voice mail on it so she's contactable wherever she is, but let her go to people rather than them come to her.'

'House calls? Isn't that an inefficient management of resources? And it isn't how you run your service.'

Paige sighed. OK, she was pleased to be talking work. It dulled—slightly—the tingling in her nerve endings caused by having Marco in the vicinity, and took her mind off things like never seeing him again.

'Our service is different. It's a drop-in place which is convenient to all the people it serves. That area once had streets of huge old houses which have now been turned into low-cost flats or rented rooms. Most of our clients are within walking distance. Here, you're trying to cover two separate geographical areas separated by a very steep and winding road with a bus service that never seems to fit into appointment times.'

'So you're saying put Lisette in a car and let her visit. It would never work. Italian people will always welcome visitors, but the women are embarrassed if they haven't finished their housework. They would be uncomfortable, not relaxed.'

Uncomfortable—how she felt when he was near. Yet

more alive than at any other time, her blood still singing in her veins.

'Lisette explained that to me, so we thought if she had two mornings a week in the upper village and two down here, then afternoons she can visit in either area and, theoretically, on the fifth day do book-work and follow-up calls. Although the service has been working American hours, as you call them, from nine to five, no one ever comes in the afternoon so there's no point in having her in an office after one.'

'Will this suggestion be so different to what is happening now?' His eyes scanned her face as if seeking an answer there, making her feel even more uncomfortable.

'I think it could be. For a start, you could make set days for different people. Down here she sees enough mothers and babies to have a separate baby clinic one morning a fortnight. On the alternate morning she can run other programmes which need regular attendance—quit smoking, weight loss, nutrition classes for those who are interested.'

'Nutrition classes in Italy?' Marco objected.

'McDonald's in Italy?' Paige countered. 'It's a worldwide problem, particularly in the younger families where fast food has become a way of life.'

She smiled at the disbelief in his face and said, 'Well, we can scrap the nutrition classes, but I'm sure you get the idea.'

'I suppose you are right,' he admitted, so grudgingly she wondered how to bring up her next suggestion. 'Go on.'

'Like nutrition classes, other things are changing in Italian society,' she began, treading very carefully this time. 'Lisette explained how important the family has always been, and how the care of the aged was usually undertaken by younger family members.'

He nodded gloomily and she wanted to reach across and pat his hand in sympathy because for his over-developed sense of responsibility must have made the decline of this tradition seem criminal.

'Now young people, particularly young women, move away to find work. They live apart from their parents and grandparents and that's where the holes appear in your net as both generations are affected. Some of the young ones are missing family support and some of the less able older people have no family to care for them. Lisette and I have talked about meals-on-wheels. Do you know the concept?'

Another nod.

'It's been tried in many parts of Italy—even the government has given money to community groups for this purpose—but I don't see what good it can do.'

'It puts someone in touch with your more isolated villagers on a daily basis—well, six days a week, we thought. The priest already has volunteers who visit housebound villagers on Sundays, but if the service can organise something for the other days, without making it look like an incursion into the older people's privacy, then that's another hole closed. The priest is very supportive. He's offered to lend the church facilities for meal preparation and has a number of men and women already rostered to cook and deliver them.'

'To the old village alone?' Marco sounded suspicious, not excited, but as Lisette had explained how quickly welfare services could break down Paige wasn't entirely surprised.

'No, to both villages. The doctor—and I think you'll have to find a way to get someone to stay permanently

in town because this locum business is half your problem—will refer people to Lisette, who'll check on any
special dietary needs then list them with the volunteers.
It can be done on a temporary basis for people just out
of hospital, say, or where the wife is ill, and on a permanent basis for those who are having trouble coping on
their own.'

'Hmm.'

The noncommittal sound stung Paige to anger.

'Well, that's a nice reaction to a lot of hard work and
thought. Lisette and I have spoken to dozens of people,
all of whom managed to sound a lot more excited than
"hmm".'

He smiled, sending her heart into spasms of delight.

'I was hmm-ing over the doctor problem, not your
idea, which is great if we can keep it working. The problem is that the population isn't big enough to pay a doctor
the kind of money he expects to earn. Patients must be
listed with a doctor, but even if every inhabitant of both
villages listed locally the numbers don't add up to a lu-
crative practice.

'Did you know that Italy produces more doctors per
head of population than any other nation bar Cuba, of all
places? No? Well, it does, but the majority want to specialise, to work in places where promotion is possible
then move into private clinics, even build their own eventually.'

'And you don't? Didn't specialise? Aren't you working in a private clinic, owned, if I've understood correctly, by some family connection?'

He shrugged and raised his hands—resignedly, not defensively.

'I was interested in surgery,' he protested, but she
sensed his heart wasn't in it. Or his mind. It was as if

her words had awoken some sleeping worry which went deeper than keeping a doctor in the village.

Not that his worries were any concern of hers. She talked on, telling him about the availability of the former schoolhouse in the old village where Lisette could hold her morning sessions, of the other rooms in the building, ideal for activities like a playgroup or a drop-in centre where older people could meet, play cards, be entertained, possibly cared for in a form of day respite for their regular carers.

'Once they sat in the square and talked and argued, played their games there,' Marco told her, his indignation at the changing ways barely hidden.

'A lot still do,' she reminded him, put out that he was meeting each idea with doubt. 'But it's hardly a peaceful meeting place these days with traffic zooming through, the bus coughing out exhaust fumes, kids on mopeds weaving in and out of the café tables and groups of youths "hanging out".'

He gave another shrug, and a nod of what she took to be agreement.

'You don't have to be so excited about it!' Paige snapped. 'If you want things the way they were, then leave it at that. These are only suggestions, which, I might remind you, you asked me to offer.'

She snatched the plates off the table, realised he'd left half the meal she'd cooked—the beautiful Castelvecchio lamb—and felt more aggrieved, slamming the dirty dishes onto the bench and controlling an urge to yell at him.

Then his hands rested on her shoulders, very lightly, but any touch of his could hold her motionless.

'I am sorry,' he said, his voice deep and warm. 'You have done so much for me, for all my family, and I treat you in this way. It is not your ideas which trouble me, Paige, but a personal problem which I must eventually resolve.'

His fingers tightened and he drew her back so she rested against his body.

'Two personal problems, in fact.'

The words were breathed against her hair and she thought she felt his lips move against it, felt the warmth of his breath on her neck. She shivered at the contact, and his hands slid down to her upper arms, brushed up and down as if to warm her, his touch so gentle it made her want to cry. Or turn and face him, let his lips touch her mouth instead of her hair, feel the kiss she longed for in every atom in her body.

But deep down she was aware that such behaviour would shock him—that, for all his worldliness, this prince's attitudes were moulded by the past when gentlemen took responsibility for their actions. They might also have taken mistresses but both sides had known the rules, respected the boundaries.

Not that she was mistress material anyway! She knew herself well enough to know that 'happy ever after' was the ending she wanted in her fairy story.

'You won't change your mind? Come to Roma with me?'

He used the Italian pronunciation this time, making it sound so much more seductive, and she wondered if she was wrong about his moral views. She hesitated, tempted. Should she throw caution to the winds and go away with him? Experience the magic of the fabled Italian city with the man she loved? Wasn't that what life was all about? Living for the moment? Seizing whatever happiness was on offer?

'No,' she said, answering him, not her tempting

thoughts. 'Lucia and Alex are coming for the weekend to say goodbye, and your mother is planning a big lunch on Sunday. I couldn't disappoint them.'

His grip tightened on her arm, his fingers no longer caressing.

'But you could disappoint me?' he demanded, and she knew she had to face him. She moved with difficulty as her body had been comfortable against his. Now she had to shrug off his hands and turn in the confined space so that he was very close, his mouth within kissing distance, his eyes asking questions she couldn't understand.

'Would I, Marco?' she asked, and heard the quavering note of hope in her feeble words. Tried again. 'Does it disappoint you?'

'Of course,' he said gruffly, then the unthinkable happened as his head tilted downwards and those lips, which she'd watched and had wondered about how they'd taste, closed in on hers, touching them gently at first, then with a growing pressure until she stood helpless beneath the onslaught of a single kiss, her body fired to flashpoint by its power.

At the time it seemed to last an hour, perhaps a day— a week—but later, when he'd gone, she knew it had probably been less than a minute before he'd lifted his head, looked into her eyes and said, with what had seemed like grave sincerity, 'Will you marry me?'

'W-will I what?' she'd stuttered, certain that the effects of the kiss had had severe repercussions in her brain.

He hadn't responded immediately, stepping back a pace and looking even more confused than she'd felt— if that had been possible. Then he'd ducked his head in a funny kind of gesture and had said stiffly, 'Marry me! Stay on in Italy. Here. Help Lisette sort out the service.'

Her arms had flown upwards in the gesture of utter disbelief she'd seen so often since arriving in Italy.

'Oh, don't be so ridiculous, Marco,' she stormed. 'Even your princely principles couldn't dictate that you have to marry every girl you kiss! And if you consider trying to sort out your villagers' health service is an enticement, forget it. I can do that at home!'

A harsh laugh escaped the tightness in her throat. She'd been asked the one question most women in love would have given their front teeth and possible an ear or eyebrow to hear, and she'd said no! Was she going mad? Was she the 'ridiculous' one, to want love from marriage, not an offer of employment? 'Oh, why don't you go home? Get out of here. Take yourself and your stupid questions somewhere else.'

She waved her hands at him, as if to see him on his way, but was surprised when he shrugged one shoulder, hesitated only fractionally longer, then spun on his heel and marched towards her door, an effect which was spoiled when he had to return to retrieve his jacket.

'I shall see you at the family lunch on Sunday,' he said, turning as he reached the door a second time. But he didn't offer his hand in farewell, and nor did she move to offer hers. She stood where he'd left her, watching him walk away, her heart already asking why she was so angry.

And why she'd been so quick to say no?

He was affronted, that's what he was. Marco tasted the English word he'd never used before, rolling it around on his tongue. She'd treated his proposal as an insult! Worse than that, a joke! Yes, she'd laughed! At him! A man whom many women would feel honoured to be married to.

No, that didn't sound correctly put. Now his English was deserting him! He steered the car up the winding road, a jumble of thoughts in his head, some mocking his own folly at coming out with a proposal in such an inept fashion, others congratulating him on a narrow escape, memories of his grandparents' unhappiness still vivid in his mind for love had not been enough to satisfy his nonna, her love of her home always gnawing at her spirit, making her restless and difficult then bitter, until, even when she'd returned to England, she'd been unhappy.

But that didn't excuse Paige. She did not know about his nonna—well, no more than bare details given as the reason all the family spoke English. She'd said no as if he didn't matter to her, yet could she be so appealing to his body and her body not be equally responsive to his? It was his experience that such strong physical attractions were usually mutual.

And beyond the physical was the fact that they were friends. Hadn't he established that with his visits to her apartment? And hadn't she acknowledged it by welcoming him in?

He felt an ache of longing in his body and knew he shouldn't have kissed her, shouldn't have started something he'd had no intention of finishing—even if she had been willing.

Or perhaps that was the problem? Perhaps he should have used more physical means to show his feelings for her?

He reminded himself that he'd held back because he'd wanted her to know his feelings went deeper than a physical attraction, then laughed aloud at such nonsense. He'd fought the physical attraction with every fibre of his being because he believed a match between them was not possible.

Tonight he'd lost the fight and, having kissed her, wanted more, wanted it to last for ever, if truth be told, hence his, as she had said, 'ridiculous' proposal!

He groaned and stopped the car at the bottom of the steps leading up to the wide terrace, remembered walking with her there the morning she'd arrived, captivated by her delight at the beauty of the view. Since then they'd walked the terrace often, usually after dinner, the scent of roses from his mother's garden weaving magic through the air, the gentle, blonde-haired woman weaving spells within his heart.

It wouldn't have worked, Marco reminded himself, climbing wearily out of the car and trudging up the steps, the music of the spring mocking him with its careless watery notes, the moon a travesty of a symbol of a romance that never was.

Now the time to move had finally arrived, Paige found she no longer wanted to travel in Europe, or even see Rome. When Marco walked out the door she shut her mind on Italy, phoned the airline and asked about flights home.

'Monday,' the English-speaking operator told her. 'We could offer you a first-class seat on Monday.'

Privilege for those who could afford to pay for it, she thought cynically as she confirmed she'd travel on that day and took the details of the flight, a late one, giving her time to travel down to Rome on Monday morning. No need to tell the Albericis she was going home. They knew she was leaving and would probably ask about her plans, but if she said Rome then waved her hands vaguely in the air they'd accept she was still undecided—probably offer innumerable suggestions about what not to miss.

Which is what happened. Anna, Paola and the signora

all talked of their favourite places, the husbands chiming in, only Marco not offering suggestions.

But he'd made his—two, in fact—and she'd said no to both. He was gravely attentive, punctiliously polite—and as distant as Antarctica! In contrast, she had gone the other way, almost Gallic in her excitement, her speech and gestures, revealing her fondness for this family who had welcomed her to their home but making it plain she was equally excited to be moving on.

Huh!

The very thought of leaving the two villages filled her with pain, while the knowledge she would never see Marco again made her insides clutch in helpless agony. Pathetic! That's what she was! But at least she could still pretend.

Marco drove her home, much later, when twilight was settling over the mountains and the valley was thrown into their shadows, the fields a darker green, the poppies already washed from sight by night's approach.

'My family has grown very fond of you,' he said as they approached the lower village and he turned the car towards her temporary abode. 'They will miss you. They also find it hard to understand your independence, refusing even to accept a lift on the first stage of your journey. How will you travel?'

He sounded put out—offended—and she touched him lightly on the arm—perhaps for her sake, too.

'Lisette's husband is driving me to Terni when he goes to work,' she began, and realised she was adding insult to injury that she'd accepted Benito's offer when Marco would have done the same. 'From there I'll get a coach. I'll be all right—my Italian has come on enormously since I've been here. I've always had an ear for languages.'

What a stupid conversation to be having with a man you loved and would never see again.

He stopped the car but made no move to get out—and nor did she.

'I want to thank you for all the suggestions you made about the service. I know Lisette is keen to implement them, although she is more a hands-on nurse than an organiser.'

'I enjoyed doing it, and hope it helps.'

Stupid or not, it was best to keep talking.

'As you refused to take a consultancy fee, I have donated money to your service back at home as I know it is dear to your heart.'

'You've d-done what?' she stammered, then knew she didn't want to hear it again. 'No, don't repeat it. I heard the words, I just can't believe them. Is it not possible in Italy to do something because one wants to—without hope of monetary reward? It's like your medical situation here in the two villages. You say no doctor will take the post because he or she will not make a fortune. Doesn't job satisfaction count for something? Wouldn't living in a place like this—with clean air, smiling, friendly people and such rich spectacular natural beauty—be worth more than money to the right man?'

She flung open the car door and stepped out, bending over to look back at him.

'Don't bother to get out. Princely manners are all very well, but there's more to life than good manners, Marco Alberici. It's been—interesting, I guess about sums it up! Goodbye.'

She slammed the door with a satisfying thud, then strode across the pavement and into the foyer of her building, angry with him yet furious with herself for letting him get to her.

Not that he didn't do it all the time—one way or another. Particularly since the day he'd made that abrupt, unloverlike proposal.

Paige went to bed, but couldn't sleep, haunted by the feeling that she was running away, leaving too much unresolved. Yet her heart told her she couldn't stay.

On the beautiful drive to Terni she answered Benito's questions mechanically, her mind on the village, the family, wondering about Lucia's baby, which she'd never see.

'You don't seem very happy to be leaving,' Benito said when she'd answered '*no*' instead of '*si*' once too often.

'Well, I'm not. It's a beautiful place and everyone has been so kind to me, but I can hardly stay there for ever.'

'Lisette is,' he reminded her. 'She is proof a foreigner can be accepted. She has grown to love the villages as much as I do.'

'I know,' Paige told him sadly. 'But she has you.'

Benito seemed to accept this statement as an argument-clincher and didn't mention her departure again, which was just as well because the closer they got to Terni the weepier she felt. So unsettled, in fact, that when he dropped her at the *capolinea* she went off the idea of taking a coach to Rome then working out how to get to the airport from there, and splurged, hiring a car and driver to take her directly to the airport.

Once through the departure proceedings and on the plane she allowed herself to relax. As it rose above the Eternal City she felt tears prick behind her eyelids.

I'll come some other time, she promised herself. When I've been home, settled down, got over Marco. Brave words when in her heart she knew she would never get over Marco.

Then why had she said no?

The question kept recurring although she knew the answer.

He should have whispered 'Ti amo'. Or more correctly, according to Lisette who had included love in every language lesson, 'Ti voglio bene'. But, no, it wasn't love which had prompted that strange proposal, just some outdated sense of chivalry—or a desire to see his precious health service running more smoothly!

She put her head back against the cushioned headrest, glad there was no passenger beside her, and tried to sleep. She ate when food was pressed on her by attentive hostesses, drank a glass of wine—Italian—determined not to think of Marco. Flying through the night in a metal capsule, high above the turning world, her sadness flew with her, an unwanted fellow passenger.

At Singapore she obediently left the plane, walking in the file of passengers to a transit lounge where they would sit and wait while minions of the airline dusted and vacuumed, refilled food trolleys and fuel tanks. Beyond the windows of the transit lounge the sun struck against the brightness of bougainvillea and purple orchids, but the colours seemed lurid and over-bright after fields of green with poppies scattered through them.

Having nothing better to do, she turned towards a row of seats set in front of a television screen. The commercial was in a language she didn't understand. Chinese? Singaporean? Did Singapore have its own language? Someone switched channels and she saw pictures of tilted houses, panic and disarray, heard words in English—Umbria, Spoleto, and the names of villages to the north.

In 1997 an earthquake had struck in Umbria, badly damaging the town of Assisi as well as many mountain villages. Again and again she'd seen pictures of the devastation, tilted houses, panic and disarray.

The thought carried her across the concourse to the airline's desk and she heard herself saying, 'I must go back to Italy.' She pushed her ticket across the counter with her boarding pass and a gold American Express card. 'Please, I must go back as soon as possible. Can you arrange it? Or someone else? Who should I see?'

CHAPTER TEN

IT WAS another thirty hours before Paige was back at Rome airport, where she once again employed a credit card to hire a car and driver, this time to take her directly to the village, wondering if her credit would stretch this far and how she'd pay for everything if the projected sale of her house to the community service fell through.

Not far beyond Terni, the driver told her, the valley roads were blocked to all but emergency traffic, but by the time they reached that city they'd become friendly enough for the driver to offer to find someone who could help her.

'Finding someone usually requires money,' she told him. 'I don't have much in lira—or notes of any kind.'

'You are a nurse, willing to help in the emergency. No one would dare take money from you when you make such an offer.'

Paige smiled at his indignation. Even in the welfare system, it was common practice for 'presents' to be offered—why would helping earthquake victims be different? But apparently it was, and she was the winner for he managed to get her as far as Spoleto, then, within an hour, she was on the move again, this time in the high front seat of a water tanker, trundling along the road towards the mountain villages which had been shaken by the earth tremors.

On the way she learned that the area around the factory had been hardest hit, the new village all but destroyed.

'The gods have spared the old village,' her driver told

her—or that was what she guessed he'd said, his English being worse than her Italian.

Had they spared Marco and his family? It was the question which had filled her head since Singapore, becoming more insistent when she'd learned the quake had indeed been centred around the one part of Italy she knew well.

'Fabbrica—pouf!' the man said, waving his hand towards the pile of rubble which had been the Albericis' business. She didn't need a translation to know what he was telling her, and her heart jittered at the thought of what might lie ahead.

She remembered the mothers and young babies of the lower village she'd seen in Lisette's office. Had they escaped? Been saved? The limo driver had told her the estimate of deaths was forty-seven, including those still missing.

Let Marco not be one of them, let him have been elsewhere.

At six thirty-two on a Tuesday morning?

Like so many people, he'd have been in bed, or just up, preparing for a working day. Definitely at home and unaware of the terrible danger about to strike.

The truck coughed its way into the square and Paige shut her eyes then opened them again. The streets leading off the square had disappeared, filled with rubble from houses which had collapsed. *Carabinieri* and soldiers patrolled, guns slung across their shoulders or hanging from their hips. Three ambulances stood in a row across a cleared space at the far end, and beyond them she could see people moving.

She thanked the man and left the truck, heading for the line of ambulances, wanting to do something, anything, to help. Excited voices yelled to each other, hope, not despair, in the tones. Paige found herself praying that another person had been found alive, the toll reduced by one, death cheated.

Now she was closer she saw men digging furiously, ahead of them handlers with dogs and people with probes moving cautiously, poking into the piles of bricks and mortar, seeking the softness of a human body.

Were heat-seeking devices being used? She assumed they would be. Everything was called into play in such emergencies—and the Italian people were among the best in the world at handling these natural disasters.

Stopping by the most forward of the ambulances, she waited, her legs wanting to carry her further up the hill—to the old village and Marco's house—but her professionalism reminding her she might be needed here. After a rescue operation which was into its third day, most of those helping would be tired, would perhaps appreciate a fresh pair of hands.

'Tre!'

Three alive?

She moved closer, found a man wearing a white arm-band with a red cross on it—internationally recognised—and introduced herself, explaining that she was a nurse and would like to help.

Her Italian must have sounded good to him for he rattled off a reply, or explanation, but at that moment the first limp body—a child's—was lifted from the mess of twisted wreckage and passed gently from hand to hand along a line of waiting men and women.

'Vivo!'

Alive! The word everyone wanted to hear. There were muted shouts of joy, the digging more determined now as one child recovered gave them hope. Paige took the space blanket from the driver and wrapped it around the small boy, then another woollen blanket on top of it, for comfort as much as anything else.

'I will hold him for you,' she said in her halting Italian. The man seemed to understand, seemed pleased the child would have the warmth of a body against him instead of a cold stretcher.

She sat on the ground behind an ambulance and cuddled the frail form, brushing dust from his face and then holding him more tightly as a medic inserted a catheter into the boy's arm, started a drip and taped the needle in place. He handed the bag of liquid to Paige who realised she would be acting as a drip-stand as well as a provider of warmth. Already there were shouts signalling that another person had been dug out so she was glad she was there to be with the boy, to murmur soothing Italian endearments to him, calling him brave and precious.

Then the commotion beyond the ambulance told her that yet another person had been rescued, and this time a huge shout went up, as if those who'd toiled were savouring their victory over nature. People milled about— that particular cave of safety must have been emptied now for rescuers were getting food and coffee from a van, stretching, talking and laughing, relaxing a little as they waited for the dogs or men with probes to call them into action again.

She held the boy closer. When the two other victims had been stabilised, no doubt all three would be ferried down the valley to Spoleto, or even Terni. Then she'd have to find something else to do to keep her mind off Marco.

'What are you doing here? This is a restricted area. There is danger of more movement, aftershocks, a second quake. *In nom di Dio*, at least I thought *you* were safe.'

It was hard not to think of Marco when he was there,

towering over her and roaring at her, swearing in Italian and throwing his arms about. Then his emphasis on the word 'you' clicked in her head and she stretched her free hand towards him.

'Oh, Marco, your family? Were they hurt? Not...?'

She couldn't say the word, bit it back as memories of the Alberici family's kindness brought tears to her eyes.

'No, they are all right, but you must go. Aftershocks are still occurring, could go on for days more.'

He was kneeling beside her now and she could see exhaustion in the dusty greyness of his skin, could see the blood on his hands where he'd torn his skin, digging through the tangled bricks and steel and concrete with the other villagers in the desperate search for survivors.

She took his right hand, the one she'd shaken so formally so often, in hers and lifted it to her lips, kissing the wounds, the blood.

'I had to know you were alive,' she said simply. 'I couldn't go on living until I knew.'

He said nothing and she knew it had been a mistake to reveal so much, so she tried for lightness as she added, 'And, apart from that, I'm a nurse. Extra medical personnel are usually welcome at these times. See, I can hold a child until the ambulance is ready to take him.'

She took her eyes off the child long enough to check Marco's face, to see if there was any reaction to her words.

Big mistake, that! His eyes were burning into hers, ablaze with something she couldn't read but which made her heart flutter wildly.

'You had to know I was alive, Paige? You came back because of me?'

So he hadn't fallen for the 'nurses needed in emergencies' routine—and why should he when the first explanation was the truer truth?

'Yes,' she said, then met his gaze once again.

'Why, Paige?' he asked, the blue of his eyes making his skin look even paler.

She looked around her, saw the damage, felt the pain it represented, thought fleetingly of life—and death—and knew only the truth would suffice at this moment.

'Because I love you,' she said, her voice almost lost in a new clamour further along the mounds of rubble. Another body located—perhaps alive.

'But you said no when I asked you to marry me,' he argued crossly, 'and now I must go and dig again before you can explain such irrational behaviour.'

'Well, go!' she muttered at him, fearing for him as she knew he'd put himself in danger. Angry with herself because she didn't want him taking risks she knew he might have to take. 'And saying no was no more irrational than you asking me the way you did. As if I meant nothing to you at all! Like it was another example of your politeness to a stranger—another way to repay some imagined obligation!'

'Meant nothing to me?' He echoed her words in amazement, but another shout brought him to his feet, looking indecisive—which was very unlike the Marco she knew.

'I have to go now, Paige,' he added sternly. 'Please, accompany the ambulance to Spoleto and wait there. My family is at the Hotel Gattepone. They will find a bed for you.'

Having issued his orders in his usual princely fashion, he departed, but Paige had no intention of leaving. Having seen Marco's wounds, it had given her an idea. She'd get a first-aid kit from one of the ambulances, and would tend the rescue workers' minor injuries as they took coffee- or meal-breaks. In any situation where water and sewerage services had been disrupted there was a grave danger of infection. It wasn't much of a contribution but it was something, and it would give her an excuse to remain close to Marco.

She asked for and was given what she'd need, but when she saw her first patient she added sutures to the list. Fortunately her patient spoke enough English to understand that if she didn't stitch the jagged tear he'd sustained, lifting bedsprings off one of those rescued, it could become infected and not be able to be stitched for a week.

She cleaned the wound and hurried to the closest ambulance, asking for sutures, using her hands to mime what she needed and getting a large pack of supplies in return. The driver walked across to where she'd set up her makeshift clinic and watched her work, and she wondered about the training of ancillary personnel, something she'd never asked either Marco or Lisette about.

'You do this kind of work?' she asked him, putting the Italian words carefully together yet knowing they'd probably end up in the wrong order.

He held up his hands in horror, shook his head and mimed driving. Which, she decided, was fair enough. As far as she was concerned, driving an ambulance through Italian traffic would require more skill and training than nursing.

Three men came in with burns on their hands and arms, reddened skin with blisters yet to form but which, she guessed, would be classed as bad first degree rather than second-degree injuries. In a halting mix of English and Italian, she discovered they were the results of a flash fire when a small pocket of gas from a leaking LP tank had exploded close to them.

Gas! Explosions!

Her stomach churned uneasily as she imagined a larger pocket of gas exploding—pictured Marco somewhere near it and closed her mind against the thought.

None of the men were willing to go to hospital and, lacking any medication she could confidently use, Paige wrapped the wounds in dry, sterile dressings and let them return to work. If infection occurred it could be handled later—at the moment these men were too intent on their rescue mission to be feeling much pain.

Word must have filtered through the rescuers that she was there for them, and by the time dusk threw its shadows over the square she'd treated innumerable cuts, gashes, burns and sprains, set a dislocated shoulder back in place and sent that volunteer home with his arm in a sling. She'd even dressed a leg wound on a dog someone had found, buried beneath his dead master in the ruins of his former home.

The dog lay beside her, his head on her foot, as she wrapped up all her rubbish, taking care with used suture and hypodermic needles, winding discarded packaging around them.

The activity had moved further from the square and she could see lights being set up and the hear the roar of electric generators kicking into life.

A bus arrived bearing a new load of rescue workers, Lisette's husband among them.

'You've come back? To help us?'

He kissed her on both cheeks then hugged her warmly just as Marco reappeared, the glower on his face suggesting he wasn't nearly as pleased to see her as Benito had been.

'Come,' he said abruptly. 'You have done enough for one day. Tiredness makes for carelessness. We will return to Spoleto, eat, sleep, then I will come back for tomorrow's early morning shift.'

His eyes dared her to argue, but the effects of the long flights, the changes of time zones, the despair and worry were beginning to take effect. Tiredness was pressing on her, as heavy as a wet blanket around her shoulders, and she knew he was right. She needed sleep.

She knelt down and lifted the dog into her arms.

'I can't leave him here,' she said defensively, when Marco frowned and shook his head.

The frown cleared almost immediately, replaced by a soft smile.

'No, of course you can't, any more than you could have not taken Lucia into your home.' He reached out as if to take the dog from her but the animal snarled and snapped at him, so instead he put his arm around Paige's shoulders, steering her across the square and down the road leading into it, eventually turning off to where cars where parked in a grassy field.

'Where were you when you heard about the quake?'

They'd driven in silence for ten minutes, Paige remembering that stupid confession she'd made hours earlier, realising how embarrassing it must have been for him, thinking how awkward it had made things between them.

When he asked the question she was so relieved to be able to talk of other things that she answered without conscious thought.

'Singapore. I was in the transit lounge and saw a news report on the television. I remembered the pictures we saw at Assisi—'

'Singapore? You were going home?'

Uh-oh!

'It seemed like a good idea at the time,' she mumbled limply, scratching behind the dog's ears, pretending an indifference she was far from feeling.

'I thought you intended to travel once you were over here. You said you'd considered spending time in Europe while you weren't working, even if Lucia hadn't crashed into your life.'

'Well, I changed my mind!'

He glanced her way, frowning fiercely as if he couldn't comprehend the language. Then he flung up one hand and said, 'I cannot understand the English!'

'I'm not English, I'm Australian,' she retorted. 'And there's nothing to understand.'

'No?'

This time he was smiling as he looked at her—a teasing smile which made her body think all manner of things she'd forbidden it to think.

'You went home because of love,' he accused, 'which does and does not make sense to me because already I had proposed to you.'

'Which meant nothing,' Paige fumed. 'Not a single thing, without some indication of your feelings. For heaven's sake, Marco, we'd been together for what? Six weeks, on and off. For the last three of them you'd called in nearly every evening and the closest we'd got to personal contact was a goodnight handshake. Even Benito greets me more warmly than that.'

'I saw Benito greet you,' he said stiffly. 'He is too familiar by far.'

If she hadn't been so confused she'd have laughed, but fortunately she didn't because it seemed his pride was already suffering.

'You were my guest as well as my responsibility—and I know you hate that word, but it is how I was brough up to act. I could not take advantage of such a situation by pressing kisses on you or furthering my suit. And as well as that, there is another matter which has been concerning me—'

'Furthering your suit? Oh, really, Marco, would you say that in Italian?'

She *was* laughing now, but more from nervousness than mirth. Did he mean what she thought he meant?

There'd still been no mention of love. And what other matter? Perhaps she'd let that dangling sentence pass and continue her attack on solid ground.

'And what's more, you followed up your proposal by mentioning the health service. It sounded as if you were offering me a job, not...'

Love? She couldn't bring herself to say the word again.

Wondered if he would.

Silence stretched between them, so palpable that even the dog must have felt it for he began to whimper.

'This is nonsense, all of it, but it is not the time or place to talk of this, any more than when I asked that question was the right time. It evaded me, slipped out or up, whichever.' Marco slapped his hand against the wheel, his confusion showing in his, for once, less than impeccable English. 'There is your home, of which you are so fond, your country, so far away... My grandparents... The medical situation...' Again his hand rose and fell in frustration but this time the dog took exception and growled again. 'And now the dog! No doubt if I so much as lay a hand on you he will sink his teeth into my flesh.'

'Oh, I'm sure he would,' Paige agreed, smiling as the ridiculousness of the situation struck her. Though what her house or his grandparents or some unknown medical situation had to do with anything she didn't know.

'It is not funny,' Marco told her, guiding the car carefully through the winding streets of Spoleto towards the top and the modern hotel where they'd had lunch on her first visit to the town.

'No, I suppose not,' she agreed, confused herself by the emotion vibrating between them in the car and explanations she couldn't understand.

He stopped in the square by the *rocca*, the ancient fortified castle which dominated the town, his fingers tapping impatiently against the steering wheel.

'I am too tired to think,' he admitted. 'To say the things I wish to say. And now we must go into the hotel where once again, without a doubt, my family will take you over, and will fuss and be all around the place.'

He sounded so aggrieved that Paige forgot her own tension and smiled again.

'Come,' she said gently, resting her hand on his arm. 'Right now, you need a hot bath, a meal and a good night's sleep. We can talk when the crisis is over, when we know for certain there's no one still buried in that rubble.'

He turned towards her, eyed the dog warily, then placed his hand on top of hers.

'Sensible Paige Morgan!' he murmured so gently, so softly, that in her ears it sounded almost like a declaration of love.

Not that 'almost' was enough but it would do for now!

She let go of the dog to open the car door, then took back her hand from Marco's arm so she could lift the injured animal as she stood up, but before she could move Marco spoke again.

'You will not run away from me again? Before we have time to talk?' he asked. 'Disappear when I return to the new village in the morning?'

'Like Cinderella from the ball? No, Marco, I'll be here.' She grinned at him. 'In fact, I'll be down there with you—or not far away. Even you have to admit I was quite useful.'

She saw his chin tilt into its determined pose and the lips thin in disapproval, and she touched his arm again.

'Wasn't I?'

He heard the smile in her voice, saw it dancing around her lovely lips and groaned aloud. If it hurt this much to contemplate her back down in the village—in possible danger—how much more would it pain him to *know* she was there?

'If I asked you not to go?'

The words sounded harsher than he'd intended and he saw her flinch—just slightly—then she turned to him and those gold-flecked eyes looked deep into his.

'But you wouldn't ask it of me,' she said calmly, not challenging him but stating a fact—leaving him no option but to agree.

Well, not to agree but to say nothing, which was just as bad as agreeing.

She moved, clambering awkwardly out of the car with the dog in her arms and, exactly as he'd predicted, his family closed in.

Well, Lucia closed in, racing across the parking area with scant regard for her condition and flinging her arms around Paige and the dog.

Which didn't growl at *her*!

He climbed out stiffly himself and locked the car doors, then crossed to the hotel steps where Lucia was now holding the dog while talking nonstop to both the animal and Paige alternately.

'I will take the dog home for the hotel will not like it,' she announced as Marco drew near. 'I would also like

Paige to come and stay with me, but she says she will be leaving early and needs a lift with you so perhaps she's best staying here, although I don't know if there are any more rooms available.'

His sister's eyes lit up and she smiled mischievously at him.

'She might have to share with you,' she added.

Just as he'd guessed. Already the family was taking over.

'She can share with Mamma,' he said repressively, but repressive had never worked on Lucia and all she did was smirk and make silly disbelieving noises at him.

'Well, I must go, for Alex will be home soon and will be worrying if I am not there. I will see you tomorrow, Paige, for I will be having dinner here at the hotel. I will tell you how the dog is then.'

Then she moved towards Marco, stood on tiptoe and kissed him on the cheek.

'*Ciao, Marco mia,*' she whispered, her lips pressed against his skin.

It was Lucia's usual farewell, but tonight it irritated him for she was still smiling in a silly way, as if she knew things he didn't.

'She's totally impossible!' he grumbled as he watched her walk lightly away from them, the dog cradled in her arms.

'But very lovable,' Paige added, and a hint of sadness in her voice drew him closer to her. Close enough to put an arm around her shoulders and draw her body against his, feeling her suppleness, her strength and warmth.

'As you are, Paige,' he said, wondering why exhaustion hadn't alleviated the sexual responses of his body to this woman. 'I—'

'Paige, you have come back to us!'

'I'll talk to you later—or tomorrow—or in a week, when all of this is over,' he muttered as his mother bore down on them, her arms outstretched in welcome to the woman by his side. 'Promise me you'll stay!'

She looked gravely him in the eyes, stood on tiptoe and kissed him gently on the cheek.

'I'm not going anywhere,' she promised, then turned to greet his mother.

Who acted exactly as he'd predicted, sweeping Paige off to her room, talking about luggage and finding clothes for her to wear, leaving him to find his own room, to shower away the dirt and tiredness, then, just for a few minutes, to rest on that soft wide bed...

'The hotel staff are run off their feet with all the extra people packed into their rooms so I brought you breakfast.' Paige's voice, piercing fogs of sleep, penetrating the blankness—probably a dream.

'Just rolls and coffee, but plenty of both,' the dream voice continued, then a slight movement of the mattress suggested she might be real, and he forced his eyes open and peered blearily into the gloom.

'Paige?'

'None other, and complete with breakfast,' she said, smiling brightly and sounding so nervous he had to look again to make sure it was her.

Paige Morgan nervous?

'I'll be right back,' he mumbled, hauling at the sheet to cover his nakedness and escaping to the bathroom where he tried desperately to get his head back in working order, piecing together what he remembered of the previous day.

Including her return!

And the reason for it!

He showered quickly, singing under his breath, ten feet

tall—at least. Then he remembered all the other problems and shrank back to normal size.

'I wish you to know I am going to give up being a surgeon and return to be the doctor in the village,' he announced as, with a towel knotted around his waist, he finally emerged.

Paige frowned as if she didn't understand what he was saying. Or didn't like what she was hearing! He hoped it was the first and explained further.

'To do away with locums, to be there and advise while they rebuild the village, to be a general practitioner not a surgeon.'

'Out of a sense of responsibility, Marco, or because it's what you really want to do?'

'What kind of question is that?' he demanded, thrown by the fact that neither of his surmises had been right.

'A sensible one,' she said. 'Is it a decision you have made with your head, or with your heart since devastation struck the village? If you take on the job for the wrong reason, it won't work. You'll be unhappy and the villagers will sense it.'

He scowled at her.

'I have been thinking of it for a long time. In fact, I was ready to make the move before I travelled to Australia.'

'And travelling to Australia changed your mind?' she prompted.

He threw his arms up in the air, remembered the towel, and brought them back down very quickly.

'You are being deliberately obtuse, Paige Morgan. I have told you of the problem with keeping doctors, but if I must spell it out then you should know it will make a difference to my income,' he muttered, 'especially now the factory has been destroyed and all family money must go into its rebuilding. I will be able to provide for you in comfort, of course, but not as well as I would have hoped.'

Now she smiled at him, eyes sparkling with mischief.

'Is this proposal number two? Or is your stiff-necked pride preventing you from asking me now you won't be able to drape furs and diamonds over me? Do you want me to say I'd as soon marry a pauper as a prince?'

She was teasing him again, but gently, and he remembered her words of love as she'd sat in the ruins of the square, holding a boy she did not know in her arms. More than anything, whether they married or not, he wanted her to know his feelings for her.

What to say? And how to say it?

'I love you, Paige Morgan. Will you marry me, Marco, neither prince nor pauper but myself?' He'd blurted the words out. No class at all!

He saw her smile, the sheen of tears in her eyes, and fell apart inside, unable to control a rush of physical desire so strong he had to clench his fists and press his fingernails into his palms to stop himself from seizing her in his arms and frightening her with his ardour.

He wanted her to answer his question, not respond to the physical attraction. Wanted her mind and heart, as well as her body.

The silence clawed at his skin, so bad he had to break it. He pretended he was far calmer than he felt. Tried for lightness in his voice.

'Did you bring enough breakfast for us both? Shall we share and make plans so when all this chaos in the villages is over we shall know the direction of our future?'

She chuckled and he felt the physical reaction kick in again.

No time for that now.

'Well?' he demanded, coming closer but not too close. But still she didn't reply.

'It is your turn to say something,' he growled, as the indecision gnawed at his heart. 'To say, "Yes, Marco, I will marry you." Then after that we will work out all the details and talk about your house and the love you have for your home country and how we shall resolve it.'

'All over one continental breakfast?' she teased, her lovely eyes gleaming so brightly he realised he needed more cover than a towel.

He grabbed clean clothes from the cupboard where some hotel person had placed them and headed back to the bathroom, reappearing minutes later to find Paige had opened the curtains and set the tray on a small table in front of the windows.

A much better position than near the bed from his point of view.

'I am still not doing this well,' he complained, moving towards her, seeing the way her hair moved like the swish of a curtain as she turned from the view to face him.

'You're not doing too badly,' she assured him.

'Then why are you laughing?' he demanded. 'I can see the laughter in your eyes.'

'Oh, Marco,' she said, smiling through the words. 'Come, sit down, have some coffee and a roll, relax.'

He flung his arms into the air and muttered a short prayer.

Relax?

When his body was on fire with wanting her, his mind in chaos with so much unresolved between them, and people waiting in the village to be rescued?

'I'm not going anywhere—except down to the village with you. We've the rest of our lives to sort things out.'

'The rest of our lives? You mean that? Are you saying what I think you're saying? Ah, Paige!'

He reached out and took her hands, drawing her into his arms and clasping her against his body—desire giving way to a flood of emotion so strong he thought it might burst out through his skin.

'*Ti amo,*' he whispered. 'Aren't those the two Italian words all foreigners can understand? I could say it in a thousand ways, in a dozen different languages, and none could express the way I feel about you. You are my light, my sun and moon and stars. My love!'

Paige let the words filter into her consciousness, accepting them but even happier to finally be in Marco's arms, held in their strength, protected and cherished. She felt him move and lifted her head, met his lips as they descended and welcomed the heat of their physical attraction.

'*Dio Madonna!* This must stop,' Marco whispered an eternity later.

'Yes,' Paige agreed, pushing herself firmly out of those entrapping arms. 'You have responsibilities!'

She spoke gravely but he must have seen the smile trying to escape, for he put out a hand to cuff at her. She caught it in hers and they moved together again, knowing they must hurry, that they were needed in the village, yet unable to tear themselves apart just yet.

In the end it was breakfast that suffered. Cups of coffee gulped down, the rolls spread with jam and taken in one of Marco's large handkerchiefs to be eaten, picnic-style, on the drive.

'About your house,' Marco said, as he twisted the car down towards the gate leading to the village road.

Paige shook her head and turned to face him.

'What is this obsession you have about my house? Do

you feel, in giving up your surgeon's job, you'll be stripped of your title and dispossessed? Utterly destitute? Are you marrying me for my house?'

She asked the question lightly, but inside a quiver of alarm was building. Not another James scenario!

But Marco glanced her way and smiled before he said, 'I am marrying you for love, Paige Morgan, and you must never forget that. But I am concerned you will be unhappy in my country—that your love for your house, your country, will draw you back there, away from me. It happened with my grandparents, who were unhappy in the extreme. I could not live with myself if I were to be the cause of such unhappiness for you.'

Paige was so relieved by this strange explanation that she laughed aloud, touching Marco's shoulder.

'Oh, Marco! If you must know, my house has just been sold—to the community service. Well, I'm presuming it's been sold—that's how I've been paying for all these flights around the world. Yes, I loved it, because I grew up there, but it's a building, nothing more than that, and now put to much better use than I could make of it.'

'And your country? You will pine for it?'

She hesitated, knowing she must answer truthfully but not knowing what the truth might be.

'I suppose I might get homesick from time to time, I don't know, but your countryside has already stolen its way into my heart and filled my soul with its beauty.' She paused, aware there was more—a final commitment to be made. 'And you, Marco, will be with me. Wherever you are will be my home.'

They drove into the field below the square of the lower village as she made this declaration, which was just as well as he stopped the car and kissed her soundly, only releasing her when the clamour of a car horn behind them forced him to move to a more suitable parking place.

She opened the car door but he was there to hold it for her as she alighted, reaching out to take her hand, to steady her or just to hold it.

'So, Paige Morgan,' he said, when they stood together in the square, about to part, she to tend the workers, he to join them. 'Will you be my wife?'

She grinned at him.

'Is that a title or a job description?'

He smiled, then bent his head and briefly touched her lips.

'It is a pledge,' he said gravely, 'of a shared life together.'

'No orders? No taking over of my life? No over-developed sense of responsibility?' Paige teased.

'Of course not,' Marco replied, then he frowned at her. 'I must go now, but you must promise me, Paige, you will not venture further from the square than the food canteen, or get yourself involved in anything that might be remotely dangerous.'

She shook her head, chuckling at his words.

'Go and rescue someone, Prince Alberici. We'll work out the sharing stuff later.'

Modern Romance™
...seduction and
passion guaranteed

Tender Romance
...love affairs tha
last a lifetim

Medical Romance™
...medical drama on
the pulse

Historical Romance
...rich, vivid and
passionat

Sensual Romance™
...sassy, sexy and seductive

27 new titles every month.

*With all kinds of Romance for
every kind of mood...*

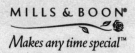

MILLS & BOON®

Makes any time special™

MAT4

Medical Romance™
6 brand new titles each month
...medical drama
on the pulse.
Available on subscription every month
from the Reader Service™
GEN/03/RS2